We Are Not Gathered Here Alone

A Novel of the Creek Nation

Donovan Hamilton

*. . . the Indian, raising his eyes above
the earthen walls about him, found
spiritual release above them in the
reaches of the blue, where, in his fancy,
the Great Spirit walked . . .*

Champlin Publishing

Library of Congress Catalog Card Number 96-95510

Hamilton, Donovan 1926-
     We Are Not Gathered Here ALone
     Historical Fiction: the Creek Nation
     The City of Tulsa; a branch of the Perryman Family

ISBN # 0-9656141-0-7

First Edition
10 9 8 7 6 5 4 3 2 1

DEDICATION

To My Grandmother
Louise Amelia "Lula" Dunbar Perryman Jordan

and

To My Mother
Alice Faye Jordan Hamilton

ACKNOWLEDGEMENTS

Terry A. Baxter; Wes Dickinson and Family; Chris Dykes and Jean Grabill of the Tulsa City-County Library; Barbara Childers Gillespie; The Moore Funeral Homes; Muskogee Public Library; Oklahoma Historical Society; Donna Perryman and Patricia Massey; Robert Powers and Dick Warner of the Tulsa County Historical Society; and Stanleys Funeral Service.

PART ONE
January, 1901

Chapter One

The young clerk put down his pen next to a short pile of frayed papers, rubbed his eyes gently, then placed his hands before him on the table top. The cold room with its high ceiling was not new to him. It had only one set of tall windows which, at the moment, was insufficient even for winter light. "Now," he said softly to the Indian who waited. With a heavy sigh of relief and a quick glance at the long line of enrollees yet to register, and to the loud clock on the bare wall, he continued, "what can I do for you?"

At first, the short Indian peered over his right shoulder at the noise behind him. Outside the building, two horses with loose reins had come untied from the front railing and a young boy was trying to calm them. With a gloved hand, the Indian brushed the lint and dirt from his moustache, cleared his throat, and sat in a wicker chair at the table.

I'm here to enroll my daughters," was his reply. He gathered three documents from the right pocket of his mackinaw and placed them so the clerk could accept them.

Interrupting these two, another clerk from the second of three tables, pushed a wide paper in front of them. "Excuse me, Noah, where do I put nineteen one? You told me once."

Silently, with the tip of his pen, he showed his co-worker and then, with a nod of agreement, the second clerk returned to his table.

"Let me begin now," he continued, shifting his feet below his desk. He studied the documents and smiled. "First, your name. I mean, as it is, already on the roll."

"Moses Perryman," and as the Indian spoke, the clerk was writing in an easy manner, voicing the words as he did so. "I enrolled right here in Muskogee, roll number two six three six. You can check it. I've been waiting a long time."

"Yes, well," agreed the clerk, "we manage to enroll about ten an hour, here. It would help me if you answer some questions, Mr. Perryman. Has an engineer already given you a townsite number? On your allotted land, I mean?"

"One did. We got it. You want it?" Moses presented it from another paper that was handy.

"I'll just jot it down, too." He coughed and rubbed his hands together, for warmth. "Are you Cherokee?"

"He's Creek," came the loud reply from a stocky man to his right. Both clerk and Indian looked up! "Hello Mose, how are you?"

Moses rose. "McIntosh, you old sonovagun, I didn't know you were here, too. Who you got to enroll?"

The clerk was accustomed to interruptions.

"Just passing through, this time, Mose. I hear your wife had another kid, about three or four days ago, wasn't it?"

Efficiently, the clerk wrote answers that were common to the occasion. He had on the page in front of him the name of Moses, but he heard Mose from the old Indian, so he waited while they talked.

"Another daughter, "Moses laughed and pointed to the papers in front of him. "Enrolling all of them on this trip."

Slightly perturbed, Noah remained as calm as possible, his pen poised above his ink well.

"Makes three, doesn't it? What did you name this one?"

"Edith Monetta. Born January twenty-ninth, it was."

"Two days ago!" McIntosh congratulated him with a pat on the back and a handshake. He leaned against the table, disturbing a sheaf of papers. "Lula doing well, is she?"

Reassembling the assortment, Noah became eager to continue. "Let me study those documents, there, please, if you will."

"Happy to know that, Mose." With a tip of his black hat, McIntosh departed through the crowd, waving to others as he left the busy building.

Having already written the year at the top of his page, he dipped his pen again to finish his line. "I see these are the proof we need for your children, sir."

Moses hardly ever asked questions about this service, but he became interested. "You're new here, aren't you? Working for the Dawes, I mean."

This clerk looked up at him, surprised by his curiosity. "My home is in Ohio but I've been here for about four months. My name is Noah Pringle. I'm happy to meet you, Mr...." and again he looked at name. "Perryman." And then he paused. "Might I ask, regarding your first name. I have it as Moses."

"That's right. People call me Mose, just Mose."

"Well, then, I'll keep it Moses on the register."

"I was named after an uncle." Moses saw a name on a sign on another desk. "Who is this Crosthwaite man?"

Again, Noah paused. "He is an executive, sir, who has been here about as long as I have, I think. From Washington D.C."

Every time anyone came into this room from the hallway, a blast of cold air chilled the interior. Noah produced a pair of fingerless gloves, for the one stove in the crowded room had exhausted the wood logs and a small lad was bringing in another load for it. "You say you're the father?" He waited for his answer, but was stalled by a second interruption.

"Hey, Mose, I seen you out front. How are things in Tulsa?" This time, Moses stood and tried to recognize this man. "I'm Harley Bohannon. I haven't seen you and the missus since...well, since way last November, I guess. I live here in Muskogee, now. She was about to have a baby wasn't she?"

Moses removed his right glove to shake hands and he selected his answer carefully. "Lula had Edith."

"How is she, Mose?" Harley was always a casual man. "And Abner? I wasn't able to go to his wife's funeral. I'm sorry, I am. Tell him that, will you?"

Noah already wrote the date, and he was reading the documents while he waited.

"You got a nice family, now, Mose! I hope your wife is recovering fairly well. Come by and visit." With a tip of his hat, Harley Bohannon departed as quickly as he had appeared.

"Registration," Noah Pringle announced, "should take only a minute or more.

I'll give you roll numbers."

Moses removed his hat and placed it to his left and unbuttoned his thick coat. As the clerk proceeded, Moses identified each one. "First girl, Rachel, born April fifteenth, eighteen-ninety-five. We call her Dot. She's the oldest."

"This second paper," said Noah, looking at him, "is for a son."

Lula had put the papers all together neatly in a box in her cupboard, behind her pictures. Moses had forgotten that he had brought all of them with him for this errand. On the face of the one Noah held was written, with an ink unlike the balance of it, 'Died. Infant.'

"I'm so sorry, Mr. Perryman," he replied reverently. And as Noah continued his work, he verified it. "The second document says, Cozetta Muskogee Perryman. I notice you spell the middle name with a k and not a c." When Moses confirmed, Noah proceeded, again neatly placing each certificate to his right as he accounted for them. "Edith Monetta, hhmm, just a baby." Noah could see enthusiasm return to this Indian's face. "All born in Indian Territory. I see that the mother's name is Louise Amelia Dunbar Perryman. Is that right?"

Before Moses could answer, another gale of cold wind swept into the room. Those waiting outside, in the hallway, peered through the door. "Yes," he answered, "That's right. Name is Lula, though. We call her Lula."

"I beg your pardon?" Noah Pringle halted, for he noticed a tall Indian standing a mere two feet directly behind his customer, the man who brought the cold air with him. Noah returned to his work, blowing warm air into his own gloves. "Did you say 'Lula'?"

"She's called Lula. Write it any way you want."

"Creek Indian, too?" Again, his pen was poised above paper.

Moses turned slowly to look at the man behind him. Then, reassured, he turned back to the clerk. "White. A white girl. Born in Kansas."

"Very well, Mr. Perryman. Here are your papers. I ask you, sir, is this date, July twenty-four, eighteen-seventy-nine, correct for your wife's birth?" He received a nod. "And I shall require your birthday, too, please."

"July thirteen, eighteen-seventy."

"The fourteenth, Mose," came the correction from the man behind him. "You were born on the fourteenth." Again, Noah stopped. He blinked his eyes, making the change on the page. In the back of his mind, he hoped that the information he had taken was correct. "Here are the enrollment numbers of the little girls." And he presented a sheet of paper to Moses who rose, claiming his hat and gloves and buttoning his coat. "Good luck, Mr. Perryman. We're finished, here."

As Moses reached in his pocket for a handkerchief, the two of them stepped away from the table, for the next customer had already seated herself.

"Pick up the papers, Mose, and let's go." It was said with a touch of urgency. When Moses looked back at the clerk who was, at once, engaging the attention of the lady, he asked, "Anything else, Mr. Perryman?" He reached for his documents shook his head, said "no", and walked out of the room with his companion.

"I see your brother found you, Mose," came a quick remark from an Indian standing by the white picket fence. "Glad to help you." As they passed him, he offered, "Oh, Abner, I just want to say I'm sorry about your wife. Word didn't get to us till way late. Nice to see both of you."

Moses's brother tipped his hat. "Much obliged, Aaron. It's nice to see you, too. I understand."

Very soon, the two brothers were walking briskly away from the two-storied building. "Well, that's all, for the Dawes." The crowded street was full of members of the tribes who waited to register. "What time is it, Mose?" Abner asked. "I don't think you have much time, do you?"

"Before I forget it, here, take the papers for Lula," and he placed them in Abner's hand. "I'm going to be in St. Louis just as long as it takes to plan for the summer." He looked at his watch. "I've got about an hour before the train leaves." To a full blood who passed them, Moses spoke in Creek.

Abner Perryman was taller than his oldest brother but was younger by eight years. While Moses had been exposed more to the Creek language, along with their sister, Emma, Abner had never given full attention to speaking and studying it. This younger brother had a good education in the missions, but his marriage to Gracie, a full blood daughter of a Eufaula family, took precedence over much of his plans for his future. She died suddenly during the beginning of a smallpox epidemic that had passed through the Muscogee Nation. This winter had been most severe, and Abner was most concerned with his new niece.

They came to a livery stable where they had parked their buckboard. It had been a long, cold drive from Tulsa, but so far, their plans were complete. After enrollment, Moses was to board the train, change at Vinita, and arrive in St. Louis for his business. The summer was going to be a good one with plenty of cattle to fatten and then shipped. It was to be their best herd. "George made me come with you today," Abner confessed, "and I'm glad he did. Are you going to be all right up there? A lot of money rides with you on this deal. We got a lot planned here, you know. With Papa dead, now, you are the head of the family." He patted his brother's shoulder. "Mama is real proud of you, Mose."

"You don't have to tell me that, Abe, I know that. Did you buy my ticket?"

Abner nodded and extracted it from his pocket and handed it to him, while an old livery attendant smiled through his dirty teeth. "You ready for your buckboard now, Mr. Mose?"

Abner answered for him. "Not yet, Billy, I'll be back in an hour after I put Moses on the train."

"Okay, Mr. Abe," came the answer, "glad to help." Billy was one of the Freedmen who owned his own business. "See you then."

They walked yet another block, past the usual traffic that filled the dirty streets of this old town. "Emma and Ella don't know too much anymore, I guess. You got a home, Mose. You and Lula and the three girls. Nice family. I'm going to see Lula on Friday, so she'll be all right." Abner thought of Gracie. "I guess I wasn't as fortunate, was I?"

From the south came the long wail of the train's whistle, with its sharp warning for horses, buggies, and men to stay clear of the rail crossing. It seemed mournful and low. When they did see it pull into the station, the usual crowds clamored onto the wooden platforms, eager to feel the warm steam on such an afternoon. All day long, a crew of construction men worked diligently to finish the huge MKT sign that lay majestically over the door to the waiting room. When Abner and Moses passed them, they were admiring their work.

"George hopes you do okay in St. Louis." They were at the platform where they waited for a hack to pass them before going into the depot.

"George and I had a nice long talk last week," Moses said while he tipped his hat to the gentlemen and a lady as they passed. "He knows pretty good what is to be expected in St. Louis. Our Papa taught us this business real good and I told him, and I can tell you, and all of our sisters, too, that I know exactly what I'm doing. Don't need to worry your handsome head about it, Abe, not a bit. I've already had a talk with Mayme. She's more inquisitive than Emma and Ella put together. I'm thinking for the family."

Abner extracted his pocket watch. "Seems to be on time. It'll be here for thirty or forty more minutes. Want to get something to eat before you leave?"

Moses took the satchel that Abner had been caring for him. He chuckled when he recounted the conversation with his own mother. "Mama made me sandwiches and I got some coffee."

"I'm glad you had that talk with George."

"I know what I'm doing, Abe, I do!" He paused to select a word or two. "And for a long time, I knew that Emma and Mayme, maybe Ella, haven't been too close to us 'cause I married a white woman." He monitored Abner's response.

Such was true. Animosity came and went within the confines of the Perryman clan. Each one had been an adult for such a short time. The father wielded a strong influence over the lot that in no time, the siblings became accustomed to proper discipline and good order. Their uncles, too, maintained a healthy Christian attitude. Despite these two areas of training, each, with the possible exception of Oliver, the youngest, only twelve now, manifested an independent streak of an individual behavior. And through it all, the animosity felt most severely was reflected in the early remarks from Emma when she, and the rest of the family, first learned that their oldest brother was going to marry the Dunbar girl.

Both brothers mulled over their history. Moses had stood on that plot of ground on which he had the Homestead built. With his father he had dreamed of the design, the architecture, even where the big barn would be located. The house was constructed for his bride, situated as it was upon a wide knoll of fertile land, the hill being distant from the main road to the east.

Sturdy teams of horses and mules had pulled a dozen large slabs of rock, tons of sandstone from as far as Kiefer and beyond it, northward on the country road, up the gentle hillside to the main house. With these rocks, Moses prepared a walkway from the front porch to the south gate. He built a stile block by which ladies could climb two steps to mount their steeds. From his father he borrowed a long horn bull and a dozen cows. In the last five years of the nineteenth century, Moses managed to breed a great many cattle, as many as he wanted. He had a ranch now, and a wife and three beautiful daughters. They were there, now, waiting.

Even his mother was pleased. Creek blood was surging all through their veins. Mrs. Rachel was always Mrs. Rachel.

"Tell Mama I'll be all right, and not to worry about me." He stopped just outside the station, under the new sign, to pick up a piece of cloth that idly had fallen from someone's bag, or from packing crates near the loaded freight wagons. With it, he began to polish his boots, knocking the dust of Muskogee from them, spitting on them for homemade polish.

By this time, the train had come to a complete halt, its engine softly purring as a big cat. Few passengers stepped from the cars. In the short span of time, with practically everything said that was to be said between them, when Abner saw a couple he knew, Moses thought again of Lula and home.

By now, this young wife stood on her front porch to gaze affectionately toward the eastern horizon, thinking that she could visualize the town of

Muskogee through the trees some sixty miles distant. But it was too cold for dreaming, or even hoping, or for working toward the good plans they had for themselves. She heard here two oldest girls in the kitchen so she turned and entered, making certain that the back screen door was not rattling as it would do, often, with the least breezes from the north. She cradled her newest in her arms, and she knew, she just knew that she was the happiest woman on this planet.

When Abner completed his visit with the couple and walked toward his brother, Moses knew it was time to get aboard. If Abner had not called him, then surely it would be the three Indians from Wealaka Mission who commanded his brother's attention. They were loading freight that had come all the way from Paris, Texas.

"Okay, Abe," Moses conceded, "I'm ready."

"You're a good businessman, everyone knows that." Abner smiled. "Don't worry about a thing. I'll take care of home while you're up there."

"Get the work done as soon as you can and come back home." In one respect Abner did not want his big brother to see how greatly concerned he was about business. "We have that nice store, now, and I suspect that stockyard is going to be bigger than it is now, one of these days, the one half a mile west of the train station. Do you ever think that yard will be more useful than Red Fork?" He saw how Moses still concentrated on the Wealaka group as they climbed aboard their wagon, loaded as it was with freight. But with the surge of traffic, Abner's questions went unanswered.

The conductor, occupied as he was with his lantern, verified the time from his pocket watch, looked forward to see the engineer climbing up to his window, and nodded his approval. "Board!" he called proudly, "all aboard."

"I've always looked up to you as my big brother, Mose, you know that." Abner removed his hat.

"I know that." Moses spat on the ground. "I know we got a big family but I also know we got problems. But Lula is good and she comes from good stock. You be sure to give her those birth papers whenever you see her." Other passengers passed by them and stepped into the cars. "I got papers in my case that will make the whole family a wealthy one. Father taught us that. I'm going to make us rich. All of us."

"I wish Papa could see us now!"

Moses looked directly into Abner's eyes. "I told you, Abe, that I was going to be okay. You tell Mayme to mind her own business if she squawks at you. You know what? I think her no good husband, Shirk, is up to something. I never did think much of him, anyway so Mayme doesn't have any cause to complain about Lula. Tell Emma I'm sorry about her losing a baby like that. I forgot to tell her, myself."

Abner watched his brother closely, for he had always been a guide, a counselor to determine what was best. Moses, the first born, the wise one, grew up with a set jaw and an eager brain that worked well under all circumstances. He was always there with his father, before a camera when a picture was to be captured, with the farm crew, or with Indians who came to visit, or as evidence that some important decision was made that day concerning cattle, or health matters for sickness among the herds.

Moses listened to the language and he heard it from his uncles, but he was subject to English, according to the wishes of not only his father but of his uncles as well.

"Don't forget to give Ella the book I got for her." This sister astounded everyone with a mild disposition among the more tempestuous ones. She was the fourth child, a lovely little thing, and Mrs. Rachel, when too busy to care for her, placed sorghum on her forefingers and gave her a feather to keep her entertained as a toddler. Ella grew up being exceptionally curious. In eighteen-eighty-six, dressed in a pretty black dress with a big ribbon in her hair, she held her father's hand when the largest of locomotives slowly came into Tulsa's new railroad depot.

"The railroad is all the way to Sapulpa, Papa," Ella announced. "Isn't that right?" Her big brother, Moses stood beside them, and Ella heard him say that their cattle could be herded to Red Fork for shipment to St. Louis and this little girl saw her father nod his wise head in agreement. From that day forward, Ella developed an inquisitive interest in history. "Papa comes from a long line of Perrymans," she told her sisters, "so that makes us coming from the same line."

Emma was a bit irascible at times when they were growing up. "You go on and talk Creek if you want to," Ella would say, "but I'm going to learn to speak English very well, I am!" But, according to Moses, her enthusiasm waned when the choice for her husband, Mr. Horner, was not their father's choice.

And then, of course, Mayme, the youngest daughter, was the strange one, so unlike their mother, secretly attending the care and household duties of the big house and so very proud of her uncle being the first postmaster of Tulsa. She had desperately tried to understand why the location of the original post office, in the house, was moved to a store when she was nine years old, for she had always been intrigued by the pony express. When that ceased operation, Mayme made the comment, sarcastically, "that it would be moved to the Perryman Store, but no, old H.C. Hall had to go and put it in his own store, and I don't think that was right. No!" As young as she was, then, Mayme even confronted their father with her complaint. "I remember when you and Uncle Legust and Uncle Josiah moved the store from one location to the new place. You called it Perryman and Reed. I remember that. And then Uncle Josiah had to die."

The train whistle sounded and departure was imminent.

"Oh, and another thing," cautioned Moses, "little Oliver will want to ride my mare while I'm away. Hold her at Mama's house until I get back so he can ride. That's okay, as long as he grooms her and takes care of her, like he was taught. Tell him to watch her left rear foot. I think she'll need a new shoe. She had a case of disease there, I reckon." He took his brother by the arm. "And Mama. She's more healthy than you and I put together."

They felt the whole train lurch. "I don't know why I couldn't have come with you. I've never been to St. Louis."

Suddenly, the engineer pulled the release rope, and two sharp whistles filled the air.

"You stay in Tulsa and take care of things. Tell George I said so." Moses again felt the long train begin to inch forward slowly. He grabbed hold of the alcove doorknob. "Now you go on," he called loudly above the turning of the wheels, "and do as I say. Goodbye."

The younger brother saw him step into the passenger car and select a seat. Walking fast to keep Moses in view, Abner soon lost sight of him as the cars gathered speed. An MKT employee pulling one large freight wagon filled with mail sacks and baggage stopped behind him. "Hey, mister, let me by." Abner stepped around him and went to the end of the platform.

He felt the rush of cold air follow the train as it gathered speed, leaving the depot with few people waving goodbye. Abner turned up his mackinaw collar and repositioned his hat as he returned slowly to the livery stable. He watched the rear car disappear around the bend in the tracks.

"Abner!" someone called from across the frozen avenue. He looked through the crowd. "Abner Perryman!" The sound came from behind him so he looked again. He saw who it was waving at him from across the busy street. Three long wagons passed between them before the man came to his side. "Abner," came the call again. "I'm real sorry about Gracie's passing." The man speaking was elderly, one of the many Indians who attended her funeral, from Eufaula. When using English, his accent was proof that his Creek was more proficient. He extended his hand politely, and Abner accepted his condolence. He continued. "Did I just see Mose get on the train?"

That month of January had been a crowded one for him. He saw so many devoted people and relatives at the funeral in that week after Christmas that a mirage of faces passed before him, of cousins, full bloods from Okmulgee, and friends of various dimensions, who knew not only the family, but of the Perryman uncles who had made such outstanding names for themselves across the years. "Thank you very much," Abner replied, with hands holding the collar close to his chin. "I can't remember...seem to remember...."

I'm one of the Stidhams," the old man answered loudly, above the noise of traffic. "You can't remember all of us, we are so many! I'm Uriah, Noble's uncle. Noble was at her funeral, too."

Yes, of course. Abner did remember the Stidhams, for his father had mentioned them when he was much younger. It was Noble's father who gave him one of the finest horses to ride when he was younger than Oliver. The Stidham Family was all around Broken Arrow and as large in scope as the Childers Family. This old man standing before him, with a blanket of many colors wrapped about his shoulders, was the last of the breed, it seemed. Mr. Stidham's wrinkled face reflected many stories that his own father passed on to the clan about the Trail westward, stories that contained references to treaty after treaty that were considered secured only to be broken later.

"Yes, sir, that's right. I put Moses on the train just now."

"Your family still shipping cattle?"

"Yes sir, we are. Mr. Collins and the drovers bring them up the west side of the Arkansas now and we herd them to Red Fork. It's easier than through the stockyard at Tulsa. Saves fording the river. This summer's going to be a big one for us."

"I'm glad for you and your family. Abe. I am! Tulsa sure is growing." Uriah Stidham nodded silently as old Indians usually do, to show politeness and concern, in quiet agreement with good fortune. He extended a hand so calloused with wear and age that Abner looked at it as he accepted the handshake.

By this old Indian's sincere gesture with a genuine smile of concern, Abner felt the return of an emotion he had not experienced in the interim of time since the funeral. Even at pow-wows, Abner sensed a camaraderie when the men would group themselves around the fires, even around the Council Tree in Tulsa. Ever so long, he believed that such a feeling was fading away, as if some harsh wind was dissolving this old man's memories, just as the present January was quick to invade a person's bone marrow.

"All you Perrymans have had a time of it, haven't you? I mean, with your father dying a year ago, wasn't it? How is Mrs. Rachel?"

"Walk with me to the livery, please," Abner invited him, but did not want to sound impatient. "My wagon and horse are there."

Mr. Stidham straightened himself and agreed with a nice smile. "Sure," he confessed, "I'm heading that way myself."

Their strolling took them past some new building, one of which was Muskogee's newest hotel with a wide wooden sidewalk and two large oak doors. The livery stable, which was owned by the same family for twenty years, had now grown to accommodate ten horses with room at the rear to park ten wagons, easily.

"You asked about Mama," continued Abner as they stopped in front of the office. "She's fine, Mr. Stidham, more healthy than any of us. That's where I'm going now, as soon as I can get away. Going as far as Porter or maybe Tullahassee tonight, then spend the night, and go on home tomorrow morning early. Abner looked for the attendant. "Mr. Sellers?" he called and when no one came, he called again.

Once more, the old man shuffled himself forward through a big door that separated the stalls from the front area. He spat his tobacco, wiped his chin, and spoke haltingly. "You are getting busy, I see."

They parted with a tingle of regret, for this old Indian's farewell left a wake that haunted Abner while he hitched the horse to the wagon, climbed aboard, and paid his bill. Not very many such elderly full-bloods were as conversant as Mr. Stidham. They preferred to be adamant, to walk along with only their thoughts, their memories, their fond reminiscences of when they, too, were twenty-two years old, riding their ponies and listening to exciting tales from their own wise elders, of chasing deer and eating wild hares in Alabama.

Abner moved his wagon onto the busy street. As he was about to turn westward and head for the river, his glance to the east caught Mr. Stidham who had stopped and was talking to someone else who would listen to him. Catching his eye, Abner waved a final goodbye.

Driving as he was, he would be in Porter at nightfall and a good super at a friend's house. And he was tired.

By late afternoon the next day after enduring ice on the Arkansas River where he had to cross on Clark's Ferry, Abner felt more at ease viewing familiar territory in which he was born. His wife had come from her clan who lived in Porter, but he elected not to call on his in-laws until more time had elapsed. He wanted to reach home, to his mother and Oliver.

His littlest brother sat on the south porch all bundled up, his cap a Christmas gift from his mother, his new scarf and mittens, two gifts from two seasons ago, when he was a mere ten years old. His patch of sunlight, its rays making their way to this porch through the cottonwoods, was fading fast, now that the afternoon had lengthened into early dusk. Two of the dogs were cuddled next to him to keep warm. Now, of course, he was a big twelve and most eager to be older. When a dog failed to fetch a stick he had thrown, he saw Abner's wagon appear on the road south of the pond. With a gleeful smile, he threw away the rocks he had stowed in his pocket and ran to meet him, joyful all the way. Something genuine and warm was always inside this boy's bearing, himself, the product of a thorough Creek culture, mixed with English from a mission school in Tulsa. In no time, breathless from running he was at the wagon and eager to board, to sit beside his brother to ride back to the house. So Abner stopped, reached down and pulled him up to the seat to ride 'shotgun.'

All this ritual of greeting was not new to Oliver, for he learned to be cordial to anyone who came up that path to see the family. Visits among the tribe often lasted for days. Regardless of weather, if he saw a buggy with people in it, he would inevitably run to meet them. Already, at this age, he was thoroughly knowledgeable of horses. Having older brothers and with an inherent talent for horsemanship, this youngster asked to take the reins. When Abner consented, Oliver climbed over him, took the leather so Abner could exchange places. Past the pond they rode and up to the front porch.

Oliver tried to peer backward into the wagon. "Did you get the big table from your friend, like you said you would?" It was there, but in pieces, parts that were once a nice drop-leaf mahogany, large enough to have a nice doily and a large coal-oil lamp which Abner wanted to place on it. It had been promised to Abner but no one had a means of transportation until now.

"That's why we took this wagon," Abner remarked, "so I went by Porter to pick it up and bring it home. I'll show it to you after I put it together. I've got to fix it, first."

Oliver drove around the house and into the barn. The path was worn and by sheer habit, the horse led the way. Their mother heard them pass her kitchen window. With the squeak of leather, she knew her son was home. Setting aside her bowl of sofkey which was ready for supper, she dried her hands on a tea towel, opened the rear screen, and lit a lantern that hung on the back wall of the rear porch. Careful with herself, she ambled to the barn with the light and called to Oliver to take it from her.

Their mother was called Mrs. Rachel by some, Aunt Rachel, by others. A widow for over a year, she was never alone at her home. Years ago, her husband had named it the White House and this title remained as fresh as when the house was constructed.

Her three daughters visited her the day Abner returned. Emma had already departed but Ella and Mayme were there, bundling themselves in their preparations to depart, now that Abner was safely at home. Ella shuffled about the large house making certain that everything was in its proper place that the doilies were straight and even on the sofa in the parlor and that the beds were made.

With Abner and Oliver in the barn, Ella turned to Mayme, this time, with another question. "Are you planning to go see Lula? We have a new niece now, you know." Mrs. Rachel glanced at her daughters while she finished the dish of food. Never at any time had this matriarch learned English in formal education, even though much of the family already accepted the fact that this tolerant woman understood every word.

Mayme pulled on her gloves and placed her hat on a table. "That's what Emma said before she left. Poor Emma. I got my own family to take care of, Ella." She looked at her mother to see if that remark would elicit a reaction from her. The sisters started for the front door, leaving their mother to her cooking. "Goodbye, Mama," they called. Adjusting her hat, Mayme finally answered. "I may go see her, I don't rightly know, now. I think I'll wait until Mose gets back from St. Louis." But then, she changed her mind, retreated down the hallway and out the back door, blocking Abner and Oliver as they came from the barn.

"Did you see me, Mayme?" Oliver said quite proudly. "I drove the big wagon with the table in it." The cold wind knocked her hat askew and the boy grabbed it.

Ignoring the rescue, she confronted Abner. "Well, I guess he's on his way to the big city." This sister spoke slowly, keeping her eyes upon his face. "I can imagine he's up to no good."

Oliver fled into the house as Abner, tired and hungry, shifted his bag from one hand to another. "Hello, Mayme," he said, "thank you, I have had a good trip." He brushed past her and welcomed the warmth of the hot kitchen and the smiles of his mother who had preceded them.

"Why didn't Mose come by and say goodbye to Mama and us?"

"Cause he asked me to go to his house and leave from there that's why. There's a good road now east from Kiefer. It took a lot of time to get all the papers ready for enrollment, especially so for little Edith."

Her departure interrupted, Ella returned to the kitchen. Abner poured some hot water into a wash basin by the door. He was lathering with a small cake of soap with Oliver waiting behind him.

"Too bad Emma's not here. She could tell Mama about your trip." Mayme again adjusted her hat and straightened her gloves. "I'm leaving."

Abner dried his hands and face and brushed his long hair. Oliver followed him, asking for his comb because he had lost his. "Mayme," Abner said softly, "I wonder what Papa would say if he knew you didn't care for Lula?" The remark stopped the sister and prompted a frown.

"What brought that on?" By this time, Ella shrugged her shoulders with a look of contempt, fearing another argument that always ensued when Abner and Mayme would converse.

"What would happen if I went and married again, this time to a white woman? Mose certainly knew what he was doing."

"You certainly aren't thinking of that, now, are you?" Mayme changed her stance and removed her gloves.

"No, I'm not," he confided, "at least, not now." Oliver quickly returned the comb and stood at the far end of the kitchen to see how this would develop.

Unknown to the boy, but understood by his brothers and sisters, was the fact that Moses had been astute enough, at an early time in his life, to establish a wide and prosperous spread of land, and he managed to have a house built on it. After all, any Creek Indian was entitled to as much land as he cared to cultivate. And in the back of her mind, Mayme Perryman Shirk was the hostess to a minimum section of wheat and pasture land which her husband had had no direction in mind when he allocated that portion when they were married. Abner presumed that Stewart Shirk came along, had seized the opportunity of marrying into money, and had given no thought at all how he could improve his own lot in life. But Abner had never pursued that premise with his sister. It was certainly not his business to do so.

It was that which haunted this tall woman. And too, it was the white lien from the new white majority that had begun to superimpose recommendations that the Creeks should break with their tribal traditions, that of communal living.

Her big brother, Moses, gratefully followed that statement from the agent that the communal system of agriculture become obsolete. As a result Moses Perryman and his new wife developed their own land, their own ranch with a commodious house, a huge barn, and their own line of Texas long horns. And now, Mayme was

stifled with Stewart Shirk, a small house, and a patch of land that amounted to
practically nothing. In his own words, for a great while, Abner inferred this again.

"I'm glad Mama didn't hear what you keep telling me. And I'm glad Emma
has gone home so she couldn't translate for her. That's mean of you to say all that,
Abe, and you know it. I will stop coming here to see Mama if you persist in what
you just said." She slipped her hands into her gloves quickly. "Okay. So that's
what you think. So when is Mose coming back?"

Oliver sidestepped from the door that led into the hallway. Without any type
of answer, Abner moved to the front of the house. Then, he stopped and offered a
reply. "Well, he didn't say, but I reckon it would be yet a week, maybe more." Ella,
ahead of him, was first through the front door, followed by Mayme. Neither said
too much of a goodbye. It was Ella who called loudly as she stepped off the porch.
"Oliver, honey, get a match or two and light my lantern on my buggy for me, will
you, please?" And then she turned to Abner who paused at the front door. "Abe,
don't worry so. You worry too much."

Oliver burst past Abner and hurried for the large buggy that was parked just
to the right under his favorite tree, with the horse still in its harness. He struck a
match, lifted the ornate chimney of the elegant lamp and lit the wick. He joined
Abner, shivering in the cold weather.

Mayme adjusted her hat again. "I hope you're all right, Abner." She conceded
as she prepared to climb aboard. "I've got things to do and I can't keep up with
everything."

"I'd light your lantern, Mayme, if you had one on your buggy." Oliver was so
innocent in his remark that the sister could only say no. When she settled and took
the reins and turned her horse toward the pond, she waved once only slightly with
out saying anything more.

Ella was the last to leave, with a genuine 'thank you' to Oliver as she drove
into the night. Her lamp swayed gently as she finally rounded the little hill and
was soon out of sight.

Abner remained on the porch until he could no longer see Ella's lantern. He
blew warm breath into his cupped hands as Oliver ran into the kitchen. Then,
when the winds became all too bitter, he joined his mother and brother. "I'm going
to see Lula tomorrow. Tabor's Crossing has a new ferryboat."

Their mother had already lit a lamp and placed it in the middle of the dining
room table, full of a hot supper.

"Mama," Abner was at her side, "why did you come back to the White House?
Papa built you that big House downtown for all of us." But she either did not hear
it, or she did not prefer to answer, even if she could. Everyone in the territory
knew that the White House was the first constructed in this expanse of wild terrain. The other dwelling was merely an ornament. Emma once said, to everyone,
that their mother wants to remain here from now on, with only a casual trip to the
other place. In fact, at the moment its future was never a substantial topic of conversation.

Both brothers then waited patiently as their mother came slowly from the
kitchen to take her place at the head of the table, now that her husband and father
was no longer there. She had not yet learned to disregard tradition, to sit and eat
with her sons.

Outside, it was quiet, except for the friendly barking of one dog, teasing the
others. The soup was good that evening.

Chapter Two

Mrs. Louise Amelia Perryman, who was Lula to her husband, her friends, and the Dunbars, stood on the front step leading to the south porch of her large house. Ever since it was constructed some five years ago, Moses had preferred to call it the Homestead. The design was Victorian, with a wide central hallway from which the parlor extended eastward, complete with a short black stove. Bedrooms were on the west side all with high ceilings, large windows, and all on one level. A second story was in the original plan, but it was negated as the house began to take shape. It was impressive, built on a crest of a sprawling hill just west of the main road, highly recognized by everyone traveling along that route.

Lula carried her youngest Edith, in her right arm and with her left hand she shielded her eyes against the bright February sun. Weather this time of year in Indian Territory, was perplexing. One day, the wind would bring cold dampness and a chill, and the next, the sun would tease everyone with a false promise of an early spring.

Moses's foreman, a tall lanky man with a rugged face and large gloved hands, came around the east side of this house, past the area where Moses planned to build a large fireplace for the parlor. He carried a shovel as if he were momentarily interrupted from his work. Both he and Lula were attracted to the arrival of a surrey up the hill carrying a stout woman in the driver's seat and a young delicate lady to her left.

"I saw them on the main road," the foreman said "and I just supposed they'd turn up our road. Sure 'nough. You think she's a woman you know, ma'am?" The surrey stopped at the south gate, at the stile block.

"Well I don't know. I don't think so anyway." Lula watched as the woman dismounted carefully and tossed the blanket she had tucked over her lap onto the seat.

Pete, too, noticed their arrival and was instantly at her side, taking the reins and tying them to the railing. This woman gestured for the other lady to step down, as well. Then, after Pete had nodded his head in a silent hello, the ladies approached the metal gate, straightening their dresses as was necessary after a long ride. Once through the entrance, they paused to admire the rocks that formed the long sidewalk to the porch. This flat-stoned sidewalk had been worthy of much conversation by many people as a hearty greeting to anyone who was visiting the Homestead. It was Moses's idea to have it just that pattern on the ground, with slabs of that special kind of rock that only comes from the Eufaula area.

To her foreman, Lula signaled with a simple gesture and said softly, "that's all right Mr. Collins. I think I know who she is. That was nice of Pete to run to help, too. You might tell him to water their horse and wipe the dust from their buggy while we talk."

And with that, Mr. Collins waved to Pete with his shovel to join him behind the house.

A reason to monitor this arrival was embedded in the foreman's psyche. Mr. Collins, as Lula was instructed by her husband to call him, was not new to unusual occurrences at this ranch. Long ago, he had learned to be alert but judicious to the sudden appearance of any strangers. His presence at the side of the lady of the house was by his own volition, especially so when he could be there almost instantly. As the two visitors neared the porch to come into earshot, he and Pete disappeared, to resume their chores. This, obviously, was a social call.

"We just can't tell anymore about February, can we, Mrs. Perryman?" came the caller's first words. "You have a right nice home here, ma'am." She was dressed well, even for a winter buggy ride, that Lulu was embarrassed in her own calico house dress. This lady had a large feathered hat with a fur piece around her bejeweled neck. The charming girl, walking delicately on the rocks behind her was resplendent in a long red coat. She stumbled slightly on the uneven flatness of the rock sidewalk, laughed gaily at this, and reached for her hat that had slid to one side. "Careful, Vera," said the matron.

"Don't I know you?" Lula called as she shifted her daughter onto her left arm.

By now, the ladies had reached the steps, "I'm Mrs. Louise Clinton. My name is Louise, too." And then she turned to the little lady. "And this is my daughter, Vera." The young lady curtsied quickly. "Mrs. Perryman, I think we met about a year ago in Red Fork. I think it was at a house warming that your daddy built for some friends of mine, I believe. He's making a nice name for himself as a carpenter, now." She gazed at the wide expanse of land south of the house, past where Pete had parked her surrey. "My goodness, but your pasture land goes on forever, doesn't it? I bet it's pretty in summertime."

"Please come on in, out of the cold." Lula opened the door and indicated the hallway.

"Things are sure changing, aren't they?" Mrs. Clinton remarked lightly as they were ushered into the east parlor. "I heard you were birthing that infant you're holding so I waited until now to call." She peered lovingly into the baby's face. "That makes three, doesn't it?"

"Sit down, if you will, please, on the sofa." Lula smiled. "My other two are back in the kitchen. Three. Yes. I'll get Pete to light up the stove here. Mr. Perryman is going to construct a fireplace when he gets back from his trip."

"This house sure looks grand from a distance! An obvious and remarkable landmark to the countryside, I've heard tell. Coming from Jenks we could see it fairly well when we turned south from the other road. Your daddy build this one, too?"

Lula placed Edith in her cradle. "No, that is, my husband had some full bloods build this with a professional overseer, of course. I've had a lot of people around here say they can see us from a distance, all right, from the north as well as from Kiefer. On a nice day, you can see this house clear from Tibbons' Hill.

All of the populace in its immediate area knew of this Perryman Homestead from the family's reputation as great cattlemen to the splendid cowboys and ranch hands that this empire commanded. George Beecher Perryman, the patriarch, brother, himself, to seventeen other siblings, had been determined to rebuild this devastated land after the Civil War. Moses, his firstborn, followed his father's careful instructions. This house, the barn, the sheds, the bunkhouse in which Pete, Mr. Collins, and a fellow whom they called Laredo lived, were the tangible result.

Totally astounded, Mrs. Clinton gasped. "What a story!" Just as she regained herself, slowly and inquisitively, two little girls meandered into the parlor to see who had come calling.

"I'll have Pete light the stove in here for us, so excuse me," Lula announced as she tucked a blanket around Edith. "My husband is away on business, and we don't use this parlor at all." She looked at her other daughters. "This is Rachel, Mrs. Clinton," speaking slowly so the girls would hear. "We call her 'Dot' and the other is Cozetta. Sometimes Mose calls her 'Cozy'." And then, to the girls, "Come along, now, let's go back to the kitchen where you were and finish your soup. Now I'll go get Pete, and I'll warm up some coffee if you like."

"Mama," Vera Clinton said excitedly, "look at the furniture! Isn't it pretty! And the antimacassar on this sofa. I bet someone took a long time crocheting it."

Mrs. Clinton's attention was on the cradle which she moved slightly to and fro, singing a lullaby. "I remember when you were born, Vera. My goodness, but that wasn't so long ago." She fingered the small blanket. "Just look at the work that went into this tiny quilt, will you, all the love you can see there with each stitch! And the baby! She sure is a pretty little thing."

Presently, Pete entered through the back door, banging the screen. He appeared in the parlor, his arms full of logs cut last summer from some big trees on the north side of Coal Creek. He was a small man of twenty years, with a healthy look about him, with a nice smile after he removed his hat. As he assembled and lit the fire, his big blue eyes quickly darted to where young Vera sat, her gloved hands neatly before her, her lovely hat tucked around her long black tresses. She was very much the proper Indian maiden which had long ago accepted the style and mode whose patterns appeared in the latest editions of the catalogs from a shelf at Hall's Store.

But Pete was white, born in the area around North Fork Town where the Missouri, Kansas, and Texas railroad penetrated the north/south route. He tested the fire, making sure that the heat was properly permeating the parlor, and then he rose to nod his head to the ladies. "That's it, I think," he said.

"Thank you, young man," Mrs. Clinton replied graciously, opened her big coat and let it fall beside her, but she did not remove her wide hat.

Lula reappeared, carrying a tray with cups and saucers. "Pete," she said, "go get our coffee for us, please." And the boy, unused to inside obedience, fled into the kitchen, grabbed the big iron pot and returned to the parlor.

"The whole Dunbar family is well known around Sapulpa. I don't use the word 'intruder' anymore like some others, I know. I, myself, came here and married Mr. Clinton so I guess I was an intruder, once." She accepted the coffee. "Charles is gone, now, bless his heart. He died in 'eighty-eight," She glanced at Vera who was unbuttoning her coat, now that the fire was blazing. Pete nodded to the ladies, and to Lula and left through the front door.

"I'm sorry," Lula confided, "I guess I didn't know of his passing." She smiled at Vera.

"I didn't remember my father, either," the girl said. She took one sip from her cup, placed it on a nearby table, and rose, leaving her coat on the sofa. Around the room on wallpapered walls was a selection of pictures, and she was eager to view them all. Two large oval prints of George Beecher Perryman, senior, and his brother, Thomas, were at eye level on the north wall which also contained the wide flu for the big stove. At the end of this room, on the east wall, beside one large window were two smaller prints of the two girls, Rachel and Cozetta, standing togeth-er wearing pretty dresses in one, and with their parents in another, pictures, evi-dently that were not too long ago. Through the east window, Vera's eyes suddenly spied Pete standing in the yard, peering at her. She turned away to find her mother still concerned with Edith, monitoring the cradle again. Vera returned to her coffee and placed more sugar in her cup.

Louise Amelia Dunbar Perryman was a handsome woman of twenty-two years, a stalwart pioneer who came from strong Missouri stock, with her father, mother, her own brothers and sisters. In 'ninety-five, she accepted the proposal of a determined and virile full blood of the Muscogee Nation, eight years her senior. Much to the chagrin of both families in that the Indian siblings looked askance upon the white woman. Lula herself was just as determined to make her marriage a successful bond. She was the oldest of the Dunbar children, and in all fairness to her own brothers and sisters, she gladly accepted this bond at the young age of six-teen.

Her father, having grown a walrus moustache since his own puberty, decided he wanted to be a carpenter. On that strength, and with the hearty Illinois blood in him, and with the name of Waller Cornelius Dunbar, his new trade made him immensely popular in Kansas where he met Lula's mother. Together, they decid-ed, also, to come southward for Texas which implied that they had to pass through Indian Territory. It was here after the birth of his seven children, and much travel, his wife died.

"I'm so sorry, Mrs. Perryman," Mrs. Clinton said. The remark was genuine. Since she had come from her native Alabama, this lady herself had become accus-tomed to learning about the rigorous life of pioneers, be they white or Indian.

But Waller Dunbar was consistent in building many a new farmhouse across this countryside including Red Fork, Sapulpa, and as far south as Kiefer. But he did not construct this one in which her guests were now seated.

Vera cleared her throat and, without rising pointed to an oval frame. "Who is that, I mean, which of the Perrymans?"

Peering down at them in a picture that was slightly askew was a dark face with short hair and a thick moustache. "That is my father-in-law," Lula said, and rose to straighten it against the wall. "He was a grand" ...and she hesitated merely to search for words, "..Indian." He died in 'ninety-nine. But he did help with this house, here, and dug our well. He was good at knowing all about well water and how to dig one. Oh," and she paused, "he made that little wooden bridge you drove over when you left the main road and came up the hill. He was more a cat-tleman than a carpenter." She laughed. "And best of all, he brought those rocks that form the sidewalk. He told me once that a lot of horses pulled those pieces. I'm talking about those pieces out at the back porch." Lula again looked at Edith.

Through the south windows across the front porch, they saw the men crossing the yard on their way to work a fence that needed mending. "Not much work this week. Today is a pretty winter day for us. Mr. Collins told me they want to get that fence fixed. And the cows, you know. We got a lot of milking to do, all the time, it seems."

That is the way it had been with the successful work of shipping cattle for twenty years. Moses Perryman's father and his uncles were extremely lucky with business brought to the area by drovers from Texas whose herds ventured north-ward through Creek Territory, through personal land owned by a variety of

Indians. Here, on their land, a system of maturing cattle for the East had expanded with herds that were insignificant, somewhat, at the onset, some twenty or so years ago when Moses was but an inquiring lad. Standing with his uncles, he learned to oversee the beginning of it all.

"You must be very happy with your home here," Mrs. Clinton said as she took the last of her coffee and declined more. "When do you expect the return of your husband?" She placed the empty cup on the table before her.

"In about, oh, three more days, I reckon."

"It's a nice opportunity for Vera to meet you, Mrs. Perryman," the matron said, "and for me to see you again, I'm sure. You are quite a strong person and I've heard this from other ladies we know." She folded her hands in her lap. "I admire you, my dear. I guess I feel like this is something you already realize, living up here on this hill and away from the crowds. I mean, from Red Fork, and Tulsa, and Sapulpa, too."

Red Fork had become a rather exciting town itself, some ten miles north of the Perryman Ranch. From its railroad station, Moses, his brothers, and his uncles had shipped cattle with growing success. People of all sorts predicted that the new city of Tulsa would surrender its economy to the burgeoning traffic of this community, especially after the railroad bridge was constructed across the meandering Arkansas River. That wide portion flowed in from Colorado and turned dramatically southward, separating the businesses near the railroad tracks, including Tulsa's one big hotel, from the stockyards across the river. Even the town of Sapulpa felt the increase in the number of cattlemen who came in from El Reno, far to the west.

It was this bit of information which the pleasant visitor shared with her hostess that prompted further remarks about the entire area. "My husband wanted to bring good education to our fair Red Fork," Mrs. Clinton continued, straightening the black lace on the front of her dress. "I've been soliciting help from practically all of the cattle families between Kiefer and Red Fork to establish a good school." She looked at little Edith. "You're not far from Sapulpa, are you?"

"It's just down the road a piece and past the Beaver home place, west of here, "Lula answered while she lifted her baby from her cradle. "I'll mention this to my husband when he returns." She smiled. "Mose is a good one for wanting education."

"Do you get into Tulsa much?" the visitor asked as she adjusted her hat. Some of the chickens began to cluck in the back of the house, rather loudly, because someone came into the kitchen from the back porch, slamming the screen door. Lula rose, holding Edith securely.

"You need any more water, Mrs. Perryman?" came the question from Laredo. He came on into the parlor but stopped suddenly, seeing the guests were seated. "Oh, I'm sorry, ma'am!" He retreated into the hallway and disappeared.

"That was just one of the hands, Mrs. Clinton. He came with Mr. Collins, our foreman. A good Texan." She sat again, in a different chair. "About Tulsa, you ask. Well. We don't get up there very much, I suppose. Mose spends time there, of course, and we see his mother from time to time, at her house."

Vera rose to look at the wall pictures more closely. Mrs. Clinton nodded her head, "I heard tell." This lady began to slip on her coat. "Mrs. Perryman, I do hope I may call again and, may I call you Lula?" She rose. Lula did the same. "I'm fortunate to have a family, myself. Vera's three brothers, you know. Fred is a doctor, now, and is living in Red Fork, but he plans to build in Tulsa, I think. Lee, my middle son, has a brand new baby girl whom we call Celia. Then Paul, the youngest. And then, Vera, of course, who is presently engaged to be married." Vera, joyfully, claimed her own coat, and together they all ambled into the hallway, and on to the porch. A sharp wind greeted them as if the weather changed its mind from the sunny day that it was to a bitter cold spell. This forced Lula to throw a shawl over her shoulders. Seeing the ladies there, and walking to the stile block, Pete was well ahead of them. He untied the reins and turned the surrey around, facing the east so the ladies could board by stepping on the stile block. To answer Vera's question, Pete graciously obliged with sparkling eyes. "It's for ladies to mount horses or get in surreys!" And to that, Vera laughed.

The afternoon was late but the sun was disappearing behind clouds. A wild flock of blackbirds cruised low over the south gate as Pete pointed to three black crows sitting in the top of a large maple tree. Without their leaves, the trees were often home to a multitude of birds that came and went in the winter sky.

"Can you come to church this Sunday?" asked Mrs. Clinton as she ascended the block with Pete's assistance. "It isn't too far to Red Fork, is it?" She lifted the blankets before she settled in place. Pete handed her the reins before he turned his attention to Vera who was waiting for him to escort her into her position.

"Shotgun!" he exclaimed, and the young girl could not keep her eyes off his smiling face. "Bundle up good, now!" was his quick reply. The horse grew impatient and pranced, squeaking the surrey.

"I go to church when I can. I'm on good terms with the Man upstairs."

"Young man, " called Mrs. Clinton, putting on her driving gloves, "would you please check the harness?"

"Oh, yes ma'am. My name is Pete. Just call me Pete."

"Yes." She cleared her throat. "And Lula, thank you for a pleasant afternoon. I must say you have a beautiful home here. I noticed you have some winter pansies across the fence there. Still pretty." She clucked at her horse as she lifted reins higher. "Goodbye, Lula!"

Just to the west, the milk cows were herded by Laredo and Mr. Collins into the barn as the surrey departed. With a tip of his hat, Pete ran to join the men.

Lula waited to return to the house until the surrey passed over the wooden bridge. She looked once into the sky to the sun beyond the barn, and to the birds that again returned to the bare trees as quickly as they fled. The crows were circling or pausing to rest wherever they found room for all three.

The cows were always in the south pasture and hardly ever strayed too far, out of sheer habit. But sometimes when they could not be seen, the men had to mount up and ride to find them. Their path, which came from an arroyo far to the south proceeded past the stile, past the barn, and disappeared to the west into the heavy line of scrub oak, which also waited for spring. But now, after seven years, this path was becoming another wide roadway on which many a buggy and horse had traveled. Moses Perryman and his bride had welcomed an illustrious host of cattlemen, Indians, Texans, the population of Keifer. They welcomed all, all of them, everyone. Moses himself has specified the same kind of sentiment which his mother had always professed at her White House. No one was ignored. No lonely cowhand was denied food, no orphan was dismissed. Mrs. Rachel had set the precedence. The very words of Mrs. Clinton, uttered no more than thirty minutes ago, echoed in Lula's mind. "Mrs. Covey once told me that your mother-in-law,

Mrs. Rachel, was the kindest lady she ever knew."

So said Mrs. Clinton who had heard not only that reference but other stories about the Perryman clan. But being the fine lady that she was, and with her daughter present that afternoon, Mrs. Clinton did not pursue much of the turmoil that existed in the subterranean areas of family life. Her sons, Lee and Fred, had heard from the gossip and strife of Red Fork society. She could almost hear Lula comment about her in-laws. "I've got some who don't quite care for me, I suppose."

Whether or not that sort of subject matter lay just below the surface of conversation that afternoon, over coffee, was not especially pertinent to Lula at that moment in time. Lula never ventured to take any time to place those particular thoughts into audible words, anyway, even for this woman and her daughter who came calling. Such supposition was a tiny idea in her Caucasian mind when she her father, and her sisters, had agreed that Moses S. Perryman, though he were a full blood Creek Indian, would be her husband some six years ago.

She paused in her thinking to see if the surrey had made it to the main road or was, by now, out of sight. She did notice other traffic there, a horse and a rider, far away, heading southward, but they were too far to discern who he was.

Lula walked to her porch giving thought once again to this matron from Red Fork. Mrs. Clinton had been prepared to meet a frightened young miss who was afraid of the atmosphere and stark ritual of farm work. Instead, this matron had discovered a diligent woman with a strong will and a warm heart. Mrs. Moses Perryman was a determined lady pleasant indeed, but capable of managing her house and land extremely well while her husband was away on a business trip to the Big City.

Lula set about preparing her stove for a big fire. Then, she went to Edith and saw that the baby was sleeping well. She tucked a little red blanket more tightly around her, lit two lamps, one for the kitchen, and one for the dining room. Dot and Cozy greeted her from the hallway. A noise from the stile block made her look out the door. Through the dusk she heard the neighing of a horse, the birds, too, as they swooped in concert, flying far to the east, against the the wind.

She opened the screen despite the cold air of early evening. The dark figure she saw on a horse was now at the south gate. "Hello!" she called. She quickly recognized her brother-in-law. It was Abner, carrying a satchel and looking tired as he came into better view.

"Well, for goodness sake, Abner," she called loudly as she briskly made her way off the porch. Dot and Cozy, from their play, stopped at the front door. "I was thinking about you just today. Come on in. I'm about ready to start supper."

"Oh, Lula," Abner began, trying to steady himself once his horse was tied. He removed his big hat, allowing the cold wind to sift through his long black hair. He entered the gate and removed his gloves, pausing to catch his breath.

Lula met him with a smile. When the little girls opened the front door and stepped onto the porch, she turned to caution them. "Go back in the house, you two, it's your Uncle Abner. Go on, now, it's cold" She welcomed him, walking arm in arm back to the house as the girls obeyed their mother.

He was unusually silent and Lula perceived a sad glint in his brown eyes as he offered a meager grin. Lula was accustomed to reticent Indians who had visited Moses at the ranch, those silent creatures who either knew no English or refused to learn it, those handsome elders who were all too quiet in their own ways, and who did not say very much, at the most. But Abner was of the current generation, one who knew merely a semblance of his parents' language but was, himself, well versed in English. Mrs. Clinton, once a student at Tullahasee, had remarked just that afternoon that, of Lula's in-laws, Abner Perryman was an intelligent and vociferous young Brave, as she had stated it.

Lula interrupted her thought by calling out to Laredo who was riding swiftly toward the house. He stopped abruptly to hear what she said. "Tell the men to start getting ready for supper. Tell Mr. Collins that Abner is here."

"Yessum, I will."

The girls were waiting for them.

"How's my Edith?" Abner asked, in the hallway and he lifted Dot first, then Cozetta.

Lula went to the cradle. Gathering the baby in her arms, she showed her to him. "I'm not going to lose this one like I did with my boy."

Abner placed his hat and gloves on the kitchen table and smiled down at the two nieces who were vying, once again, to be lifted and hugged. Presently, he told them to run into the other room for a while. From the back porch, they heard Pete who was the first to arrive with two buckets of milk.

"Sit down, Lula," he said as he grabbed a chair for himself.

"You can wash up in a minute" she offered. "Take this towel when you go so the men will have a new one." She was at the cabinet with a fresh cotton cloth in her hand. Edith began to squirm in her cradle so Lula put the towel on the table and looked at the child. She did not notice how immobile Abner had become, sitting there as if he, himself, were waiting for something to happen.

Mr. Collins joined Pete on the back porch. They commented on the milk, their words sounding through the back door amid their laughter. Lula poured some well water into a glass and offered it to Abner and then cradled Edith in her arms. Then for the first time, she noticed Abner's quiet countenance and sat opposite him.

Lula rocked the baby but suspected some odd situations as manifested by his sober face. To break this spell, she rose to replace Edith, reclaimed her towel, and again she focused her eyes on Abner as he finished drinking the water. He set the empty glass to one side as she remained standing. Abner cleared his throat while hardly moving a muscle. She took another lamp, removed its chimney, and placed coal oil in its base. She realized he had not spoken, except to dismiss the girls, something he hardy ever did, especially upon arrival. She put the lamp on the table and sat down.

"What is it, Abner?"

They heard the men walk away from the porch and into the milk room where the temperature, hopefully, was as cold as all outdoors.

"Let's go in the other room.," Abner answered, rising and forcing Lula to do the same. "Come on. I got bad news."

Lula grabbed the lamp she had just filled and they passed into the hallway. "Bad news?"

Dot and Cozetta were in the front bedroom talking to themselves. But when Abner stopped under the archway that led to the parlor, she also hesitated. The coffee cups were still on the table where, just an hour ago she had had a pleasant conversation with a woman and her daughter whom she hardly knew.

Lula passed him and walked to that table, moved a cup and saucer to make room for the lamp. Then, mystified, she turned to him. "I'm ready." The lamp's rays filled half the room.

Abner forced her to sit on the sofa with him, and he held her hands gently. "We got word on the morning train." He took a deep breath. "Mose is dead, Lula. He died in St. Louis. He must have died accidentily."

The mahogany clock on the other table in the room chimed its lovely melody before it struck the sixth hour.

"He's gone, Lula."

She sat there, alone, save for her three daughters.

Chapter Three

The winds were cold that day, for it was February again with her return to winter. The bright, deceiving sun of four days ago, when Abner wept, decided to mourn also, and it hid behind dark clouds that threatened rain.

But still they came, those loyal to this branch, those who had known the uncles, the aunts, the cousins, the in-laws of so many limbs of this family tree. They came to the designated plot of ground that was their own cemetery and they were standing in droves, in multitudes, ever respectful, with the buggies, their horses, their carriages, all along the narrow frozen road that led northward into town and southward into barren fields and blackjack hills. The birds were there, flying in their large clusters as they ordinarily did, but they did not land in the trees as if they too, knew a funeral was in progress. The winds grew strong and forceful that day.

Mrs. Louise Amelia Perryman stood just to the west side of the open grave, holding Edith in her arms with Dot and Cozetta to her right, standing in obedience without totally understanding the solemnity of the day nor did they comprehend why they would never see their father anymore. But the people always joined together, under any circumstance. They were always there to help each other, as in this case, as in this ritual that the Creeks wanted. And they came for all reasons and occasions, for all businesses, for all recreation, even for funerals. They were there.

They had waited for the arrival of Legus Perryman and his wife. This leader of the Tribe stepped down from his wagon. He first ventured to the grave of his own son. The mourners understood. All eyes were on him as he continued, walking quietly, hat in hand, directly to the widow of his nephew.

Lula watched this impressive figure come nearer. He reached down and patted the little girls' heads, cupping his left hand under Dot's chin to whisper a sweet condolence in Creek and then in English. Then, it was Cozetta's time to look into this kind face when Legus repeated the words.

"I am so sorry, my dear Lula. Since yesterday when we ate together I have been in prayer for your Moses. Please allow me to stand on the other side of the grave, opposite you and the girls. I want to help with the blanket over the coffin."

On the east side of this cemetery nearest the wide street, a buggy had not dislodged its passengers. Remaining there to keep as warm as possible but not to draw attention to themselves were Mrs. Rachel and her oldest daughter, Emma. She hardly ever preferred to be called Mrs. Clifton Drew. Since childhood, she was wary of funerals. The death of her oldest brother was still bearing down on her and her mother. But Creek traditions were exceptionally strong in her veins. She was willing. Now that the ex-chief had arrived and was consoling her sister-in-law, Emma began the task of escorting her mother over to the grave with but a few young boys to help the ladies up the steep incline.

One of the lads assisting them spoke softly and reverently. "I'm one of the Childers boys, ma'am. You're Mrs. Drew, aren't you?" He tipped his black hat as he took her arm. Emma only nodded her head. "My Mama and Papa told me to get word to the family that they couldn't come this time. We are all awfully sorry, ma'am, about your brother. My Papa knew your brother." He tipped his hat the second time.

They were at the top of the little knoll where Mrs. Rachel wanted to stop and rest. "You tell your mother and father we thank them most sincerely," was Emma's reply. Then she spoke in Creek to her mother, identifying the boy to whom Mrs. Rachel extended her gloveless hand with a nice smile.

Emma told her mother to put on her gloves. A bit dazed in grief, she was drawn to the spot where only recently she had placed two little babies in their graves. To return to this cemetery, for whatever purpose, reestablished fresh tears in her eyes. It was for that reason that her husband, regardless of the dimensions of his own personality, did not wish to attend the funeral in so short a time. But on the previous evening, at the White House, he did extend his condolence to Lula. With Emma standing beside him, he went into the dining room, took Lula's hand in his, and said how sad he was. This was a man Lula had hardly known, but he was sincere and she could discern this in his eyes and the manner in which he moved about the house. Mr. Drew was strangely distant and shy.

Legus Perryman saw Mrs. Rachel coming his way in slow steps wearing a heavy shawl about her shoulders, with a black hat tied under her chin. She was regal, he could see that. After speaking inaudibly in Creek, she guarded her own hands. And being the grandmother, she blessed the little girls with her genuine smile and reached down to kiss Edith on the brow.

Ella Perryman Horner was a sister who kept to herself for the majority of time. But she and her husband and little Leo were there, themselves thought to be always on the outskirts of any family development. But Ella persisted in being friendly as much as possible, whenever she had visited her mother. Ella's complexion was darker than her siblings, and her husband, being full blood Creek himself, was darker, yet. They remained just behind Lula and the girls, standing next to Mr. Collins, Laredo, and Pete, in the background.

Mr. Horner was such a quiet individual that Ella was unable to attest to his mourning. He was less vociferous of all the Indians she knew and as he approached middle age, he was content to remain so. He refused to provide opinions of what happened by accident in St. Louis, if indeed, anything did happen that was akin to a misadventure of sorts. Before stepping from his buggy, he produced a quid of tobacco, bit off a large bite, much to the chagrin of his wife. Ella glanced at Mayme who was alone since Mr. Shirk decided to remain in their buggy for the sole purpose of draining the last drop of whiskey that he bought in Sapulpa, just for the occasion.

Mayme Shirk, the tall, heavy woman with a large bosom, was quite displeased about the whole affair. At the White House, just prior to coming to the cemetery, she argued with anyone who would listen to her. She was noted for making quick angular gestures with her caustic remarks, so unlike the subtle relationships of her brethren. So in the cold weather of the next day, she was shocked to find Oliver suddenly at her side. He had come to her with Abner, and he had grabbed his sister's hand, and she looked at his in disbelief. His little mind did not accept what had happened to his oldest brother in that far away city, and he could not understand what everyone was saying in whispered corners of their minds. At one point, he was crying so that be began to shake, even in the cold. It was then that Abner pulled him away from Mayme, to himself, and he reached his strong hand around Oliver to assuage the boy's grief.

George junior, the bright, young businessman of seventeen years, even in grief, was proudly standing next to his fiance, Orphia Reynolds, who had just consented with the agreement of her own family, to become Mrs. George Beecher Perryman, junior, come June. Some time ago, a doubt entered upon this announcement. Mayme Shirk, being a staunch believer in pure Indian blood, contested the blood line of this fine Caucasian sixteen-year old. Long before Moses departed for St. Louis, George escorted his lady out to the Wrangler Ranch and introduced her to Lula. Together, Orphia and Lula went all over the property there, to the barn, to the well, and the young girl was introduced to Pete and Laredo while George stayed in the house and talked to Mr. Collins over coffee.

"You don't possibly think we are too young, do you Mrs. Perryman?" Orphia asked Lula on their way back to the house. This question was brought to mind when Lula's eyes gently caught Orphia's look at her, across the open grave, and Lula nodded to her as a swift breeze passed over her head. "I was sixteen when I married Mose, my dear."

Now, Lula turned to her father who stood directly behind her. She handed Edith to him because she had suddenly felt tired. He replaced his hat on his head when he took the baby in his arms.

The many full bloods who were near the open grave began to sing their Creek song, and a prayer was uttered. Then, as if a silent director was taking charge, the coffin was lowered into the hole not too far below ground level. The men pulled out their ropes and stood away from the edge. Ella, who had elected to be the bearer of the burial quilt, joined four young men who had come to the casket, standing two on each side. They accepted it from her and placed it on the outside of the coffin, smoothing down the edges so that the top was neatly in place, over it. This gesture brought great comfort to many mourners, some as far as the road. The old ones nodded in agreement. Despite the cold sprinkle of rain that came in from the north, the soft verbal contentment accompanied the kind words of the minister.

To complete this rite, two other men from the tribe held shovels of dirt and stood at the opposite ends of the grave. As the Indians sang again, each of the crowd, one by one, removed a glove and scooped a handful of dirt and dropped it into the vault. The family was first. Before she did so, Orphia whispered, "George, why did those men put that lovely blanket over the coffin like that?"

He could do nothing but shake his head, for the tears welled in his damp eyes as he let slip the grains from his fingers. The line was slow but the winds were threatening rain. Since that morning, the winter black birds circled above them, darting in and out of thunder clouds, so unlike a February sky. Shortly, a blast of colder air passed over the mourners. Some concern for snow had softly entered the conversations, for the winds persisted and the horses began to whine and paw the hard ground.

Mrs. Rachel found three full bloods with whom she was able to speak. One of them reminded her of earlier years when he learned to call her aunt, a gesture which sustained the title across the many months. She stopped a quiet man with a subtle nudge from her hand to thank him and friends of the family for digging the grave. Not at any time was it ever necessary for the bereaved family to ask remuneration for this service. George junior finally had a moment to respond to his fiance's inquiry. "Tradition, my dear," was all he said.

It was time to cover the grave. The tombstone would come later. As the people dispersed, a slab of flat concrete was placed, hoisted by sixteen men because of its weight.

Of Lula's siblings, only one brother came all the way from Sapulpa with their father. He was her youngest, fifteen years old, a bit shy, but polite, and enraptured by the unique Creek burial. He came to stand close to his sister and he took his nieces' hands. At one point, Lula took Edith from her father. "There's Oliver!" Lula said, pointing.

Sometime ago, the brother had become acquainted with Oliver. Often, they played together at the ranch, proudly showing each other their horses even though Oliver was not at the time, in possession of Moses's mare.

"Hey, Walter Clyde!" Oliver called in greeting.

"Hi, Oliver," and again the two boys were friends. They walked away together to the buggies to talk about horses.

The umbrella affect of the grandiose scrub oak trees with the less dignified elms was a great comfort to the ceremony that just finished. The old trees had surrounded this small plot of ground longer than anyone could imagine. These oaks were similar to the great tall one on the Council Oak area in Tulsa, inviting not only the few Perrymans to consider placing the graveyard at this location but others to protect and respect this area. For miles, nothing was around it, no buildings, no tents, no ranch homes. Only the north-south road, aiming itself toward Tulsa, was evident that some profound concern had been given to this hallowed ground.

Soon the commitment to the ground became a fresh memory. The pallbearers with the men who worked the hard sod and the singers stepped away from this place, to their own thoughts, to their own buggies and horses, to their own homes. They did not move fast, for the rain was slight and the departure was silent. Filing past the widow, a few spoke to her in Creek.

Lula and the girls climbed into her father's carriage to receive the handshakes, the condolences, the kind remarks, and the simple nod of the head form those in line. The same Childers boy, whose face was familiar but whose name eluded Emma, escorted her and Mrs. Rachel back to their own buggy, turned the horse in the direction of the White House and tipped his hat in a kind farewell gesture.

"No, wait a minute," Emma said as her mother whispered a word to her. "Mama says for you and the others to come have a bite to eat at the house, now. You're expected."

"Thank you, ma'am," he said, looking to the others who had remained. "Just two more of us who helped dig. I'll tell 'em."

"She wants you all, now you know!" Emma removed her glove to wipe the rain from the boy's face. "Put your hat back on, it's cold."

"Yessum, thank you," and he waved as she raised the reins, clucked at her horse, and got in line with the others.

George and Orphia were the last to leave. They sat in the special black surrey borrowed for this occasion. He held the reins loosely for the while, still thinking about when he had reprimanded all of them for even having a convoluted thought in their minds. "Don't think like that," Uncle Josiah said, once, when Abner was angry at Moses, or when George did not see eye to eye with what both of them were thinking.

Just before they dispersed, Mrs. Reynolds came to Waller Dunbar, noted the care he was giving to Edith and complimented him. "I'm Orphia's mother," she said, taking the baby for a moment. "I'm used to carrying little ones like this."

"Well, I am too!" he responded.

With Edith in her arms, Mrs. Reynolds walked with him to his carriage and surrendered the baby to Lula. "I'm riding back with Orphia and George, Lula."

Ella's attempt to remain calm that day finally gave way to her husband's second remark that he volunteered about Moses's demise. En route with the rain having stopped, she sat to his left while he commanded the horse. "Mr. Horner, I wish you'd stop. Now don't say a word, anymore, do you hear, about what happened." She was forceful, he was silent. "We just do not know what happened in St. Louis. And do not go making any accusations about Mose's body not being embalmed. How on earth do you know that?"

He glanced her way. The unusual and astonishing remark that his body was not prepared for shipment could be a shock practically to everyone. This was nineteen-one and a degree of civility was very assuredly a part of this new city of Tulsa. She allowed a myriad of thoughts to invade her mind as her buggy followed the others toward the house. How could anyone in his right mind place a corpse in a tacky wooden box and ship it, bloated and ugly, if that was indeed the case, on a freight train to Indian Territory and not feel in some form, some compunction for the people to whom it was being shipped? Moses was not embalmed. And this was why, even with the threat of rain or snow, the funeral had to take place that very next day.

"Now you just be quiet about a lot of this, do you hear?" Ella was explicit and never did her composure return until she and Mr. Horner stopped by the pond to relax.

J.M. Hall, at his store, agreed with the city undertaker that nothing, now, could or should be done to make the body presentable before entombment. Supposedly, Lula had not been told. Ella suspected that even her mother was spared this information. But somehow, some way, Mr. Horner had heard pieces and bits of what occurred in St. Louis.

The crowd was at the White House. "Now," announced Ella, ready to proceed, "when we go inside just act like you didn't hear anything about that trip....all that untrue information." Despite the cold damp weather she removed her gloves and hat and held them in her lap as Mr. Horner clucked at the horse and found a place to park under one of the big oak trees.

Oliver sat in his favorite chair in the kitchen, watching the ladies come and go. He was eating some stew which Mrs. Covey brought to the house before the funeral. Through the window he saw the farm hands going to the barn to milk and he was glad he did not have to join them because it was cold.

When he was a mere boy of six or seven, he once complained to his grandfather why he had to rise early to milk. In order to provide as logical an answer as possible for the boy, the old Indian called Thomas over to them, and it was Oliver's uncle who translated the advice. "Oliver," replied the amused uncle, "we have to milk early so you can leave for school." But he also added, "Now that your father has the new house downtown, you and your mother will live in it while you are in the first grades. You will like that. You will have a short distance to walk and you won't have to help with the milking anymore. Won't you like that?"

A boy of twelve had thoughts about all this, too. He enjoyed the House, but he liked being out here at the White House even better. He had room in which to ride, and he suddenly realized that maybe Lula would give Moses's mare to him! He looked at the food and toyed with that thought, and the spoon.

Abner came into the kitchen, pulled up a chair next to his side of the table, and sat. "Is the soup good?"

"It's stew, Mrs. Covey's stew."

"Oh." Abner nodded affirmatively. "May I have a bite?"

Oliver pushed the bowl toward him. "Sure."

Abner dipped into it with is spoon and swallowed a big portion. He nodded again. "Hhhmmm, good!"

The overwhelming event of the day was still with Oliver. He had no one at such an hour on whom he may rely, other than Abner, for any degree of logic about it all. He had heard of violent death in Tulsa, but for it to occur to his oldest brother in a far away city was confusing. With his hands in his lap, he stared at this brother for a long time. Abner offered his spoon to him and made a small indication to "eat up", a gesture by which this closest sibling had been joking with him for a great many months. When younger, Oliver played the game of "whistle" with him, in that the child would whistle a tune and Abner would "grab" the melody from his lips with a quick hand and place it in his own mouth. With the food game, Abner always made certain that Oliver would eat practically anything set before him.

"When you finish the stew, you might want to come into the parlor and sit beside Lula for a while. She'd like that." Before he rose, Abner leaned closer and whispered, "you know, I think maybe she'll give you Mose's mare. I know you'd like that!"

About to dip into the bowl again, Oliver poised his spoon above the food. His eyes grew wide and he grabbed Abner by his arm. "You think she will?"

"Even his saddle, too, if you ask her right." Oliver jumped up from the table. "No! You finish, first. I'm going back in the parlor myself. Now, you come in a minute, all right?"

Oliver ate fast. Many people passed through the kitchen, into the hallway and mingled on the crowded back porch despite the damp weather. The men sipped coffee and exchanged stories about this one who was dead. A few laughed, but not overtly, nor were they disrespectful to a memory.

Through the doorway leading into the hall, Oliver viewed George and Orphia. He got a quick glimpse at Stewart Shirk, talking to another man, with his hat still on his head. Mayme was there to complain, to remove it for him with some kind of remark Oliver was not able to hear.

Waller Dunbar sauntered into the kitchen with a plate of half-eaten food. Walter Clyde was with him but Waller talked to a white man who followed him, with both leaning against a cabinet.

Walter Clyde sat down opposite Oliver and selected an apple from a blue bowl on the table. Food was everywhere, and it was difficult for either boy to select which desert each should try. Four separate pies waited on the counter behind the two men. "I think this one is mince, Walter Clyde," his father announced "You want that apple or do you want a piece of this pie?"

"What are you going to have?" Walter Clyde asked.

Oliver confronted his problem as best he could. He would either leave now, go into the parlor to talk to Lula, or he could sit with his friend and have a piece of mince. "I guess I'll have a piece if you will!"

Presently, as the late afternoon, with its dampness, turned into early evening, when the Indians began to leave, Lula remained in the sitting room after putting the girls to their naps. Mrs. Covey and Arnold waited patiently to talk. She buttoned her flimsy coat as she spoke. "Oh, Lula, I'm so sorry you lost Mose, but..." and then, she hesitated to compose her words. "Well, I guess that's all I can say right now. Come on, Arnold, let's go. I'll come by and see you soon."

The people who had been so courteous, who had sat next to her, who held her hands, who imparted their sorrow were all leaving the house. Old Indians spoke in Creek. Even the singers had a moment of farewell for her and wished her success. Someone brought a lighted lamp and placed it on a table near the front window. A lady whom Lula did not recognize paused in front of her. "I'll take the coffee cup from you. You want more? Mrs. Rachel is finally eating something. You better come into the dining room and try some of my chicken."

Lula would have done just that, for she was finally awakened from her prolonged and quiet time. Many families were represented. Many had spoken only to Mrs. Rachel. She could not remember them all.

Oliver appeared just as she was about to rise. He paused at the archway and Lula saw him amble toward her, his hands behind him, the most solemn look on his little face. It was that image that made her wait. As he drew near, she raised her arms for a loving embrace as he sat down next to her on the sofa and leaned his head onto her shoulder. With her arm around him she managed a soft pat on his cheek. Nothing much was said among any of the remaining mourners.

"Indians are usually quiet aren't they, Lula?" was Oliver's only offering.

"Yes, honey, most of them are. But that's all right. They show their concern, just the same." Lula suddenly began to sing, softly, a hymn that her own mother had taught her long ago. It was to Oliver, yes, but it was, at best, merely to give herself added courage, some semblance of the type that provided her family with a degree of immeasurable hope. Oliver turned to look at her as she sang. It was actually the first time he had ever known her to raise her voice in a melody of sorts. He had hardly ever heard his sisters sing, unless it was at church where no one was solo of any kind. Eventually, his eyes fell away from her profile and he returned to her warm shoulder.

Ella was in the kitchen with her two sisters. The question of their husbands entered their simple conversation. She put the dirty forks into the dishpan and began to wonder. Her husband lost himself in the crowd at first, and then, later, had managed to seclude himself in the far corner of the hallway where she finally discovered him, alone, and in thought. "What is it, Mr. Horner?" She dried her hands on an apron and looked directly at him.

"Well..." he began, hesitant to speak his mind because he hardly ever did so. "Here I am the white man, and you're the full blood...Just the opposite of Mose and Lula."

Ella had a habit of listening to him more than she did of returning his meager conversations. One of the intruders who came into the territory at a very early date, Mike Horner had brought with him a wife and young son as part of the land rush. It was not altogether successful. They then settled on a farm south of Tulsa in Broken Arrow, but that failed miserably. Just as they recovered, with Perryman assistance, he lost his young son in a sudden accident involving a team of horses. Within months the boy's mother died of grief. Perhaps all that was still reflected in his deep set brown eyes and dark hair that was streaked with gray.

"I'm glad we got Leo, Ella," he said softly. "These winters we been having took Emma's little babies. I'm glad Leo is all right."

"I'm glad too, Mike. Come on. You go get the buggy ready, and let's go home."

He put on his thick mackinaw. Stepping past the other two husbands on the south porch, he said nothing to them because they were arguing, picking their teeth after a big supper, and swearing, and waiting to go to their own homes.

Chapter Four

For a week after Moses Perryman was buried, the weather remained so unbearably cold that few people ventured to the Wrangler Ranch to console Lula. But one day a small wagon approached the house from the south, crossed over the little bridge and came up the incline to the stile block. Bundled against this chill, and driven by sheer willpower, was a group of five full bloods. Their driver was a young Creek who never forgot the kindness of Moses when, three years ago he was in dire need of rest and food. The Creek boy, then eighteen, had lost his way in the worst snowstorm that Eufaula had ever had. Moses had seen to it that he was fed and clothed. The youth promised never to get lost again. Moses had not forgotten the incident nor had he mislaid the name of the boy's family. It was this wagonfull that made the trip to see the widow. And it was ironic that powdered snow accompanied their tribute.

The mother and father and the other two children were ushered into the kitchen while the oldest boy, with his hat now balanced on his back by his chin strap, spoke eloquently in English to Lula. "I shall never forget your husband, Mrs. Perryman. And my parents do not ever forget, either. We live in Eufaula now, and we could not arrive in time for the funeral. We are sorry, please, and we want you to know that his memory with us will not perish, as we all are bound to do so."

Present at this incident was Ralph Collins who, with Laredo and Pete, had come in, out of the cold, to help prepare food, and then, reluctantly for the visitors, to send them on their way. The snow had ceased by the time they boarded their wagon, but they again wrapped themselves well with their blankets and with wide strips of cotton tied around their hats.

In the month that followed, with the wild winds of March, a dark pall settled over the large house on the hill. Eventually, activity that concerned itself with the upkeep of the ranch resumed. The gate between the steps to the kitchen and the pathway to the bunkhouse became noisy when anyone tried to open and shut it while passing through it. At one time, Pete presumed he could erase the squeaking with proper oil, but none seemed to do the job. As with so many other complications arising from time to time, Lula surrendered to fate, and the portal retained its title as the noisy gate.

By spring of that year, nineteen-one, Lula ventured to Tulsa, fording the Arkansas River by herself for the sole purpose of selecting a lawyer to help her in legal matters. She thought of an attorney whose name came to mind, wisely enough, a portly gentleman who had lived in Indian Territory for ten years, and who was recommended by several tribal leaders. In one small stack of business papers found in Moses's desk, she encountered his name, Jedediah Parker, written in her husband's neat scribe. "I'll be all right. I've forded the river before, Mr. Collins. You don't need to come with me." So with the three daughters intact, she managed to meet him at this time.

"By Creek law," he had told her, "all property goes to the children of the deceased, and not to the widow." It was a thought to ponder.

At a distance, so as not to impose, because he was always aware of grief, even for a short while, Ralph Augustus Collins remained aloof, but always present, eager to assist when he could do so, but ever respectful of his position at the ranch. His background was not strange, only elusive to some of the settlers. He was a Texan, tall and strong, born in eighteen-fifty-three, in some nondescript southeast town whose name Lula could not remember. His dark face, sunburned by countless days on the prairie, and his wrinkled skin made everyone presume that he too was Creek. He was, so he said, at one time on a snowy day after milking, the third child of a Mexican mother and a hardy drifter from Tennessee who died in the Civil War. Lula later learned from Moses's uncle Joseph that the mother died before Ralph Collins left Texas and his older brother and sister disappeared in the long rambling years as they were growing. Even this drover never did understand where they eventually strayed, much like the many longhorns brought into Texas by Mexicanos. Somewhere now on a paper on which some educated rancher had written the name, Ralph Augustus Collins, he was told to keep the first name and forget the middle one. And so he did. But he folded the paper and tucked it away with a picture of his sister and brother and placed them in his satchel. He forgot his middle name and he also forgot where he placed the paper.

The rancher who wrote his name was the successful cattleman, James Daugherty, a Texan, too, who had been purportedly in a more lucky station in life than the poor Ralph Collins. Where Daugherty obtained his original money, no one knows. By eighteen-eighty-three, he was into Indian Territory his latest trip with his fourth herd, having arranged a legal lease from Legus Perryman. For one-half-cent an acre, James Daugherty rented a large tract of land, brought literally hundreds of longhorns and beef cattle on a trail other than the Chisholm, and he established a kingdom for himself. And with him came Ralph Collins.

This thirty-year-old, a bit awkward at first, hesitant about taking on any new responsibility, talked well into the night with his new boss before actually leaving Texas. So Mr. Daugherty was well aware, indeed, of what Mr. Collins aspired to do for himself. As a drover, coming north into Indian Territory even for the first time, naturally took charge of his own care and his own future. Honest and quiet, he came to be the best cowhand James Daugherty hired.

"You're all right, Mr. Collins. You're a good man!"

After leasing the acreage for grassland, Daugherty spoke favorably about Collins when the latter applied to become a ranchhand for Legus Perryman. The time had come, so was the mutual opinion, that the young cowhand liked the country here. Even Daugherty himself admired this drover for that thought.

Despite the charm and open-mindedness of his countenance, Ralph Collins was adroit master of his gun, with a quick draw and an inherent awareness of what his gun could do. He had never used it, lately, to any degree, even, in self defense, but he had been taught by an old cowhand who had come north with Daugherty's herds long before the boy was hardly old enough to master the technique.

It was not this elderly cowpoke who taught him everything. The first Mr. Collins, their father from Tennessee, began the rudiments of firing pistols when Ralph and his brother were mere lads, shortly before their father became an unknown soldier. When others asked, the old cowpoke remarked that Ralph Collins handled his piece well. Very well.

Ralph was forced to make a decision about his own life and his brother agreed. He was to leave. So, with hardly any education, so to speak, he found that he was en route northward with a new trend of herding cattle to Kansas, but not on the Chisholm Trail. There was a new direction for him. The old cowboy and Mr. Daugherty saw to that.

"Mr. Daugherty," Legus Perryman responded after hearing the request from both the men, "I don't need a man, but let me tell you," and the Indian shifted his weight to another foot, peering into the questioning eyes of the Texan, "my brother, George Beecher, needs a foreman and needs one like right now. I'm going over to see him tomorrow on some cattle business and I'll take this here man with me." This was a valid recommendation from the man who was soon to become the principal chief of the Creek Tribe.

So the next morning, Ralph Collins stood awkwardly before another Mr. Perryman, with his dirty brown hat in his rough hands, but wearing a clean denim shirt washed the previous night by Legus' wife, herself.

"Yes, sir, that's right," Ralph was saying, continuing the involved procedure of being hired. "I actually came into the territory in eighteen-seventy-eight, with this here Mister Daugherty, so I know this entire area pretty well. I know you have been thinking about fencing your own property. I have been back and forth now for about four separate...with four separate herds, Mr. Perryman. And I know how to use a gun."

"I'm sure you do," Perryman smiled, "after seeing the demonstration today, after what Daugherty told me. Now come on inside. If you want to wash up first, go around in back. I want you to meet my family. You've already met my brother Legus. We've got a dozen or more it seems. And we got some sisters, here and there." Then he stopped as they approached the first steps. "You don't mind working for a full blood, do you? This is a big day for us, Mr. Collins, it is! My family is here to celebrate the birth of yet another son for me and my full blood wife, Rachel." From the hallway, he called his children into the main sitting room where Rachel had positioned herself earlier. The two men walked over to where she was sitting on her sofa, with their baby in her arms.

"This is my wife, Mr. Collins, with our newest baby boy. She doesn't speak English so wait a minute, if you will, and I'll introduce you to her." The gentle words whispered, were along with the soft touch of his hand on her arm. He said he was their new foreman by the name of Mr. Collins. Then, taking the baby, he said, "and this is George Beecher Perryman, junior!"

Once the introduction was over, Mrs. Rachel reached again for the infant so that the farmhand could look into the boy's eyes. Ralph Collins could see how proud the lady was!

To the others who came into the room, the father acknowledged them, one by one. He singled out his oldest son. "This is our first son and his name is Moses but we call him Mose. He is twelve now."

"Thirteen, Papa," Moses politely corrected him.

"Oh yes, oh, yes," and he turned to another. "And this is our first daughter, Emma, who is seven." She curtsied and stepped back to allow others to come forward.

"We lost a boy, Mr. Collins. His name was John. He would have been, oh, I guess, eleven by now." And then he placed a hand on another son's shoulders. "And this Abner who is....how old are you, son?"

The child raised his hand and counted five fingers.

"Then, Ella, who is only four. I guess that's all except our new one." But it was Mayme who, herself, was only three and silently standing in the archway, unable to object to her father's innocent forgetfulness. It was Legus, their uncle, who brought this mistake to his brother's attention. And then little Mayme, greatly relieved that she was still a part of this important family ran to her father's arms as swiftly as she could manage, with joyous laughter.

"Wife, and family," the head of this clan began, "this here is Mr. Collins and he is going to be our new foreman effective right now." One by one, politely, the brothers shook his hand as the little sisters peered quizzically into the wrinkled face. "Now, Mr. Collins, you may join us in the celebration of this new child of ours. We are going to proceed into the dining room yonder and have a nice repast."

Legus came over to talk. "Mr. Collins, you may put your hat on the halltree while we eat. We have a lot on our minds, today but I want to say that you are welcomed into a fine family. I don't think you've ever been in this house, have you? This place has a name. It's called the White House. My brother grew to manhood on this land just as I did, sir. My place is in Eufaula, now. I have three children, Andrew, who is twelve, and Henry, and a girl, Leah."

They began to seat themselves around the big table, bounteously filled with food, and Legus did not have time to complete the story of his own ranch nor the story of how their own father died in Kansas during the War. "That is another story, Mr. Collins. Perhaps I can tell you some day."

Ralph Collins, in his chair, turned to Legus, his hands in his lap. "Thank you, Mr. Legus Perryman, for what you did. I guess I owe you a big debt of thanks." He started to shake his hand, but hesitated.

"That's all right, glad to help when I can. I'm sure my brother will want to take you out back to have you meet the boys. Say, did you know about the new bridge constructed over the Arkansas? It's clear to Red Fork! But let's wait. It's time for the blessing now."

"Legus," invited George, "if you'll lead us, please."

He stood, waited for everyone to bow his head, then uttered a pleasant prayer in English first, then, in Creek.

Ralph Collins, who had been to Kansas twice with James Daugherty, and who knew the rigors of hard work in getting the herds over rivers, arroyos, gullies, and mesas, began to eat quietly. His brown eyes sparkled at the reference that shipping cattle to market would become far easier than bringing the herds across the Deep Fork west of Okmulgee. Red Fork was the new tent town.

Momentarily, he was caught off guard in his reverie by the sporadic glance from time to time of Moses who peered at him over his glass of tea. This new foreman was glad he had this roving experience behind him, all the dusty trails, learning where the best places were to ford, and other locations that were known to be difficult and dangerous.

For some reason which eluded this reserved cowhand, now, as he sat at this table, Ralph Collins had never understood the cause James Daugherty had in mind when he directed their herds by way of this eastern route to Kansas despite the arduous crossings and rolling hills here. Daugherty may have thought of working the Chisholm, but not recently. And for some equally strange account, this drover began to realize a blessing, sitting as he was, with this family all about him, this cattleman, his wife, their children. Something stirred within him. During the delivery of the prayer with the arrival of another brother, Josiah, he suddenly reverted to his Mexican mother, that delicate and sweet woman. He recalled, ever so subtly, the Catholic foundation for her three children, so long ago. Josiah's voice filled the room with a final "Amen" after Legus finished grace. Ralph surmised that God works his wonder in mysterious ways indeed.

With Josiah Perryman had come an angular young man who was a stranger to all but only for a short while. This tall Indian, his long black hair neatly groomed, sat politely to Josiah's left and responded well when the head of the table began to ask of his background. "Did you say your name is Shaw? Of what tribe?"

"Yes, sir," this man replied, William Shaw is my oldest brother. My name is Robert Shaw, the youngest of three. We are Shawnees."

During desert, Legus Perryman confided in Ralph Collins. "We're proud of our brother, Josiah there. He is the new postmaster here in Tulsey-town."

"Actually, Tulsa, now, so everyone says," corrected the other brother. "I'll show you the office if you want. It's right here over on the west side. You probably already noticed the extension of this house."

But then, when they rose from eating, and Josiah translated his gratitude to Mrs. Rachel, the woman smiled, nodded, and gladly received his hand. Noting this, Ralph Collins ambled on to the south porch. At one point, he leaned against a pillar as if all the land he was able to encompass was his property. This cowboy was still in awe, wondering just how he could ever repay all this kindness.

Just as he pondered, he felt a sensation he had not had in a long time, that someone was watching him. The boy, Moses, was eyeing him from afar with a curiosity that was born out of an eager attempt to learn as much as he could. Ralph Collins noticed this silent admiration when he turned to him.

I'm Moses," he said, slowly making his way toward him from the doorway. "You can call me Mose. Everybody does. I'm the oldest. You got your own horse?"

Ralph Collins politely nodded, folded his arms and pointed toward the pond. "He's right down there, see him!" The gray pony, complete with a handsome saddle and rifle attached to it, was nibbling at tall grass. "His name is Bill."

"Can I ride him, please?"

The cowboy straightened. "I suppose you can, but I'm waiting for your pappy to take me to the bunks. I'm waiting...."

Moses's eyes darted from the horse to the new foreman. "I'm getting a pony for my fourteenth birthday coming up in July. I'm hoping for a mare, they're the best!" This boy was quite certain of himself. He took a step nearer. "Can I go down and pet him, please, Mr. Collins?" He moved off the porch.

"Well. All right. But I'm keeping my eye out for your dad. Like I say, I got things I want to do."

Others came through the front door onto the porch, some children who skipped onto the ground while Josiah and Robert Shaw remained to talk by the Welcome sign.

By this time, Moses walked well ahead of Ralph Collins to where the horse was tied to a low limb of a big scrub oak, similar to the ones that lined the entire pasture onward toward the south and west. Beyond the pond, with the ducks, Mr. Collins noted only the smooth even hills to the horizon. They were good grass and pastureland, all right.

They passed Legus's buggy that was moored on the same limb. Ralph Collins stopped to see if the horse needed water. Moses watched as he verified the teeth and eyes and then on to his own horse. "How long have you had him?" Moses was at his side. "Is he a father, himself?"

In all his born days, Ralph Collins had never encountered such an inquisitive Indian boy. The Texan had heard of cases where, ordinarily, the young braves remained quiet but attentive, with beady eyes that kept constant awareness of all that occurred. For the first time, he was at odds how to keep answering all the questions of this son of his new employer. This boy was always a step or two ahead of him.

Moses slowed as he came nearer the pony. With a respectful touch, the lad essayed the leather, the pouches that held personal belongings, the cinch that cir-cled the belly, and, finally, the rifle that protruded from a strap of darker cowhide. Ralph Collins was about to object when he realized that this boy was ready to mount. His left foot was already raised for the stirrup. The appearance of his uncle, his father and one of the children in his father's arms caught his attention. "Come on, boy, let's go back to the house. I see your father."

Reluctantly, Moses shuffled along beside him and picked up a rock, tossing it toward the road as far as he could. "My father is taking me to St. Louis on the next trip." He thought he could delay the walk by quickly mentioning another birthday gift. "I'm going in July with them."

Before Moses proceeded to his usual Sunday afternoon adventures, his father requested he say goodbye to his Uncle Josiah and Uncle Legus who were late com-ing from the house. While he heard them discussing further business for the week coming up, Moses trailed behind them, keeping his respectful distance as a young Indian would in matters of family protocol. His mind, too, was on the foreman who was disappearing around the east side of the house with his father.

But Josiah's remark about fences brought the boy back to the uncles at hand. Or was it the remark about Christianity? Half of the conversation as they walked to their own buggies was in Creek and certainly Moses was aware of the sounds, and articulation of this language. While in the company of his father on different occa-sions, Creek was spoken more than English, so oftentimes he was excluded from any progress of subject matter. At Tullahassee, the instructors made it a point to speak English all the time so naturally he kept Creek on the edge of his education. When that school building was totally destroyed by fire just three years ago, Moses shifted to a new arrangement at a school in the town area. That was why he always presumed that a horse of his own would suffice his coming and going those twelve miles round trip. That was most logical to the boy. Now, his goal was to make it just as obvious to his father.

"What do you think about the on-going problem of the 'Intruders', Legus?" came the question from the brother. "The white man keeps coming into our nation with one purpose or another. With their own reasons." As usual, out of sheer habit, they paused between their buggies to talk as if their topics were not exhaust-ed in the house at dinnertime. Moses found another rock which he elected to put in his collection since it was of a remarkable color.

"I guess we've finally been colonized," Josiah said as he reached to pat the nose of his horse. While he spoke, he verified the cinch, the harness, and the reins. "Mose, son, will you go fetch a bucket of water for this one, please."

Hiding the rock in his pocket, he ran to the house.

Josiah placed his foot on the buggy to pull himself up into position. "We're really lucky, Legus. With father gone, now, it's been twenty years since Kansas. Look what is happening to us here. Compared to the other fifteen or so tribes around us we're fortunate all right." Then, as if he were waking from a dream, Josiah spoke to the Shawnee who had come along the path behind them. "Mr. Shaw," he said, "we didn't mean to ignore you, sir."

"Perfectly all right, sir," the young man answered. He was more concerned with nature, anyway.

To Legus, his brother remarked, "Did you hear what George said about getting a franchise for another ferry?"

Josiah removed his hat and wiped his face. They saw Moses return with a bucket brim full, splashing a bit of the water as he ran. Holding it to the horse, the boy carefully watched the water disappear.

The Arkansas River had been a major conversation piece for fifteen years when this whole area east of that stream was subject to growth, yet the grounds on the west and southern banks became a stumbling block for future herds from South Texas. The settlers, too, from Okmulgee, Nuyaka and Wealaka Missions had to ford the river at various points where a few enterprising businessmen planned to improve the shipments of materiel and traffic. The Indians had been the forerunner of such a trade. Creek Law had stipulated this.

"Such a law, Legus, has become even more vague since the white man has gained revenue for ferry crossings. If you intend to be a chief, then be a good chief!" Josiah was referring to the political aspirations of this brother. "You'll have to compete against our cousin, though. Joseph is the brand new chief. I'm sorry, Legus. You'll have to wait if you want to be a chief, too." Josiah was laughing now at how close he had come to the truth.

The horse moved his head out of the bucket so Moses ran to the house with the empty bucket.

"The bridge at Red Fork will do away with ferryboats won't it?" Legus was concerned with the railroad plan. But twelve miles south of this rail construction, where the river began to meander aimlessly eastward, the drovers swam their cattle across the shallow parts especially if they were destined to graze on Cherokee land, far to the east.

"Josiah," continued Legus, "the cattle I have at Eufaula, and the cattle you have at Wealaka remain west of the water and can head for Red Fork. In that sense, yes, we're lucky. Before you and..." and Legus glanced at the guest, "you and Mr. Shaw, here, arrived, George mentioned that we're not too worried about ferry crossings. We're going to take our cattle north from Okmulgee, just like always." Since this conversation had been in English, Moses, having returned, was listening intently as his uncle continued. "So now we can head for Red Fork. I hear tell some mighty important people there already think it will grow faster than Tulsa." He turned again to Mr. Shaw. "You and your parents come from somewhere there, don't you? What do you think Mr. Shaw?"

"I am listening and learning, sir. I wish I had the proficiency of the cattle business that you do. I have felt right at home in your brother's house, sir." He circled Josiah's large black horse. "I enjoy your comments, especially about fences. I am recently acquainted with Mr. Hall at his store. One day, I overheard the remark between three Creeks that as long as you lived no fence was ever necessary among your people of your property." He climbed aboard. "Am I right, sir?" he asked Josiah.

But Legus answered. "It is coming to a more serious concern, I'm afraid."

Moses was still engrossed in what his uncles and this stranger were saying. Without Ralph Collins, his father reappeared from the east side and joined the men at the buggies. "Moses! Come, son! Back to the house."

That was an invitation to return for errands. Obeying gladly but disappointed that his uncles were leaving, Moses called, "Goodbye, Uncle Josiah, goodbye, Uncle Legus," and he sped onto the porch where his mother had come to watch the departure. He stood by her to wave.

"Well George, this is goodbye for a while. I will see Joseph and Thomas soon and give them the good news about their newest nephew." Josiah clucked at his horse and pulled at the reins so that he made a complete turn. Waving to Rachel and the boy, he began a slow trot toward the pond and onward to his home.

"I must see to business myself, George," replied Legus as he too prepared to leave. "I think we had a splendid talk today about cattle. I miss father, don't you?" He paused to wave to Rachel. "But we'll have a new chief with Joseph and, hopefully, a new future. But I am definite about being a chief, too, one of these days. Grayson and Stidham were talking to me. Goodbye, George."

Soon he too was swiftly passing the pond and frightening the ducks. In another second he was out of sight.

George started for the front porch. "Go change your clothes, Mose," his father said softly. "I want you to go with the boys and Mr. Collins to round up the milk cows. You may ride to his left. Stay on his port side, behind him. Watch what he does."

Then, George joined Rachel and together they went inside the White House to look at their new baby again.

Chapter Five

In Okmulgee by late June of eighteen-eighty-five, the town already had experienced its abundant share of Creek History. Little more than a trading post after the Civil War, the village became better known than its predecessor, Shieldsville, three miles to the northwest. The Muskogee Nation, changing the "c" to a "k" by that time, also constructed its large and impressive Council House. In that building, the council was to enjoin themselves with yet another session this time to oversee what the agenda would be when this group would be together for its next meeting.

At the end of that particular day, after a lengthy conversation, and because of the warm day that it was, four men remained, still involved with topics. The thick walls of their room retained the cool air inside it. That was sufficient reason for them to stay after everyone else departed.

George W. Stidham, who had come all the way from Red Fork, knew the language well for he, too, had been instructed by a young woman from Tullahassee Mission. The woman, Mr. Stidham had learned much later, was now married to a businessman in Sand Springs where she assisted any full blood who wanted to learn English no matter how advanced in age he was. Others, too, from the south of Tulsa, from Broken Arrow, from Coweta, some of whose own fathers had been on this council since before that War, preferred English, but even they courageously held to their original tongue. Many women, who were endeared wives, were also faithful to the Creek language. Many a household now were bilingual.

The Green Peach War had come and gone but Unrest of some dimension was still apparent on the subject of Tribal government. One of the two men who were still seated at the table turned to the other and put down his pen.

"George," he began, placing some papers in a neat stack before him and folding his arms, "if we are to hear this man, then let us hear him. It's still early enough, I suppose, and supper is not until seven-thirty."

George Stidham by now had stepped over to the window for some fresh air. It was open but he opened it further. "Before we do, then, are we agreed that we have reached the only decisions we can reach at this time?" He turned to address the other men. "Chief Joseph Perryman gave us authority to meet the challenge before us. I don't know that animosity exists between Joseph and this man, but anyway, so be it." Mr. Stidham frowned as he spoke to these others. In previous sessions this council always was reverent and helpful when it came to discussion of any topic. Tired as they were, Mr. Stidham and the men sat down opposite each other, turned their chairs so that they could receive the one remaining person at the head of their table, and waited. While one wrote some additional words on is tablet before him, another member wiped perspiration from his hot face. Mr. Stidham cleared his voice as he became comfortable in his high-backed chair. "John, are you all right?" But after he received an affirmative nod, George continued. "Gentlemen, let me remind us this day that when we hear this man that we must forget any and all problems relating to Isparhecher and the conflict of two years ago. That is history. While it divided our people considerably at that time, we must consider it part of our past and not necessarily the course of quelling the revolt. We must not presume in hearing this man that those problems are still with us."

One member was not at all aware of the man who waited in the hall. Even John Berryhill could not remember when last he saw him. Mr. Stidham noticed the frowns on their faces, as if to ask about whom was he talking. "Gentlemen," he continued, glancing to the other three to see how his remark was accepted, "I refer to Captain Daniel Childers."

His companions were visibly moved. John Berryhill, who had laid aside his handkerchief and who was writing a note about another matter, stopped his pen poised in mid-air. With slight agitation, he capped his ink well and turned the page over as if he decided to finish his information to himself later. Mr. Berryhill had already spoken to this council about this captain's endeavors long before this June date. Mr. Childers had earned respect of a few but he had also developed his reputation as being a most unusual and very distraught veteran. "He is weird." John Berryhill whispered to the companion on his right. "It's a shame, an outright shame. And to think he was adopted into our tribe long ago." Before the Civil War, and as early as the eighteen-forties, the Muscogees resumed the ancient practice of incorporating alien tribes within their own nation and some of them were admitted to the council.

George Stidham, then, after another quick poll, raised a little silver bell and rang it vigorously so that its sound was heard beyond the thick wall and closed door that separated this room from the hallway. John Berryhill looked quickly at his pocket watch and heaved a big sigh.

A young clerk, who had waited at his own desk, rose, cautioned the captain to wait a moment, and opened the door. At a signal from Mr. Stidham, the clerk pressed himself against the door and nodded to the captain. This man, whose violent reputation was always preceding him, bolted into the room, after bumping into the clerk. This tall figure with a nervous walk was Daniel Childers, carrying his knapsack of food. He stopped just after the door closed behind him. He removed his stained hat, as requested by the clerk before he entered, placing it with his food on the floor to his right. He wiped his mouth with his sleeve of his cotton shirt, eyed the men before him and took a deep breath. He started to step nearer but was stopped by Mr. Stidham's quick greeting.

"Good afternoon, sir, Captain Childers." He waited to see how this man would react. "There is a chair over there for you to sit before us, if you want it."

"I'll make up my mind about sitting down in a minute," was his curt answer. "My being here today has nothing to do, as you might think, about that war a year and a half ago, I ain't a rebel anymore no sir." He started to retrieve his knapsack but he changed his mind, shifting his eyes from one member to another. "It's true, I was with Isparhecher once and I guess I did..." and he searched for a word, "...I did object to what was going on, just as ol'Isparhecher did, mind you." He smiled. "But I'm an inspector now, up Tulsa and Catoosa way. Up in Cherokee country. I'm watching brands on cows and horses now. And on hides, too."

John Berryhill spoke quickly. "That is history, Captain, sir. The war, I mean. The authority at Fort Smith and the Indian police took care of all that." John hoped that when he stopped to breathe, that the dirty man before them would not begin another long statement of sorts. "I believe the council is fully aware of your present occupation."

Mr. Stidham, Mr. Berryhill, and the third man, Mr. Monroe, recalled the insurgents who were led by Isparhecher. He operated against the Nation as well as against the white man's slow and sure manipulation of political interference in the territory. This leader outwardly protested against the constitution in that too much leeway was given to white traders and emigrants from Kansas. Nuyaka Square, west of Okmulgee, was the center of this uprising. This person standing before the four members became a trusted lieutenant in Coweta District. When Federal troops were requested by the chief, they moved quickly. Isparhecher fled westward to the Plains Indians. By February of that year, these same revolutionaries were delivered back to their own nation, disheveled, out of order, their courage broken for ever presuming that they could overpower the Creek government.

As if to clarify again for those present, this man continued. "Daniel Childers, that's me! And I don't mean to carry this message any further. No, sir."

"Then don't!" put in Mr. Stidham.

Childers again eyed the man who uttered those words with a sharp stare as if to relieve him of duty right then. "It's true. I was part of that mess. But I ain't, anymore. I got a good job now, yes, sir, yes, I do have."

His audience who listened remained patient as if they too were waiting for some moment when discussion would break and a more favorable venue would ensue.

"I'm with the new cattlemen's association now." A noise of some kind halted his thinking. "I got a wife and six kids."

John Berryhill changed positions in his chair. He removed his wire glasses and rubbed his weary eyes. This man before them, his arrogance and temper, everything about him were already known long before he came into this big room. Captain Daniel Childers' bearing and countenance, even his style, were universal, with cheap whiskey furtively purchased at a small shop in the country south of Red Fork, and a temper that was silent only when he was sleeping. Any minute antagonism could ignite it. Without delay, the man and the council members, his pistol was waiting for him on a table to the left of the guard who sat beside the clerk in the hallway, both of whom were to leave as soon as this appointment was concluded.

Daniel Childers straightened his crude corn-husk badge that he had pinned to his old shirt. "I found some of Charley Clinton's cattle, you know, the S Brand, mixed in with some of the ones that come up from Texas, just about two months ago."

As he continued his harangue, Mr. Grayson, the fourth member, sitting opposite John Berryhill, picked up his pencil to make silently a half circle with an S below it, showing them all that Childers was not altogether correct about the brand.

"It might have been Fred Severs' cattle for all I know." At this point, Childers slumped in the chair. "There's some kidnapping going on. And another thing, what about the fence? I thought you people were going to make everyone fence their lands. I thought that was the case." Then, as if to change the mood of his plight, he turned to one of the members. "I bet you're one of the Grayson family. Ain't you a Grayson?"

"I am," said Mr. Grayson who returned his stern gaze.

"Yep, I just figured," Childers countered, scratched his face, and resumed his diatribe.

As he did so, Grayson whispered to Berryhill, "Did you say this man is a citizen of the nation? To which Berryhill nodded. "Too bad we adopted him. It was a mistake."

Again, Childers ran his hand through his black hair. "And another thing, let me say about them ferries crossing the Arkansas. I got a franchise, you know, and I still operate my own boat."

This was true. Apart from his receiving a salary, meager though it may be, for minding the business as inspector, he managed a popular crossing just west of Coweta, a lawful permit when he learned some months ago that the Lochapoka Crossing was to become a valuable source of income. Childers' pole ferry was just down the hill from the Wealaka Mission, and a great deal of full bloods lived in that entire area.

"And I've been watching the loading pens. I've even been keeping my eye on hides, you know. I've been reporting every stolen animal I discovered. There's not too many brands that I don't know one from the other."

Mr. Grayson reached quickly for a wire swatter that waited in the center of the table and aimed for a pesky fly.

While this visitor continued to ruminate on the past misadventures of his strange existence, the clerk knocked on the door, opened it, and came over to Mr. Stidham. After whispering in his ear, the clerk waited for an answer that came with a gentle nod of the head. The young man nodded an affirmation and, with a hasty glance at the captain, he sat at his desk after closing the door.

Childers's eyes darted from the men at the table to the door and back again. After Mr. Grayson cleared his throat and Mr. Stidham leaned forward as if to anticipate more remarks, Childers stood and began to move about in the space between the chair and the table. With a determined voice, barely audible, once again he returned to his subject matter, with the allusion to being mistreated by Mr. G.B. Perryman. He made derogatory references to the White House which had become widely known as a haven for many a destitute Indian. Childers inferred that too many cattle which he had encountered in Mr. Perryman's herds had brands which were not his own.

These four men, who had been politely listening, began to conceive how this Daniel Childers could wreak such mistrust throughout his own life. From where he had originally come no one rightly knew. Part of the Childers clan lived near Catoosa, but that was in Cherokee Territory and Daniel Childers was not Cherokee. To the question where he lived, he answered that he had his own place south of Tullahassee and south of Muskogee. He finally placed his location southwest of Porter.

"Mr. Perryman," he ventured to say, "this Mr. George Beecher, as he likes to be called, has got his own ferry, now, and he's been mixing his cattle with those he's stolen. This man has..."

Instantly, with grave concern, George Stidham raised his hand silently, stopping the statement half-way. Others at the table agreed with the interruption. Daniel Childers had been talking too long, too assiduously, about such a variety of complaints that the table reverberated with the hammering of open palms against the wood.

Mr. Monroe spoke first, signaling silence. "Do not speak of the Peach, Captain Childers, sir." Then he rose and stood proudly on his side of the table. "I believe you have made a moot point, sir, in fact, several of them."

Mr. Stidham agreed. "We feel that you need not continue."

Perplexed at this answer, Daniel Childers sat slowly, his eyes still on the speaker. For a moment or two, from the avenue outside the council hall, sounds of buggies passing came to them through the windows of the thick walls. Horses' neighing told them traffic had increased. Mr. Grayson was the second to stand, and then Mr. Berryhill, with Mr. Stidham last, as if all four were intimating that the captain's departure was imminent.

So Daniel Childers did stand, also, after this last remark from their leader. He blinked his eyes, wiped his face with a dirty bandana he took from his shirt pocket. He put it around his neck and tied a quick knot, pushing it to the nape.

The four men waited for a word from their visitor. "Well," was all Childers could utter. Mr. Monroe detected a frown emanating from the captain's cold eyes.

Mr. Stidham raised the bell the second time, rang it, and waited for an answer. Another clerk entered, leaving the door ajar. He looked directly at Mr. Stidham.

"Captain Childers has reported to us and he is now ready to leave us." This clerk waited patiently while the visitor realized what the men inferred. So with a mounting anger and little attempt to cover it, Childers sauntered over to where he had dropped his hat and knapsack. He paused to make a slow exit, peering again at the men but saying nothing. The clerk had to move away from him to escape the swinging movement of his bag. He was out of the room and down the hall, past the stairs, having claimed his gun and holster in a matter of seconds. He was at his light wagon before the clerk could sit at his desk again.

Mr. Stidham sat again at the table to collect his satchel. Mr. Berryhill and Mr. Grayson joined themselves at the window to watch in which direction the captain was going. Soon, the men terminated their business and were in a quandary, each silently troubled about how to explain what had happened.

"What can you say, George?" John Berryhill was at his side with his logical question.

Assembling papers into his briefcase, Stidham paused. "Our chief will be expecting a full report. After supper, I'll try my best to write something on paper for him." He placed his chair neatly at the table and joined the others as they sauntered for the hallway. "It's time to eat, now anyway. Smith's Hotel maintains a schedule."

George Stidham was fretful when he was last to leave the Council House. With Mr. Berryhill, he tried to piece together the statements, the image, the disparaging threats that had come from the captain's mind. The look in that man's eyes and the words that emanated from his coarse mouth had not necessarily been a shock to them but it was Stidham who voiced his concern. "I've known the Perrymans so many years before they and their father had to flee to Kansas during the War. I have never known any of them to warrant the remarks that Mr. Childers implies." They stopped outside the main doorway to feel the wind. "Did you see the glimmer in that man's eyes, John? What do you think?"

The early June breezes caught John Berryhill's large grey hat when he tried to place it squarely on his head. He held it against the wind which jostled his long black hair. "Well, I remember once when President Porter came to see me, and he talked at length about this captain. Even then, over eight or nine months ago, it was, he told me "Goob" Childers had a violent streak about him, in thought, in deed, in fact. Both Porter and I presumed the captain would mend his ways. His wild appearance worries me."

The early evening traffic of Okmulgee was more predominant here, in front of the House because the building was erected in the middle of the square on the same plot of ground where the first wooden structure sat. Being of stone, this new house was more impressive. They waited further while a wagon and horses sped down the dirt road and out of sight, beyond the new buildings that formed the side streets of their town. "It sure is dusty today," was a comment. But the passing of this swift wagon was not the only movement that made them wait at the gate. Berryhill grabbed Stidham's arm to halt him in his place, for he pointed unobtrusively to other movement at the end of the block, just east of them, and opposite from where they were going.

When the traffic cleared both saw Daniel Childers stepping out of his wagon. He had parked it on the same street and was tying the reins to the side. Evidently he was conversing with someone whom they could not see for several pedestrians covered their line of vision. But the business tract where the captain had stopped was an undertaking parlor, complete with a large sign which they could read from where they stood. It stated, in gawdy but legible letters, that cemetery lots and tombstones were for sale.

"Isn't that Witherspoon's place?" questioned Mr. Berryhill. The crowd thinned and he saw the man about whom he spoke. "Yes, yes, it is." 'Goob' Childers was gesturing, gawking at a display of upright stones placed side by side on the lot. Presently, as if a decision had been agreed upon, both men disappeared inside Witherspoon's store. More traffic came between Stidham and Berryhill and the storefront, and with its dust other wagons and horses obscured further view.

George Stidham pulled his companion to one side and waited for a moment or two. "Let's see what's going to happen," he offered, "I don't think Mrs. Smith at the hotel will mind if were late for supper. Besides I think Grayson is there by now anyway."

John Berryhill surmised that he had better continue to the hotel if his friend wanted to pursue this situation. "George it's enough that we heard Childers' case. Maybe you had just as well forget it and come have a nice supper."

"You go on ahead, John," Stidham announced with his eyes still glued on that wagon. "And tell Grayson what we saw. I have an idea that I should see about this myself. Tell him. Tell him that." The wind was stronger now and both the men held to their hats. "I believe I'll wander down and ask Mr. Witherspoon just what it is all about. After the captain has gone, of course."

"All right. Just be careful, George." So with the other members well ahead of him, Berryhill crossed the road and was soon out of sight.

Keeping his eyes on the light wagon, where the horse was pawing the dirt, Stidham's goal was suddenly interrupted by a man who called to him from across the street. Cordial, but a bit wary, Stidham conversed a short while in Creek. He stood so that he could visually be unencumbered by this full blood. With a smile, the man finally went on his way. Stidham, yet alert, hid behind a tall oak tree that lined the thoroughfare and peered again toward the wagon and horse.

Two mischievous Indian boys stopped to appraise the animal and verify its hooves. One even climbed on board, picked up the reins to admire the sight of the crowded street from the driver's seat.

Presently Mr. Stidham noticed that Daniel Childers himself reappeared, angry, replacing his wallet in his shirt pocket.

He scolded the boys at once! The one in the seat fell in a frenzied rush to flee and together they escaped. The captain checked the tautness of the harness and the reins and patted his horse's nose. He walked all the way around his wagon to see if the two urchins had vandalized any of it. In the back, his shovel and axe, a satchel and his knapsack were still in place. With an insane gesture that was his trademark, and in a foul mood, he seated himself and called to his horse. With loose reins, he turned completely around so that he departed in the direction that he came. He did not see George Stidham behind the tree as he raced by him in a thick cloud of dust. Soon he was lost in the west side of the square.

After he was certain that Childers was out of sight and over the hill of the road, well past the hotel, Stidham made his way quickly to the undertaking parlor, holding his hat in the wind. With an occasional glance westward to insure that the captain was not returning, he approached the tombstones and knocked on the front door which he discovered was open. He knocked the second time and decided to enter.

Mr. Witherspoon came through an archway that was robed with two black draped curtains. "I heard you, sir. I was coming. What may I do for you?" He was coatless.

"Mr. Witherspoon, sir, I believe. Permit me to introduce myself."

The shopkeeper raised both hands. "It is I who know you, sir. You are a noted figure on the council, are you not? Mr. Stidham, I believe!"

"Yes, sir, I am George Stidham," he confirmed, and the undertaker was greatly pleased. He was also relieved since his last customer.

"If I appear distraught," Witherspoon said as he grabbed his long black coat, "it is because of a previous transaction." Witherspoon knew his customer. He remembered him as one who was involved, ever so long ago, with the deaths of several men who were arrested and executed. He remembered the look in the eyes of this man, in the attitude that did not seem normal.

"That's what I wanted to ask you, Mr. Witherspoon, sir, if you don't mind. I would like to know what the business was of that man who departed just now." Stidham removed his hat and mopped his brow with his wet handkerchief.

"Oh, then you mean Captain Childers sir. Well. I must say that his being in my place of business upset me tremendously. Just a moment." With this, the nervous owner excused himself to disappear behind the archway and into the area from which he came. And then, just as quickly, he returned with an order form in his right hand. "This, sir, is what Captain Childers ordered from me not more than ten or twelve minutes ago!" He offered the sheet of paper to Mr. Stidham. "You see, it is an order for a head stone. A rather large one, I might add." He pointed to the contents with a palsied forefinger.

Mr. Stidham held the order in his hand and read all of it. Just as the captain had stated, it read: "Capt. Dan'l Childers served as a U.S. scout during the war of the Rebellion." Below this, was the remainder of what this man wanted. "Daniel Childers, Born May 13, 1833, Died — Remember friends as you pass by/ As you are now so once was I/ As I am now soon you may be/ Prepare for death and follow me."

"He already paid for it, Mr. Stidham. He paid cash. I must get to the bank right now before it closes. It might have already closed. What time does it close?

Do you know?"

"If it is," the council leader mentioned, "we can go back to the council house and I'll put your money in a safe place."

Mr. Witherspoon was frightened. "The captain was muttering something as he left. I didn't hear what it was. I couldn't understand him in the first place." The mortician was quite sure what he was about to say. "When I was counting the money, I heard him, definitely, clearly."

"As you were counting the money?"

"Yes." Perplexed, he continued, hardly realizing what he was saying. "the Nuyaka Square west of here. Tuckabat - something and a name Neha Harjo. I remember Harjo because I know some Harjos here in Okmulgee. Some Negroes, too, all against the Creeks. I'm not Indian, Mr. Stidham, but I do know what I heard from this man. And how a man name of George something, Beech, I think it was..."

"George Beecher Perryman!"

Mr. Witherspoon gathered his cash and was placing it in a small bag with his initials on it. "Yes, that was it!" By now, both men were at the front of his shop, the owner grabbing his hat. "Something about how this Perryman and a great deal of others had managed to capture him and others outright. I'm sure that was it."

Instantly, reviewing the situation that had elapsed last April, after Isparhecher and the insurgents fled to Anadarko, Mr. Stidham remembered that Perryman with twenty-five men were in fact at the start of the arresting party. It was the troops from Fort Gibson with their officer that actually squelched the uprising.

They began their way to the bank. "What is going on, Mr. Stidham?"

It was this question that haunted the leader. He smiled sullenly, nodded his head in thanks, and confirmed that the light was lit in the bank and that someone there would help. He turned to take his leave from this concerned little man. Witherspoon was grateful that he was escorted by such a dignified gentleman. The bank clerk locked the doors and pulled down the door shade. The mortician was his last customer for the day.

George Stidham had indeed been an impressive figure in his time. Middle-aged now, and with a family all his own, he had always been aware of the Perrymans, all of them, including a sister whom he had, at one time, thought he may wish to marry. But it was not the reputation and energies of this clan that concerned him. With his head bowed slightly against the warm wind and still holding his hat in place, he approached a busy intersection. A fast buckboard sped down the street. Standing to Stidham's right, a young lad reached out to halt his movement from the crowd. Had it not been for that gesture, Stidham would have been trampled by the fierce horse pulling the family in its wagon.

In uncontrollable noise amid a lady's scream, the driver slowed and stopped. Some children who rode behind their parents jumped to the ground. As Stidham stood there, breathless for just a moment, he watched as the father dismounted. With only a quick and fretful glance at Stidham, he called to his children to follow him into a store. His wife, stepping to the ground was more thankful that the accident was averted. She stood there, helpless, but grateful.

"Intruders," Stidham thought, "children of a white family and no school to attend." A myriad of other thoughts raced through his mind.

"Sorry to grab you like that, Mr. Stidham," replied the boy who, even yet was holding onto his arm. "Are you all right?"

To him Stidham nodded and quietly responded, "Yes, thank you...I...thank you indeed." The boy then retrieved the hat that had fallen to the ground.

With no further delay, Stidham increased his step toward the hotel. Most assuredly after supper, a flustered George Stidham decided that he must get a message to George Beecher Perryman at the White House. By some perceptive omen, as if this afternoon had not been strange enough, Mr. Stidham was certain the activity of that hour in the Council House pointed to the fact that the Perryman family was now in danger.

Chapter Six

The following month, young Moses Perryman completed his fifteenth year. He was certain that every young brave in the Creek Nation was to hear about it. Already in possession of a sorrel mare for these past two years and with the saddle of dark mahogany leather, with a matching bridle, he pestered Ralph Collins to see if this foreman could make an enquiry what his new gift might be from his father. The foreman did not want such a request to deter the growing friendship with the boy.

The young Brave, as Moses wished to be called, grew tall and healthy, noticeably large for his age. That trait was common among the uncles he and his siblings had. Moses rode his mare well over all the south and west pasturelands, all the way to the river. The neighbors, far and wide, were able to sight him coming over a ridge in the road, or down an embankment where so many of the busy ranchhands were tending longhorns. In the summers, Ralph Collins rode with him at George's personal request to keep an eye on his oldest son. "Make certain that Mose does not show too much enthusiasm and conceit." So Moses would ride with his new friend when the foreman allowed him, or he rode with one or two other ranchhands when he was not in school. "Now that Tullahassee has burned, you can go to mission school in Tulsa. I'm even thinking of building a nice house there in town anyway, sooner or later." That was his father's early remark.

Apparently, some type of new township was forming in the area west and south of the river where much of their cattle roamed. The question of fencing was to become a more important and urgent topic at the Council House, for the land the Perrymans possessed extended far beyond those visual borders which George and his brothers maintained. Those stretched as far as the bend in the river but certainly not nearly as far as the northern border of the community of Okmulgee.

Moses Perryman was happy to comply with his father's wishes. With several drovers, he would traverse this entire acreage with its shallow ponds of fresh water and its ample supply of dog-tooth violets and bluestem grass. They would return each evening of this summer, tired and dusty but pleased to report to his father that he was learning every conceivable lesson to be learned, many of them taught him by his favorite friend, Ralph Collins. So all this riding everywhere, and saddle sores, and surveying, and monitoring what all the men did began to seep into his consciousness despite the hot days. He remembered what this man Collins was telling him every day that they ventured away from the White House.

"I'll be glad when I can go out there with you and ride," sighed a younger Abner, who, only seven at the time, began to doubt if he would ever own a horse, himself, as pretty as the mare or even to ride as well as his oldest brother. "Why don't you let me ride the mare, Mose? All you have to do is lift me up so I can hold on to the saddlehorn. Please!"

"You'll get there, little brother, I'm sure of that!" And Moses would often stand in the doorway of the bunkhouse holding Abner's hand to say goodnight to Ralph Collins and then they would casually walk up the path to the main house. This foreman was good to this family. He was grateful. The manner in which he rode, in which he spoke to everyone, manifested this gratitude. And he believed that this family realized it. He saw that all too often on the face of the beautiful woman who was Mrs. Rachel, with her healthy brood of children, her quiet life, her consistent and purposeful ritual of home care and family pride. Being a Creek Indian was predominant. The bearing of her children brought her much happiness. Even when her second son died at only ten years, she was already pregnant with the baby whom they called George.

One of the ranchhands, another Texan, who had come north on the last roundup with James Daughterty, and who wanted to move with the Perryman family cattle, spoke Spanish but he handled English equally as well. He used to say, "Cattle was six dollars in Texas and we got sixty dollars in Kansas. I'm called 'Laredo' 'cause. I guess, I was born there."

This lanky Texan, Laredo, took a message to the family of Robert Shaw who had explained, two years ago, when the young Indian visited the White House, that he, his brother, and the sister were grateful to the Perrymans for many reasons. This message, given orally as well as written on paper in English, was for the Shaw family to visit again on this date, the Sunday following the return of Mr. Perryman, the foreman and the son, Moses, from a recent trip to St. Louis. This son celebrated his fifteenth birthday on that trip but that a dinner was planned on that Sunday, and the Shaw family was indeed welcome to attend. Laredo was to carry it for the benefit of the parents because they did not understand English. Laredo returned, after his round trip of twenty miles, with an affirmative reply that they would gladly be there.

"They right nice people, the Shawnees. I thought they were Yuchi. Whatever. They gave me some stewed rabbit."

Some time ago, before the young boy, Robert, knew much of anything, except tracking, and plowing, and some sickness, he professed that he was Shawnee when he stood on the long sidewalk leading to the front door of Tullahassee Mission. That was at a time in his life when his mother told him that she wanted him to learn from the ladies at the mission. His deep dark brown eyes were fearful, for while he was hopeful of receiving a good education at this church school, he did not know how to speak well enough to enter the classes.

Miss Baldwin saw the forlorn child on the walkway through a tall window on the first floor of her classroom, so she excused herself, stepped into the long hallway leading to the front door. An older student, during this interruption, who had also seen the boy, motioned for him to come through that door into the cool building. He rose from his chair to stand by his teacher.

"Does he speak Yuchi or Creek?" Miss Baldwin asked.

The older boy, who muttered Creek to him, received a soft muffled answer that sounded like the Shawnee tongue. While this lad waited in the cool hallway, Miss Baldwin gestured for him to remain where he was and raced upstairs to knock on her supervisor's door.

"Yes? Come in."

Miss Baldwin smoothed her brown hair with her palms before presenting herself. She entered. "Sir," she said, "we have a new Indian on our doorstep. Benjamin and I have supposed that he is Shawnee or possibly Yuchi. But, I think he understands Creek too."

A lady was in the office. "May I, Mr. Loughridge?" this woman asked.

"Very well Miss Robertson," the gentleman replied with no problem. "I must see to other matters, now, myself. Thanks."

Together, happily, they rejoined Benjamin and the anxious child. "Remember Miss Baldwin," Miss Robertson whispered as they stopped in front of the Indian, "many of the Creeks incorporated alien tribes within their own nation. If Creek doesn't work we have three girls from the Yuchi Tribe right here at the mission who can help, I'm sure!"

That first day became a fond memory of Robert Shaw as he stood and watched the messenger from the Perryman home return that day. Part of that memory was when he learned that the great two storied school burned. So it was that when he made that trip with his parents, the journey eastward would be arduous. Once the Arkansas was forded, the rest of their trip would be simple. But doing so, especially in the heat of a July day, meant arising well before dawn, to hitch the one horse to a delapidated wagon and to inform the neighbor that they would be gone for two days, at the most.

His mother worked diligently to prepare for this moment. She washed garments to reflect a neat appearance, and she prepared a bag of food to eat en route in case they needed it. Her soft voice was always carefully modulated, never to sound urgent or harsh, much like Mrs. Rachels attitude, especially in the kitchen. A Shawnee wife was just as orderly as Creek wives. Since she had borne three children, this mother was disciplined in every gesture she committed. It was an honor to be invited for such an occasion, and the son whose birthday they were celebrating knew to expect them.

After feeding the chickens and a reminder to the neighbor to repeat the food the next day, they left. Their route took them along a road which paralleled the long line of maples, the trees that bordered a small stream which the local tribe had named, long ago, coal Creek. This wide section of land, dotted with scrub oaks, pointed their way to a fairly flat area that was easy to cross. Once they were out of the shallow water, the horse found the pathway again that led them through open space toward the larger Arkansas River, directly in front of them.

Robert asked his father if he were tired, to which the old man answered negatively.

Robert thought it best to rest after fording the river, for at least a short while. The pathway broadened, an indication that a great many teams and wagons had entered the stream at this one given place. Many of the ruts appeared old and deep. The sand of the river was thick and hot as far as they could see. They forded without incident, with Robert guiding the steed easily through the warm water. Once across it, however, their journey took them along a road which only the local people knew, a winding, desolate path making its way in valleys that formed the everlasting hills of the Creek Nation. The mid-morning sun by now was extremely hot, and the mother who sat on the floor of the wagon, behind her son, found her cotton shawl to place over herself.

At one point the trees became forests which were a part of the entire area, known throughout by virtually every member of the tribe. Robert intended to rest here, among the trees. He stopped the wagon in a wide shade and hopped down to aid his mother as his father tied the reins. A flock of arrogant crows welcomed them into the dark cove.

But the arrival of this family was not instrumental in the sudden flight of these birds. As they found seclusion among the scrub oaks, they noticed a pack of hounds dart across the path, frightening their horse so that the father waited until the neighing subsided. Out of nowhere stepped a figure.

From a clump of bushes came a ragged and dirty Indian with a large brown hat and a staff to help him walk since he was obviously old. This quaint character stopped as the dogs circled about him, a few yelping and squirming, their tails as busy as they. He squinted gingerly at the trio who was as surprised and shocked as he. No one spoke.

In the language of Shawnee Robert softly explained not to be too fearful, for this elderly man, with his hounds and a local reputation, was known to him and to all the nation. In the manner of being hospitable which was a significant trait taught him by the Creeks, they invited this old man to have a bite to eat with them but that they soon should be on their way.

Their son said that this hermit was a Tuckabatchee and not to be afraid of him, and that his name was Efa Harjo. So, eager to be moving, Robert checked the harness and the reins. With a bucket, he brought water from their own container from home as did his parents. With a wave of their hands, the family was saying good-bye, turning northward on a corridor between more trees. The great pastures on which the Perryman cattle roamed and grazed, on which Moses and Ralph Collins rode their horses, were far to the east side of the river. Robert and his parents would soon be at the White House.

On this day, with minor chores already accomplished, including feeding the hogs and chickens early, which was the work of the Young Braves, Laredo washed himself at the spot so designated behind the bunkhouse. Naked from the waist up, he lathered himself, shaved, and splashed water he pulled from the well. As two new colts scampered by him on their way to make sure that all the milk cows were out to pasture, again. Laredo enjoyed his own kind of gratefulness because he never had been so fortunate. Ralph Collins had found him alone and hungry about a year ago near the stockyards west of town.

"If you come up with Daugherty," Collins echoed, "then you are all right as far as I'm concerned. I'll take you in, and see how you work out! I want you to know that the Perrymans are kind. I want you to know that when you come to work with us, you'll be working for the best men. They got a big ranch."

And that was the way Ralph Collins introduced the family to Laredo. This happy little Texan, with a cheery smile, put on his clean jeans, combed his hair, tucked in his denim shirt and wiped his boots again for the third time. Standing as tall as he could, he came to the farm and worked with an air about him that made him as much a part of this family as the children themselves. At one time, about two months ago, Mr. Collins mentioned that he wanted to speak in English, along with the civilized Indians.

"Do you ever want to go back to south Texas?" Laredo asked Mr. Collins one evening. It was last spring when warm winds through the trees made both of them dream of home. But at the moment, Mr. Perryman sent word for Mr. Collins to join him at the White House so Laredo's question was never asked again.

On that particular Sunday, immediately after church, little Abner was on the front porch. He was the first to notice the Shaw wagon approaching. He hopped down the steps, threw down his orange ball, ran down the path past the horses that were tied to the railing, eager to say welcome to the Shawnees. Even the ducks on the pond had sounded their greeting. When they met, Robert stopped the wagon, reached down, and pulled the little boy to sit between him and his father.

"Let me take the reins, please, please, mister!"

Gladly, Robert obliged, seeing that the child's eyes were too gleeful. "Mose's birthday was when Papa was in St. Louis and Mose got to go. So that's why we're having a big dinner today." And then, most politely he turned around and greeted the mother. "She doesn't know English, does she? My mother doesn't know English, either. Does she understand Creek?"

By the time Robert confirmed this, they were at the south porch where others of the household gathered to meet them as well. Laredo had a bucket of fresh water and dipper to offer the guests as they dismounted. He helped Robert's mother up the steps and into the house.

Mr. George Perryman, himself came to welcome them, with a big handshake and an obvious word. "Come in and welcome, and are you hungry? I bet you're hungry!" And he repeated all this in Creek.

Ralph Collins came around the east side of the house with Laredo and two other ranchhands. Young Moses, on the south porch with his mother, waved heartily at the men and they returned the greeting as they passed. Mr. Collins came up to Mr. Perryman with the news that the women were ready at the back of the house to serve.

The entire crew assembled there, under the wide trees, with the food ready in covered dishes on tables, with so delicious an aroma, that even the horses came to their corral fence to investigate. Two of the Perryman women aunts, who had arrived the preceding day, were standing waving big fans to ward off the hungry flies.

After a long discussion with Robert Shaw, commenting on a great success this Shawnee made of himself with his study of English and history, Josiah Perryman called everyone to sit.

"He's one of the elders of the Presbyterian Church, you know" whispered one of the aunts to a drover. "Practically all of the Indians at Wealaka Mission are now members there."

Everyone, including the little ones, waited politely until Josiah raised his hands to offer the prayer. "Merciful God." he began, "and Robert translated for his parents, "for this blessing, we are forever grateful. And we pray in the name of our Lord and Savior, Jesus Christ."

By this time the family and even the drovers were accustomed to being present, removing their hats automatically to eat at their own table not too far from the others. They all began, with Mrs. Rachel seated at the south end of the long table with her oldest son to her left.

One horse, enticed by the food, nudged himself through the corral gate and proceeded to meander around the west side of the house, with a threat that he may invade the dinner. With his change of plans, however, he began to nibble the grass. Mr. Collins asked Laredo to fetch the animal and bring him back. Excusing himself, he rose and grabbed a rope from the fence.

Presently amid the joy of the day, Laredo captured him far to the west of the wing that housed the old post office. As he slipped the noose around the neck, turning around to retrieve him, he noticed a wagon far down by the pond. The noise of the ducks is what made him look in that direction. So not to upset the dinner, Laredo quickly brought the animal around to the north end of the corral, and he captured Mr. Collins' attention while doing so.

The foreman rose and walked to Laredo who spoke in a muted whisper. "Step over there where you can get a good look at the pond."

"The pond?"

"You expecting anyone else for dinner?" Laredo fenced the horse and together they walked to a vantage point.

His friend squinted his eyes against the glare of the sun placing himself in the shade of the nearest trees. "I don't think so. Why?"

Laredo whispered so that he would not interrupt the occasion. It was enough that he stopped where he did to rope the animal. He did not want to attract too much attention.

"Well for one thing." Laredo spoke softly, "the ducks made a lot of quacking and I noticed this here fellow down by the pond. He must have parked his wagon...and he was just sitting there. He had even taken off his hat, I see him do that, and he didn't move at all. Least not when I spied on him." Laredo looked toward the tables to see if he had caused any alarm. "I don't recognize him, not at all. I don't think he's been around these parts. Maybe you better go and see..."

After another view to the south from under the trees, Ralph Collins quietly slipped over to the head table where George Beecher was relaxed chatting with a full blood. "Mr. Perryman, sir, I think maybe I better go check on something." He stared into the faces of the two men. "If you'll excuse me." George returned the stare as his foreman reversed swiftly to where Laredo waited. He paused underneath the eaves of the roof of the far west end. Leaning slightly for a better view, he saw that this man had not moved his wagon but had placed himself in shotgun position of the seat.

Laredo was back of him. "What do you think?" came the eager question.

Without waiting any further, and realizing that Perryman was still looking at him, Collins turned and drew Laredo to one side and still secreted from the dinner tables. Just as Ralph Collins was about to make his decision, the man in the wagon emitted a loud grotesque scream, yanked on the reins so quickly that his horse bucked. The ducks scattered. The two cowboys reacted as quickly with Laredo running beside Mr. Collins to enlist the aid of two of his drovers. This commotion caused everyone to glance their way as they raced by the tables. Others blinked and several rose, including Moses.

Giving direction, Ralph Collins was en route to the bunkhouse with Laredo following as far as the east side. "No, don't come with me," he shouted, "get to the front porch, keep an eye out, and I'll bring your pistol for you."

Moses heard that and started in that direction, but Ralph Collins stopped him with his gesture. He disappeared through the side door as several men joined Laredo with a multitude of questions. Two remained beside Mrs. Rachel and her husband. One shouted, "I'll get my gun," and off he went.

Mrs. Rachel, gathering George junior in her arms, sought protection from a situation that was yet unknown to her. At once the dinner guests were perplexed as they stood by their chairs. Laredo had vanished with others to the far east side yet out of sight. George Beecher himself dropped his fork and was about to retrieve it when two cowboys established their perimeter around him. Two other hands joined them, herding the children into their care.

Collins soon reappeared and handed Laredo his pistol while he loaded his own rifle. With the help of four others, they formed a narrow line away from the house. All had an unimpaired view of the wagon and its driver who, very slowly was moving toward the house. The sun was bright. "Driving the wagon from shotgun is kind of crazy, if you ask me." Laredo wiped sweat from his brow.

The wagon and driver stopped just thirty feet from where Collins and his men were standing. The driver reclaimed his hat, placed it on his unruly hair. His long white coat, dirty from wear, flapped in a small wind. He remained on his feet in his wagon.

By this time in anxiety the head of the household appeared around the corner of the house but stayed behind the line of men. The driver looked directly at him.

"Be careful, Mr. Perryman, sir," Laredo cautioned, at once reaching out to guard him. "Who...who is he, do you know him, sir?"

"Of course I know him," George answered, hardly believing what he beheld. "Yes. I know who he is."

This man jumped to the ground and with his right hand, he quickly exposed a pistol in its holster. "Hey you, Mr. George Beecher. I know you stole some cattle. You know who I am, Mr. George Beecher? You know why I'm here?" He did not wait for an answer. "I bet you don't know who I am!"

"I know you, sir," was the loud answer. By this time, the other men including young Moses had carefully made their way around the far west side of the house. They learned long ago to keep their distance.

"You're not going to steal anymore cattle, no, I'll see to that. You shouldn't have come after us like you did, you and your men that day." Instantly he produced his pistol. He fired so quickly at his target that he missed, the bullet hitting a pillar on the porch. He fired again and the bullet whizzed by a cowboy who dodged as the crowd fled to the rear. A third bullet came from a rifle held by Ralph Collins. It found its mark in the intruder's chest, making a red spot on the coat. This man slumped over, his pistol fell from his hand, and for just a short moment, he was on his knees, an agonizing look on his stunned face.

The foreman advanced steadily with his rifle ready for any sudden movement from the body on the ground. Laredo and the other men cautiously joined him, one, with his right arm extended to guard Mr. Perryman if something else should occur.

"It's all right, people," someone called, "he's down."

The crowd returned to the front area and Moses ran to the side of his father. Chattering in Creek, Mrs. Rachel remained with the ladies at the tables.

Ralph Collins put his rifle to one side, reached down and closed the man's eyes. "Yes, sir." One of the men gathered the hat. Another took charge of the horse and wagon which had bolted backward when the shots were fired.

"Keep the ladies back at the dinner tables please. Will one of you men see to that?"

Ralph Collins rose and looked at Mr. Perryman. "I'm sorry sir, but he would have killed you sure if I...."

With frightened eyes Moses looked at the foreman, hearing him speak, and he also heard the reply.

"I know. I understand. You leave this to me." His father was looking directly at Collins but others heard him too. "If I report that you fired, then we'd have to go to Fort Smith for prosecution. I don't need that. and I don't want that. I fired, you hear? I shot and killed this man." Then he announced it to everyone. "the council can hear me on this one. Let me handle it. Does everyone understand that?" His eyes lit on those nearest him, including Moses. "I'll be all right."

The men retreated, patting the foreman on the back. "You did the right thing, Mr. Collins," one said, the others agreeing. "You sure did, we can see that."

Still shocked by his experience, George turned to go and noticed that Mrs. Rachel was now approaching, along with two girls by her side. The winds had risen and were blowing dust from the parched earth.

Then, most graciously, after embracing his family, he returned to the business at hand, studying the face of Mr. Collins. "Well, sir," he mused, "you did the right thing, I agree. Will you get some of the men to lift the body and place it in the wagon?"

Signalling, Laredo obeyed unhesitatingly. He called for three of the drovers who helped lift the corpse and carry it to the wagon. The nervous horse had pushed it farther to the rear. The rusty tailgate was lowered so that they could load the body easily.

Suddenly, Laredo shouted. "Hey will you look at that!" He halted the movement by staring into the narrow bed. His loud voice stopped those who were returning in the food. With the helpers, the Texan peered long at the contents resting on the wagon's floor on a large piece of tarpaulin. What they saw was a brand new coffin still shiny and clean but with a thin layer of dust on its top.

Ralph Collins joined them at the wagon's side where Laredo grasped the gate. Lying on the floor next to the coffin was the body of a woman, placed there, surely, just after she was killed, for the blood on her blouse and arms confirmed that she died on that day.

And it was this hot Sunday afternoon in the month of his birthday that Moses remembered for the rest of his life. He was fifteen years old then. He ventured to look at the contents of the wagon with his father, and he held his father's hand, and together they agreed that his mother need not come to look at all. And for the next fifteen years he would remember and respect the fact that this man saved his father's life. He would definitely remember that.

And he would remember who it was who tried to kill his father. At first, he would not recognize the name even though he heard it for the first time. The dead man who lay sprawled and uncovered at the rear of the wagon beside the dead woman was Daniel Childers.

He would remember everything.

PART TWO
Spring 1901

Chapter Seven

Spring of nineteen-one came with the threat of rain storms but that was not unusual. The ranches that sprouted across the landscape, from Tulsa on the east side of the Arkansas to the far west border of the nation, were often inundated by sporadic showers. Since her husband's funeral, Lula had persevered with more than merely the ordinary chores of farmwork. Appraising thunderstorms, concurrent with a change of weather, become part of the daily ritual.

Lula resisted communication for a long while. But she was ever grateful for her three men with her on the ranch. Standing at her kitchen window with Edith in her cradle, she allowed a soft memory to invade her thoughts.

"I want Mr. Collins for my foreman, father," Moses asked when his own house was constructed on this spot. "He saved your life. Please, father." With that short plea from his son and new bride, George Beecher Perryman asked what Mr. Collins thought of this idea. And so it was that Ralph Collins, with his meager belongings, his dapple pony, and his noted rifle, and, at his request, with his friend, Laredo, six years ago moved to the Homestead.

"Or, I may call my place the Wrangler Ranch," Moses had remarked to Lula. "What do you think? Well I can't call it the House because that is what father calls the big new home that he built for Mama in Tulsa."

"That's a mighty nice big sign you've got at the gate down by the main road, Mrs. Perryman." It was Mr. Collins, commenting on the archway over the wrought iron gate, through which many a guest had driven his teams and wagons. "You all right, ma'am?"

"Oh, sure," Lula answered, washing her dishes. "I was just thinking about when you and Laredo first came here. I sure am glad you did, after all."

The Perryman Farmhouse, this acreage, the rich grasses for the longhorns, the wide expanse of scrub oak trees, the pastures that contained the answers to their prayers, were all for their definitive future. But their future lasted only six years.

Almost once a week, now, in order to organize work and determine what must be done to continue, Lula, without Moses, would ride with Mr. Collins out to the north, to the east, to the west. They stood on hillsides and exchanged ideas on what must be accomplished.

"See," Lula pointed, "this is where Moses wanted to build a dam, if it was possible, for another lake on Coal Creek." Or she took Mr. Collins to the south end of the land. Turning their horses so that they could view the panorama, they saw their majestic barn to their left, the house itself, snuggled among the many large trees which prompted Moses to build his home there, in the first place. To their right, gracefully falling to the east, the ground formed a small stream over which Moses had built the wooden bridge to the main road.

"Well, that's it," Lula concluded, kicking her horse gently. They rode slowly back to the south yard where Moses had placed his stile block. "He thought of everything, Mose did," she said as they paused to look at its symmetry. "Those big pieces of rock weighed out a hefty pound I reckon. Same thing for those flat chunks to make my sidewalk." She laughed. "I told him what I wanted all the way", and she pointed from the south gate to the front porch, "And he sure did it. That's a pretty walk, don't you think?"

Laredo saw them coming from where he was drawing water at the well. "Milk time!" he called when they dismounted at the west side. "Mrs. Perryman," he smiled, "I put you some fresh water in the kitchen. You making that pie tonight?"

Lula patted her horse. "Yes, Laredo, just for you."

Together with Laredo, who was sitting opposite him at the bunkhouse table, Ralph Collins practiced his writing. Robert Shaw had first interested him in learning to read and write, but the foreman had not seen the Shawnee in a long time. He was writing well, now. By the lamp which spread its rays for both of them, Laredo, too, was accomplishing much the same.

By now, Mrs. Moses Perryman had become, simply Lula to her friends, drovers, even to her Indian family. Ralph Collins and Laredo both insisted on retaining the Mrs. If Moses were yet alive, they would have called them by the formal. Lula's brothers, including Walter Clyde, her sisters, and father visited her more frequently than others, all strong Dunbar stock, and had always called her that ever since she was a small child. "It was my Papa who called me that," she told Mr. Collins one day when he asked. "I can remember they came from Missouri, so Papa told us, and they stopped in Kansas where I was born. I think Papa was destined for Texas. Some people began to go there before the big War. But we stopped in Sapulpa. I don't think the Indians liked that idea very much, no siree!"

Waller Cornelius Dunbar, tall and stout, with a moustache that had been growing since well before Missouri, did not particularly defy the Creek Nation and its statements regarding the white man's invasion of the territory. The Creeks wanted a specific definition of the Treaty of 1856 and they demanded a better and more concise explanation of the one of 1867. Of course, all this was a foreign language to the big man of Missouri. The white man had invaded and was settling on the Creek Nation. All the while, he started building houses.

Over the months this problem increased. For full bloods, even for those of mixed blood, their chief, representing the tribe, once met with Legus Perryman on the front porch of the White House some ten or so years ago when his brother, George, and his young nephew, Moses, were off to St. Louis to barter cattle. They had talked for hours.

"It's a dire threat," Pleasant Porter commiserated, "and we have a great deal more important situations to solve than to tolerate the mounting invasions of these emigrants, no matter what. I'm, saying, it's about as bad as what happened to us in 'seventy-four, with that serious drought, and that terrible plague of grasshoppers." This type of conversation across the years was one which still haunted the White House long after Josiah died.

The young, eager Pete had come to the farm from the area around Sapulpa. Within this section of the Creek Nation noted for its heavy crime with so many murders going unsolved, disreputable ruffians found sanctuary outside the law by hiding, in one way or another, in the back streets of Red Fork. When Ralph Collins found this frightened youngster, he brought him to the ranch, made him take a bath in Coal Creek, put clean pants on him and gave him an old shirt. Then Collins went to Lula and asked her outright if he could stay.

Such came at a time when this stalwart woman, young, herself, had to make a decision of this kind without her husband.

"Bring him into the kitchen and let me feed him first," she concluded. "then I'll make up my mind."

But two days later she called her foreman to her one evening after supper because she always had one more cup of coffee waiting for him. The baby, Edith, was in her cradle, and the other girls were asleep in their room. "We've got a lot to do here now with Mose gone. I can do it 'cause I feel like you and the boys can do it. I don't doubt that at all." She sat at the kitchen table in her calico dress, with a bonnet thrown casually across the back of a chair. On the oil cloth she used for a table covering were the salt and pepper and a large lamp with a new supply of kerosene, its own chimney dirty with soot. From the bunkhouse came raucous laughter from the two boys. "How's the new one, Pete working out?"

"He's a good milker. Just where and how he learned to milk he didn't say. He's all right." He took one last sip of his coffee. "He keeps thanking me for hiring him when it was you who did the hiring."

The delicate moment registered with her, but her thoughts were elsewhere. "I'm going to Tulsa tomorrow so I'll need my buggy harnessed early. I plan to stay overnight. Did you say something about the hogs, yesterday?"

"We'll have the biggest ready for slaughter around November, I guess. That was what I wanted to tell you." He rose and put his cup on the cabinet. "Are you sure you can make this trip by yourself?"

En route to the water bucket, she stopped. "I don't see why not," was her soft reply. She reached for the dipper and drank as she spoke. "I've got to get up early, Mr. Collins. I'll be taking the girls with me, of course."

"I mean fording the river that way, Mrs. Perryman. The river is up now, you know with all the rain. Is Mr. Tabor's ferry working, now?"

The realization that she was alone filled her with a tender sadness. Around the ranch, of late, she drove a small buckboard down by the south forty, across the gullies and rough terrain, feeling the fragile wagon veer, and shift its weight when the ground was so uneven. Long before Moses died, she managed herself on the prairie fairly well, often with one of the drovers, either Pete or Laredo by her side. Long ago, she learned to handle the horses, especially the nice gentle stallion Moses gave her, and to guide him by different pressures on the reins, the separate and subtle tug, push, and pull of the leather to talk to him.

So now Ralph Collins learned to agree with her on certain matters. When he felt compelled to disagree, it was with a physical hesitancy by the way his body moved and his arms became nervous. As he grabbed his hat from the nail on the kitchen wall and he opened the screen door to the back porch, Lula saw again this air about him. "I wish you'd let me go with you. Or Laredo, maybe, ma'am."

"I knew you'd want to go with me, but I'm going to be all right, yes sir. Now don't you fret and you stay here and take care of everything, and those other two, and I'll bring you all some of those peppermints you like."

"Ah, now, Mrs. Perryman..."

She pushed him through the door. "Mind you now, you do as I say." She nodded to him. "Goodnight, Mr. Collins."

Reluctantly he smiled. "Goodnight, ma'am." A lamp was burning in the bunkhouse. He heard a horse neigh to another as he turned to Lula, cleared his throat while she shut the screen door and reached for her shawl that waited on a nail next to where he always placed his hat when he came inside the house. The air was brisk and cool and for just a minute or two, he thought he heard some thunder far off to the west. "Well," he finally agreed, "all right."

He found his way to the well, lowered the bucket, and poured the cold water into a pail that waited for him after his sojourn into the kitchen. Thunder sounded again. This time, he saw a sheet of lightening across the heavens which brought a curious Laredo out of his bunk. Pete was awake, too.

"I thought we'd get lightning," Laredo said looking upward past the trees. "You going with her tomorrow?"

But Ralph Collins did not answer. Now shirtless, he headed for the washstand with his water.

"There's no more soap. Here!" and Laredo threw a new bar to him. "I meant to take some, myself." Even when he caught the soap, Ralph Collins said nothing.

When he stationed the buggy for her near the stile block the next morning, Ralph Collins was still quiet. Laredo was with him, holding the reins. Lula had given Edith to him, to hold until she herself eventually arranged her satchel. The other girls were waiting in the rear seat. The night had passed with no rain at all but the sky was dark and gloomy. It was early. Summer birds were already flying high above them, calling to others in trees to the east.

Again, Lula made another trip into the house because she forgot her fancy hat. Attired in a pretty black dress, wearing the boots that Moses gave her for her birthday two years ago, she carried a bonnet which she wore when traveling. The hat was for her arrival. Dot and Cozetta were squirming, eager to travel. "Sit still," she called as she climbed into the driver's seat.

Once settled, seated on a cushion, Lula reached down for Edith from a willing Laredo. She placed her in a box to her left designed by her foreman as a good cradle for travel. Her big hat was already anchored near it. She tied her bonnet, adjusted her driving gloves, and took the reins from Laredo. The look in Ralph Collins eyes halted her. "I know you don't want me to go alone but I've done it before!" She glanced back to see why Dot and Cozetta were so silent, just sitting there. They were little ladies now, looking straight at their mother with prim white caps tied about their brown hair. Dot carried her newest doll and Cozetta fussed lightly with her nice new black dress.

"We talked about this last week and again last night. You worry like a wet hen. I told you not to worry none. I said to both of you, and the new one, that you will not have to leave." She looked directly at both of them. "I'll think of something with your help." Then she chuckled. "Daugherty probably would not want you back anyway." She laughed aloud. Then she bent over to pat Mr. Collins on his arm. "Did you ever wish you had stayed with ol' Jimmy Daugherty?" And then, facetiously, she winked, "you two don't want to go back to Texas."

Ralph Collins eyed Laredo quickly and then he asked, "Will you tell me, ma'am? I've often wondered if Mr. Perryman was sorry he took me off Mr. Beecher Perryman's place like he did. I mean, time passed so fast we never did talk about that, you know, least, not to my knowledge, I guess."

Lula rested the reins on her knees. "Mr. Collins," she said selecting her words carefully, "I've known about that story since I first met Moses so long ago, now." Must have been when we first met at a barn raising. I can't remember. But what I do remember is that my father-in-law took the blame for you and was freed by the council. That, I do remember. Mose knew you were a good man, Mr. Collins, and, by Heaven, you still are. Now," she finished, "the three of you mind your manners while we're gone." She reclaimed her reins and clucked at the horse. "Who is that down on the main road yonder?" She saw a lone figure of someone on his horse, silhouetted against the early morning sun.

"That's Pete, ma'am," Ralph Collins answered, "he's going to be with you as far as Jenks. He's buying some supplies and coming right back. We need some three-penny nails."

She smiled a secret smile and Ralph Collins smiled back. "Okay!" and she nodded her goodbye and clucked again. A breeze was apparent from the south as she started down the hill. Across the wooden bridge she nodded to Pete who was instantly at her side. "Say, Pete," she began, loudly over the clatter of her carriage. "Did you ever run into my daddy in Sapulpa? Name is Waller Dunbar. Thought you might know him, a carpenter, made a lot of houses in the last six or seven years."

"Can't say as I do, ma'am." To her right, trotting along evenly with her speed, he noticed how she was holding reins and sitting properly. "You ride good, Mrs. Perryman. Yes ma'am, Real good!"

Lula only smiled at that. The old road into Jenks was over a number of loosely fitted hills, past an assortment of small houses where a few white farmers rented their homes from the Creeks who owned the properties. She did not stop nor give a greeting to anyone she saw, but she did wave as they passed. Pete was always slightly ahead of her as they made their way through the little town toward the river. This portion of the land was damp, for rain had fallen here in the night.

"One of these days we'll have a bridge here," Lula spoke lightly to Mr. Tabor. "Then you'll be out of business."

"You be careful what you say, Mrs. Perryman," Tabor returned the joke, and then when he saw that Pete was there, "you going too, mister?"

"Mr. Tabor," Lula said pleasantly, "this here is my new man and his name is Pete." He's turning around here." She drove her horse and carriage aboard herself, feeling the weight of the vehicle press into the water. "Thank you, Pete," she said as he waited until they shoved off. "I'll be back tomorrow."

With a wave of his hand at the tip of his hat, Pete smiled at them and waited an added moment before he disappeared. In a matter of minutes, they floated across smooth water.

Mrs. Mayme Perryman Shirk was Mrs. Rachel's youngest of her three daughters, often a morose little girl who grew up with her own brand of temperament, who rode well, but who always bothered her oldest brother, Moses, for all kinds of favors, either at the the new House or at the White House. But Mayme had married Stewart Shirk on a dare as most people presumed. He became her husband, so she presumed, because of her allotment of land west of the White House directly on the east bank of the Arkansas and on a road that ostensibly became a thoroughfare for all traffic northbound from the ferry dock.

Lula made the trip several times, either by herself, with one or two of the girls, or with Moses. And when he was with her they would inevitably stop at Mayme's modest home on the small acreage for talk with his sister and eat dinner. Their destination, in all cases, would be the White House.

This road had become so flat and smooth that she picked up Edith from the cradle to sing to her. Soon she saw the Shirk house on her left as the trees thinned.

Every time she made the approach she remembered what Moses had told her what his sister thought about this farm of hers.

It was a simple one-story dwelling, constructed well some two years ago after Mayme's allotment was secured but it did not have the image that she preferred even when it was built.

"I don't like it." Mayme always said that it was finished with wood that was left over from the White House, but that was only an unfounded remark based upon her own opinion, and not on the lumber cost that came from the white men who were contracted to build it in the first place. Moses's opinion, which was never appreciated, was that the whole household was a result of not doing anything at all well. The location for their one buggy was not a shed but more a ramada with a weak roof. The chicken coop to the north was too small for the purpose Mayme had in mind. But the thick line of tall trees on the north kept the cold winds away from their house. As Lula's buggy neared this home, the dust from the road announced the arrival. The wind was stronger there than on the west side, nearest the Arkansas.

A lone figure of a young Indian girl was standing on the two steps, her hands balanced against her forehead to shield the bright suns rays. This was Mayme, a mere twenty years old and already pregnant with her first child. Lula saw her amble from the shade of the trees with an unwelcome air about her. "What are you doing here, Lula?" came the hard question.

Reining to a halt in front of her, Lula untied her bonnet. "Did you get my message I sent last week?" Dot and Cozetta both begged to get out of their seat. "Of course, girls, wait while I get down and I'll help you."

The dust settled and the girls scampered across the side yard and disappeared. Noises from the chickens told Lula they were at their favorite place. Lula sighted a sorrel pony tied to a tree limb. "Is that Abner's horse?"

Mayme tried to control her hair in the wind. "He's inside drinking some coffee." She seemed uncommitted as she folded her arms. "But I think he's leaving soon."

Lula left her bonnet and hat in the front seat. "I sent Laredo over to tell you about a week ago. That I'd be on my way to Tulsa." She was preoccupied with retrieving Edith from the homemade cradle. The girls reappeared, running and laughing, Dot already having lost her new cap somewhere in the process. Following closely were two Negro children of a neighbor who lived not far from Cline's Corner, just beyond the turn of the road. "He told me he left word with you."

"I guess he must have told Stewart cause I didn't get the message." Her hands were busy warding off the flies that waited near the front door. "Ab," Mayme called, "Lula is here."

With a cup of coffee on the table before him, Abner rose with a genuine smile when they came into the small kitchen. "I heard the girls outside so I guessed you were here, Lula!"

"Where is Stewart, Mayme?" Lula asked, going first to the water bucket. "I haven't seen him since the funeral. Here," she said to Abner, "take Edith for a minute, will you?"

Abner pulled a chair to the table and accepted the baby as Lula joined them. Mayme glanced at her brother, sat opposite them, and began to fan herself with a piece of an old calendar. "I don't know," Mayme confided, "I really don't know. I guess downtown, mostly." Abner returned Edith to her mother. He rose again and left the kitchen by the back door to scout for the girls, whistling for them, as was his habit, as if he were calling his dogs.

Mayme looked down at her bulging belly and perceived it much larger than it actually was. "I'm so sick of this," she said. "I'll be glad when it's over." Then she looked at Edith with a tired smile and a heavy breath. "How on earth did you birth four babies, Lula?" And to the mother whose daughters were outside with their uncle it was a most logical question in all the days she had been Moses's wife.

"Well," Lula answered, "how on earth did your mama birth eight of them?" But whatever Mayme thought did not bring any smile this time. She rose from the table and ignored Lula and Edith. Hospitality in this household was not at all in keeping with the family in which not only Abner and Mayme matured, but their brothers and sisters as well. Mayme had married quite young but so had Lula. Mayme was now part of the Shirk clan, a somewhat notorious group of mixed-bloods. It maintained a reputation for a sadistic slice of morality in keeping with earning a living and building their own society in clandestine ways and means. Any more, Mayme refused to visit her mother often. She was even late at her father's funeral.

Gently rocking Edith, Lula managed to get to the back yard to monitor the girls with Abner. In the kitchen, he had appeared ill at ease, himself, but attentive with his nieces. Now that Lula was present, Abner excused himself to speak to the Negro lady who came for her own children.

"Come on, kids, time to go see Grandma." and with this, Dot and Cozetta squealed with glee. Lula returned to the kitchen to say goodbye to Mayme who, by now, was lost in thought at her cabinet. "I guess you don't want to talk about any-thing do you?"

Mayme sat again in her same chair. She lazily scraped a few crumbs from the table onto the floor. She offered no reply and stared at Lula so forlornly that a tear dropped from her eyes. "Ab will go with you when you go."

"I have to, now, Mayme," Lula responded softly. "I'll tell Mama you said hello. All right?" Mayme nodded. With Edith in her arms, Lula left quietly through the front door.

Abner was turning the buggy toward the road. He had tied his own horse to the rear of it and he had placed Cozetta in the rear seat and was lifting Dot when Lula stepped off the porch. The Negro and her children were out of sight by now.

Abner helped Lula sit so she could manage the cradle again. He took his place behind the reins, squared his hat on his head, and clucked twice. Without inci-dent, the horse surged forward leaving a cloud of dust in the early afternoon sun. Mayme had not risen to bid them goodbye.

For a long while neither spoke as they began an easy trot on the even patch of road. Abner put on his gloves and pushed back his hat. Edith woke from a nap. Tired as they were, the little girls became drowsy and quiet. The thrill of seeing their grandmother no longer excited them. A whippoorwill, usually singing at night, decided to call to them from across the pasture.

"Father was a good organizer," Abner said softly, but his statement sounded so loud, coming as it did with no pretext. "He made sure Mayme's land was secured. Emma, too, for that matter." He pointed to the left. "He put the allotments side by side." He laughed, "I never did know what ever happened to Ella's side of the bargain. Her land is farther up the road."

Abner looked at Lula, anticipating some kind of a remark but her attention remained on the baby. Three buggies passed them going south. After a while, Abner turned east where the road was less smooth. This was part of the pasture-land belonging to the original family after the trail from Alabama.

"This part was desolate." Abner voiced as an extension of his thoughts. "As far as you could see. Father told us he and his brothers, like Uncle Sanford and Uncle Thomas, had a difficult time. Grandfather Lewis died in Kansas before the war was over."

While they bounced along often on hard rocks, Lula grabbed the arm rest still clinging to Edith. She had not yet become accustomed to her brother-in-law's fast pace. Her bonnet, still tied around her neck, slid to her back.

Lula was actually thinking of Mayme. Since Steward Shirk was not at home tending to his cow, or plowing the field between their land and that of her sister, or tending to a garden that his wife needed, or rebuilding a shed for their buggy, then where was he? Strangely, she presumed her thoughts became audible, and that Abner himself would provide answers. Astonished, she looked at his left profile but his concentration on the horse was necessary as they approached the White House. His own pony was merrily following along.

Mrs. Rachel became more than merely the mother of her eight offspring. To many citizens of the nation, she was even more than a matriarch. This lady of the big familiar home on the rise of the hill toward which they were moving, and the one daughter whom they had left in the kitchen, weeping, were two separate and distinct personalities, now. The former respected the trait, so inbred with the nation, that once something of value was yours then you must take responsibility of caring for it, no matter what it was. But the daughter.

"If' it's worth having, then it's worth taking care of."

Abner did look at her this time. "What did you say?"

"Oh," Lula tilted her head, "nothing especially. Just something I was thinking about. I think, something your own mama said to me once after Mose and I were married. I guess I'll always remember it." And then, so as not to embarrass him, she returned to her own pensive mood, Mayme had lost that concept somewhere along the way. The sun was lower in the sky. They could feel a more intense cool-ness in the air, brought on by the weak promise of some rain. Dark clouds had fol-lowed Lula and the girls from Tabor's Crossing but all too often, these clouds did not mean much at times.

Abner looked at Lula again who raised the question, "What?"

"Nothing," he said, "I thought you said something."

Steward Shirk was his own kind of farmer and Lula had been trying so well to dismiss the gnawing supposition that this mixed-blood was a threat to the nation's honorable and distinguished character. And she would never force that thought upon even the closest of this family. And, she felt, Abner was the closest of the entire clan, now that Moses was gone.

Rachel Alexander Perryman was now, not only the provider of honor and the propagator of the nation's reputation, whose own parents had been forced to come west, but, she was also the noteworthy semblance of material sustenance. No per-son, white or Indian, was ever ignored by this lady. No person had ever been turned away from her doorstep, a trait undoubtedly taught her by her own par-ents. If anyone were sick or unable to work, she maintained help. If a neighbor needed to plant a crop or mend a fence, it was Mrs. Rachel who saw to it that the chore was finished.

However, in the case of her own daughter, Mrs. Shirk, a solid phalanx parlayed against this philosophy in the form and being of Steward B. Shirk. He was not always easily located.

Even when death occurred as it most certainly did when Josiah died and, more profoundly later, when her husband passed on, the Tribe was always present, was always willing to console. That is just the manner of the Tribe. These traits were ever more astutely delineated as Lula, the girls, and Abner came nearer to his mother's threshold, in thought and deed.

For the short distance, while they listened to the summer birds, they were quiet. To break this silence, Abner began to speak aloud, as if what he thought was so overwhelmingly pertinent that his words he uttered required an audience, even if there were only pasturelands on both sides of this avenue of trees.

"Father is gone. He was not like some of the tribe who were contented with life or little labor and small return." Lula was surprised that her friend may be alluding to his own sister's marriage into a nondescript branch. "And just look at Josiah, too. They were all willing to accept the white man's ways." To Lula, Abner appeared to ramble with his comments. "Certainly not like old Efa Harjo. I remember him. That old Tuckabatchee who, with his hounds, refused help and lived out in the open somewhere this side of Sapulpa."

A man on horseback, to their left, called to Abner, waving his brown hat, but Abner did not see this greeting. Only Lula nodded a hello as he passed. Abner continued with a sigh. "I was just a little kid but I remember ol' Harjo. Too many of us, Lula were content to live in log cabins with an outhouse or two, a meager existence, but not for me."

Lula Perryman was actually more concerned with Edith in her arms now than in any philosophy that Abner endorsed with his oral recital. Abner was the scholar of this family. He had a valid interest in history and the uniqueness that set this family apart from the others of this famous nation.

Gracie had just died the preceding December of influenza. For a long time Abner saw no one and talked very little with anyone. Both Lula and Moses were the only ones. it seemed, to manifest any degree of sympathy. Very likely Abner was still in some sort of depression at the passing of his young wife, and his uncle, and his father, combined.

Then, just as rapidly Abner changed his tone. He licked his lips and with a free hand, he removed his hat and wiped his forehead, feeling the cool summer breezes pass over his long black hair. "I was just a little boy", he mused, but I remember when Mose told me about Mr. Collins when he came to work at the Homestead. Mose told me, years later."

Lula was hesitant to recover thoughts about this for fear they indeed would become audible and Abner would not wish to prolong that portion of family history. They were at the home by now, with its pond, the ducks, the trees and the imposing barn to the rear.

Even though his father constructed the big House downtown fifteen years ago, this house here, in the country, this huge acreage, was home to him and to Moses, to their sisters, too. No matter how many times they arrived or departed, everyone felt akin to this amity, to this togetherness, everyone that is, except Mayme Shirk.

Daniel Childers came up this same road sixteen years ago. He had parked his wagon. Laredo, or someone, had noticed him. But now, the one more incisive piece of news, far more compelling than what Ralph Collins had so unceremoniously done, was what had happened to Captain Childers' children. Orphans they, and they were so graciously accepted into the Perryman household, to be cared for, fed, clothed, and sent out, much later by the matriarch whom Abner and Lula would see soon, a woman who still lived in this very house that was there, looming ahead of them. It was discovered eventually that the dead woman in the wagon was Jane Owen but her relationship to the captain remained a mystery, one that was lost in the surge of time.

As rewarding as their arrival was, to recover the warm and tender beating of her heart, here, Lula did not deny another premise, short as it was, that she considered herself a case of unworthiness. It disappeared as quickly as it arrived. She had become unworthy to possess a dead Indian's land, that she was outside the realm of this Creek Nation's panoply of living. Emma and Ella, those two strange sisters, themselves, had discussed this theory. George, junior, was as eager to succeed as his oldest brother. Abner, who had voiced so much of what was on his mind on this journey, was closest to her than all the rest. It was the second time such a thought had penetrated her psyche. Oliver, now eleven, was too young to realize the depth of concern. And Mayme had already exerted more discontent than what Lula was able to perceive that morning.

The quiet and not so quiet nation still felt a deep distrust of the white man's culture even though that same culture, with all its inherent violence, had altered virtually all of the abiding traditions that had been theirs since Alabama. It was Lula, then, who thought that this Change that everyone feared was personified in herself.

"Look there, Lu," Abner called softly, pointing to two little boys running past the ducks toward the house. "There's Oliver with a neighborhood kid."

Abner slowed the gait of the horse so the two boys could run beside them, smiling, gleeful, without a care. They all arrived in front of the house together, where the welcome sign was balanced against the newel.

Oliver bounded eagerly to Lula and carefully parted the blanket in which Edith was wrapped, to look directly into her eyes.

"She's awake. Go on and look." Lula smiled at the boy. His curious playmate stood under the trees to observe their arrival. Dot and Cozetta both stretched their pleading arms in a big request to be removed from the rear seat.

"Take them out, Oliver," Abner suggested, "and then I'll take their carriage to the barn. Lula gave Edith to Abner, dismounted, herself, and then took her baby again.

Coming through the front door, standing with eager arms, was Mrs. Rachel with a sweet smile on her wrinkled face. The granddaughters ran up the steps to her.

Taking her satchel from the driver's seat before Abner could get away, Lula was home. Here.

Chapter Eight

Main Street of Tulsa, so designated by the populace because it was by far the only predominant thoroughfare, was full of mudholes due to the slight rain that fell the previous evening. It pointed southward at right angles with the railroad tracks which had been the focus of economy and business locations. The Frisco requested permission and was brought into the territories in eighteen-eighty-one. The Tulsa House, purportedly to being the earliest hotel facility, was directly on the north side opposite Archer's Store. Even so, on this hot June forenoon as many as one hundred business establishments were vying for attention. Gambling was a major attraction at every corner and in every tent, before tents began to disappear. Businesses favored the one-story wooden frame building. They began to sprout up overnight. The remark that this little town was becoming a city now that the new century had arrived to be exact, was already a cliche'. Other parallel avenues were growing southbound as well, on both sides of Main. Three large private homes had already been constructed including the city dwelling that George Beecher Perryman planned on this street just six blocks from the railroad station.

Lula Perryman, accompanied by Abner, rambled down this avenue northward in a stylish carriage, complete with a new top to ward off the hot sun. They came from the White House over a narrow street that led them on the west side of the cemetery. Lula thought, perhaps, of tending to Moses's grave, but she had other matters to consider first. She left Dot, Edith, and Cozetta with their grandmother while she attended to business. As they felt their vehicle bump along the puddles of water, Lula swayed with each vibration. At one time, she dramatically grabbed at Abner's left arm for fear of falling into the mud. With her satchel still beside her, more than once she had to adjust her new hat and rearrange her tresses.

A few people recognized them as they trotted past the Oak Lawn Cemetery, heading to the small hill that was on the extreme south end of the area known by everyone as downtown.

"It seems to me," she said casually, "that every time I"m in Tulsa I see new houses. Well, I'm glad I'm where I am, still out in the country even if it is twelve miles south of here!" She nudged Abner as they proceeded. "Whose house is that going up over there?"

Abner, having become a citizen of this fair city by virtue of the fact that he is in it often, responded with authority. "That, dear Lula, is the new modest home of Dr. and Mrs. Fred Clinton. Didn't you tell me his mother and sister called on you the day we learned about Mose?"

Lula agreed, recalling an afternoon in her life that had been pleasant in one way, but too alarming, in the other. "I think she is a nice lady, his mother, I mean." And that was all she could muster at this moment, when the pedestrians around her, the horses, the buggies commanded her attention. They trotted slowly past the House on the corner. "Your Mama hardly liked the place that your daddy built for her, isn't that right?" Lula always made a point either to walk by this beautiful structure, stopping to drink from the deep well out in back, or ride by it.

"Well," answered Abner, removing his gloves now that they were getting closer to their destination. "In one sense, this place, there, was good, 'cause we all had to go to school which was right over there," and he pointed to a building to their right that had become a public school for Indian children in the last ten years. "But Emma told us Mama wanted to go back to the country. I can understand that. So, she did."

"There!" exclaimed Lula, indicating a place to park their carriage and tie the horse. "Park there. We can walk. Would you care to look at that!" As she dismounted, she noticed the new wooden sidewalks around some of the store fronts. "Guess I won't get my new shoes muddy after all!"

They both started to walk northward after they waited for a buckboard full of lumber to pass them. The driver waved at Abner and tipped his hat. "Howdy, ma'am."

Painted in large neat letters on the facade of one of the newest buildings was the name, Jedediah P. Parker, Attorney at Law. His bold letters could be distinguished from a block away, they were so predominate.

Before they could proceed to this office, a sudden surge of activity, a melee of sorts, of several men, bursting from a shanty building, ran down the street toward the train station. Four in all, they apparently had a great piece of news which they shared as they made their way out of sight.

Lula straightened her hat and her dress while Abner stomped mud from his boots. Jedediah Parker exited his office and threw some dirty wash water into the street just as Lula and Abner were about to enter. "Oh, hey, ma'am I'm sorry! I just about washed my clients, didn't I?" With the empty pan in his left hand, dripping water, he extended his right. "You must be Mrs. Perryman and, let's see, you are Abner or are you George?"

The lawyer was in shirt sleeves, nice looking, with a great smile and a laugh behind his moustache and small beard. His bow was genuine and he permitted entry before he too came into his office. He placed the wet pan in its location, in a corner under some old newspapers.

The room was neat but his desk was not. Small and untidy, its top was full of several sheaves of loose papers anchored by a frosted glass ball which, when lifted and shaken, would manifest a rather cool image of children in a snow scene. On his wall opposite the two windows to the south were two well framed certificates explaining his authority and degree as a lawyer in Indian Territory. He reached for his suit coat and put it on, without attention to a vest which remained on the back of his tall leather chair.

"I've got that one chair there for you, Mrs. Perryman, and Mr. Abner Perryman, if you do not mind, you may pull the box over just a bit to the desk and you may sit on that." Jedediah sat behind his desk and shifted some papers so that his file on the present clients was before him. "I'm glad to see that you received my letter, Mrs. Perryman," he began, looking from Lula to Abner and them back to her. "I sent it with your foreman, I believe he was, a Mr. Collins, when he was in Tulsey." He coughed. "I guess we citizens of this fair city can call it Tulsa, now." He adjusted his glasses and opened his dossier.

Abner remained standing for a while but as the conversation lengthened, he sat on the large wooden crate that was, at one time, a box containing personnel effects of this lawyer. On one side, printed in thick letters, were his name and Fort Smith, Arkansas.

Mr. Parker scratched his chin before he spoke. "I returned from Okmulgee recently after speaking to the proper authorities and I learned a bit about Mr. Pleasant Porter, the current chief. A grandson of one of the Perrymans, I mean. Quite an illustrious history, there, I might add. He would be a cousin, would he not, of your late husband?" He smiled graciously, shuffled a few papers, and extended to her an important page. "As a result of your attendance in court with me on the second of June, nineteen-one, I am pleased to report that the case of the late Moses S. Perryman has now been adjudicated."

A startling noise from outside his office, on the street, drew his attention and was causing alarm among some horses that were tied onto the railing just south of the lawyer's front door. Mr Parker breathed heavily, rose, and went to see about it. Four large Poland China hogs clamored onto the wooden sidewalk that ran the entire distance of this block. They rubbed against the side of the buildings as they fought each other for space.

Above this din, Mr. Parker called to a small lad of sixteen who tried corral his animals down the street. "How the devil did they get up here on the wood in the first place?"

"Oh, I'm sorry, Mr. Parker," he exclaimed, beating them with his stick, "but I'm trying my best."

The lawyer dodged them as they squealed past his door. "Try to keep them in the middle of the street if you possibly can. I have some clients here." The remaining hog, a straggler, struck him in the leg as it lumbered by him, leaving mud on his pants leg. "Say hello to your mother for me, Billy, will you?" who replied as politely as he could under the circumstances. "Her cake was good. Thank her for me, please!"

While Mr. Parker was at the door, Lula read the page, signed it, and gave it to Abner to read. As the lawyer returned to his desk, Lula brushed lint from her collar. "I think I already know about the inheritance. About the girls getting everything, I mean. That's Creek law, isn't it?"

As Abner agreed, rising because the crate was uncomfortable, Mr. Parker answered. "I think so, yes, it is. But until the girls are matured, I believe, you are in total possession of the house and lands, but the girls will be given a guardian and his name is..." and he consulted a sheet, "a Mr. J.H. Simmons."

Lula opened her satchel and accepted the paper from Abner. "Is this my copy, then?"

"It is, Mrs. Perryman and if you will sign my copy, I will give you these other papers for your possession." He pushed at desk level another copy of the transaction which she read quickly. After signing, she placed her papers in a side pocket of her bag and balanced it on her lap.

"Please date my copy, if you will." He rose and moved his chair back from the desk. "Today is Tuesday, June twenty-fifth. The year of course is already on there, at the top."

"Lula," Abner whispered, "be sure and date your page too." With his hands clasped behind him Abner looked at Mr. Parker. "Are we finished, then?" He claimed his hat from the floor.

"We are, indeed!" the lawyer replied, making his way from his desk. A pervading breeze made its way through the window and Jedediah anchored his work with the paperweight, arousing the fake snow. "A little something from my nephew and niece from back home."

Lula rose and straightened her calico dress and was about to adjust her hat when the lawyer raised his hands to delay their departure. "Oh, Mrs. Perryman, I would like to suggest one other bit of news, if you will."

Abner was already through the door but he stopped, his hat in hand. Mr. Parker allowed Lula to precede him, and stepped through the door to get some fresh air. The sun was hot for this time of the afternoon but traffic was increasing with the imminent arrival of the train from Vinita. A host of cowboys, drovers, and cattlemen made their way into Owen's cafe. All too often on days when herds crowded into the corrals at the far west end of town, these men on horseback hollered at each other. Today one jovially called out to the lawyer who waved back at him. "He may some day be one of my clients! I'm used to the noise, myself, now."

As the boisterousness subsided, when the cowboys followed each other into the cafe, Mr. Parker took his handkerchief and wiped his forehead. "As I was saying, Mrs. Perryman, and Mr. Perryman, too, of course, I have an invitation for you if you wish. I, myself, am going, and you are welcome to come with me." The three ambled to the railing where the buggy waited. The horse recognized Abner with a rattle of his harness.

Lula extracted her fan from her satchel to cool herself. "And what might that be, Mr. Parker?" Abner proceeded to untie the reins and pat his horse's nose.

"Mrs. Louise Atkins Clinton is a client of mine. When her own husband died in 'eight-eight, she was my very first customer. I had just arrived in Indian Territory with a blessing of the chief of the Creeks, I might add. Mrs. Clinton reared four children, all adults now of course. Young Dr. Clinton is a practicing physician in our fair city. His new house is going up right over there." He pointed to the east. "She also has two other sons, Lee, and Paul, and a daughter, Vera."

Two late riders on perspiring horses, obviously of the crowd that had already passed them, fled down the street and around the corner. Mr. Parker waited again for the drovers to disappear. "Mrs. Clinton is entertaining this afternoon from one o'clock until four, so my invitation says, at the Stivers residence." This time, he pointed southwesterly to an imposing structure with a wide front porch and a high gabled roof, easily seen from any direction. Their line of vision was just to the west of the big Perryman House. "There," he said, raising one hand to his forehead to shield his eyes from the bright sun. "See where some buggies are parked. It won't be a cotillion, of course, but I'm sure you would be equally as welcome."

Abner waited a moment to hear what Lula might say but the lawyer continued. "I saw Mrs. Clinton last Saturday and she would like you to attend when I explained I would be seeing you. She did not know how to correspond with you."

Lula placed her satchel in the carriage on the rear seat. "Mrs. Louise," she reflected, aloud, "I remember she said she had the same first name as I did. "Oh, yes, her daughter."

"But people call you Lula," put in Mr. Parker quickly.

"My papa called me that. Mose liked it, too." She started to change her stylish hat for her bonnet. "Well, I'll tell you, Mr. Parker, sometimes I get the idea that I'm not the kind of woman who enjoys that sort of get-together." She glanced at Abner whose expression at this remark disagreed with her.

The lawyer turned to Abner. "I believe, sir, that an uncle of yours has also received an invitation. A Mr. Thomas Perryman, sir. Is that your uncle?"

"Yes," Abner nodded, "my father's brother."

Lula had not yet climbed into her seat. "What's the occasion, Mr. Parker," she asked.

"I think it has to do with the announcement of her daughter's wedding. I believe that is the case."

Remembering the young girl whom Pete had mentioned from time to time at the dinner table, Lula smiled. "Well!"

Abner extracted a small envelope from his trousers pocket. Holding it carefully in his left had, so he could soothe his restless horse, he spoke quietly to both. "Lula, if you don't mind, let's go. I'm sure Mama is taking care of the girls all right." He hesitated as he displayed the card. "I got an invitation, myself."

"You got an invitation?" She was surprised. "To Mrs. Clinton's party?" The wind caught her hat and she reached to control it. "I didn't know you were going to parties!"

Abner laughed when she laughed. He had the card from its envelope, now wrinkled and a bit worn from having been in his pants pocket for a long time. "It's actually from Miss Lucy Stivers but it's for this party Mr. Parker is talking about."

I don't know the Stivers family at all," commented Lula dryly. She took his card and read it silently, noting a personal touch of finely written words, bordered by an elegantly printed ribbon with hearts and Cupids.

"If I may explain, ma'am," interspersed the lawyer, "this Miss Lucy M. Stivers is the young daughter of the household where the party is taking place. Mrs. Clinton still lives in Red Fork and it is she, Mrs. Clinton, who will be announcing Vera's forthcoming wedding. This is a social occasion, if I may add." He could see questions reflected in Lula's eyes.

"Well," Lula hesitated while she thought about it. "Isn't it about going on four now or something like that? I bet the men back home are getting ready to round up the cows. That party will be over..."

"It's just a matter of five blocks in that direction," the lawyer insisted. "If you'll permit me, I will just get my hat, close my door and ride with you over to their house. If I may."

Lula looked at Abner and shrugged her shoulders. She had heard of the Stivers family only once over a year ago, when Thomas Perryman asked Moses and her to come hear the sermon by their new minister on New Year's Eve. "On the last Sunday of the last week of the last month, of the last year, of the last century." Thomas was poetic at times. At that time when Mrs. Stivers and Lucy were introduced to the minister and his wife, they thought it more of a social necessity rather than a worship service. But Lula and Moses attended. She remembered waiting for Moses that Sunday while he talked with some cattlemen. That was the first time she saw the two women.

By Moses, Lula learned more. Mr. Stivers had come from Missouri, too, with apparently a strong intention to make a name for himself. He had posed as a trader or possibly a marshall for the judge at Fort Smith. So the story went, after church that cold day. Lula did not give it much thought since then.

This man John Jacob Stivers, with only a dollar and a half in his thin pocket, elected to settle in Red Fork. For a short while he cavorted with outlaws and a prostitute or two. but he did end up an inspector of cattle and hides, along with a mixed blood by the name of Daniel Childers. Both of them made their way into the

Broken Arrow area where, alone and destitute, he met a Miss Thomas and courted her, thinking she had Creek Indian blood. He had always connived his way into any business that inspired him to make money easily, endorsed as well by this flamboyant woman whom he eventually married. So too, eventually, John Jacob Stivers succeeded in getting everything he wanted either legally or illegally with the consent of the lady who became Mrs. Stivers. Anyone could assume that with the passing of these ten years, with the arrival of their two sons and their daughter, that the Stivers clan would gain respect among the population of Tulsa. People soon learned whose house that was on the second street west of the main avenue. It was home to all. Quietly, all too quietly, their means of livelihood was subject to doubt and argument, more so that of Mayme and Stewart Shirk.

That is what Lula recalled when Mr. Parker retrieved his hat.

"I want to stop at Mama's well and water my horse," Abner said softly as he saw the lawyer join them. "It won't take long." He was laughing, then.

With Jedediah Parker perched in the rear seat of the big carriage, Abner helped Lula to her seat. He took the reins for an arrival in style after a stop at the well. The trio could discern an exodus from the porch of the Stivers residence, a mere three blocks from the watering trough. The guests were on the wide terrace around the northeast corner. Their own surreys and wagons occupied all the shady areas for the entire block. After bouncing through potholes, they stopped at the high front gate where Lula and her lawyer dismounted.

"I see a place under a tree," Abner said. "I'll park there and hustle back. Wait for me."

Lula straightened her dress and hat as she muttered a tiny greeting to several people who were leaving. "I believe you are Mrs. Moses Perryman, are you not?" inquired a matron as she passed them. "My dear, I'm so sorry for you. Please accept my condolences." Lula smiled at her. She could not remember her name.

Mr. Parker waved at Mrs. Clinton as she stood on the porch with a lady whom he accepted as Mrs. Stivers. They were equally busy with their pleasant farewells to a stream of people who were still coming from the house. It was already four o'clock by Mr. Parker's fob watch. The summer sun was still high in the western sky. Abner joined them at the gate, dodging the crowd.

At first, Mrs. Clinton did not recognize either the lawyer or the two people with him. When the line thinned she became exhausted and longed to find a chair. Hatless but wearing a long black gown with acres of lace at the throat, this lovely lady whispered to Mrs. Stivers. "My dear, I see Mr. Perryman now, I believe, coming up the walk. Your Lucy wanted to know when he arrived. I was about to give up on him!" With that, Mrs. Stivers fled into the house with this news.

"Mr. Parker," shouted Mrs. Clinton, eager to greet them all. She practically ran to meet them. "You missed the most outstanding news of the day! Or have you already heard?" And to Lula, she beamed, "have you heard the news?" She ushered them inside the door rather quickly. "Did you hear the news about the oil well?" Inside, the laughter was more apparent with several guests who lounged in the sitting room. The tumult of her forthcoming explanation was still very much alive. Mrs. Clinton continued as if it were her solemn duty to repeat to all, again, the case.

"Yes, yes, I know the reason for the party." and her exuberance was contagious, "I'll get to that. And thank you, by the way, for coming." She made a point to nod her head toward Lula. "I see you did bring Mrs. Perryman, I'm so glad you did, really, I am!" She smiled at Abner and brought them from the hallway into the sitting room despite the noise.

"We just heard the confirmation just thirty or forty minutes ago!" She dabbed at her mouth with her handkerchief she carried with her. "Last night, about midnight, oil! In Red Fork! Can you imagine right there in Red Fork! It was on Mrs. Bland's property. Sue Bland, the wife of the doctor." All attention was focused on this vibrant lady as she glanced from guest to guest as if others, still present, had not heard the impressive statement.

Maybelle Stivers, as many had learned to call her, brought a tray of tiny cups filled with strawberry punch. It was true. As Mrs. Clinton explained the whole story, Abner eased himself around the room and peered into the dining room opposite the hallway to determine where Miss Lucy Stivers might be hiding.

In an attempt to subdue the whole incident of the oil on Bland property, Dr. Fred Clinton bottled the precious fluid and departed on that morning's train to Muskogee. He had to do so primarily to make an official claim on behalf of this woman. He wanted also to discuss the future of this discovery with his friend, Dr. Fite. The opposite side of the case was to place the well in the Bland name before those who drilled it would think that the oil actually should be theirs. This bit of reference was not included in Mrs. Clinton's report.

"He had some kind of power of attorney or something like that" she said, finishing the story. By this time, she was on the settee facing the front windows, a bit out of breath, but still most excited about the information she bore. Maybelle, after serving all the punch, returned to the kitchen for more.

Abner peered down the hallway but saw no one he knew. But another group was still in the dining room. Above the noise of conversations, he heard Mrs. Clinton's remark about the Dawes Commission. "That's why my son had to run off to Muskogee like a flash! Mrs. Bland's land! It had to be done right then and there."

The ebullient Maybelle Stivers placed her tray on her kitchen cabinet and fled to the back porch where her daughter was chipping ice. "I told you ten minutes ago that Abner was here, darling! I thought you wanted to know!"

"Oh, I do, I do, Mama," Lucy giggled, with wet hands, and water splashed on her newest dress. She then calmed, thanked her mother, and grabbed the nearest towel she could find.

Abner once again looked into the sitting room to see that Mr. Parker and Lula were the only two still engaged in this bit of news. A maid had brought them a plate of cookies. When Lucy finally appeared in the hallway, Abner practically collided with her.

"Mr. Perryman, sir," she gushed, smoothing her tousled hair and rearranging a blue ribbon at the top of her head. "you may not remember me but I did speak to you last February at your brother's funeral. I even tried to see you again at your mother's house." She stopped the maid and took a cup of punch. "Here is some real good punch for you, if you'd care for some, that is. I made it myself, yes sir!" While he accepted the cup she continued. "I can see how the news of this oil business has blocked out the real reason of the party." She smiled at him. "Come. I want you to meet Vera and Mr. McBirney."

But they were too late. Mrs. Clinton had risen and fetched the bright young couple, herself, and escorted them into the sitting room. Properly, Mrs. Clinton also brought with them Maybelle Stivers. "Mrs. Perryman, I believe you remember my daughter, Vera. We called on you some time ago at your house in the country." She escaped the direct reference of the very afternoon when Lula learned of her husband's death. "And may I present Mr. James Hugh McBirney, her fiance'." Then she took James' hand. "Jim, dear, these are Mrs. Lula Perryman and Mr. Jedediah Parker, our lawyer." She looked about the room. "I don't know what happened to Mr. Abner Perryman, oh, dear!"

Graciously, Mr. McBirney took Lula's hand and, with a splendid authentic Irish accent, replied, "Sure and I am pleased to make your acquaintance, Mrs. Perryman. You don't appear an Indian lady."

"I'm not, Mr. McBirney. I'm as white as you." Lula surprised them all with her directness. "It was my husband who was a full blood." Prompted by his genuine laughter, she smiled at him. "My best wishes to you both, Miss Vera."

"Yes indeed," agreed the lawyer. Maybelle, perhaps more flustered by what Lula had said than by her position as hostess, began to laugh softly while she continued to look for her own daughter. She did, however keep her own eyes on Lula as one who could easily become her nemesis. She had a gnawing fear that this Mrs. Perryman could easily ask her where her own husband was at this moment, even though, assuredly, Lula had never had an occasion to learn anything, anything at all, about where he was while this afternoon had been in progress. The elusive Mr. Stivers was nowhere to be seen.

Mrs. Clinton spoke well of the future of her daughter and her new husband and how the wedding was planned for the fall sometime after Mr. McBirney established his career with a local bank. Then it was Maybelle Stivers who rose and accepted the farewell gestures of a few who were nearest the entrance. Refusing another cookie, Lula managed to find her way to Abner as once again the two mothers sauntered onto the porch.

Lula found him drinking another cup of punch. He spilled a drop and laughed. "Lula, this is Miss Lucy Stivers."

The young girl smiled sweetly, pushing a strand of hair from her wet forehead. But before Lula could return a remark, her eyes caught the image of a familiar figure standing in a corner of the dining room, surrounded by three other guests. "Nice to meet you, Lucy," Lula said but she interrupted with a soft question, "Abner, did you notice who is over there?"

Abner placed his empty cup on the window sill and glanced in the direction where Lula nodded. The man was Thomas Perryman, Abner's uncle, now sixty-two years of age, still a spry and healthy gentleman. "You better say hello to him, I think." Then to Lucy, she whispered, "Excuse us a moment, will you?"

Their departure was so sudden that Lucy was left with only her cup poised in mid-air.

Lula and Abner walked over to where Thomas stood near an open window, feeling the breeze slip over him. A gallant and wise man, this Indian commanded the attention of anyone and everyone, easily, who came within his presence. With only a rapid glance toward Lucy, as if to apologize for this interruption, Abner was first at the side of this paragon.

Thomas Ward Perryman, a reverend for a long time, once a willing student at Tullahassee, was determined to become the great success that his brothers and sisters expected him to achieve. Both Abner and Lula were aware of this man's feats. Gladly, while remembering that Moses appreciated him, Lula embraced this uncle. She had not seen him since Moses's funeral when he delivered a masterful tribute at the church.

"My dear, Lula," he returned, "and how well you look!" He turned with a sly grin. "And who is this fine looking nephew of mine?"

In a split second while Abner was laughing at this remark, he remembered all the important accomplishments of which the uncle was guilty. And humor was one of them. This man's life was dedicated to the spiritual welfare of his people, for he was implacably attuned to the Muscogee Nation, in his church as well as in the political arena. His brothers, Josiah and George, were gone now. Lula could discern a sad character in the lines of his tired face.

"Your wife, Uncle Thomas," Abner mentioned, "Aunt Eva, and my twin cousins, Tom and Arthur, how are they?"

"They are all well, Abner" he replied, "but I suppose you know that Ida has moved to Philadelphia with her husband. We probably shan't see them for a while. And dear Lula, God Bless you! Oh, it is so good and grand to see both of you. What a nice surprise!"

Vexed at what she beheld and by the manner in which Abner ignored her, Lucy did not stay to hear the rest of this conversation.

"I am going to leave tomorrow on the train for Washington D.C." Thomas claimed his hat which was resting on the fireplace. "This is yet another journey for me on behalf of the tribe. Pleasant Porter comes and goes too. This time, he has asked me to pick up the work that so many others have begun." He hesitated, in search for words. "And of course I am happy to do so. A little tiresome but I will make it again for sure."

Lula prompted him to sit on the settee in the parlor where they continued, the three of them, to cover all the news since the first of the century. Thomas had always been an excellent conversationalist, attesting to his impeccable ability to preach. In politics he was no different. A district attorney, a teacher, and a member of the Creek Council in Okmulgee, he never ceased to amaze those with whom he came in contact. Abner, seated next to him, with Lula on the other side, had not forgotten the kudos.

Maybelle Stivers pulled Mrs. Clinton to one side away from the sitting room. Only the lawyer was with the ladies but he excused himself to join the Perrymans.

"Now that we're alone, for just a moment," Maybelle began, "I want you to tell me just what is all this business regarding Sue Bland. I heard she was ill. And her oil well. The fact that she did not know, at this moment exactly where Lucy was did not keep her from extracting as much information, if not more, from her friend, as possible.

"Where are Vera and James?" Mrs. Clinton asked. "They were here a second ago."

"Never mind, Louise." This hostess was in agony. "They are probably in the kitchen. Now tell me."

Louise Atkins Clinton, having surveyed the empty portion of a corner of the dining room, noting only the presence of the three Perrymans with Mr. Parker, caught the strange insistence in the eyes of this matron which, perhaps, she had not previously noticed. She was hoping that nobody would detect this odd curiosity.

As a widow living in Red Fork, it was not convenient for her to present her daughter to the public. "There's just too much riff-raff in Red Fork here," someone said. At the onset, Mrs. Clinton did not actually wish to tell this woman much of anything. Again, the threat was that Maybelle was not at all the complete person in whom she wanted to confide. It was indeed true that these two women developed some type of friendship. Even Madame Stivers, at times believed herself to be a widow. This was before anyone began to realize a certain undercurrent of deception that surfaced. Soon everyone learned that she was just plain Maybelle Stivers, lacking the sincerity that she discovered this day in Mrs. Perryman's face.

So it was that Maybelle simply allowed the entire town to come to know her as that, rather than Mrs. John Jacob Stivers. A few ladies at the church never did actually know the name of her husband, anyway. In an effort to gain some degree of respectability, she was also prone to open her house for any tea, or church meeting, or Tuesday afternoon Bible study. Or, for that matter, on that fateful June day, the reception for Vera Clinton and Mr. McBirney. With all this in mind, Louise Atkins Clinton began her explanation.

"I didn't quite know what happened, myself. I only know that my son fled on this morning's train. I begged him to wait since his sister was so aggravated that he decided to run in stead of staying this afternoon. Lee and Paul were here."

"Lee and Paul, yes," echoed Maybelle fanning herself with a damp handkerchief she pulled from her ample bosom.

Mrs. Clinton waved at someone in passing and returned to her narrative. "I thought all the Blands, being Indians, had already filed for their allotments. Somehow, though, Sue, bless her heart, has been claiming that land without her official papers so that's why someone had to run real quickly to Muskogee to claim that property before anyone else got to it. Especially now that there is oil on it. Dr. Bland himself wanted Fred to hustle down there. To file the oil strike with the Creek agent."

To gain her breath after her long dissertation, Mrs. Clinton sat on a nearby chair that was borrowed from the church. Maybelle, more concerned now, grabbed another chair, placing a guest's empty cup and dirty napkin on the floor. "Go on!"

"Well," Mrs. Clinton was at a loss for words, "I'm sure he is seeing Mr. Allison Aylesworth. He's the agent with the Dawes Commission."

"What's that?" The question came quickly from Maybelle. Mrs. Clinton simply gawked at her. "I've never heard of that."

Carefully, dear Mrs. Clinton chose her words so not to confuse the issue any further. "Maybelle dear, your lot on which this house sits had to be, at one time, allotted to someone, and it's this someone from whom you and Mr. Stivers rent. I take it that this house is , actually, not yours but that the Indian whose allotment it is, is actually the owner." Louise, dear Indian woman, felt embarrassed that she had to offer an explanation of sorts to a woman, purportedly her friend, who should already understand the Dawes Commission. Perhaps not, though since she, and her daughter and sons were Caucasian. "You see, Maybelle, Sue Bland is Indian, and she had never legally claimed that property until now, of course. Why she waited, I'll never know."

For just a split second Louise saw in the face of Maybelle Stivers many avenues of thought that were converging in one thoroughfare of significance which, at this time this simple woman elected not to share with anyone.

Vera Clinton, still fresh and pretty in a dress that came from a shop in Vinita, appeared suddenly, her little hand at Mr. McBirney's elbow. "Mother," she announced, "Jim and I are leaving now. The dinner is at his parents' house."

"Yes!" gasped her mother, rising suddenly, "Of course!" She looked lovingly at them both, noting the happiness that surrounded the excited couple. "Give them my best, will you, James?"

"Oh, sure, I will," he replied, fascinating this lady even yet with his Irish tone. Hand in hand, they escaped the heat of this house and raced happily down the rock sidewalk, past the iris to their buggy. All this left Mrs. Clinton profoundly pleased. Maybelle retreated to the confines of her messy kitchen, full of half-filled cups and a big elaborate punch bowl, borrowed from the lady who had just given her a world of thoughts within her frazzled head.

Thomas Ward Perryman escorted Lula to the front door as Mr. Parker waited on the porch. Hardly anyone else was present in the house. Lucy Stivers appeared from nowhere, grabbed Abner by the arm, and together they made their way past the two Perrymans, the lawyer, and into the front yard.

"I'm glad you attended today, Mr. Perryman," Lucy confided almost furtively as they paused under the trees on the north side. "I'm pleased we had this opportunity to become better acquainted." Abner looked into her perspiring face. "My mother told me Jacob met you once. My brother, Jacob." Then, shifting her position to the other side, she nodded to the porch. "I didn't know Mrs. Lula Perryman was white. I had actually presumed that she was full blood like you. You are full blood, aren't you, Mr. Perryman?" She pinched his arm. "A real full blood?"

"Yes, ma'am, we are. I mean, yes, I am. My brother married Lula. I was about sixteen and I remember the wedding. My cousin's husband performed the ceremony." Abner noticed a strange gleam in her eyes. "At our house," he continued, "south of town. He was Mr. Broyles. Ida married Reverend Broyles."

Somehow this demure girl had a way of extracting information from him which had lain dormant for so long a time. The end of the century brought so many changes that he dismissed much of what pertained to the family's opinions on matters both social and political. Ella had not really complied with the idea of Moses marrying a white lady. George junior was a youth who was too young to object. Oliver was only four when the wedding took place. "Mama and Father both gave consent." Abner finished his thoughts audibly.

"Oh," was all Lucy could say.

Maybelle Stivers was on the porch and called her daughter. "Come in a moment will you dear? I've something to tell you. Please excuse her, will you, Mr. Perryman?" So Lucy gave his hand a tap and skipped into the house behind her mother.

Abner stood by his buggy alone watching the bright sun in the west and noted the traffic on the other avenues, the passing of wagons and pedestrians to a street where Mr. Hall still operated the corral for the steers, the longhorns, the cows, and a few horses that nobody claimed. Abner thought about going into the store soon to see Mr. Hall or at least call on Mr. Reed.

As he wiped dried dirt from his reins, his eyes fell on several rocks that were resting behind the seat on the floor where they had been gleefully collected by Oliver, no doubt. The boy had polished each one before putting them in a corner with a piece of cloth so that they would not bounce out of their location.

Voices interrupted his reverie. He essayed the two people on the porch, Lula, and his brilliant uncle, and he waved at them both. They were talking even yet. Three large trees along this side of the street spread their shade where he waited.

His thoughts once again returned to the family. For some reason, he thought of Emma. "We're still a family," her words echoed in his memory. "Papa is gone.

Mose is gone. but we've got Mama. George, bless his heart, wants to marry. All those problems with Uncle Legus being a chief no more." Her reasoning sounded like something Mayme would conclude but not necessarily Ella, although at times Ella was indeed recalcitrant. but it was Emma's words that returned when he least expected them. "Look at all the people coming in from everywhere and Lula and her brothers and sisters and Mr. Dunbar. There's not enough Indian spirit anymore. It's a sad state of affairs if you ask me." In a sense, in a great sense, Emma was correct.

Abner stood under trees that had been there long before houses on this sparse block were constructed. His eyes looked toward his mother's home. Emma had once commented, when she and Abner were standing by a box of carpenter's tools watching that majestic house being built on the main street, that not many buildings were in the town. They were mere children when she said this. "Is this Tulsa going to be our town, Ab, or is it going to have other people here, too?"

Abner noticed now, that Lula and Thomas were slowly making their way from the porch down the walk to the gate. His uncle's gentle but strong voice penetrated the air. "Pleasant Porter is a good chief, after Legus, I mean." His comment almost was a duplicate of what he was thinking, remnant words that Emma had said to him, often enough. "Pleasant wants us to become contented members of the white man's society."

Again, Emma's words, exactly, because she was very much an adherent of the old traditions. But it was Thomas, standing with his hat in his hand, who continued his own contribution. "We could have had a civilization which would have suited us better than the one which has been thrust upon us. Pleasant Porter, God Bless him, said that, more than once. I remember him saying that, in my presence. Now: all that is gone. My brothers, Sanford, Lewis Wesley, George, and Josiah, my sisters Lydia, and China. Oh, I saw my nephew, Reubin Partridge, just this morning."

"May we take you somewhere, Uncle Thomas?" Abner turned the buggy to face north.

"Thank you, Abner, but I'll walk. My bag is already at the station and I'm taking the evening train to St. Louis. Well, dear Lula, it is nice to see you again. I pray all goes well with you. Abner, you must be alert to her needs." He embraced them both, tipped his hat, and departed leaving them staring at this tall figure who stopped for a drink from his sister-in-law's well.

Chapter Nine

Shortly after her return to the Homestead, Lula pieced together the remnants of her marriage with the future for herself and her daughters. She went about her chores in her own way, gladly and resolutely, with an eye to making certain that her family was well cared for, her house was clean, and her plans secure and bright. Being a young widow was not too uncommon, for many women had been left alone. Accidents plagued households, husbands abandoned families for one reason or another and common law wives maintained a sudden degree of independence. A few of Lula's acquaintances were married and divorced two times and some, even three.

Lula visited Mr. Parker two separate occasions, each to establish an orderly plan for financial strength which, apparently, was becoming a viable argument among her sisters-in-law. Every time she left the ranch, Ralph Collins devised a reason for having Pete accompany her as far as Tabor's Ferry and not an any time was Lula ever aware that his riding with her was a ruse.

"The river is up today," he would announce, or "Leave the girls at home this time, Laredo and I can take care of them."

Once, about two weeks after the oil discovery at the Bland location, so quickly authorized by that sudden but necessary rush to Muskogee, Jedediah Parker came to visit Lula at the ranch. He brought with him a lady who had professed an interest in wanting to see the beautiful Homestead. She, herself, had heard so much from the lawyer. This woman, who claimed a strong talent for investigating historical data, specifically wanted to know about the land, this house, and a general explanation of the Indians. The lawyer and she appeared, unannounced that day at the south gate. So while she sat in the kitchen drinking coffee with Lula, he went to chat with Ralph Collins about a variety of subjects, pleading to show him how to milk.

"You must be very courageous," this lady said, more that once. But her conversation was not at all boring, for Lula learned more about her home in Ohio than the lady learned of courageous pioneer widows. After a bite to eat at the round dining table, attended also by the three cattlemen, as Lula preferred to call them, now, Lula and her new friend sat on the front porch and whiled away the afternoon until Jedediah Parker called for a departure. Rain clouds were gathering along the western side of the row of trees by the barn. They climbed into their buggy, said goodbye, and went down the hill over the little bridge and vanished on the main road. Lula walked over to her bed of iris along the east fence to ascertain their care before she went back to her kitchen.

One of the topics of conversation, more so with this lady than with Mr. Parker, even though he did confess interest in it at first, was the coming nuptials of George Perryman and his own bride, Orphia Reynolds. He was only eighteen and she confessed to being fifteen, the matter certainly not odd in that day and time. Lula her-

self was fifteen when she married Moses. The whole subject may have been somewhat compounded because Mr. Parker's lady friend was not married and already
she was well past the mark of fifteen. But she was certainly gracious and sweet and
she was instantly popular with Dot and Cozetta. Lula meant to write her name on
a list that she kept for future reference, but it slipped her mind.

But the impending marriage of Lula's brother-in-law and this full blood Creek
woman was more to her personal interest than the Clinton-McBirney nuptials.
Abner came to visit for a day and returned to the White House with the consent
that the wedding could, indeed, take place in Lula's big south yard, under the
trees.

George had already brought his fiance' to meet Lula some time ago. She was a
petite and tender little lady who was shy only at first, until she saw Lula's children. They charmed this Indian and were fascinated by her long braided hair
beneath a dainty hat. "Yes, I am going to be your aunt," was the word that delighted Dot and Cozetta. "Can you say my name?"

"Orphia! Aunt Orphia," they echoed and giggled and ran out to the stile block
to wave goodbye when they departed.

"What happens if it rains?" Ralph Collins asked Lula that evening at supper.

"We'll transfer to the bunk house!" was Lula's reply, covered with contagious
laughter.

"Two weeks more puts it the end of July," surmised Laredo. "It's be hot, all
right, even under the trees."

"Mr. Collins," Lula stated softly, "you and the men can slaughter a hog early.
We still have two, then, in the fall. It shouldn't be a problem, feeding everyone
after the ceremony. We can put two tables out under the oak trees."

Lula then had another guest show up at the house, not altogether a stranger,
but not expected at this time. When a buggy came up the hill and stopped at the
south side near the stile block, Ralph Collins was already walking out to meet
them. From her kitchen window, Lula saw him pass, so she dried her hands on a
nearby towel, looked once more to Edith in her crib, and then walked down the
hall and out the front door to see who was calling.

The buggy, with a wide roof, was new, but the lady in the seat was family.

"I remember you, ma'am," Ralph Collins said, holding the reins. "You're Mrs.
Perryman's sister, aren't you, from Sapulpa?"

"Call me Daisy," the girl replied, "everyone does!" She was Mary Cordelia
Dunbar until she married last year. In fact, it was Waller Cornelius Dunbar who
provided the surrey as a recent birthday present. It was he who called her by that
name since she was a baby. "I got a new baby boy, Mr. Collins, since I saw you last.
I was big as a barn then." She dismounted as she saw Lula coming down the sidewalk to meet her.

"Well, I swan, Daisy," Lula chuckled, "you're a sight for sore eyes!"

After Daisy removed her baby and the satchel, Ralph Collins steered the horse
toward the barn. "Thank you, Mr. Collins," she called and then she turned to her
sister.

Lula chatted aimlessly as they made their slow way to the house. Daisy gave
little Richard to Lula as she straightened her dress and removed her bonnet. She
was most jovial at seeing Lula again after almost a month. "You okay, Lula?"

"Well sure," was the reply. The dogs arrived to bark and make certain Daisy
would notice them.

"I can't get over this big house, Lula. My goodness, but Mose really did build a good one for you." She placed her bag in the hall for the time being, fanning herself with a small handkerchief she took from her bonnet. Daisy had been in the house often in these last four years with their father, even with the man she married. "It's all so big, Lula. You have a nice home. Mose left you with a nice place." She started into the sitting room but changed her mind. "Sure is hot!"

"We can sit on the back porch. I've already started the stove for supper so its hot in there." Lula returned the baby to his mother as Dot and Cozetta came bounding over to greet their aunt and look at their new cousin. "If you want a drink of water, I can go to the well real quick."

"Let me catch my breath for a moment. Can I put Richard in Edith's crib if she's sleeping in the bedroom now?" She moved in that direction but hesitated. "You asked about Dad...?"

"I was going to," Lula answered. For just a moment she began to suspect something was amiss with her sister. A subtle sense of disorder was apparent in the manner of movement, in the way she sat in the porch rocker, the way she shifted the fan Lula gave her, from one hand to another. Daisy asked her nieces to leave, something she had not ever done at all. "Dad is okay, I guess. He missed Mama so much until he married again. Do you miss Mama, Lula? I bet you miss Mose."

"I put Richard in the crib in the kitchen and I guess that I didn't hear your questions. But you look fine. I'm glad you're here." She offered a glass of water she got from her bucket.

Lula settled in the chair that had come from Mrs. Rachel's White House. This chair and the rocker had been on the porch so long that they were withered and rough.

Pete and Laredo were at the well, lowering the bucket for the ration at the bunkhouse. They were laughing and preparing to milk. The summer birds flew all around them and a breeze slipped through the north woods and onto the porch.

"It's always cool this time of the afternoon here on the back porch." Lula took the empty glass from her and set it on an old white table that was part of the furniture there. "I'm glad to see you, Daisy." The statement was, more or less, a question to her well being. She looked directly at her.

Daisy finally gathered enough courage to announce why she made this journey. "I'm pregnant again." She stopped fanning herself to see what Lula would do or say.

The long and involved story of Mary Cordelia Dunbar raced through Lula's mind. The older sister had lived it, too, with her own marriage to Moses, moving into this large estate at such a young age. But with Daisy, another story emerged from the Dunbar clan when Richard Childers became her husband.

The incident at Mrs. Rachel's White House sixteen years ago was often reoccuring on Lula's mind, sometimes for no reason at all. It echoed again, this time when she noticed that Ralph Collins had joined the drovers at the well. In the back of her foreman's mind, harbored there for all those years, was that incident. Moses had recalled it all too often, himself, especially so when Lula first learned of it.

George Beecher Perryman took the blame for the shooting. The council had exonerated him immediately. That was the decision of the council. When Ralph Collins departed the White House to become Moses's foreman at the Wrangler Ranch, or the Homestead, as Lula called her home, Moses asked her to forget the incident and so she did. It was, indeed, forgotten until Daisy met and married Richard Henry Pratt Childers.

"Mr. Collins doesn't know who I am, does he?" Daisy asked softly, fearing that her voice would carry as far as the well.

"He knows you are my sister and he's met our brothers and sisters. Walter Clyde comes by here once a week. He sits and talks, right there in that chair."

"I mean," Daisy whispered, "my name now that I'm married."

"What if he did." Lula rose to fetch a fly swatter from the wall. "There's a thousand Childerses all over the nation." She struck at a fly but missed. "Oh, I see." And indeed she did. The situation arose again, the Childers incident, the orphans that were left, the body of that woman in the wagon, eternal questions arising now and again as if the ghosts of Daniel Childers and her were as much a part of the Perryman psyche, through all the years, through all the sorrow that had come and gone.

Moses explained it all at one time. And his sisters and brothers grew up with that explanation. The two orphans were two boys but there were four other brothers; Mrs. Rachel was aware. Only these two, Richard Childers, aged eight, and the older one, James, arrived one day on the Perryman doorstep, bedraggled by the rain that day, lonely, frightened, escorted by the patriarch himself who followed the Christian concept that had been inherent in the tribe's character.

While the boys may have been unable, then, to comprehend the extent of their poverty and hardship thrust upon them by their father, they came to the White House in a stupor as all orphans did until Mrs. Rachel's love and care molded them into grateful children. From as far back as even her own mother remembered, being a Harjo from Alabama, widows and orphans with nobody, were never ignored. This Creek persona was present, even in their ability and willingness to build a house or make a fence, or plant a field for any unfortunate tribal member. This lady was never known to dismiss anyone from her kitchen.

As she listened attentively to her sister, Lula reached for a garment that she was mending. She also supervised the girls as they played near the rear gate. The light reflected on the porch was less harsh than direct sunlight on the south porch. So with her needle already threaded Lula worked and listened.

"I don't know why I ever married him in the first place." Daisy looked down at her hands. With her left thumb she softly massaged the right palm. "I guess I should have known better. But Papa gave his okay for you to marry an Indian. And I was real happy when Dick asked him for my hand." She glanced at Lula and finished with "Creeks are strange people."

Daisy was always talking about something to her sister. It did not startle Lula for silence between them was rare. They were always remarking about a house that their father built, or that one of the Covey girls was engaged, or what was going on in the big city of Sapulpa.

The little daughters ran around the house in play and the afternoon sun was noticeably lower in the sky. They heard the men as they entered the corral, especially when the wind was from the northwest to bring the sounds more closely to them.

Lula slowly raised the swatter again and handed it carefully to Daisy. "See if you can get that pesky fly."

"Dick said he stayed with Grandma Rachel over a year or about eighteen months, I think." She aimed too and missed. "And he just left and didn't come back."

Lula appraised her sewing. "He must have been nine or ten I guess. James told me once that he just didn't tell anyone anything." She snagged her thread and had to correct her mistake. "Too many homeless Indian kids as it was."

Daisy lowered the swatter. "Jimmy told you? Why on earth would Jimmy say something like that to you when he wouldn't even tell me?" The baby in his crib, not far from the back door, cried. Daisy rose to investigate and then stepped over to the large block of granite rock that formed the back step from the porch to ground level. The laughter of Dot and Cozetta from the west side of the house drew her attention away from her problem.

Daisy's husband wanted to be called Pratt but the name of Richard persisted. Those in the Dunbar family used Dick. As young as he was, he fled the compassionate White House with no notice. No one could understand why. Apparently, the boy decided to vacate the comfort and love of this household. For one full afternoon, until chores made her mobile again, Mrs. Rachel sat in the parlor of her house and contemplated this sadness. Explaining to James was somewhat of a problem for he knew only English and hardly any Creek. A fourteen-year-old boy whose brother suddenly had vanished in a matter of hours sat in the parlor and wept.

But they did learn what had happened. The urchin became a water-boy for the crews who extended the railroad southwestward from Red Fork to Sapulpa. He was too small to accomplish much of anything else. The hearty men who shouldered the iron rails as a team moved steadfastly covering the empty prairie laying ties and track at a rate of two miles a day. And they yelled for water constantly. The boy was at their sides with a sense of self-confidence but always a gnawing question persisted. He could not quite understand why Jimmy did not help him learn why they were orphans. His little mind, so engrossed in his joy of helping everyone, in the pride of standing with the workers to view the finished product, soon forgot poverty but never his brothers. Alone at night nuder the meager care of a thin blanket and his cot, he remembered Jimmy, and Aunt Rachel and the big horses in the barn and the pond, with the ducks, too. But he forgot everything else.

"You can remember when I met him, can't you, Lula?"

Biting the thread since she finished the hem, Lula placed the gown on her lap and sighed heavily. She had always been the oldest sister, always someone to whom her siblings could come for an answer. Walter Clyde cut his foot on a rock and Lula was there to wrap the sore spot and pat him on the back. "Little boys don't cry, do they?" To them, Lula was always able to supply just the right amount of condolences and also the correct answers to all the world's problems. The oldest of the Dunbar brood, she was now a wise twenty-one-year-old widow. But when she herself was ever fearful or hesitant, or undecided, she never told anyone unless it was Moses. She was not able to pursue that joy anymore. But she had a commodious house, a barn, and men who worked with her. Lula had a goal. She may not have been able to vocalize it, nor could she map it on a piece of her ledger paper, but she was young, attractive, and she was stalwart. She told herself she was strong, as well.

"Well, you like to go to dances," Lula laughed, placing the garment in her basket. "So did I. And then when Mama died, I guess the family just started to fall apart." She rose from her chair when Ol' Don came ambling around the house, the oldest of the dogs, panting from the heat. He came upon the porch and settled under Lula's chair. "I couldn't keep up with all of us. I even tried to understand what was happening to all the Creeks, especially when I was ready to marry one of them. And as for James, well," she hesitated, putting her needle in its proper place, "well he was just a kid who needed someone to talk to. Jimmy is a nice kid." Lula had never been able to deduce what made Richard leave Mrs. Rachel's care and how Jimmy remained there. "Jimmy has a level head. He's careful. I don't know about the four other brothers. Benjamin I think I met one time about two years ago."

Daisy replaced the fly swatter and fanned the front of her calico dress. "He's left, again, Lula. Dick has just gone off and left me alone." Daisy was beginning to show stress from all these complications. "Here I am, pregnant with God knows what, nobody in the world to turn to except you and Daddy, I mean." Her gesture of futility worried Lula.

Ralph Collins made his way past the well and through the back gate, its noisy clatter interrupting their duet. He removed his hat and with a gentle smile said. "I'm sorry, Mrs. Perryman, but Pete forgot to get more buckets. I'll just get them and hustle back to the barn." Then he turned to Daisy. "That sure is a handsome buggy you got there, ma'am."

"My daddy gave it to me for my birthday, Mr. Collins."

On his way from the milk room he paused again, "Mrs. Perryman, the mare hasn't foaled yet. We're waiting, along with you. She should foal any time now. Pete's staying with her." Then, as he turned to leave, "I got two buckets, that's all we'll need." He nodded to Daisy.

Lula sat on the rear step and patted the area by her. "Now you sit down by your Ol' sister," she laughed. Daisy did so as she watched the foreman make his way to the barn. Their feet rested on the immense rock that formed the step. "Where do you think Dick might go?" It was the only question on her mind, the only thought Lula could conjure.

Ol' Don rose and came to Lula's lap for a pat on the head. For a long time, neither sister spoke but merely watched the clouds sift in from the west. The men were leaving on horseback, first to round up the cows from the south forty and to escort them, two or three at a time through the east door of the barn. The other cattle, reserved for beef, had, as their home, the balance of the range before they were herded to the pens in Red Fork. This procedure was all the backbone of the estate, from Josiah Perryman and his home in Eufaula to this station, here, from as far as they could see on a clear day any time of the year. Every time Ralph Collins would ride by himself, some ghost of a plan that he learned from his days with Daugherty would haunt him. It would help him conceive of a better method of herding. He remembered the times with Moses to make this ranch the best in the nation.

In the pleasant hours after supper, this foreman and Laredo, with Pete, would sit in the doorway of the bunkhouse to chat and discuss the success of this homestead. How fortunate they were was always a good topic. A doubt sometimes arose.

"With Mr. Perryman gone now, it might be hard for us, especially for Mrs. Perryman," Laredo mumbled.

"Oh, I don't know. We don't have too huge a spread but we got a nice farm and a nice lady to work for." Pete smiled as he nodded in agreement to the foreman's statement.

Lula gave her sister a hug as they sat there. She saw the men depart, each on his own pony harnessed, roped, Mr. Collins leading, wearing the new hat that Moses gave him just last Christmas, with Laredo calling to each other, as they disappeared around the barn. Laredo laughed broadly.

"She won't give birth, now, will she, Mr. Collins? While we're rounding up I mean." Pete was nervous an he yanked his reins. From where she sat, Lula heard the reply.

"You can sit with her after milking." His words were loud coming clear from the corral.

"I don't know where he is." Daisy broke their reverie. "He can be away six or seven days at a time, leaving me with the little baby there and me pregnant like I am. One time when he came home he said he went all the way to Texas and back on a train." She scratched her arm after a fly bit her wrist. "I guess I just needed someone to talk to." After another spell of total silence in which they could feel a breeze and hear the chickens talking to each other, Daisy cleared her throat. "Jimmy is a nice man like you said," and it was with a shrug of her shoulders since many weeks had passed since even she had seen her brother-in-law. "He's got no family, other than his brothers. He just works somewhere in Red Fork, at least, he worked as a carpenter until he got the job with the railroad in Sapulpa." She paused to think.

Lula was curious. "How do you know all this?"

Daisy laughed softly. "Well, Daddy told me once and I saw Jimmy at the station about a month ago." Then, suddenly, she offered, "Maybe Jimmy knows where he is." The baby began to cry so Daisy rose instantly to tend him. Lula followed to see about her own child resting in the crib in the front bedroom beside her own bed. Through her wide windows across the south yard she could see Dot and Cozetta playing with Ol' Don. The collie had ventured around the house to where the girls were talking to the birds.

After supper that night, after the girls were bathed and put to their beds and with Edith in her own cradle, Lula was in her kitchen again. Daisy sat near a window with her son in her arms, almost asleep. The weather was cool with another threat of rain, a noticeable change from the heat of the day.

"Daisy," Lula started, quietly, "I don't know if you realize it or not, but James knows it was Mr. Collins who killed his daddy. And of course naturally being brothers he was sure to tell Richard." She folded her tea towel and placed it on a corner of the table. "Did you know that?"

"It doesn't make much difference now, I don't think," replied the sister. With her son asleep, she rose, walked to the crib that was posted momentarily in the kitchen, and put him gently under a blanket. "What's the difference?" Lula was at the table so Daisy sat opposite her. "But I don't think my Richard knew that, no, he didn't know that. I know for a fact they are close to each other. They got four brothers, including Benjamin, but Richard doesn't know what happened to them. My daddy-in-law was a wild one. He had a wild streak in him. Even I knew that. His little sons didn't know a thing that was going on, at that age." Daisy toyed with a spoon beside the sugar bowl. "Poor little kids. I suppose no one ever learned who that Owen lady was that Mr. Childers killed. Too late now."

They heard the back gate open and slam shut and footsteps reaching the back porch. Lula rose and went to the door just as Ralph Collins was ready to knock. "Come on in, Mr. Collins."

"I seen your light, ma'am." Hatless but with a clean face and hands, and wearing the new shirt that Lula bought for him the last time she was in Tulsa, the foreman nodded hello to both of them. "Just wanted to say that you got a new colt in the barn." He had a wide grin.

This happy news smothered the sad story the ladies shared. Right away, Lula chuckled gaily, slapped her thigh, and Daisy jumped with a yelp! Ralph Collins laughed with them. "Yessum, he was born 'bout thirty minutes or so ago, with Pete and Laredo in attendance. Mostly Pete, I might add. He seemed to know what to do. He said he'd been a midwife before." He exploded with glee! "He wants you to know that if you have another foal, I mean, if another mare ever gets..." and again he stumbled over words. "Well. We can call Pete the doctor, and Laredo the nurse. You want to come see for yourself? You want to? I'll fetch the lantern. It's right here, hanging on the porch wall."

Lula again faced Daisy. "I think I will, if you don't mind. I won't be long. Watch the babies and I'll tell you all about my new baby in the barn!" She untied her apron and threw it on a chair while Ralph Collins checked the oil supply in the lantern's tin base. Then he struck a match and lit it.

"Come along then, just follow me." Together, they passed through the noisy gate, turned west along the path toward the well, and down a small incline bordered by old pieces of lumber used to repair a shed. Rain, again, was imminent and Lula blithely ignored the few sprinkles that fell even though she had no shawl or bonnet.

"If it really does pour," Ralph Collins bemused, holding the lantern high above them, "we'll both get wet!" They neared the east door of the tall handsome barn. By habit, Lula paused and asked her foreman to hold the lantern near the jamb. She wanted to see the marking that Moses had carved in the wood just above the Dutch doors. The initials were hers with the year, eighteen-ninety-five, and they were still there.

"My daddy was right here, standing where we're standing, Mr. Collins." Lula felt the wet breezes against her face and her hair fell about her forehead. "He didn't help build this barn but he sure thanked the men the day it was finished. You didn't know that, did you? Mighty good barn, all right!"

Before he could answer, Laredo met them there, all smiles as they made their way to the stall where the new colt waited on his feet, feeble but upright. "See there, Mrs. Perryman," Laredo said, "it was Pete. Pete and me. But Pete did all the work."

"I reckon the mother helped a little bit, too!" Lula eyed the baby.

"I reckon so, ma'am," Pete laughed, "I reckon so!"

With another lantern already lit and prominently hanging on a rusty nail and with hay carefully banked away from the wall, the space was clean and neat. Lula looked at her new possession. The mother was just as proud as she. Slowly, and with great admiration, Lula reached out her hand toward the nervous colt to touch its nose and to peer into its startled eyes.

"See the white spot on his head, Mrs. Perryman?" came the question from the joyous Pete. "I think it's a good sign!"

"Where on earth did you hear that?"

"Oh, I heard it, all right, I did! Yessum!"

"Well," Lula continued, "if you say so, then I guess it's right. But I bet you anything his daddy had something to do with it." She reassured him with a pat on his back. "But thank you, Pete, thanks a lot! On behalf of the mother." She looked at them all. "Now, Pete, you name him!"

"What, me?" and again Pete became shy which was his usual trait when cornered by Laredo or by Ralph Collins when a decision was his to make. "Well," and he was flustered, "well, let me think on that one, please, Mrs. Perryman."

"All right sir," Lula nodded, "all right, we will! But you come up with a good one!" She turned to the aisle and paused by the ladder to the loft. "We got plenty of hay upstairs?"

"Oh yes ma'am." Laredo was first to answer. "Lots of bales."

"I'll take the lantern, Mr. Collins, Please," she said. "I'll make it back all right."

"I'll walk a way with you, please ma'am. I got something on my mind." After he said that, Ralph Collins looked at Laredo.

This trio of men who worked for Lula were subconsciously aware of their future that lay ahead of them. That Lula was able to discern this subterfuge was a trait she acquired almost immediately after Moses was buried. The multitude of so many others who came and went, who worked for Moses and Lula, those drifters who proved themselves good stable hands, helped on the hay fields and at different chores. Elsewhere, they had their own living quarters, places which were not altogether pertinent to their employment as long as they were there on the land, willing to work, and respectful of the ranch. A few of them had been with Moses's family for sometime, cowboys who worked for a small salary and a dinner at noon time. Before Moses died, still others, many homeless, were grateful for a job that lasted only one harvest and no more. So many drifted as if they had a specific plan for themselves.

Laredo exited the barn with them, closing the door while Pete remained to talk to the horses and to make certain that all was normal with the mother and her child. Laredo had always been with Ralph Collins for one reason or another. This Texan was loyal Across the miles, they developed an abiding friendship that surpassed brotherhood or mankind. And Lula noticed that a tacit adherence to this trait existed between them. There was even something monumental when all three rode together, with Pete often galloping ahead of them as if they were teaching this young one how to ride, to rope, to laugh! The Texas lineage of the first two never escaped them. While they longed to ride southward to the Nueces River, a thought that had been paramount once in their minds, they did, eventually realize, some time ago, that their lives were now better lived in the Muscogee Nation. With Moses Perryman gone, this thought became more obvious when they stood respectfully on the edge of that crowd at the Perryman Cemetery on the cold day last February. When Thomas Ward Perryman came over to shake their hands, they felt as much a part of their family as was the man who died. They were no longer intruders.

Laredo entered the bunkhouse alone.

"Are you all right, ma'am? Ralph Collins and she stopped at the well to pull some water for morning. He lowered the bucket. "Laredo wants to know, and I guess I do, too."

With the lantern put beside the bucket she had brought en route to the barn, Lula saw her foreman's profile clearly with his rough hands guiding the rope. When his bucket hit bottom and filled with water, he pulled it gently upward.

"The boys and I were wondering," he hesitated as he spoke, "just what your plans are, ma'am." He poured the water into her bucket which she started to lift but he took it from her. Then, with the lantern in his other hand, he quickly moved toward the noisy gate, allowing her to precede him.

"You all are good men, Mr. Collins," Lula answered, for she knew what was on their minds for well over a month. She felt a wind come up from the south as she opened the gate for him. "I expect to work hard at keeping my farm. It's my farm, now, according to Mr. Parker. He said he mentioned that to you when he and that Missy lady-friend were here. I forgot her name."

The gate banged shut as they climbed the step to the porch.

"He's proved that abstract, and I signed the papers."

"By Creek law, thank God, this land is mine and the girls'. She took the bucket of water from him as they waited before the kitchen door. Daisy had left a lamp burning on the cabinet. Ralph Collins lifted his lantern, extinguished the flame and hung it on a nail on the porch wall. Lula noticed a smile on his lips.

"Let me tell you something, Mr. Collins. I guess you know what I'm going to tell you but let me tell you anyway." Leaning against the screen door, she folded her arms. The light from Daisy's lamp filtered through the door onto both of them. "You know, Mose's family and all the Creeks, as a matter of fact, are under that law. My father-in-law took the blame for that man's death, that Mr. Childers."

"I guess I sort of knew something like that," was his reply "but I never knew just how it worked out, I mean."

Lula reached through the door to get a dipper. "Well. the council knew and understood it all. This all happened a long time ago, as you know." She took a drink of cool water.

"Yes ma'am, it was, all right!"

With her right forefinger she tapped him on the chest. "If a deputy had come for you, then Mose wouldn't have a good foreman for this here home of his. I'm talking about a deputy from Fort Smith much like Mr. Sizemore or maybe Roley McIntosh. You would have been gone, g.o.n.e. gone." Her gesture emphasized the meaning. "Mose told me time and again that when you shot Mr. Childers, he wanted you right then and there for this place. 'Course, he was a youngun at the time, you understand."

In the shadows prompted by the one remaining lamp, their faces reflected a sober image not so uncommon to farm folk. Still attractive even though her hair was mussed by the wind that had increased, Lula nodded assertively. And Ralph Collins though handsome, had finally reached that point in time when he accepted those summers that had begun to make deep ridges into his face, that his own hair was turning white, that he was conscious of this new century's mark on his mind. He had come a long way from south Texas.

"I've got to take care of my family, you understand? Seems like I get worried, sometimes being by myself, as I am. Sometimes I just don't exactly know what to do and how to do it. So I guess, that's why I need you and Laredo, and that young squirt, Pete." For the first time they heard distant thunder. "I'm not a very religious person, at least, I would like to think that I can do better. I pray though. Mr. Thomas Perryman told me to be sure to pray. That helps but I don't reckon I learned that yet." She passed into the kitchen to verify the amount of coal oil at the bottom of Daisy's lamp. She returned to the porch in time to see Pete walking from the big barn, carrying his lantern in his left hand, casting its own shadows against the trees.

For one still moment they heard the summer katydids chirping near the henhouse. One of the dogs began to bark possibly at Pete who stopped to pet him.

"Mr. Collins," Pete called, "is that you on the porch?" As he came through the gate with its squeaky hinges, he called, "Oh, Mrs. Perryman, ma'am I didn't see you." Ol' Don, who had been sleeping not too far from where they stood, became awake and joined in conversation with the dogs.

This was Lula's home. This was the Homestead as she preferred to call it now, and this was the Wrangler Ranch, too, in memory of Moses, this fertile landscape that took on more profound dimensions these days. And as young as she was, she became more determined to keep it. With her foreman on the porch, and with Pete at their side, Lula peered into the north line of dark trees and then to the east where the dark horizon melted into the blackness of the cool summer evening.

Ralph Collins stretched his long suntanned neck, rubbing it with a gloveless hand. He passed her and stepped onto the rock that he and Laredo, with Pete and some others, along with a team of ornery mules, managed to drag up the hill and place there for a step off this porch.

"I'll just go on," Pete called, as he disappeared with his lantern. Without turning to Ralph Collins, but folding her arms, again, as she usually did, often, before her, she spoke. "I guess you are my family now, Mr. Collins." She waited, not expecting a reply, and then she reentered her kitchen taking the bucket of water this time with her. He watched her from the gate as she claimed the lamp from the cabinet and proceeded out of sight, with the shadows of the rooms darkening her swift image.

Ol' Don returned to the porch, waging his tail happily as if he had won an argument. He waited, looking into the face of his friend.

Ralph Collins reached down and scratched the dog's ears. "Family," he said, and moved away, passing through the rear gate unobtrusively so that the hinges would not destroy the pleasant beauty of the moment. He saw streaks of lightning as he walked toward the bunkhouse.

Chapter Ten

The day before the last day of July was one of turmoil and confusion, the former because of the threat of rain to spoil the wedding for the next day, and the latter, because of the arrival, too early, of relatives from the fartherest reaches of the Muscogee Nation. The father of the groom even yet had become well known over the years. He had established his own empire of cattle with an honorable reputation and his children were of great concern, especially when each was allotted land of his choice on which to build and develop his own station in life. When this father died at the end of the last century, these same relatives came up the roads from Eufaula and Broken Arrow to mourn this loss. This time, they were here to celebrate marriage.

As uncles of the groom, only Legus, an ex-chief of the tribe, John Ward Perryman and Thomas were invited but not necessarily expected to attend. The aunts were all dead by now, and much of their families were scattered geographically and socially, which was a blessing to many and a prayer answered for Lula. Old Josiah Perryman, deceased, was at one time an elder in the Presbyterian Church and others, not invited, had become ministers. With due respect to such a memory of his father's siblings, the groom and his bride decided to request the services of the current pastor of this church. They had visited him recently.

"Dr. Kerr," George spoke politely, with Orphia at his side, "I'm glad you are going to perform the ceremony, but...." and he hesitated. Dr. Kerr looked quizzically at him. "But we want to know if you will perform it outside the church."

"Oh?" the pastor questioned.

"Yes, sir, if you will. We want to be married on Perryman land at my brother's place, just south of Jenks a little way. He waited until the pastor began to nod his head, as if the movement were necessary before he could answer. "It's where he lived before he died. His widow still lives there."

"I understand."

But George did not totally think that the good pastor did, actually. "It's to be outside, on the yard."

And so it was to be. Electing to have it on the grounds, rather than inside, was a decision that was made some days ago. This occasion would be more comfortable on the southeast lawn under the big trees than in the confines of a hot sanctuary on a dusty street. But this youth and his future bride were ready to face a negative reply if this pastor would object. Not everyone was aware exactly where the Wrangler Ranch was located, but a great deal of the population of the city, both Indian and white, were knowledgeable of the precise location of Tulsa's first church.

But the pastor did not object. "Rumors abound anyway, that our..." and he cleared his throat and smiled, "dusty streets would soon have their names."

The Hall Store, the train station, that church, even the Stivers residence and the Perryman House downtown, would all have designations by which they could direct the population. But Lula's Homestead was in the country, literally surrounded by cattle, pastures, rolling hills, an abundance of trees and her large, majestic barn that could be seen from a distance of a mile or two, even a small stream meandering down from the north that someone, long ago, named Coal Creek. How that came to be was forgotten in the previous decades.

George and Orphia were lost in their own dreams, walking from the church just two blocks to the House. Their schedule for their betrothal was broadcast among those invited. After the wedding a sumptuous dinner was to be served, so the noon hour was most appropriate. They spent the rest of the day engrossed in preparation.

"Wonder why they want to have it on a hot day in July?" Pete asked as he carried his share of milk that morning from the barn. Actually, his mind was on the new colt. Frisky and healthy, he did not need the full attention of either Pete or Laredo. Bailing hay was delayed for just those two days, and Ralph Collins consulted with Lula, busy in her own right, concerning the location of the oak table in the yard before any cloth was placed over it.

But the early arrival of cousins who appeared on that late afternoon prior to the wedding day was a source of confusion. Not all the relatives came but those who did in their wagons and clean carriages represented, in many respects the entire eighteen siblings who had been, at one time, the groom's uncles and aunts. These cousins, tired and dirty, had halted three buckboards on the main road with exhausted horses, hungry relatives, and the big question of not knowing exactly where they were.

Thomas and Arthur Perryman, the twin brothers, walked from this entourage across the wooden bridge and up the hill to a spot under two trees where they could make an enquiry. They stopped at the stile where they recognized Lula who had come out the front door to welcome them.

"We're Thomas Ward's sons, ma'am," Arthur volunteered. We be a day early, I guess, but we're here. We're kin!"

Lula shook their hands. "Did your daddy make it to D.C. all right?" She was astonished by the sameness of the boys.

"Yes, ma'am, he did. He's still there, talking." And the other replied, "We don't know when he'll be home." They both were amazed at the large Victorian house. "Cousin Mose built that for you? I'm Arthur, ma'am. He's Thomas."

With a slight nod, Lula raised her hand to her forehead, for the sun was bright. "Oh yes." Then she looked to the road. "You got three wagons?"

"One is for sleeping." Thomas continued the explanation. "The second one has the Smiley kids, some more twins, ma'am. Little Ernest and Emmett are just eight years old. But they wanted to come with us. The driver isn't related, ma'am. Our cousin Nora Smiley became ill and died recently, so they are without a mother. Just their father, but he couldn't come."

"Don't forget the other Nora, too, ma'am." The twins had been schooled well. They were willing to offer explanations. Arthur knew that since Lula had not met some of George's cousins, that she might not understand his meaning. "That Nora is Nora Scott, 'cause she lost three of her little babies and her husband. Tiny infants, they were."

"Nora didn't come to the wedding," Thomas replied.

Lula thought to change the subject. "How old are you boys?"

"Twenty-one," was their reply, almost together.

She looked at the road again. "And in the little wagon, I see two maybe three kids there."

"That's the third wagon, ma'am. Edmond and Tecumseh Perryman. Just tiny lads. Just two of them."

"Well." Lula began surmising best what to do about the situation. "You bring your wagons on up here and park them south of this stile block." She pointed. "Over there. You can set up camp over there. That'll be all right."

"Thank you ma'am," Thomas smiled as he signalled the first driver to begin their movement. "We brought our own food. We be all right. We be fine, like a visit." Their trek continued.

But all those invited were not nearly as cordial. Early the next morning Mayme Shirk and Emma Drew arrived in one of the old buggies that Stewart Shirk discovered somewhere without telling anyone how he obtained it. He brought it to their house late one evening and parked it behind the ramada. At a moment when Mayme was on the front porch, he covered it with a soiled tarpaulin. Two days later, Mayme saw it when she was feeding the chickens. Its yellow wheels protruded beyond the edge of the short cover.

Emma Drew did not know that story until they were en route to the ranch. She became as incensed about it as Mayme was, after it was discovered. They came up the incline of the hill and drove all the way around to the west side, away from the cousins who stood by their wagons to observe the arrival of their relatives.

"I've never seen so many buggies in all my born days." said Mayme as she removed her traveling bonnet, straightened her tousled hair, and put on an elegant new hat, complete with a bright fancy feather. "Can you see George's buggy, already?" But Emma was too occupied with tying the reins to answer. The lawn was full of people. "Who is that coming toward us?"

"I believe that's Mr. Collins who used to be foreman for Papa." Emma changed her bonnet for a new hat. Mayme remained in her seat and caught her breath.

Ralph Collins tipped his hat as he approached. "Welcome to you both, ma'am. I guess I can't remember which you are since you're so grown up ladies, now."

"I'm Mayme," was the first reply as she hoisted herself out the left side, holding onto the sideboard until she gained her proper stance. She sheltered her hair from the wind.

"Emma Drew," came the other answer as she stretched her arm in a quick exercise. "You're getting old, Mr. Collins, since you were with Mama and Papa." The foreman started to collect the satchels from the rear but Emma stopped him. "Leave 'em be, if you will, Mr. Collins. We can get them later."

With a kindly gesture of agreement and a big smile again, the foreman stepped back, allowing the sisters to proceed to the main house. He started to unhitch the horses.

"Leave 'em be, Mr. Collins," Mayme coughed, "just keep him harnessed, please. We'll be going right back after the ceremony."

As occupied as she was, Lula observed this arrival from the front door and waited on the lawn to greet them. "Glad to see you and Emma," she called, "this is a pretty busy place, now." She was not accustomed to making small talk with these two sisters-in-law. Their husbands had obviously not come to this event.

"Well, Lula," Mayme said, as she adjusted her hat, "I guess you're happy now that George is marrying." It was so inconsequential a remark that Lula pretended not to hear it. Mayme was always the brunt of argument on any level.

"Come on around in back where George is," was Lula's reply. "Orphia is inside getting ready and I guess Abner and Oliver are around here someplace."

"Is Ella coming?" Mayme asked as she adjusted a long earring to her left ear. The dogs were there sniffing at everyone. "Keep your dogs away, Lula. This is a new dress." And she added a quick remark. "I bet that husband of hers won't show up!" She slapped her hands to ward off one of the dogs.

Someone called for Lula so she excused herself and disappeared into the kitchen as the sisters greeted their brother quietly. This group managed to remain sequestered under the shade trees that populated the north yard. The rear gate became a source of anger, banging open and shut when children passed through it. "I couldn't stand that noisy gate all the time like that," Mayme objected. Then she smiled at a gentleman their brother was escorting to them.

"Pastor," George said softly, "I want you to meet my sisters." Each smiled graciously as her name was called. "This is Dr. Kerr who didn't have much problem finding Lula's big house after all. His wife is around here someplace too."

At the rear window that overlooked this crowd, Ella drank water from a dipper. "Well," she said to Lula, "I guess it's time for me to say hello to the whole mess. Ol' Shirk didn't come, I can see. And I don't spy Clifton Drew, either." She placed the dipper into the bucket, dried her hands on a towel, opened the screen door and stopped on the porch. "Hello Emma." She hesitated before she greeted Mayme.

Daisy Childers, who had maintained a quiet time for as long as she could do so, came from the front bedroom where she had placed her son and Edith. Once in the kitchen, hesitating, not knowing when to speak, she finally caught Lula's eye. "I bet you'll be glad when all this is over," she said as she investigated what lay under a pan cover. "I just noticed that the table out there is about ready. What time is it?"

Lula straightened the lace collar around her sister's neck. "My, you look pretty! You changed into that pretty dress like I told you. That sets off your dark eyes." To the other ladies helping her, Lula said, "I guess that's it. I'm not the director of this shindig but I'm telling the pastor were ready. In another hour they'll be married and we can eat." She went to the back porch where she gained George's attention. "I'm ready with the food if you're ready to get married. You go on about your business and we'll follow right along." Then she returned to her kitchen.

Daisy casually stepped through the back door, viewing the Perrymans as if she had never seen them. Keeping quietly out of the way, alone, leaning against the side of the milk room, her mind was observant only when she heard them bicker with themselves or disagree about a minor problem. These were the usual lot, the sounds of insignificance amid the laughter of happiness that somehow accompanied siblings, the nondescript attitudes that paved the avenues of thought, of grouping together to go to their prescribed locations on the lawn, again, the laughter and the friendliness that normally becomes a necessary enjoyment. With all the preparations, the pastor attempted to keep up with the hurried pace of people and with their trend of conversation.

Presently, Daisy passed among this crowd, nodding to each one, but she secretly was glad she was not a party to any of it. The day was bright and the mood, happy, but these did not remind her of when she and Richard Pratt

Childers were married. That was only a year ago, but even so, memory had faded and she saw nothing today by which she remembered her moment at the alter. She was aloof to these requisites, this hour. She lost herself wandering westward to the rim of the crowd, under the lofty trees and around to the south, past the line of modest buggies that waited beside elegant carriages. She looked west to see Laredo as he escorted two horses from one buckboard that had just arrived, the guests scurrying to find a good place to stand. The wedding was about to begin.

She had made certain that her son was asleep in his crib in the bedroom. Her stroll was not to be too long for she had to return, she was certain, especially if he awoke and needed changing.

The cousins who camped south of the stile block sauntered onto the lawn. Some men were helping Ralph Collins anchor the cloth on the table. A cool breeze came up from the east and ruffled the pretty decorations.

Dr. Kerr stood with the groom at the portable podium. "I'm ready." he called to his wife who then walked into the house.

Amid the pleasant sounds with the crowd waiting impatiently, with the cloudless sky on such a hot day as this, a matron passed cardboard fans to the ladies. Daisy was still at the edge of the crowd at the far west end of the house. She could essay all that happened and not permit her mind to wander to the question of her own husband. The tiny bride appeared at the front door with several attendants, all dressed in their finery with pink hats each carrying a small array of flowers, giggling but serious as if they had no care in the world.

It was not like that for Daisy. Soon, very soon, all this frivolity would be passe'. Frighteningly so, the bride would become a matron with a wrinkled face much like the woman who handed everyone the fans.

"Dearly beloved," Dr. Kerr began.

And then, from a far corner of that crowd, stepping away from it and toward Daisy was a young Indian lad, coatless, but with a big gray hat on his head, looking directly at her. She hardly noticed him at first but his stare was persistent and she looked again, recognizing immediately who it was. He removed his hat, smiled sincerely, and said hello when he was but a foot away from her.

"James!" Daisy uttered it so softly that she was completely enchanted by her own emotion. She glanced quickly in the direction where Lula stood but other people blocked her view. "Jimmy! I'm surprised!"

The ceremony continued without their attention. "Hello again, Daisy. I knew you were here."

"What on earth? I mean, well, I don't know what I mean." She stayed under the trees, out of the direct sunlight that lit all the crowd, the wedding party, and the yard. She could hardly believe the moment. "I didn't know you'd be here."

They walked to a place where they could talk above a whisper. "I talked to your father and he said you'd be here." He placed his hat on a limb. "I knew George was getting married, but I really didn't know when."

"Of course. You and Dick grew up with all of them, didn't you? Of course." She was so flustered that she did not quite complete her thoughts. "Well! Shall we...go...?"

He stopped her with a gentle hand on her arm. "Let's just stay here and talk if you don't mind."

Again Daisy tried to see where Lula stood. From where they had moved, they could not hear Dr. Kerr speak. The dogs were making such a racket at the rear of the house that his words escaped them.

James Childers looked a lot like his younger brother but with hair that was always much shorter. Richard's eyes were brown but James' were dark blue, something a bit odd for being an Indian. He was taller than Richard. He stood erect, with one hand guarding his hat from the wind, peering into Daisy's eyes while keeping a discreet distance and a lookout for the end of the ritual.

"My goodness, Jimmy," Daisy stammered, "I just am so...Surprised!" She laughed heartily.

"Where's the baby? Inside?" James was purposely slow with his questions. She only nodded. "My job came through. I have a real nice job with the railroad now at the Sapulpa depot."

"Oh, you do! Well! That's nice." Her handkerchief served as her fan. James improved it with his hat, waving it to and fro in front of her. Then she stopped. "Jimmy, I haven't seen Dick in six days. I just don't know where he is. Daddy went to the deputy, you know, this Mr. Sizemore to tell him to watch out for any report about him." That sounded so drastic to her. "I don't know what to do?" She dropped her handkerchief and James stooped to retrieve it. "What is it, Jimmy?"

He put the handkerchief in her hand and tried to choose words in an even manner so as not to draw attention to themselves. The couple was married, joined together by the kind of holy matrimony that was amenable to both cultures, Indians and whites. The full bloods gathered around Mrs. Rachel, agreeing with the entire ceremony.

James Childers was the more sturdy and astute of these two brothers. Both had no knowledge what ever happened to their other siblings. They had just vanished, especially the older ones who were more concerned with their father's demise. But it was James who helped Dick in menial tasks with a place to sleep, the clothes on his back when he was but a child. They were shy at first under the watchful care of Mrs. Rachel. It was from the House downtown that she escorted them to school.

But at the age of nine, Richard learned other lessons, that of a wanderlust spirit prompted by stories of older boys who knew of the railroad. After all, the bridge across the stream was completed. It was possible to walk across the stream on ties and tracks, even to place a penny or two on the rail and wait for the engine and cars to flatten the coins. By the influence of such antics, the lad pestered the rail foreman until he became the waterboy in Red Fork. So when he left the House, he did so surreptitiously as James discovered later.

"I never could understand how a nine-year-old kid could just get up and leave a household that loved him." That was what James told her, under the trees. "I don't know where he is, Daisy. It's been a week since I've seen him. I even asked around maybe if the railroad is planning to build toward the south but no, they don't have authority to do that. It takes some kind of authority before a railroad does that. I asked everyone I know." He waited and a smile came on his face. "I did learn that he had been a good waterboy when he worked. He cared for the men who built the line to Sapulpa."

They could see the crowd dispersing readily, some milling about, waiting for dinner, joyously congratulating the couple.

"He's gone like this before," Daisy whispered when she noticed other people looking at them. "He'll be back..." She pressed his hand over the wide brim of his hat. "I'm pregnant again, Jimmy. He's got to come back."

"I'm glad to hear that." Her friend could see tears beginning to form. The wind from the south began to shift through the multitude promising a cooler afternoon. Two men dismantled the alter. It was time to eat.

"Mr. Collins," Lula called "make sure the alter is put in the Kerr wagon. Tell Pete to help me with the food now." She remembered her own wedding. It was Reverend Broyles who had attended because he was planning on himself becoming the husband of Ida Perryman shortly thereafter.

Mrs. Rachel, with the help of Emma, honored her son and his new bride by wearing the simple ritual garments of her tribe. Without English which Emma provided, she was beaming with joy for both of them. Abner was Best Man and Oliver, just as excited by the event, stood enthralled beside the family. Abner noted the moment silently and commented that he wished their father would have lived for this moment.

The jubilation spread across the lawn. The ladies brought the big bowls of salad, sofkey, green beans, and a large ham that Lula baked just for this feast. Three children were designated to stand with large fans to ward off the flies while Oliver and Emmett Smiley were the first in the line.

James Childers hardly spoke when he waited with his plate. Daisy waited with him. He saw the concern in her features, her worried looks when she tried to smile, and the way she moved from the table with hardly any food. They sat at the edge of the south porch on the steps with their feet on the sidewalk and their plates in their laps.

Mayme and her two sisters preferred not to eat. Only she insisted on returning home. She was pregnant after all which was not an altogether original reason. Mayme did not particularly care to remain in the presence of the mistress of the ranch any longer than necessary. "Come on, Emma," she whispered again, "let's go home. I don't feel well."

Lula surmised correctly but offered no further remarks. Emma Perryman, though married three years to Clifton Drew, had lost two infants at birth or shortly thereafter. Lula recalled what Arthur, on of the twins, had explained what had happened to their own sister, Nora. As the new Mrs. Scott, she had also lost her husband to the epidemic as well. This reflection was overwhelming for Emma. While Emma was grateful for seeing the twin cousins again, she was first to climb into the buggy to leave.

The turn of this century brought two separate cold winters and with them, all across the nation, families had lost their children. For Emma to hear the natural crying of a boy child whose surname was Childers or a girl whose name was hers was difficult to accept. Even Ella could not convince her sisters to stay and eat. The task of saying goodbye to their brother and sister-in-law was given directly to Ella and she was not as good a communicator as was Emma. So with the assistance of Pete, who was relegated at the last moment and who had to put his plate of food down on a rock with a napkin over it, Emma and Mayme hurriedly made their exit with hardly any word to Lula. That action was all a part of what Lula had learned to accept long ago.

Daisy did prepare a plate for herself at the insistence of both Lula and James. "That ham does look good. I guess I'll take some."

The pastor, his wife, the matron who had collected all her fans, and everyone who was associated with the preparation of the wedding were leaving. George and his bride had fled only moments ago with the help of a new surrey and horse.

Oliver and Abner assisted too. This activity did not delay any further conversation for Daisy. The cousins' wagons moved out of the south pasture. The women, those who remained to help Lula, tidied the kitchen as a few men carried the table back to the shed near the bunkhouse. The dogs ate the leftovers.

"I'm glad you're eating something, Daisy," Lula said, patting her sister's hand. "I'd stay but I got things to do."

"I'm afraid I'm not very good at talking this afternoon." Daisy pushed her plate aside and rose to get some water. The buggies' departure and the disassembly of everyone echoed across the lawn. The merriment of the few who remained was so ironic to what she was feeling. James followed her into the kitchen. By this time many of the ladies had themselves gone and portions of the pies and food were still on the cabinet with tea towels covering them. Daisy attempted again to speak as she placed a glass by the bucket. "Let's go back outside, Jimmy, it's too hot in here."

James could not remember exactly how he met Mary Cordelia Dunbar in the first place. Then, he did not know she was called Daisy. Often, when it came time to solve Dick's problems, he remembered visiting Moses Perryman and his new wife here, at this house, some time ago. He was twenty. Dick had announced that he was marrying one of the Dunbar girls and that was about three years ago. Time stood still all too frequently. His noticing how Ralph Collins went about his own chores reminded him that he never sat down to talk to this foreman. It did not matter, actually, now. At least that is what he presumed. A thought did reoccur. It was here on this Homestead, four years ago that he came to visit and he went directly to the bunkhouse. He heard the entire story of his father from the man who shot him.

A flood of sorrow swept over Ralph Collins. "I knew who you kids were with Mrs. Rachel." The foreman sat straight in his chair that day and looked directly at him. "But you were kids and I figured some day I'd tell you, but not then. Well. That day is here."

It was as if all that were yesterday. The Homestead was still here. The bunkhouse was still here. But a whole new atmosphere prevailed between the Childers boy and this foreman. Now, James was strolling with Daisy Dunbar Childers and for a short while he was still lost in reverie.

It was not Daisy who broke his thought but Ralph Collins who stood beside him and put his hand on his shoulder and he smiled. "Hello, Jimmy, Nice to see you again. I'm glad you could make it." So now, it was all right.

"You okay, Jimmy?" Daisy asked, when the foreman left.

"You remember some time ago," James said quickly "Dick and I were here and you were here visiting Mr. and Mrs. Perryman and your father came to get you. Dick tried to make some type of good impression with your father. It's funny sometimes how things just happen." His eyes caught Ralph Collins as he was drawing water from the well. James was almost sure that this foreman looked at him, again, from such a distance and waved his gloved hand.

Daisy looked about them to the emptiness of the afternoon, now that the crowd had dispersed. Hardly a remnant of a wedding existed. The wind in the trees returned with the birds who flocked together high in the branches. The dogs no longer jumped from one playful attitude to another. Pete and Laredo were on their horses to oversee the aftermath. It was a quiet time now.

Mrs. Rachel sat in her favorite chair in Lula's parlor. It still had the odor of old

Indian leather, she said to the full blood with whom she was talking. She smiled at every inflection, reminiscing of the last century with its hardships and joy. Oliver was with them for a while, enthralled by the sounds of a language that he had never learned. The boy only knew that the old man with her was a Grayson, one of the many who populated the Okmulgee area, much like the Stidhams. The Smiley wagon was the last to depart, he had no one with whom to play so he wandered in the parlor to listen. Cross legged, he sat on a thick rug, completely captivated.

Once on the south lawn, James gathered courage. "I should have married you, Daisy. I should have said so as soon as I felt it." She scurried away from him. "I didn't though, did I? I guess I didn't know what to do. Like I don't know, now."

Carrying Edith, Lula came through the front door en route toward the stile block. She stopped abruptly when she noticed the serious concern on both their faces. Shifting the baby to the other arm, she managed a small smile to both of them. "I didn't mean to hear anything. Daisy, I'm sorry. I sort of suspected this from the start."

"Is my baby all right?" Daisy took one step nearer to her sister.

"Oh yes, he's just fine. I have Edith because Mrs. Covey wants to see her before she leaves." Lula pointed to the barn. "That's her buggy comin' from the corral now." And then she looked at James again, noting the perspiration on his brow. "I don't say much about this sort of thing, Jimmy. Be it far from me to say, Dick is your brother. Now, he may have some faults, God knows, we all have, but he's still Daisy's husband. You got a good head on your shoulders, Jimmy. I can see that." She was shocked at what she was saying to this man whose age was the same as hers. "I'm not good at giving advice on this kind of stuff, what you were talking about, just now." James shifted his eyes away from both of them. Daisy started to interrupt but Lula raised her hand. "Just a minute, Daisy," she said sincerely, "let me finish. I guess Dick has a wandering streak in him. Papa once told me he thought that. One of the Covey boys disappeared, never did come back! Sometimes," and Lula paused, "sometimes the head of the family has to remain away for a while to help make ends meet. I learned that lesson from Mr. Collins. Now, if he ever shows up here, looking for you, Daisy then maybe even I'll be asking some questions myself. Like telling him what to do, myself. How two brothers with different attitudes can birth from the same mold is not hard for me to understand. Mose had three sisters and three brothers and they're all so different even I get perturbed at times. Don't get me started on what I think of Indians. They are quiet-thinking and silent in their speech, I know that!" She noticed how the Covey buggy was approaching the block. "I guess they're acting like they do because of what happened in the last twenty years." Her eye contact was with James. "You stayed with Mama Rachel. You learned to read and yet Richard took off like he did. Oh, I heard all about it from the family. I don't know why things work out like they do. I loved my Mose and he died. But I had to go on doing the best I can. Daisy can do the same."

Time stood still for all three of them, standing near the porch on the rock sidewalk, somewhat at a loss for words. The katydids were singing in the far south pasture as clearly as if they had perched in the grass at their feet. On the west side of the house, Abner and Ralph Collins were talking but the barking of the dogs smothered their conversation.

Lula sighed deeply, a heavy weight lifted from her mind. "When you do the best you can," she breathed, looking at Edith when she said that, "then that's the best you can do."

"Lula!" called Mrs. Covey from her driver's seat.

Saying nothing more, Lula walked forward to her block. A gentle breeze passed over them and rustled the high branches of the trees. James stood silently to survey his own area of thought. He adjusted his hat on his head and moved swiftly.

Daisy was quick to follow. "Where you going, Jimmy?"

"I'm going to the barn for my horse." He walked through the noisy gate and she was there at his heels. They soon were at the well.

"I'm going back home, Jimmy. I'm going to Sapulpa first thing tomorrow morning with the baby. I've got to talk to my daddy."

Oliver appeared on the back porch. "Daisy," he called loudly, "It's your baby. He's crying."

James stepped very close to her. "I love you, Daisy," he confided. "I'd be a fool not to tell you." She was embarrassed but she listened. "I don't really care who knows it, anymore."

"Mrs. Childers, ma'am!" Oliver made another call.

"Your sister knows it. I guess that's all that matters now at least. I'm going back to work. Goodbye."

Forlornly, she watched him striding along the path. He did not look back at her. She turned and answered Oliver's call. Once inside, soothing the baby, she carried him to a window where she saw James trotting by the stile block, heading for the main road.

Abner appeared and disappeared so frequently that Lula did not realize he was the sole caretaker of his mother. But Mrs. Rachel was content to spend time with Mr. Grayson, chatting as they did with no care at all about the passage of time. The elderly man was to ride back to Tulsa with her and Abner. Oliver had long ago found other amusements while waiting. Mrs. Rachel reached for her bonnet, placed it on her head and adjusted her hair. She was ready.

With so much on her mind, Lula walked into the parlor and sat next to Mrs. Rachel. Abner soon entered, enquiring about the boy and his mother nodded to the east lawn. At this same time they heard his laughter from midway in the large oak tree.

"Hey, monkey!" Abner called through one of the side widows, "it's time to go. Get down, now!"

In full agreement, Mrs. Rachel stood slowly with the help of Lula and they walked to the front porch. Mr. Grayson went ahead of them to harness the horse and turn the buggy toward the main road. Seeing them Oliver slowly slid down the trunk and bounded over the lawn.

"Let me stay all night with you, please Lula," he begged. He already had a defense. "Abner said he was coming the next day or so back here to see you anyway. Please?"

"Come on Mama," Abner said softly taking his mother's arm and pretending not to hear. "Come on, Oliver."

The boy was persistent. "Please, Lula?" He ran to his mother. "Mama, please!"

"He'll be all right," Lula offered. "I'll put him to work! If anything he can dry dishes. He can milk the cows tonight with Mr. Collins and Laredo and Pete. I'll wash his shirt for him tomorrow morning."

Mr. Grayson was waiting at the block.

"May I, please, Mama?"

The affirmation came easily and Oliver jumped with glee, hugging his mother, his brother and Lula before he scampered off to the tree again.

They found Laredo waiting for them, too, at the wagon. "I am glad to see both of you, Abner. Please tell her that, will you?" It was Mr. Grayson who translated. "She don't know English, does she?"

"Not a word." Abner said as he helped his mother sit down.

"Like my own mother in Texas. She was Mexican. I grew up learning Spanish here and there, but daddy he was pure Texan but he couldn't read or write English. Just speak it."

By this time, with Mr. Grayson riding in the rear. Abner adjusted the blanket that they used for comfort. Lula handed him a package of cold meats which he stowed behind the seat. The rifle was there covered by another blanket to be used in case they needed it. Time was late and the night would be on them in another hour. Fording the river could be dangerous.

Lula stood by the left side, shielding her eyes from the hot sun that escaped the clouds that were gathering. "I wish you'd stay the night and leave first thing tomorrow."

"Oh, you know Mama," Abner chuckled. She wants to go home as soon as she can, don't you, Mama?"

Mrs. Rachel nodded yes. Pete rode up on his horse.

"Goodbye, Mrs. Perryman," said Mr. Grayson, tipping his black hat and nodding his head.

"I asked Pete to ride with you," Lula said, "up to the corner on the far north end. Oh. by the way, what did Mayme say to your spending the night at her house?"

"She didn't take to the idea. That's why we're going on to the White House tonight." Abner repositioned his hat on his head. "Stew isn't there, I guess he's off somewhere near Muskogee, or Porter or Tullahassee, I suppose. She's not sure."

"Well. She'll feel differently when the baby gets here. I didn't get to say goodbye to Ella and Ed, did you?"

"We talked but that was about all." Abner flipped his reins and the horse reared. "I don't think Ed likes us."

"Don't forget Oliver. I think he's taken with my new colt."

"Goodbye, Lula. I'll see you soon and I'll pick up Oliver then. Keep him out of mischief." Then he turned to Laredo who had removed his hat. "Adios, amigo." And Laredo laughed!

Lula walked with them to her gate and watched as they descended the hill, traverse the bridge, and then turn north, with Pete just ahead of them. Laredo left to prepare to milk, calling to Oliver who had climbed into his favorite oak tree. Tired but happy, she paused on her sidewalk to survey her land again as if Moses, himself, were there beside her, with his arm around her.

She watched Oliver gleefully run to catch Laredo who was, by now at the rear gate, for she heard the hinges squeak as they passed through it. A hot wind passed over her. The ladies who helped her had all gone home. The guests, the cousins, everyone had departed. This yard that had been so occupied just five hours ago was now alone as she was, empty of the laughter that prevailed, empty of the happiness that permeated everything.

Oliver was soon on a pony that Laredo saddled for him, and all three were

riding south for the cows, joined again by Pete who came galloping back to them.
Every moment he had, he would show how he enjoyed racing his horse. The sun
was right at the crest of the roof line of the barn. From where she was standing, she
could see its rays gleaming against the spikes of the lightning rods.

She heard an owl call. It was too early for such a call. Or was it a rain crow
high in the tree from which Oliver had jumped. A flock of sparrows swooped
again over the house and flew northward where her land fell toward Coal Creek.

Then, for no reason, she paused merely to glance eastward to the stream that
branched off of her creek and paused under the little bridge that echoed the clamor
of hoofbeats, wagon wheels, and buggies and carriages of that day.

Once, not too long ago, she and Moses stood near that wooden bridge, he in
his big brown boots that he enjoyed wearing, and she in her green jodhpurs that
her Papa gave her for a wedding present. Once again, did she hear an owl call?
Did she see it fly into the treetop to her right?

From the back of the house Ol' Don barked at something, for the other dogs
had run after Oliver for a distance, and then changed their minds and returned.

Some big clouds behind the barn covered the descending sun and a wind rose,
blowing through all the trees as if it were heralding a storm that was brewing.

Chapter Eleven

John Menifee was a successful businessman of sorts who arrived from the east on one of the first trains to pull into the depot. The station was new and had only a small building to represent its rail terminus. With him came his wife, three children, and a dog to make their new home in a new section of town. In her ledger, in which she posted each and every conceivable item of purchase, so expertly organized, she also made reference to the year of arrival, eighteen-eighty-seven, as one of the most significant changes in her life. A rumor she heard was that the railroad was going to build a much larger depot. That was the least of her worries.

Much to Mrs. Menifee's dismay, the little town was not so much a village as it was a group of people huddled together in a valley between two sets of hills. But whatever it was, it was home to many families, among whom were the Dunbars. Mr. Menifee, on his rounds to become acquainted, met Waller Cornelius Dunbar because the newly arrived family heard of this man's talent with the saw and hammer.

What really brought the Menifee family to this part of the world was the spirit of adventure. Whatever else that was on her husband's mind was not at all shared with Mrs. Menifee who longed to be back in the States. Nevertheless, they were here.

John Menifee's middle initial was C but even his wife did not know for what it meant. He was so well adapted at being a good husband and father, and a provider, that she did not pursue the question. Menifee was noted for organizing tours for men from the east who wanted to hunt. Game was abundant including quail, pheasant, deer, squirrels and wild turkeys.

"This town's growing," he had often reported to his wife, "and all kinds of men, and women, are arriving on the Frisco."

"That's what I'm afraid of, John," she answered, just as often. "The Indians do not cater to that class of women, and you know what I mean." She was one who gave much voice to every avenue of thought that was relative to the burg to which they had come to settle. "I've done some study besides wash your clothes and sweep dirt from the porch."

Mr. Menifee had a habit of meeting his friends in the bar of the McAllister Hotel. Located on the north side of the thoroughfare, and south of the terminus, this popular meeting place was thought to influence the name of the street. Every city east of the Mississippi had a designation of Main, but a sign just west of the hotel called it "Dewey" in a local attempt to have its byways named before Tulsa could name its own streets.

This hotel where he and Waller Dunbar met was already well known in Indian Territory. One large room just off the lobby, and at a far distance from the saloon, had been the site for Sunday School class, on those Sabbath mornings when not very many patrons, who had revelled the night before, were on the streets.

Within the confines of this alcove area was a large pump organ set against a high wall which was played rigorously on those mornings by one of the daughters of the young matron who came with her enterprising husband from Kansas City some twelve years ago. After class one Sunday morning, when the lobby was empty, Mrs. Menifee, with her daughter beside her and her Bible tucked under her arm, was heard to repeat her longing to board the train and return to civilization.

A group of hopeful men comprised the city council and always met in an alternate room just off this same lobby. Once, John C. Menifee was asked to join this illustrious clan. He declined, though, and professed a strong interest in his own business which somehow always remained illusive. His interest however in the railroad led many of this council to presume that he partook in clandestine rituals in the night. The more conventional members were assuredly aware that Tulsa, just to the northeast, was in the center of a crime-ridden territory to which fugitives from justice fled from surrounding states, very likely hoping to proceed in their activities undetected.

"Even though Tulsa is far up the road," one council member concurred, "and so far away from us, we must still be alert to any such crime that can easily penetrate our pretty town." So when he, and the other members, would encounter John Menifee on the dusty streets of Sapulpa, each would be less willing to tip his hat in a greeting to this famous hunter. "And after all, gambling and prostitution followed in the wake of railroad men but Sapulpa hopefully was to remain a clean metropolis." The council members remained auspicious.

In the bar, raising his second glass of cool beer, Mr. Menifee quaffed his good fortune with Waller Dunbar, an acquaintance of only a few months. Mr. Dunbar had completed the carpentry work on a shed this hunter designed for himself to accommodate his buggy and his rifles. Mrs. Menifee refused to have a gun of any size inside her home. It was just as well. In the last year alone, her husband gained a favorable reputation for going on twelve-hour hunting sprees, but for having an unfavorable one for business tactics.

This hunter lifted his glass and referred to the interior of the room, especially noting the bar itself. The mahogany serving area, the large gilded mirror behind the bartender, with its fancy scrolled frame, and the orderly rows of clean beer glasses had become the toast of all who entered here. A separate round table, reserved for cards, was to his right.

"No sir," he concluded, "you don't find anything like this in Ohio!" He put his back to the bar to rest his elbows. "I'm glad I'm here, Mr. Dunbar. With the advent of oil up there in Red Fork, I just bet you we have oil right here in Sapulpa. What do you think? That doctor fella did the right thing at the right time." He twirled his moustache in glee. "Oil! Yes, sir!" Then he paused and looked at his new friend. "But you were asking me about this here Childers, weren't you?"

Waller Dunbar lifted his right leg so that his foot would rest on the pipe near the floor. Mud had crusted over it so that he found little room to place his boot. His half-empty glass was before him. "Childers, yes," he repeated, "Richard Pratt Childers."

"Oh, it's Richard was it? I thought you meant James." The man moved so that he could face the saloon's entrance archway into the lobby. "James Childers sure, I know him too. They're both just kids, aren't they? I bet no more that twenty at the most. Yeah, I know who you're talking about, now. Jimmy. The railroad clerk at the station, isn't he? At least I always thought so. I thought I saw him there last week."

Waller Dunbar sipped some beer. "I was more or less interested in the where-abouts of Jimmy's brother." He concentrated on this man's eyes to tell him what he wanted to know, more so than drinking his beer. "I think you already know Richard is my son-in-law."

"Well, no, I didn't know that. I don't think I knew that. John C. Menifee lifted his glass and drained the rest of the liquid. The bartender looked his way, raised his eyebrows but when his customer shook his head, continued drying glasses. "Well, look. Here's the final payment I owe you for that shed." He reached in his coat pocket and extended a check to Waller Dunbar. "Thanks a lot. You did a nice job, I tell you." Then he raised his hat and passed a hand through his red hair. "I got to go. I think my wife is out in front or in the lobby, waiting for me." He extracted a silver pocket watch from his vest. "It's four o'clock. It's sure hot. I wish it would rain." He left, nodding to several men in the bar as he passed them. The foyer was quiet but he stopped short of exiting, just as a couple entered the hotel.

"Oh, Mr. Enyart," he called softly, removing his hat. He nodded to the lady with him. "Mrs. Enyart, ma'am. I want to take a moment to to tell you how sorry I am about Silas in that war. I know it's been some time since that Spanish business was finished, but I only heard from Bert Gray just in conversation last week that your boy was killed...I'm so sorry!"

"Thank you indeed, Mr. Menifee," came the sober reply. "It's been three years now." Mr. Menifee stepped aside, retrieved a fan the lady dropped, and allowed them to enter.

Now, just three weeks after George's wedding, Lula Dunbar Perryman arrived in this thriving town on that same hot August afternoon. "I'm going to tend to some business," she said to the young livery boy who bounced up off a chair when she brought her wagon to a halt at the entrance. "You take good care of this horse, will you? She dismounted and looked at the boy again. "Are you Amos Riddle's son?"

"Yes, ma'am, I am," he smiled, guiding the horse through the wide door. "I'm the youngest, the baby, as Mama says." He appeared no more than thirteen or fourteen with long brown hair tucked under a wide brimmed straw hat.

"Well," she laughed, grabbing her parasol."I'm sure you will grow up fine!" She opened her parasol. As she left the stable, she was obliged to raise her long skirt so that the dust of the road would not soil its hem. Few businesses along Dewey Street had constructed wooden sidewalks. With her parasol in one hand, she untied her bonnet as she approached the hotel. Two ladies, with children in tow, waved at her.

Her journey that day included a short visit at the Beaver household in their wide two-storied brown frame house on the south side of the road that led to Sapulpa from the east. It traversed many rounded hills, the result of much traffic over a lengthy period of time. Some of the ruts were deep where wagon wheels had carved muddy tracks when rain was abundant, where the sun baked them into persistent trails. Even so, a trip to Sapulpa from the ranch was a great deal easier than one to Tulsa.

Ollie Beaver, the new wife of David Checote Beaver, one of the cousins who attended the wedding, was pregnant with her first child, so Lula was assured she would be at home. This branch of the Beaver clan stemmed from Lydia Perryman, one of the eighteen children, and Mrs. Rachel's sister-in-law. Before Lydia died in eighteen-seventy-nine, she had given birth to four Beaver children, one of whom was David. It was quite complicated in many respects with one of these four marring an Atkins farmer.

Throughout the nation, this Beaver home on this desolate road between Broken Arrow to the east, and Sapulpa, was a convenient way-station much like the stops for the Pony Express that operated westbound from the White House before the railroad cancelled operation. So, after a bite to eat and a long conversation regarding Moses, Lula was again on her way.

The hotel's facade had the high porch along the front on which was painted its name in large gaudy letters. Dr. McAlister, its owner, wanted to be the first to install tall windows in the foyer. From St. Louis, he obtained the best of interior designers who fashioned the lobby in the most resplendent decor, but the continuous entrances and exits of cowboys, businessmen, soldiers, politicos, and children wore the carpet to thread-bare existence. Once, due to a fight on the wooden sidewalk directly in front of his establishment, the railing and many of the boards had to be replaced at great expense.

Dr. McAlister himself was at his new railing, speaking to one of his clerks, when he saw Lula Perryman approaching. To balance herself, she grasped the end near the steps leading to the ground. She stomped her shoes against the new boards, watching the dust fly, and she removed her bonnet and closed her parasol.

"Good afternoon, Mrs. Perryman," came the greeting from Dr. McAlister. "Permit me to open the door for you." And then he turned to the man beside him. "Thank you, Mr. Stevens for the report." The clerk preceded Lula and went to his desk.

Lula smiled broadly. "I hope it's cool inside, Dr. McAlister."

They waited an additional moment while a trio of cowboys passed them and entered. The owner's attention immediately went to their boots which carried with them a pint of grime.

Lula discerned his agony. "You will notice that I stomped my shoes just now," was her reply. She laughed jovially.

"Well, I can say," he answered, "that the overhanging of the porch keeps the sun away from these front windows, just as the architect told me." They stopped in the middle of the lobby. "I believe your father is in the bar." Electricity had changed the interior of several public buildings. Lula noted that this was the case of the hotel. Every time she ventured into a shaded building, with porches of this kind, she hoped secretly that soon she would install the same mechanical apparatus that would bring this new wonder into her own home. Two large four-bladed fans hung from the high ceiling, churning the air, a respite from the hot breezes of summer. From her bag dangling from her arm, she extracted a small handkerchief to wipe the perspiration from her wet face.

"Now, if you'll excuse me, Mrs. Perryman," and with that he disappeared through a door.

Several men glanced her way as she looked about the room. She stopped near the desk, pausing to catch her breath and to make a mental note again of the whirling fans above her. The desk clerk smiled. A large sepia portrait of President Lincoln graced the wall to her right, and a woman was seated alone in a tan leather chair in the center of the room. From where she stood, Lula could visualize her tall father leaning against the bar in the area a great distance to her left. She started in that direction.

"I'm sorry, ma'am," interrupted the clerk who had just finished sharpening his pencil, "but no women are allowed in…"

"I know," Lula said, halting just to the side of the entrance. She listened to a conversation her father was having with an Indian. She thought how she could get his attention from the distance of thirty feet.

Taking another swallow, Waller Dunbar wiped his walrus moustache with his right hand, smoothed the ends in proper place but was not yet in position to see his oldest daughter waiting. At the Indian's invitation, they moved to a table nearer the curtained archway and sat down but her father still had not realized she was there.

Before Lula attempted to ask assistance from the two men who exited the saloon, the Indian finished his remark which she had heard clearly. "And so by the time they got back from Kansas, they just didn't have a thing left. They were Rebs, once, but then so many of them fled north when the situation got worse. That's when they went to Kansas. Are you from Kansas?" He stopped to take another swig from his glass. "And then after the way they all came back here, those that were left…" Lula was attracted by this subject so she waited a while longer to listen. It seemed this old Indian knew his story. "One family I know got mad when they couldn't prove…" and he searched for words best to describe his plight, "when they just couldn't make us accept the land business, you know, the Dawes business. Your cattle graze over there and ours can eat over here and that ridge yonder is the border. That's the way it all began. It's all different, now."

This man who spoke so eloquently appeared to be her father's age but his hair was not white. She noticed that when he removed his hat to wipe his face. But he was an intelligent Yuchi, she decided, or he could be a Shawnee. But he was not an Apache. When two other Indians passed them, heading for the bar, this old man spoke in Creek to them. Then, after a greeting from them, he resumed his remarks to her father. "Now this man in Muskogee comes along and make everyone of us say they give us land. How can Great White Father up in Washington give us land that we got already?" With his glass poised in mid-air, he said softly, "Dunbar, I think lady over there wants you."

Curiously, Waller Dunbar rose and walked to the doorway. "Hello, Lu. Wait a minute, will you?" He turned to speak again to the Indian. "Nice talking to you, Wildcat. I got to go. My daughter's here." He nodded to him and escorted Lula to a quiet corner of the lobby where they located two chairs facing each other. He waited until she was seated with her bonnet in her lap and the parasol to her right on the floor. He sat opposite her, his hat in his hand.

Lula was comfortable in a wide easy chair, with its ample arms, its thick cushion, and its high back. She fanned herself with an old newspaper that had lain on the floor.

"You want a drink of water?" he asked.

The paper collapsed, so she fanned herself with her bonnet. "I'll get one in a little while, Papa." Her attention was attracted to the Indian with whom he talked. He went from the saloon to the front door and departed. "It sure is hot! I stopped at Ollie's place today on my way over here. They're getting along fine."

"Was David home?"

"I don't think so, at least, not when I was there. She's pregnant again, due in another six or seven months. They got a nice well, now. Finally got water. And the barn is finished, thanks to you. Ollie sure does thank you. She told me to tell you hello and thanks."

"After we rest here," he suggested, "we can go to the rail station to see Jimmy if you want. He's working all day today. Daisy's at my house and she's expecting us for supper. The baby is fine." Placing his hat on a nearby table, he slid forward in his chair to speak more confidently. He waited until the heavy wall clock chimed the half hour before he measured his words to her. She was so startled by his look of confidence that she lowered her bonnet. "Are you having any problems with your in-laws?" He peered straight at her his elbows on his knees, his hands folded under his chin.

She did not answer him but only blinked her eyes while she thought of an answer. "Well, Papa. Daisy told me that Mayme was complaining about a lot of things at George's wedding."

Her father, somewhat satisfied, leaned back in his chair and crossed his legs. His demeanor was relaxed. "Mayme always complains. That's not new. Even I noticed that."

"Well, Papa, I guess that's true, all right. She has complained for as long as I've known her. She and Emma. I wouldn't be a bit surprised if both find fault with George's new wife. I don't think they like her at all. Poor Emma. She lost those two little ones." Lula sighed deeply and rearranged her skirt. "So far, Mayme has been okay, I guess. I'm certainly not one to object, but, Papa, I can't help but notice that she is .... well....so unlike her own mama."

To break this spell, Waller touched her shoulders with a big smile. "How are the grandkids?" He allowed a degree of pride to reflect the question.

"Believe it or not," she chuckled, "Mr. Collins is learning to be a good caretaker. I went to Tulsa one time, and he insisted on taking care of the girls, including Edith. I guess by now he's learned his lessons all right. I reminded him to keep them away from the new colt. Mrs. Covey was over yesterday, you remember, Merle's mother, and when she heard I was coming over to Sapulpa, she wanted me to say hello to her son Arnold. He's working at the railroad yard, doing something I don't know. I said I would. Anyway, she said she'd look in on the girls, too, mainly to see if Mr. Collins knows what he is doing!" Lula shifted her weight in her chair and crossed her legs. "I got to get back tomorrow, you know." And then in retrospect, she muttered, "Mrs. Covey had four sons and three daughters."

Waller leaned back in his chair and placed his hat on his lap. "Are you and your lawyer...what's his name?"

"Parker."

"Yes, Parker. Are you and he finished with your work now?" He waited, then added "Daisy seems to think Mayme is cooking up something."

Lula then realized what he was meaning. "You think Mayme is trying to take the girls away from me?" It was more of a statement than a question. She knew that Daisy's husband was on her father's mind as well, but that situation was far less complicated. Richard Childers, they were presuming, was away somewhere, looking for work. He was in Red Fork asking for a job with the railroad again. His waterboy experiences probably were leading to a greater fortune. "Papa," Lula added, "can she do that? Can Mayme take the kids?"

"Well, Lu," he mused, scratching his chin, "the girls are yours, but they are Indian too. Mayme may have a thing or two up her sleeve so you better keep your eyes open." And it was this, evidently, that Daisy heard during the wedding talking to Emma, or to Mayme, in the course of merely being polite, or indirectly, by just accidently hearing the sisters talk. Daisy was so near to them at one point that they did not realize they had an audience. The whole question of who the girls were and which culture was to be predominant in their little lives from this hour was to become the predominant factor in a game of wits and a battle of the minds.

Stewart Shirk came home a month ago with a tall tale that many of the Creeks were rebelling against the current trends to Anglicize even the full bloods, with a proposal of new laws that were to affect the social changes and totally destroy old traditions with which the generations even the present ones, had been born. Mixed bloods were becoming all too common, now.

"I guess we're just lucky," Waller confided again, relaxing in his chair. "Coming into this territory, I mean. Lots of us, coming here. I remember talking to your mama about going to Texas. You were too young. You don't remember what we went through. We didn't know exactly what was ahead of us." Lula listened quietly to her father speak of yesterday. The world she did remember was right here in this little town, eating homemade soup and playing with her brothers and sisters. She later realized that she was being courted by a full blood Indian who wanted her for his wife. Lula had no idea of such a relationship and what it inferred where, little by little, the Tribe was intermarrying with whites. She had no references by which to plan, or judge, or decide, other than her heart. She had not even realized that many of the Creeks had intermarried with their Negroes, even before they became Freedmen.

"I had no idea, I suppose, about Dick Childers when Daisy married him. Other than, I mean, that he came from a big family with all brothers." That statement brought her back to reality. "I have discovered a lot of Indians whose last name is Childers, many of them in and around Broken Arrow."

Lula surmised a point of conjecture. "You think Richard is dead, Papa?"

This brought her father to another comfortable position in his chair. "I don't think so, no, but that's what I'm going to ask Jimmy." Waller was by no means any kind of detective but he had been surveying the townspeople whom he knew. This village was such that, being of minimal size, in the years that he had lived here, he had become fairly well acquainted with the majority of landowners. Through his carpentry, his name was just as well known. The population which at one time was thought to outgrow Tulsa became acquainted with everyone including who owned which horse and who had the nicest reputation, who attended Sunday School at the hotel, and who became more aware, than others, when the town's Saturday night melees frightened the populace.

John C. Menifee consistently warned the sober council that something must be done to rid their city of the multitude of drunken cowboys who rode their rambunctious steeds over the dusty streets late at night and fired their pistols at lighted windows. "I'm glad we don't live in Tulsa. People up there are more disturbed than here in Sapulpa. We're going to be a bigger city than Tulsa, anyway." Mr. Menifee said that often.

"I even consulted with a U.S. Marshall, Lula," continued her father. "About Richard. He don't have time to go around asking questions."

"Go get me a glass of water, Papa, please."

Interrupting his trend of thought, he nodded silently, rose, and stepped to the bar. Lula decided to walk around the room. She straightened her dress, gazed about the lobby to see that they were alone with only a big clock ticking away the hours from the far wall. From Dewey Street, she heard some dogs barking as a wagon passed the front door full of men with a bundle of barbed wire. From one of the windows she saw three men standing on the wooden sidewalk across from the hotel, talking to themselves.

She fanned herself with her bonnet again when Waller returned with water. She drank, then placed the empty glass on a crocheted doily of the nearest table. Once he was seated in his chair again, she surmised the situation. "Dick is probably on a train going somewhere." She did not especially wish to sound cynical. "I just don't think he is treating Daisy right. No, I don't." She reached for her parasol and he for his hat. "Let's go, Papa. Let's go see Jimmy and see what he says." She placed the bonnet, smoothing her hair in the front. "I'm ready if you are."

If Sapulpa had one distinguished feature, apart from its notable Saturday nights, then that was the imposing railroad yard. The entire facility consisted of the large brown building which served as the passenger waiting room at one end of a wide, long room with a high ceiling and the freight office with its own cage for business. Cattlemen had long ago learned to transact through this terminus. Since eighteen-eighty-nine, this whole area was improved greatly. Businessmen would not have to drive their herds to Red fork, according to such a plan. The stockyards deterred this idea, however.

But the ground plan of this area was splendid. The tracks came in from the northeast, proceeding westward beyond the station to a point determined, by the railroad, for only the distance that the big engine and all the cars needed. Once there, the switchman changed gears and gave a signal so that the train could then reverse itself on a track that curved south below the depot, the caboose leading the way. That section of track extended as far southward as was necessary so that the train would then point itself in its northward direction toward Tulsa and St. Louis, chug forward to the east side of the platform and wait for traffic.

This entire yard was engineered by a fortuitous old rail architect and constructed by a hundred and forty men over a period of two years. In that length of time that was all the people knew about Sapulpa, that it was an immense rail facility that was, hopefully, destined for greatness. And along with such eminence came the odious stockyards, cow dung, and ignored petitions against such stench.

Lula and her father came out of the hotel in time to see several buckboards flash by them, the horses sweaty and hot, as if they had come from a far distance. The dust that they aroused made Lula cough, stop, and wait for the entourage to pass. Waller escorted his daughter slowly on the wooded walkway, down two steps to ground level, and to the corner where they turned to meet the track on the south side. This track abruptly ended with a large sign posted to keep everyone, including animals, away from the blunt ends. This announcement also prophesied that this track would be constructed for future service all the way to Muskogee. "A good plan," said Lula.

In a conversation of some months ago when Richard Childers was courting his daughter, Waller Dunbar remembered what this young rascal said about heritage and his family. Lula had not particularly heard of it to recall it, but as they stepped cautiously around the sign, the rails, and the wooden platform which provided the wide exterior deck, her father continued his remarks which began the moment they left the hotel.

"A waterboy when these tracks were laid in 'eighty-seven. Must have been ten at the most. I can't imagine him leaving Jimmy and Mrs. Rachel's house. Not very many miles from Red Fork but it must have taken them a very long time to lay. He told me he was going to love Daisy and build a nice family. He told me that. I remember." Waller Dunbar extracted his gold watch from a pocket of his trousers and checked the time. As he replaced it he looked upward into the hot sky, shading his eyes with his right hand beyond the rim of his black hat. "I got the train schedule from Jimmy just yesterday. One coming in from St. Louis in about an hour, I think he said."

They were on the platform where several men pushed large wagons to certain positions to await this arrival. For a moment, they watched these workers scurrying about the deck.

"Jimmy told me a wild story but I reckon that it's true." He subtly pointed to three elderly men sitting on one of the railroad benches to his left. "I bet I can get a confirmation from any one of these old cronies who while away the time at the depot arguing among themselves."

Lula sat on an unpainted bench against the wall not far from these men. "What was that, Papa?"

"He told me about when he was on duty just a few weeks ago when an unknown man, well equipped with a gun, because Jimmy saw it, well, this man inquired for a certain package and after identification was necessary to prove he was the correct man to accept the package, Jimmy let him have it. This man signed his name, Billy Mac Jones."

Lula was tying her shoe lace when he told this anecdote. She looked up with a wry chuckle, "I bet you know what was in that package!"

"Well, how did you know all that, missy?" Waller was a bit peeved that the story was not new to her.

"Oh, Papa, Mose told me long ago liquor did quite a business through here. I don't know who this Billy Mac Jones was but I bet that's his real name, all right." She rose at once and pointed with her parasol through the window. "Look, there's Jimmy now."

James Childers was inside the station at a place where he audited shipments of all sorts of material. He carried a long clipboard on which he penciled figures and weights. The tall windows around this part of the freight room were open and a breeze passed over the boxes and crates.

"I wonder if Billy Mac Jones is around someplace." Lula laughed. "You want to go in and ask Jimmy?"

"Hey, Jimmy!" Waller called to him through one of these windows. "Look who's here!"

James placed his clipboard on a nearby box and waved. After a quick remark to a dock worker, he walked into the waiting room amidst several cartons that he stacked, ready to be placed aboard the train. "Hello, Mr. Dunbar," he greeted and then he saw Lula follow her father. "Nice to see you again, Mrs. Perryman." His face was wet and he raised his hands to smooth his hair in place. "We'll be finished here in just a minute. This is my job in the freight office when the train arrives and departs."

A horde of people mingled on the platform including several small boys who played tag while they waited and a group of curious Indians who stood away from the crowd, surveying, but austere. Two couples were already in line with their baggage at their feet. The clerk behind his ticket window excused himself to gather some change. He raised his visor to see the time from the ancient wall clock on the wall above their safe. Lula found a convenient seat on one of the oak pews as a young boy dusted the remaining seats. She smiled at him.

Removing his work apron, James breathed heavily as he managed to lift one more box with the others. "Here comes Arnold Covey. He comes on duty and works all night before the train leaves for St. Louis tomorrow morning."

Hearing this from where she sat, Lula stood quickly to get the Covey boy's attention. "Arnold," she called, "your mother says hello."

The young man stopped abruptly and slowly walked to where Lula remained beside the pew. "Yessum?"

"I'm Lula Perryman and your ma came by yesterday to see me at my place." She saw a square face, scrubbed clean with his hair neatly combed when he removed his hat. "You and your family came by to see me one day after my husband's funeral."

"Oh, yes ma'am," he smiled, "I remember you, ma'am."

"You must be seventeen now since you had a birthday. Mine is in July, too."

"I'm just fine ma'am, Mrs. Perryman. I have a good job here at the station. I have to work tonight when the train comes in. How's Mama?"

"She's just fine, Arnold. We sat and talked for a while."

The traffic around them increased. Outside, dogs began to surround the depot as if they knew of the impending arrival.

"I have to go now, ma'am. Thank you!" And he disappeared in the crowd.

Another small group of spectators was coming in from Dewey Street to admire the impressive engine that pulled the cars. This was the weekly ritual of the City of Sapulpa every time the train finished its long run from Missouri. The populace, the workers, the animals, everyone stopped what he was doing to celebrate the event.

None had to wait long. Slowly coming in from the northeast, having made a scheduled stop at Tulsa and another one at Red Fork, this Frisco means of transportation, this elegant and handsome piece of engineering, while dirty from its passage, drifted into view, clanging its heavy couplings. The crowd cheered as if this one arrival, among many, was a unique moment in history.

The engine passed them as Lula, Waller, and James made their way to the other platform to see the whole line of cars come thundering to a halt. Two freight cars were directly behind the coal car. Only two passenger cars and a caboose remained.

Waller Dunbar noticed one of the council members was near the edge of the crowd. At his greeting, this member replied, "And another occasion that brings pride to our fair city, Mr. Dunbar" and he shouted above the din, "The rail company reaps great harvests from having extended the rails south from Red Fork. Can you hear me above all this noise, Mr. Dunbar?"

Once the train ground to a halt with the engine far to the west, and the freight car directly in front of him, Arnold Covey, with the laborers, began their ritual of unloading. The engineer climbed down from his perch, stretched his limbs, and instantly found a host of men with whom to tell of his work, his concentration, his talents to bring this machinery to yet another station.

James was not among those who were unloading. "All I have to do is check out." He carried his work apron as he made his way to the ticket window. "I'll be right with you," he yelled before he disappeared behind a door.

From the far end of the train, the tired passengers began to step to the ground. A man, nattily attired, peered as well as he could into the soot-covered windows and searched among the arrivals. Lula thought she recognized him as one of the men across the street from the hotel. Finally, with a big grin, he extended his hand to a buxom lady wearing a large red hat and red gloves who curtsied as she reached the platform.

"Don't tell anyone on the city council, Papa, and I won't either!" Lula chuckled when she saw them walk from the station, together, and into a waiting buggy.

Still laughing, Lula and her father sauntered to the south door to escape the hustle of the people. She placed her bonnet on her head, tied it in place and opened her parasol, for the late afternoon sun was still hot. James returned shortly, ready to go, with his hat in his hand.

All three were stepping onto the exterior deck when they stopped suddenly. There in front of them, with his satchel in his hand and his hat pushed back on his head, was Richard Childers.

Chapter Twelve

The surge of activity and the noise of the crowd around the engine and mail cart erupted into a cautious harangue when a loading cart leaned too far to the right and turned over, its contents spilling on the platform. Arnold Covey was furious. The engineer and his party of admirers stepped aside suddenly while the boy and the mail clerk righted the heavy steel wagon. Parcels, boxes, and the fat mail pouch had spread everywhere.

James Childers left immediately to help, leaving Richard alone with Lula and his father-in-law. Nervous and a bit shy which, apparently, was most unusual for him, Richard placed his bag on the ground, removed his hat, and with a big colored handkerchief he wiped his face. Quickly he turned from the man before him to Lula and then back again. "Mr. Dunbar," he grinned, "I'm home again. I've got a job, I think!"

The anxious Dunbar, his eyes never leaving this young man was silent only for a moment. While Lula stood, fanning herself with her open palm, her father escorted Richard from the confusion and held him bodily against the exterior wall. "I want to know just exactly what is on your mind, Mr. Childers."

With his back against a window so severely that the brim of his hat pushed upward , Dick was frightened for the first time. His eyes were directly opposite Dunbar whose words came ever softly. "I don't believe you've been home in a long time, or have you?" With a quick glance to Lula to excuse themselves, Waller pushed Dick farther away from her to position himself at a far corner of the deck. Waller Dunbar had raised ten of his children, Lula, being the first. She knew he was fair in his discipline tactics. Forceful, yet kind, he knew how to handle this particular homecoming.

Lula remained where she was but stepped into a shady area. Her father spoke so softly that she could only guess what he was saying for too much noise interfered. She saw the perplexed expression on Dick's face. In one short instance, she accepted innocence and not any degree of malfeasance. Dunbar always guided his family with the same approach to discipline for his daughters as his sons. It was just as well that she did not hear any dialogue for that conversation was only between those two and was not to spill over into anything that might be monitored later.

With unloading back to normal, and with Arnold Covey once again in control of the other boys who helped him, James returned to Lula, picked up Dick's satchel where he had dropped it, and silently waited for the reprimand to cease. "I've been to Muskogee," was all that Lula and James could discipher.

"Well, it certainly is not my business, I guess," Lula was saying as she opened her parasol. "But I can imagine that Papa is mighty mad right about now. Still, I don't think there's been a time, no siree, when I've seen his temper 'roused, maybe, except once when a whole bunch of studs was wrong and he made a man tear them all out and start over. I've seen him in more dire situations than this than when a wandering son-in-law comes back home." James started to interfere but Lula put a halting hand on his arm. "Not just now, Jimmy, please. Let's just stay right here and wait till Papa says it's okay."

By this time, the people had dispersed, many of them noticing the incident only in passing. Once again, the station became an empty shell with only the remnants of rail personnel. The duo in question moved toward Dewey Street after Waller gave a nod to Lula to follow them. Dick was able to look quickly just once at his brother. Even then, with eagerness to be at Waller's side, Dick appeared more relaxed, as if he were in command of his own situation. Waller had released his grip from Dick's forearm. All appeared pleasant.

"What do you think they're saying to each other?" James asked. This whole incident was perplexing to him.

"I imagine we'll find out later," was her reply. "Papa is fair." While they carefully kept their eyes upon the men ahead of them, the ensuing traffic from the station and that of the busy street separated them. The early evening was upon them. While James longed to intercede, Lula, most obligingly, calmed his fears. "It's all right. I know where they're going." They passed the hotel. "I suspect you want to see Daisy don't you?" She looked at him and could see that his eyes agreed with her. "That's what I thought."

"He's my little brother, Mrs. Perryman," came the ardent answer. "I want to talk to him too!"

The new electric lights from the hotel lobby were quite an attraction to all the passers-by. While James saw them, time and again, en route to work, or walking home, each new moment of their glitter was a surprise to him. As light and shadow played against them they proceeded in silence, a natural gesture for this man who felt uncomfortable all too often when forced to make decisions for another sibling. Lula closed her parasol because the sun, now low on the horizon, was covered by trees and the gentle hill at the end of the street.

"Amos Riddle owns the livery where I parked Old Bill," Lula remarked lightly. "Papa once told me they had a tough time when they came to Indian Territory. Papa started to build the structure you see there, for another person name of Naifeh, I think it was." Lula glanced to see if James was listening to her. But his eyes were searching the pedestrians well ahead of them. She nudged him with the point of her parasol. "Hey, you're not listening! But ol' Naifeh was shot to deathright here on Dewey Street. I'm not saying Amos Riddle did it, but he didn't last long either. Anyway," and by this time, they had arrived at the front door again. "Mrs. Riddle came to own this establishment in time. They say she's a rich widow now."

Once there, they waited while her son collected money from two gentlemen whose horses were delivered to them by a young Indian. They thanked master Riddle, mounted, tipped their hats to Lula, rode into the street, and disappeared.

"You back again, ma'am?" master Riddle asked politely. He was brushing a horse and stopped when he saw them.

"What's you name, son? Lula inquired, nodding yes.

"I'm junior, ma'am. Amos junior. Daddy's dead now."

Giving full explanation of the change in her plans, Lula waited while Amos, with James, brought the buggy forward and harnessed the horse. The clean stable had the strong odor of good hay. A lantern, unlit, was on a table near the front.

Amos had learned to maintain an orderly ledger that rested beside another lamp. When ready and with their buggy pointed eastward, Lula climbed aboard with James' help.

"Here's your money," Lula said, and with a tip of his hat the boy handed the reins to her. She tied her bonnet in place and placed her parasol and bag behind her. "Get in, Jimmy. I can drive."

They moved eastward and by now the traffic had become less constricted. "I was planning on eating supper with Daisy and Papa before all this happened," was her guarded remark, for her attention was on Old Bill. Often his equine personality was overbearing. "Right now, you and I will just sit outside and wait. I bet you anything Papa and Dick will spend a long time together and Daisy will just be sitting there listening and wanting to say something, if I know my sister!" Once out of the mainstream of traffic and after they turned southward, lamplight from the fewer houses was not as noticeable as on busier streets. But these side streets were just as dusty, ungraded, even mucky when rain fell during the springs as were the thoroughfares. Lula kept her eyes on her father as they walked on ahead of them at a distance by which she discerned only the figures against the darkening background. She pulled Old Bill to a slow walk, his little bell dangling and sounding as his head nodded with his own gait.

The buildings along this way were not on stilt-like foundations like the hotel and other businesses. Lula reined to a halt under a large sycamore tree with a wooden swing hanging from a high limb. Dusk had settled its cover over the landscape and the sky became a somber grey, from the black east to the red west where the sun was disappearing.

They waited in front of a blacksmith shop into which Dick and her father vanished. This building's silhouette was stark against a plain level field with nothing around it except a shed and an outhouse at the south. Lula remembered that her father spoke of this once, that this two-storied frame business had two small rooms above it which were the modest home of his daughter and son-in-law. A narrow stairway, leading from the back area to the upstairs door was badly constructed. Down its flimsy steps from his argument with his daughter came Waller Dunbar, hat in hand, cursing as he slipped on a broken board at ground level.

"It's not the way to build stairs," he exclaimed as he advanced toward Lula. "I'm glad you didn't come up, not now at least." He stood by Old Bill. Breathing hard, he replaced his hat on his white head. "I don't know what to make of it." He looked at the window above him. "I just don't!"

When Lula saw her father, she was cautious to speak. She knew for a long time how methodical he was about the upbringing of his children and too, of the meticulous talent he possessed in his carpentry. As the oldest of her other nine siblings, she was constantly aware of what their father would do or say when confronted by all the daily activities of taking care of everyone and growing to maturity. Waller Dunbar was specific about household rituals and especially important about Christian ethics. Each child had a duty to perform no matter what the occasion. That was all a part of growing up.

And in the case of construction, each nail, each piece of board, every length of lumber of any kind was destined for a certain end and all this made for a stronger house, a better shed, or a more attractive architectural bearing. So Lula remained quiet to allow her father to voice his concern. Even the passing of pedestrians and their greeting did not deter his mind nor confuse his rules for what his mind planned.

Waller Dunbar, without looking up at the weak lamp light shining through a window, boarded the buggy and accepted the reins from his daughter. In a determined gesture he motioned to turn the buggy back toward town. James hopped down to lead Old Bill around a protruding anvil amid pieces of metal. When James sat again, the aggravated man provided a story of which only Lula was unaware.

Richard Childers had been a product of the railroad. His young age was a challenge for him and for a foreman who decided to hire him. Surrounded by an array of misfits because they had no other predilections, this ten-year-old appeared older than he actually was. With the supposition that these tracks would be constructed south beyond Sapulpa or westward to Guthrie, the work began. The boy was fairly well known to be a responsible worker. His attribute was his water containers, so said the laborers. It was this pleasant task that kept him busy, but it also made him subject to every conceivable scalawag and vile influence. Hearing this from Waller Dunbar was new to James. At the time when the brothers encountered each other, after Richard's sojourn of six years, his sibling told of being waterboy until the foreman gave him more responsible work of unloading track and of laying it, of learning to wield the hammer that drove spikes into the ties.

James came to the conclusion without this recitation from a man whom he learned to admire, that his brother was more reckless than the most notorious conman, and there were many. As a waterboy, Richard had learned to take care of himself if not how to cheat at cards and confront all kinds of riffraff. The boy learned early. It was all part of the job. Richard's first conversation with his brother underscored the rule.

One day, not too long ago, when the new station was completed and the new track was found to be secure around it by which the strongest engines and train cars could make the reverse move, a picnic was in progress at the celebration of a new two-storied house of a council member. Daisy Dunbar sat on a pine stool covered with a pink cushion, eating a piece of white cake.

"Go on, Jimmy," Dick laughed, "you know her. Introduce your little brother to her, come on, please."

Waller Dunbar guided the buggy to Dewey Street. "They were just kids, she was about fourteen or fifteen and Dick wasn't much older." He had calmed his temper by now while he soothed his right ankle that was scratched by the loose board at the stairwell. He looked at James. "You aren't much older."

"I remember I was the oldest. Benjamin was the youngest." James cleared his throat as they passed the railroad station. The whole train by now had positioned itself with the engine pointed north ready for tomorrow's departure. "I was born in 'seventy-five, Dick, in 'seventy-seven. I don't know whatever happened to the others, not even Benjamin. I was about ten I guess when our daddy was...." and then he paused to look at Lula,"...when our daddy was killed. Mama was gone. I don't know where. That lady that daddy shot and killed was...well, I don't think we knew who she was."

Mrs. Rachel had come to be known as "Aunt Rachel" to the boys as well. The fact that she had given them a fresh outlook, clean clothes, and school books was a part of the very dim past. The remark by Miss Huntsman, their teacher, echoed from time to time. "They look to be bright children, Mrs. Perryman." She spoke through the translation of Mr. Grayson. "At the church school, here, we'll take good care of them."

"I don't know what went wrong, Mr. Dunbar," James commented sadly, "please, sir, would you stop a minute?"

Waller Dunbar reined in and Old Bill made his turn to the right as was his usual habit when obeying such a signal. "You want something?" Even Lula was surprised.

"If you don't mind, sir, I would like to go back and talk to my brother." He dropped to the ground and tipped his hat. "Thank you, Mr. Dunbar, Mrs. Perryman, for what you are trying to do. But I got to go back and see for myself."

Lula understood immediately and smiled at him. "You do the best you can, Jimmy. Remember what I said."

Waller Dunbar interjected another quick thought. It came loudly over the clatter of horses as a buckboard passed them. "What about the rifle you wanted me to help you with?" Old Bill balked at his tight reins. "Don't you want a new rifle?"

James professed a healthy interest in hunting a week ago when he met Waller Dunbar and J.C. Menifee in front of May's Feed Store just west of the train depot. The season for quail was forthcoming. Mr. Menifee knew all there was to know about licenses and seasons and rifles. "You get a nice rifle, Jimmy," Mr. Menifee had said, "and I'll let you join us come November fifteenth."

That invitation was indelible in James' mind. "Yes, sir," he confirmed the idea to Waller Dunbar, standing on the dark street. "I do want one and I will buy one just after payday, Mr. Dunbar. I already checked that out. I appreciate your offer to help, yes, I do. I'll make it, all right!"

Lula touched the satchel, "You take this back to him, will you? We forgot to leave it." She handed it to James.

"Thank you, Mr. Dunbar," and with that he tipped his hat to Lula. With a hesitant note of farewell he made his way across the wide street toward the road from which he came. The bell on the harness rang again as if Old Bill were eager to be on his way.

A myriad of thoughts raced through his mind. Almost naive yet more precocious than Richard ever was, this lad attempted to piece together the puzzle that mounted, almost daily, at his work, in the town, the chores of communication with the new breed of Indian, of men and women who came into the nation weekly. He walked swiftly southward, past two men who were talking about the Clinton Oil Discovery. Bits and pieces of their conversation were already familiar to him. The rail industry was thriving. In the back of his mind he presumed a new future for himself, away from Sapulpa, further entangling himself with the new social order between the Creeks and the white man. He even had discovered a new variety of humanity that his young mind could not yet comprehend.

He had not altogether been honest with Daisy when she came to the station. He had, indeed, followed the whereabouts of this carefree brother. He had asked questions from everyone.

Once, whenever it was, he did not remember, he did speak to Richard. "I'm having a problem, too, trying to understand things. We got this whole new white man way of doing things. I have this feeling you can't accept the white man. I mean, you had a good job with the railroad. Go back to it. You can get back onto the railroad company." Such dialog raced in his mind as he neared the blacksmith shop.

But Richard Childers disappeared again in one of his many moments when he sought adventure. He could not meet the new standards of this aberrant society that managed to overwhelm Indians with its styles and cultures.

Too, the Cherokees had balked at such weird and sensational encounters. Even the Creeks found reason to object. Chitto Harjo, with his antagonistic group of snakes, manifested an outrageous commotion that stories of their escapades found their way into every saloon and home in the nation. Once, when James was worried, he thought he heard from a conductor that his brother had joined that group of dissidents. Such was not so.

By this time, James reached the shop and turned down the little path that led to the rear. A lantern, with its weak lamplight, threw rays onto the back steps and covered Richard as he sat there. The katydids were singing their mournful tune. James stopped, put the satchel on the ground and peered into the tired face opposite him. Then he heard the sound of Daisy at the top of the stairs with the baby in her arms. She recognized the brother.

"Come on up before you go," she called, "I've got a pie." She went into the room, leaving the back door ajar.

Richard mumbled a few words in Creek.

"Little brother," James interrupted, "speak English."

"How come you didn't want to learn the language?" Richard moved the lantern so James could sit by him.

"I remember Aunt Rachel teaching you but I just never did take the time, I guess." He removed his hat.

Richard placed the lantern on the ground. Its light became brighter when he increased the height of its wick. "You remember my terrapins?"

James looked at the small rocky area just beyond the steps. One lone turtle rested quietly in the rays of the lantern. It blinked its eyes. " ' Course I do." He looked at the small animal, so still. " 'Course I do. I helped you find it, remember, when was it, about two years ago? You've had it this long?"

Richard sat so that his chin was resting on his knees and his hands were clasped around his boots. The cool August wind came in from the south easily, across the back area, with no buildings at all to stop it. A breeze rustled the screen door. Upstairs, Daisy turned on another lamp and the men heard the baby's tiny cries for attention.

"I've been to Muskogee, Jimmy. Mr. Dunbar didn't believe me, not on bit." He looked directly at his brother. "I took the baby's paper with me to prove I got a son. Since I knew I had to enroll him I went about doing that. I stood in line. That Dawes man wanted to know my roll number. I knew it! We sat there and he was writing everything down, and when I explained who our father was, another man, a Mr. Brickinridge, wanted to know more about him." Richard looked fearful. "Jimmy, I can't remember everything that I knew what happened to him. I knew that the foreman went and killed father. I know that, anyway." He extracted a piece of paper from his shirt. "I got the baby's roll number right here! I just haven't given it to Daisy, yet."

While his brother spoke, James lifted the turtle and placed it on Richard's lap when the little animal's head and feet appeared. He wanted to mention Daisy some way but changed his mind. "Did you see about that job idea in Red Fork? There's some kind of clerk's position open now that Mr. Ishmael died."

Richard extended a piece of lettuce to his turtle but put it on the ground when the pet did not respond. "Not quite yet Jimmy. I think I found something in Muskogee to my liking."

Before James could comment, they were startled by the appearance of a large white man carrying him own lamp. He had come down the path silently from the front of the shop. He wore no shirt, his hands were dirty, and his chin was thickly bearded. "You all right, Dick?" he asked, lifting his light so that its rays fell on the two men. "You home again?"

They both rose quickly. "Yes," he said, after seeing who it was. "This is my brother, Jimmy and we're having a little talk."

"Okay," and with that the man disappeared as quickly as he arrived. In silence they heard his footsteps dwindle away in the darkness.

"Who was that?" James peered after him.

Richard tried to reach his turtle. "He's the blacksmith and he and his wife live across the street. I don't know how he got into the anvil business because the full blood whose allotment this is lets Daisy and me live upstairs. That white man rents his part of the place but we live free here. A lot of white people do things like that, renting, I mean. He sat down again more tired than ever. "I guess you and I was just left out of everything. We don't have anything, like a place to live on land or anything like that, do we?"

"Aunt Rachel helped us get our roll numbers you know that. She was kind to both of us." James glanced at his brother. "After you left and got that job on the railroad." The turtle crawled toward James who picked it up. "Was two years or more before we learned whatever happened to you. Twelve years is a long time, little brother. Did you hear Ol' George Beecher died two years ago? You go by and see her. You should."

Part of the agonizing worry that infiltrated Richard's mind was not being the kind of man his older brother was. "Please don't you start on anything, Jimmy. I haven't seen her in a long time, all right. Maybe I should make it over to her house. I remember the one she liked was way out in the country."

James reaffirmed this with a nod of his head.

"Just look out there," Richard said, pointing to the west. "In daytime you can see clear to the far horizon." Now, tiny lights dotted the black countryside where fires glowed and a lamp or two flickered in the distance. "Nothing much is out there," he continued, "nothing much south of here either. That road out front stops just over that hill. Nothing. I wish I had a piece of that nothing. Why can't I go out and claim a piece of Sapulpa? I learned a lot in the last five years, I guess I have, all right. I'm just too late. We're too late, Jimmy, you and I." He laughed, seeing that his turtle was chewing the lettuce. Then, in one major change of attitude, the younger brother, who for so long had been adamant on the topic, offered, "The white people have run all over us and committed all kinds of misery for us." He looked at the stairs. "The whites were bound to take this country away from us. I never asked for anything but what I needed for Daisy and the baby. In Muskogee I heard an old Indian talk. He said that the government said it was better for us to leave Alabama. I didn't know at first what he was talking about. That land back then was supposed to be ours forever. That was an agreement. A treaty." He looked at James. "Did you know that, Jimmy? A treaty. He was an old Indian, Jimmy, from Alabama and he told me the government officials would take care of us. They promised." He lifted a stick and threw it into the darkness. As an afterthought he muttered, "I don't know why the nation has to be all cut up."

From upstairs, the brothers could hear Daisy moving about the one room that formed the kitchen with its wood stove and a little sitting area. She came to the screen door, opened it and called brightly. "You two wash up. I got some pie for you."

"I reckon I knew about roll numbers," Richard said as he stood again, lifting the lantern. "When I talked to that man in Muskogee. He asked me a lot of questions."

"You home now?" It was a gentle effort from a brother who could not disguise his concern. For a long time James was aware of what Lula had once told him about the differences of brothers.

"I got some money." They climbed the stairs, ignoring the one broken board. "But I might be leaving to check on some things. About a new job."

"What things? What new job?"

But they entered the small room before Richard could answer. Daisy's smile was radiant despite the hot stove.

Rachel Alexander Perryman, who had graciously accepted the two boys, had also received others in the ensuing years. That was as much a part of her reputation as were her long calico dresses, her shawls made of cotton, and her prolonged dinners. When Richard left abruptly and stumbled out into the reality of the railroad, she was disappointed but she never flinched from taking stock of the many other orphans who came under her care. The matriarch was "Aunt Rachel" to them all.

Many dignitaries had entered the portals of that country house across the years. Throughout the Creek Nation the White House gained a semblance of grand living, complete with Sunday dinners and intrepid discussions of the problems of the nation itself. She had sat in her chair to listen to the elders. As a polite mother and wife should, she offered no comment. She had four in-laws, great minds, to solve any plight that may arise.

But the century had expired as did all her husband's family. Sanford, Joseph, her husband, and now Josiah were no more. Even the post office had moved to town with the blessings of a new postmaster. Stashed away in the small room on the west side were the drawers and portable shelves that had, at one time, held the mail for the people of this part of the nation. These remnants collected dust, just as many of her memories did which were, at this same time, most vibrant and alive.

So many times it was on the front porch of the White House this lady stood to gaze southward at the endless hills which lay beyond her sightline. Typically, she was saying goodbye to one of her friends with whom she had shared her comments. Her friend had asked about her House downtown and it was to this lady that Mrs. Rachel explained the situation. That one was there; this one, here, in the hillside was her favorite. Mrs. Rachel preferred the quiet countryside and the sound of the meadowlarks, the bob-o-links, and the katydids in the summers to the endless clatter of buckboard and horse in Tulsa. Her trees, her pond, the ducks, the dirt path to the main road had itself become a road with countless ruts where buggies, surreys, carriages, hacks, and heavily laden wagons ventured to this home of hers. They had come in answer to eager invitations and festivities, dances, feasts. All that had remained in the century that passed, but she still had her house, that pond, those ducks, such memories. She still had those.

This known reputation blossomed into greatness as did her flowers beside the east fence but her figure had not changed in thirty years time. Everyone knew her as a short woman but a loving one, a great and unique contributor to mankind. Once when asked of these traits and the source of them by an elder of the church where Josiah worshipped, this gallant woman smiled elegantly. In Creek, she mentioned tradition that had come with her own mother and father from Alabama with direct reference to the Great Indian Spirit who governs us all. Joseph, Sanford, and Josiah had taught her how to become a Christian. Every time she went to this porch, for whatever reason and looked out to the south, those ghosts followed her. Every time she sat in her chair, there, those brothers-in-law were there also. She felt that they were as much a part of her as were the rocks and boulders, the ducks on the water, and the cool breezes on hot summer nights.

So, on this porch again, she folded her arms, petted her dog that somehow knew she was on the porch again, and called to Oliver to come in and wash for supper.

Abner came around the bend in her road and up the incline of her hill and passed her pond, riding his spotted pony. He waved at her.

Again, but not to ignore his mother's call for he too had waved to her from where he played, Oliver threw the rocks he was holding into the pond and frightened the ducks. He called brightly, raising his arms so that Abner bent down to pull him into the saddle for the remaining short ride to the barn.

Nodding her head and smiling, their mother returned to her kitchen. Mayme and Ella were seated at the table. While Mrs. Rachel went about completing the ham dish the sisters argued.

"When did your first husband die, Ella?" Mayme exclaimed as she placed the silver around the table.

"What a terrible way to say that!" was Ella's reply.

"Well with so many taken by the epidemic, I completely forgot. Poor Nora's three babies gone now. Even Mr. Scott himself." Mayme paused placing the remaining knife in its proper location next to a plate. "You're on your second husband and first child. Leo junior is about two now, isn't he?"

Ella ignored the usual mundane questions that her sister always put to her for they did not have the opportunities of seeing each other often to exchange bits of gossip. She rose from where she sat at her ususal place at this table when she came to visit her mother. Through the rear window she saw Abner and Oliver closing the heavy barn door and start for the kitchen. "Yes," she finally said returning to the sink, "Leo is twenty-seven months now." She glanced at their mother who moved from her busy kitchen into the dining room with a bowl of mashed potatoes which she prepared. "And about Lula," Ella interjected as if she decided to continue a subject that was begun ten minutes earlier, "I want you to leave Lula be, you hear?" Mayme looked up startled. "It is not your business to want to adopt those kids. Those are Lula's girls, not yours." She was so close she reached over to pat Mayme's pregnancy. "You'll have one of your own in not so very long, now."

Mayme was insistent. "They have roll numbers now you know."

"Of course I know." Both sisters ignored their mother. "I wouldn't be a bit surprised if Lula had Mose's number, too."

Mrs. Rachel came from the kitchen holding the plate of meat. Mayme wiped her hands on her apron, took it, and set it down in the middle of the clean table. "Lula doesn't deserve what she's got out of the deal."

"Has Stewart Shirk been putting ideas in your head, Mayme? Has he, huh? What do you think can happen? You two probably can't afford that one that's to be born!" Ella pointed to her sister's big waist line. Then, folding her arms, she noticed how her mother patiently waited beside her chair. That was a habit not too easily broken. Ella retrieved the green beans from the hot stove as their men folk bounded into the room.

"See, Mama," Oliver laughed, flashing his hands to show her he had washed them. Abner, less pretentiously, did the same, a domestic gesture that had become a daily ritual.

Abner sat first as was the custom with Oliver beside him. The two sisters sat opposite them at the old circular table.

"Mama, sit." Mayme spoke softly. Then, turning to Oliver, "Your turn to say Grace."

With that, Mrs. Rachel sat at her place. Obediently, with his little hands folded over his plate as taught him by his Uncle Josiah when he was but three years old, the youngest of this family closed his eyes and muttered the first words of his prayer in Creek but completed it in English. "Bless us, O Lord, this food to our use and us to Thy service, and keep us ever mindful of the needs of others. And we pray in Jesus' Name and for His sake. Amen." A chorus of Amen accompanied him.

"Sofkey." said Mrs. Rachel, looking at Ella.

"Oh, yes!" her daughter replied and rose to fetch it from the stove. The others began to eat.

"I saw Billy at school this morning," Oliver volunteered as he delved into the ham dish, "and I told him that my Uncle Josiah was one of the first members of our church. I know all about his coming from Wealaka Mission to start it." He passed the dish to Abner. "Billy's been out here a couple of times. He likes to fish." It was not unusual for the boy to ramble from one subject to another. "He's adopted."

As the dishes were passed among them, Ella glanced at her sister and both looked at Abner. All this bit of information coming directly from one his age was not new to them. Oliver had learned long ago to speak his mind at the table. It was a new trait among Indian boys who normally would have remained reticent at suppertime, some of them more so preferring to eat at a separate table in the kitchen. But Oliver and Billy were living in the twentieth century. He continued.

"Miss Huntsman taught us about the new century and that we have to start all over again with the numbers of the years."

No reaction and no objection came from the family. But it was Ella who accepted the sofkey from Oliver, and she asked, "How do you know that your friend is...adopted?"

"Oh, I know. We've been talking. I told him I'm Creek 'cause one day at school the Creeks got to stand and give our names. When Billy's time came, he said he was Yuchi. I saw his mama once and she and his papa are white."

Abner cleared his throat and asked for bread. Ella handed him the plate with three remaining slices during the silence that ensued. And for a moment or two, when the dogs, lying near the front door by the Welcome sign, barked loudly and ran into the darkness, Ella went to see who might be coming up the road. She had in mind obtaining a second lamp from the parlor anyway.

She saw only the dogs returning as if they had failed to catch a raccoon or tree the squirrels. No one was outside on the road. One of the hounds bounded up the steps to the door, panting in the heat, looking at her with great pleading eyes.

"No," she admonished him, "Not your suppertime yet." Leaving the door open but the screen latched to allow breezes to sift into the hallway, she found a match on a side table and lit the lamp she found. After one additional look toward the pond because she heard the ducks talking to each other, she returned to the dining room.

Chapter Thirteen

For seven years, J. M. Hall operated his well known hardware store on the west side of Main Street. He could call that muddy avenue by that new designation on this bitter and cold week after New Years Day, nineteen-two. The entire town received official names for its few streets in the previous autumn. Mr. Hall himself, the short man of one hundred forty pounds stood on his wooden sidewalk under an impressive sign the length of which was longer than his five-feet-seven-inch height. His store, two-stories, had a wide front porch covered by its own roof and it had a history all its own. Its merchandise included virtually every conceivable article anyone in the territory might need for sustenance, home decoration, care for cattle, plant propagation, and kitchen cleanliness. That included poisons for cockroaches and beetles.

Mr. Hall helped organize the first school system for the city. He introduced his clerk, Reubin Partridge, to one of the first teachers, Miss Huntsman. She later became the clerk's wife. At that moment, J. M. Hall was showing his store to two men on this frozen morning. Despite the chilly weather, the bright sun tried to belie the temperature.

Those two men with whom Hall spoke were august visitors to Tulsa since last fall. "I"m happy to show you my wares in my store, gentlemen," he said smartly despite the breezes, "and I may say that we are glad you are here to complete our fair city. Have you always been a surveyor, Mr. Patton?"

This man of whom Mr. Hall had asked the question nodded an affirmation as if he were too cold to utter words. "You and your store are now on Main Street." With a flourishing gesture with an outstretched arm, more to warm himself than any motive, he continued. "All the streets running parallel to this one, east of us, there," and he pointed, "are named after cities east of the Mississippi River. Don't you think that is a good idea?" He blew his breath into his hands. Before Mr. Hall could comment, Mr. Patton spoke as if he memorized a recitation. "And, yes, you get the idea! All the streets west of Main are named after cities..."

"West of the Mississippi." It was Patton's younger brother who answered that for them, getting colder by the minute. He continued, nevertheless, "These streets as we identified them are nothing but dirt roads. In time, surely, with their proper names, each will reflect the good city you want. You will see that they are all ninety degrees with the railroad. With the tracks, I mean." Through the glass windows of the front door Mr. Patton watched as Mr. Partridge poked more wood into his stove. "You've got a mighty nice warm stove there, Mr. Hall."

"It's cold out here, gentlemen," the host said nonchalantly. "Come upstairs and I have some coffee waiting for us." All three gladly entered the establishment.

"You have just about everything here, don't you?" Dan Patton laughed as he stepped near some kegs of powder. "I guess I better be careful of my cigar!" He nodded his head quickly to the clerk. "Good morning, sir."

Reubin Partridge nodded back while he wiped his hands on his work apron. He watched the trio as they reached the rear stairs. Mr. Hall paused to allow his guests to proceed him upward. "Oh," he said, "and further to comment on Tulsa being a quiet little village, I might say that we experienced a bad situation back in 'ninety-four I think it was." By this time they entered a warm room complete with sofa, three chairs, a nice coal stove whose heat was permeating the loft, and many crates and boxes. "One of the Perrymans, a young kid, the son of a principal chief, was shooting off his pistol and blew himself up! Along with the proprietor of the store. The kid shot right into a keg of powder, yessir!"

"Yours, Mr. Hall?" the other brother asked, "this one?"

"No no," came the quick answer, "A man name of Archer at his place across the street yonder. Killed him, too. Quite a mess." Eager to explain as he poured coffee into tin cups, he continued. "Archer's was the first store here. He started out with a half barrel of cider and a box of ginger snaps in...I can't fully remember, 'eighty-two or 'eighty-three." He lifted one cup. "I guess you all take it black. I guess I have some sugar around here some place. Archer was a fine man. Blew his store up, too." Hall looked at the other brother whose continence was very close to his brother's. "Are you Dan or are you Gus?"

"I'm J. Gus Patton, Mr. Hall, the older of the lot. My kid brother there was the surveyor. I was the one who laid out a grid of streets beyond those existing dirt roads we had mentioned. As of now you have a complete townsite." He wiggled the map he had rolled in his hand.

"Who is the Indian you have in your store downstairs?" Dan Patton flipped his cigar ashes into the stove.

"Oh, Reubin! That's a bright young man, Mr. Patton, one of the full bloods you keep asking about. His mother was a sister to the first postmaster, one of the Perrymans. I might say that the post office is right here in my store after Josiah moved it into town." They all three became more comfortable. "You're here to stay, then, both of you? The city commission was fortunate to get both of you in the first place."

Gus Patton drank slowly and wiped his moustache. "Dan here might say if he wants, but I got to get back."

"Well, we're a fresh new village now. You should stay a mite longer and see the Green Corn festival at Council Oak."

"Part of the Osages, no less," said the older of the two.

"Creeks, Mr. Patton," smiled Hall to correct him, "Creeks. But anyway, welcome to Tulsa if I may say so again. I don't have any more questions, do you?"

"With no sanitation, yet, and only water from polluted wells." Dan Patton laughed. "and the streets Gus named for you only quagmires in the winter time. Want are they in the heat of August?" From where he stood, Dan Patton gazed through one of the windows and raised his coffee cup to propose a question. "That beautiful house, yonder, Mr. Hall. When we walked by it I meant to ask you about it." Patton looked at the large monumental home of George Beecher Perryman. The one point of interest someone had mentioned to the Patton brothers was that this house was the Perryman home downtown but that they must take time to view the country house also. Gus Patton unrolled the map. "If that family wished to do so, they can now tell everyone that house is on the corner of..." and he pointed, "On the corner of Fifth Street and Main Street. In fact that whole square block."

"You spoke of polluted wells." Mr. Hall carefully made his point. "Mrs.

Rachel's well there," and he referred to the location behind the house nearest the intersection of Boulder and Sixth street, "which is very well known. Fresh clean water all the time."

They were laughing when they heard footsteps on the stairs. Mr. Hall opened the door to admit Reubin Partridge. "Mr. Hall," interrupted the young clerk, out of breath, "there's a Mister Shirk downstairs who would like to see you. What shall I tell him?"

Hall thought a moment. "Shirk?"

"Yes, sir." Reubin replied. "He didn't know you'd be busy today with these gentlemen." The brothers sipped their coffee and remained patient. Gus Patton rolled up his map.

"I'll be down directly, Reubin." And with that, the clerk disappeared, closing the door against the cold draft.

Dan Patton lifted the stove top again and flicked his cigar ashes quickly. "I don't reckon we have any more questions, do we, Gus?" He finished his last sip of coffee. "I was satisfied when we handed in the corporate map of the city. Good meeting, that!"

"Well, let me tell you, Mr. Patton," answered their host, "I am happy and honored to help open the townsite." He lifted the coffee pot but replaced it when both brothers shook their heads. "Too bad we don't have a stomp dance for you under the Council Oak."

"The city commission group was mighty nice to both of us, yes sir." Dan Patton patted his stomach and hoisted his trousers higher. "Nice Christmas present, my first Christmas out the States!"

J. Gus Patton smiled. "That's right, I about forgot. We are in a foreign country, aren't we?"

Dan was the first to the door. "Thanks again for everything, Mr. Hall. I guess we'll be going now." They chatted easily as they descended. "We can let ourselves out since you have the customer. I'll be careful again when I pass by those kegs of gun powder." His laughter pervaded the store. Mr. Hall waved at them and then he turned to his clerk.

Reubin nodded his head to the man who was waiting near the front entrance. Mr. Hall removed his glasses to clean the lens. He knew practically everyone of the thousand and one customers who frequented his place of business, so many of them by their first names. But he did not recognize this tall Indian. He walked forward. "What may I do for you, sir?"

"Nothing emergency like," this customer said. "My name is Shirk. I guess I never met you until now, I mean." His words were quiet. Mr. Hall for a moment, thought he knew this man. He tried to think. "My wife is Mayme Perryman, ol' George's daughter." Reubin Partridge stopped his work to listen from where he stood with his back to the men.

"Oh yes." Mr. Hall was always polite.

"She's having a kid and needs some liniment."

Remarks of this kind always startled the store owner. "You mean she's having it right now?" He passed two aisles and approached a case full of medicine. "Forgive me for asking but I need to know." He opened a glass door with a small key and searched his labels. The bottles were neatly placed forward. The request coming from the husband sounded odd.

"No, not quite," Shirk said, following him to his side of the store. "She just wants me to get some." He removed his gloves. "Since I'm ...here."

"Has she seen the doctor in town?" Mr. Hall in all his eagerness to help attempted to glean information without prying. Shirk did not respond so he turned again to the case and selected a liquid in a short brown container. "I guess this is what she can use." He closed and locked the glass door. "Take this over to Mr. Partridge and he'll collect the money." He carefully scrutinized this Indian. "Thank you, sir."

Only nodding his head in reply, Shirk obeyed. Reubin was ready, standing behind the tall counter with an ancient cash register. He pushed the required keys and a heavy iron drawer slid open with a loud ring of the bell. "Ten cents, please."

Shirk reached in his small purse that he extracted from his pocket. "Here."

The front door opened with the fury of a cold wind and a bearded man wearing a mackinaw and gloves stuck his head inside the store. "Are you coming?" he asked roughly.

"Mr. Shirk," Reubin said when he accepted the money, "I'm China's son. I'm your wife's cousin."

Ignoring this statement with only a grunt, Shirk walked out, brushing against two bolts of material. "I told you I had to get this stuff for Mayme," he growled as he pushed the bottle deep into a pocket. "Come on. I'm ready."

"What do you want with me anyway?" This man was insistent as they trudged across the popular street against a January wind. Shirk led them into Owen's Cafe.

"Listen to me, Stivers," Shirk confided as they sat at a table far from the doorway. "I want you to hear what I got to say and then you can tell me what you think about it."

"About what?" Stivers asked, sitting closely to his companion, "I'm as busy as you are. I got Lucy to see today. My ol' lady is mad at me anyway." He kept his hat on his head.

Stewart Shirk was just as much a businessman as anybody in Tulsa. He sat on the edge of his chair, pushed his black hat onto the back of his head and scratched his chin. Stivers was more successful in the new business world. Allotted land under the auspices of the Perryman name was a strong factor that Shirk had among his possessions. No one ever suspected that this Indian married Mayme for only that reason. Their property might not be as viable as they wanted, since it was so far from town, being on South Lewis Avenue at a distance designated eighty-one streets south of the railroad station. "That's a far piece away from civilization," Stivers chided, "you should be right here in the downtown area."

Stivers was a stubborn and silent man. He refused to divulge any system or method to acquire money. The new address of his house on Cheyenne Avenue may have impressed his wife but all those new numbers were superfluous to him. His source of sustenance was a mystery. He always preferred to retain a degree of aloofness.

"I wasn't even at my house when my crazy wife wanted to be hostess for the young banker to announce his engagement to a Clinton girl. I don't like things like that." That was his type of conversation, especially when he did not completely understand what it was that Stewart Shirk wanted from him at this moment in time. Stivers had ignored his own background.

He and his young wife arrived in the Muscogee Nation eleven years ago on a dare with hardly enough cash to make ends meet. In a matter of so short a time, he had prevailed somehow and sustained himself as a railroad executive. That was a fluke but lucky for all of them. The company of which he was said to be a stockholder was the Midland Valley, destined for greatness in the future to meander south to Jenks. As of that moment, traffic was thought to be nonexistent.

The Creeks called Fred Stivers and his kind Intruders, establishing a farm here and there when ownership of the acreage could not ever be proved as that of a citizen of the nation. While some of the intruders were always on the outside of a transaction, Stivers successfully fooled everyone, with his sly smile, including the council in Okmulgee. The image he purported was that he was truly destined to possess everything that fell into his quick hands, including the allotment of land upon which he built his house.

Shirk, being Indian in more respects than the man who sat opposite him, was a member of this devious fraternity as well. When they sat looking at each other, thoughts of all dimensions raced through his troubled brain. While not thoroughly political, this Indian at one time, not too long ago, complained to Stivers that these Creeks did not want the end of tribal government, but Fred Stivers was in no mood to hear this same problem mentioned ever again. Stivers, the obtuse businessman, welcomed no nonsense from this Indian this time. Mr. Shirk, as he enjoyed being called, heard from other tribal members that the tribe opposed any alteration of the present status, although this white man had not cared for the future of the Creeks. At this very moment he was concerned with only his welfare and the cup of hot coffee that was placed before him in its thick white mug.

"You still want some more property?" Mr. Shirk whispered, placing two spoons of sugar in his coffee. "You told me last month you wanted more land." In a previous conversation when Chitto Harjo and his Snakes were considered, by a great deal of Creeks, to be heroes for objecting to every phase of what the Commission was ordered to finish, these two men learned much about each other's commitments and motivations.

Fred Stivers always reserved his opinions until he heard every side of any argument, especially one that might be conducive to his improvement physically and financially. Looking at this Indian with unflinching eyes, he removed his had and placed it to one side and sipped his coffee.

"Look," Shirk began, "my wife got an idea how you and I just might make some money." Stivers sat quietly ogling him. "You want to make some money with oil?"

Stivers was well ahead of him. In these last six months, since that Bland woman had brought to Red Fork the news that wreaked havoc with the influx from the states, men and machines rushed madly into this part of the nation. Virtually no new well had ever found oil. This panic was not new. "Can't say that I do, but let me hear what you got to say. You sure you know what you're talking about?"

Shirk cleared his throat after he took anther sip. "I know what you're going to say, Fred. But it is property that I'm talking about. Not oil. Not oil right away, that is, I mean."

Stivers was certainly not ready to disclose all that he had learned about this commodity but he did reply. "And where is this piece of land? This future oil property?"

Shirk brought his chair closer to the table's edge, dropping his spoon. Ignoring the utensil, he confided. "You heard me mention Lula Perryman, haven't you?" To this, Fred Stivers said nothing. "Well. She's Mose Perryman's widow and lives on his tract of land two miles south past Jenks, way out in the country. It was his allotment, two, maybe three years before he died." Stivers leaned back in his chair and signalled for more coffee. "Anyway," Shirk continued, "Lula's got this land now. She don't need all that acreage." He emphasized what he was saying with a jab of his forefinger on the table top. "I agree, least Mayme says she shouldn't have any of it."

Stivers unbuttoned his coat. "She related to this Abner Perryman?"

Shirk found a glint of interest in this man's eyes. "Abner is my brother-in-law. Abner and Moses were brothers." The waiter brought them more coffee.

As he drank and listened, the facts of Shirk's story fell into place in Stivers' mind. His own daughter had spoken of Abner to him, explaining that she was seeing Abner from time to time. He actually had a slight talk with this Perryman but it did not register with him how the young Indian was to fit into Lucy's scheme of things. Perhaps in the back of his mind Fred Stivers merely thought very little about it, other than the on-going reference that this Indian was from a prominent family. Most assuredly, Abner reflected a better financial background than any drover, cowboy, or clerk whom his daughter might attract. Hearing Shirk speak of this Lula Perryman may be the one means of gaining a new outlook on wealth and another new source for it.

"My wife," Shirk extended his hands to warm them by the cup of fresh coffee, "just happened to learn that Lula wants to sell some of the land."

"And you want to but it," nodded Stivers smiling, "because you think oil is on it." His speech was cold and strange.

"Mayme wants to have it before Lula might get the idea oil is on it." Despite his urgency he waited until two men passed them heading for their own table. "Mayme wants it for other reasons, too."

"There's no more oil anywhere," was Stivers' flat reply.

This caustic remark startled Shirk so quickly that he lost control of his cup. It practically dropped from his hand. He frowned, "What do you mean by that?"

"I happen to know some things about the Bland find and all those men running around Red Fork like they got gold in Montana. A lot of them gave up and left for good. They couldn't find a thing anymore. There's no more oil, Shirk." Stivers rearranged his chair and crossed his legs as if he were expecting another weak solicitation. "Anyway, where do I fit in?"

In other matters with Stivers, Shirk learned that this man knew more about business, any business, than did he. And it was evident at this point that buying any property from Lula Perryman would be folly other than merely having the property for the sake of expanding their real estate.

"Well, you see, Mayme's idea is to get that piece of land," and Shirk swallowed another dram of coffee and squinted his eyes, "because Mayme's plan is to get all of it..."

Fred Stivers peered incredulously as if a major part of his own method of cheating people was now purloined from his own sacred chest that he had stowed away so no one could discover his tactics. "What's all this go to do with...?"

Shirk looked straight at him. "You want in on the deal?"

"You mean if there's oil on it." That was a statement, not a question.

"Yes." Shirk even nodded when he said it.

Stivers shoved his empty cup to one side. "How do you know if this Perryman woman will sell?"

"Mayme had already found that out. Mayme had got ways of finding information easy."

Stivers rose slowly and buttoned his coat. "I want to meet this here Perryman woman. You take me to her?"

Shirk poised his cup in mid-air and licked his lips. "You can come with Mayme and me if you want to. Sure." He pushed his chair from the table and reached for his hat. "Sure, I guess. Let me check with my wife. We don't see Lula very often especially when Mayme's about ready to have this kid." He stood. Stivers flipped a dime on the table, started for the door, but stopped. "I can let you know when," Shirk said.

"Well, don't make it too late, will you." Stivers opened the door. "I got things to do myself." Just as another customer was ready to complain of the cold blast of air, Stivers left, slamming the door. Shirk saw him make his way across the street to his horse.

Shirk frowned again for he realized that this opportunity to make money was the biggest failure in his onerous life. He was still thinking this when he felt the cold wind against his face as he paused on the corner unable to think what was next in his life.

In this little hamlet of Tulsa with its new map provided by an engineer who classified the population, the acreage, and named the streets, more than one such conversation ensued about the question of oil fields. The men who invaded this nation vowed great and monumental profits merely on the supposition that Red Fork oil was also to be discovered under the wheat and pasture lands, oak trees, and eroded landscapes of all this surrounding territory. Dry holes did not deter anyone's greed and ambition. Such dialogs as that which just occurred in the popular cafe on Main street numbered into the hundreds. Prospectors and drillers and excited producers were more than convinced that oil was to be drilled, especially after Mrs. Bland had made great stride and wealth.

Jedediah Parker, whose office was only one block away from Owen's Cafe, was able to notice Stewart Shirk as he plodded along this street with his hands in his pockets. The lawyer recognized this Indian's pace, the heavy movement of his steps. Shirk had Mayme's antagonism against failure imprinted on his brow.

Mr. Parker closed his door that morning quickly for he was concluding an involved transaction with Lula Perryman. Businesslike, she was waiting just inside the front door. "Forgive me for interrupting our talk, Mrs. Perryman, but I had to go see who that man was. I saw him come out of the cafe, and I thought I knew him. In fact, he is a relation of yours, I believe!"

Lula rose and searched among the people across the street where Mr. Parker pointed. "Oh,," she sighed, "that is Stewart Shirk, Mayme's husband. Wonder what he's up to!" Then, with his help, she slipped on her winter coat and rearranged her big hat. "Thank you," she said, "for completing this job so early. You helped me quite a bit, you know!"

"My pleasure, Mrs. Perryman," the attorney replied casually when they stepped through the door onto the wooden sidewalk. "You want to join me for a luncheon? I'm going to Owen's Cafe just over there. Ladies are always welcomed."

"Well, now, I'd like to, very much, but I'll have to decline this time. I'm going to Mrs. Rachel's now, and pick up my kids. They got to spend the night at their grandmother's house which they always like to do!" They walked to the center of the frozen street en route to her buggy. Ol' Bill was cold. She boarded and turned the buggy to the south. "Goodbye Mr. Parker," she smiled holding her hat in place. "You'll be hearing from me, soon!"

"Very well, Mrs. Perryman. Take care that you do not bump into any holes on our new main thoroughfare." He tipped his hat as he made his way to the cafe and she began her journey. After the third cross street with their newly acquired numerals, she sighted Stewart Shirk still walking but she did not greet him. She did notice, in passing, that he stopped to say hello to two Indians, one, a lady who Lula had met once at Mayme's house not long ago, the other, a full blood complete with a colorful red blanket wrapped around his shoulders.

She was soon out of the downtown area, again surrounded by the open fields that had become familiar to everyone. In the back of her mind, as she clucked to Ol' Bill, she was learning to call the road by its new name, Lewis. She remembered that Moses himself spoke of his ancestry one evening over a roaring fire in the parlor when too much snow had fallen and not much work was accomplished. Perhaps this road was named after his grandfather.

The sound of the little bell on her horse's neck was comforting and the side panels to her buggy became windbreakers. This was a time more than any other when memories came flooding into her vision. The fact that this road had the name was superficial. Somewhere along the way she learned that there was no such thing as a coincidence. That thought echoed again in the buggy.

She did remember, too, Moses's personal opinion about the Dawes Commission that had been on his mind for a long time. After one of his most recent trips to Muskogee he related an incident of which he had learned. That, too, reverberated in her mind on that cold afternoon. His voice was still prevalent and crisp as it was then. "I heard that old Craig Johnson, the one who knows Dave Sizemore, the deputy from Fort Smith, says that the commission down there had got some hair brained idea that we can't govern ourselves. 'Course we can! The council is doing a good job. Uncle Thomas told me so. My own father has whites working with him. I can agree to that because I took Collins for my foreman, didn't I? And Uncle Leagus was in favor of resisting..."

Her reverie was shattered by the shocking appearance of a boy on his horse that frightened even ol' Bill. From the crest of the steep incline to her immediate left, she glimpsed the young Oliver Perryman on his own pony who had sprung from nowhere, so she thought. The lad recognized her buggy and had come so close that he would have collided with her if he had not stopped in time.

"Oh child!" she called, "don't ever do that again, please."

His horse was wild. "I didn't mean to scare you, Lula," was his reply as he calmed his animal. "Really, I'm sorry. I was on a new part and the dirt slipped..." He pulled up along side of her and noticed the bulging eyes of her horse. "But I found a new way to get to the house. Come on, I'll show you." And then he stopped again. "Oh. You can't take the buggy through, I forgot."

"I don't know what you're trying, young man, but I'll go on ahead on this road, if you don't mind."

He plunged ahead of her but then stopped to wait for her to follow. "Come, look, it's a new way. Turn here, Lula."

Slowly she proceeded, reining carefully in the fading afternoon light. Her heart was once again beating normally.

"I've got this new road to the White House, Lula. It's wide enough for your buggy too. You can get through with it, now, I'm sure!" He smiled broadly as if he had made a wise decision. "Come on!"

Carefully she followed Oliver eastward over a narrow path which the boy insisted was wide enough for his new road. Presently they were able to see the White House with no forest obstruction. The pond was uninviting with patches of frozen weeds all around its shore but the dogs ran to meet them. On and near the front porch the ducks found safe haven from the cold. Near it, too, when she was able to manipulate her buggy to a safe stop, Lula noticed a strange horse tied to a tree limb where, originally, horses of the barn waited. The ducks waddled away, disgruntled and dismayed.

Oliver tied his own horse. "I saw you coming from a mile away so I waited for you."

"Take the buggy to the barn will you, Oliver, please." She looked at the new horse. "Whose is that, do you know?"

The boy took hold of the bridle to lead. "He's a man who came with Abner for supper. I watched as he put a blanket on his horse. I'll take care of everything, Lula."

She was tired. The sudden jolt of the incident with Oliver was still with her but she managed to examine the intricate design of the saddle when she lifted the Indian blanket. The animal was a dark brown with two thin white streaks down its nose, apparently of good stock.

Once through the front door she was able to perceive who was in the parlor. One large lamp was lit and waiting on the table. Just as she started to greet Abner and his guest, Cozetta ran down the hallway with Dot right behind her. One year older now, they were even more exuberant when visiting grandmother. Jubilantly they fled into their mother's arms laughing so that for a while, the attention of all three adults were on them. Mrs. Rachel was soon following them.

"Is Edith asleep?" she asked Abner and Mrs. Rachel nodded yes. With one girl on each side of her, grasping her skirt, Lula tried to remove her hat.

Abner was caught up in the arrival, but he managed to speak. "This is my sister-in-law, Mrs. Lula Perryman," he said to the tall gentleman who stood beside him near the stove. "And two of her three kids."

"Mama," Lula whispered to Mrs. Rachel, "take the girls." And then, just as quickly, she removed her hat and looked at the guest.

"Lula, this is my friend, Winfred Jordan." He took her hand gently. "He's going to have supper with us tonight."

Mrs. Rachel and the girls returned to the kitchen.

"My hair looks a fright, I'm here to say." She tried to press it into shape after she put her hat on the table. "That little scamp Oliver 'bout ran over me just now. Is that Moses's horse he's riding? Well, anyway." She looked again directly into Mr. Jordan's eyes. "I'm pleased to meet Abner's friend, I am." She nodded her head slightly, smiling while she fussed with her hair. "You Indian, Mr. Jordan? You don't look Indian."

This handsome guest smiles graciously in return. "No. I'm just one of the cowboys I guess, around town." Lula looked at him the second time as if she had seen him possibly once before now. She thought she had remembered his curly hair and blue eyes or certainly his height. "Enough Indians around about, I guess." He stared at her for a short time.

"Well, there certainly are!" Lula sat on the sofa. "Sit down, Mr. Jordan.

Anywhere. This house welcomes everybody, doesn't it, Abner?"

"It's sure seen a lot in its day, all right." Abner stoked the fire with an additional log.

"Permit me, Mrs. Perryman," Winfred Jordan began. "I already met your daddy some time ago in Sapulpa. I was working on a house there and he was, too."

"Are you a carpenter along with being a cowboy?" She glanced at Abner.

"I been doing all kinds of jobs lately." He sat opposite her on a big mahogany and leather chair and placed his hands behind him but Lula had already noticed their rough skin. He cleared his throat. "You from Missouri too, so I hear."

"I was born in Kansas but Papa was from Illinois." Abner dropped another log. "A long way from home, I guess. Our home is here, Mr. Jordan." She relaxed. "You got that from Papa, I bet. I can remember coming into this part when I was ten or eleven. I can remember that."

Abner swept log crumbs from the stove area with a broom. "Winfred is mighty hungry, I imagine." He laughed. "I told him all about how Mama makes sofkey and he's never tried it." He remained by the stove, brushing dust from his coat.

"You'll like it, Mr. Jordan," Lula said. "Mama Perryman makes a pretty good dish of the stuff." A strand of hair fell over her forehead and she moved it aside.

Tactfully, Winfred Jordan ventured a question. "Then, your husband...?" He gestured slightly in an attempt to piece together the family tree.

"I married into the family here," she explained. "My husband was a brother. He's dead." Again, she smiled but heaved a big sigh. "Well, I guess you've already met Mama. She'll talk a leg off you!"

Abner laughed heartily as did Lula at her own joke, leaving the cowboy wondering. "Mama speaks no English, Win," Abner explained, "and unless you speak Creek..."

"No," came the reply with a chuckle, "no, I sure don't."

Abner opened the big doors that separated the parlor from the dining room. In no time , the stove's good heat permeated the whole area. Then he stoked the fire again and went down the hall to garner more wood for the evening. "We're hungry, Mama," he said en route and he repeated it in Creek. Oliver burst in from the kitchen and politely stood beside both.

Mr. Jordan looked at the lad and then he looked at Lula. "You must have married quite young, Mrs. Perryman," he said, standing when she did. "You look very young to me." Embarrassed, he glanced again at Oliver whose eyes never left his face.

Lula was not aware of her age in any sense. Girls usually married young in this day and age. Daisy was four years her junior and she married Richard Childers when she was fifteen. Lula stepped to the stove to feel the heat while the thought of her own youth was just as warm. She, herself, was sixteen when she married Moses. "Thank you, Mr. Jordan. I feel quite young, at that." She stood in the doorway leading to the dining room. "We'll be warm in here while we eat."

"Oliver!" came a call from the kitchen. It was Abner, who with logs for the stove, beckoned the boy. This interrupted Oliver's appraisal of the conversation he was enjoying and he ran to help. He then returned carrying three pieces himself, as Abner, bearing a heavier load, followed him.

"I guess you've already met the boy," Lula suggested. "He's the last of the clan. He's riding now...has been for a long time. Oliver placed the logs quietly near the stove, brushed his hands and stood solemnly staring at the tall stranger.

"How old are you, boy?" Winfred asked.

"Thirteen now." He nodded his head. "I go to school every day at the church school. Did you know Uncle Josiah?"

After a quick glance at Lula, Winfred folded his arms. "No, I didn't."

Abner stacked the logs near the stove and stood surprised at Oliver's sudden interest.

"Do you like to hunt?" It was Oliver's persistence that delayed their movement around the oval dining table.

"Well...yes, yes, I do!"

The boy was elated. "What kind of rifle do you have?"

Abner opened the damper so more oxygen could improve the fire. "Hey, Oliver, Mr. Jordan isn't..."

"That's okay, that's all right," the guest mused, "I don't mind at all. Kids don't bother me." Then he looked at the boy again who was ready with another question. "About my rifle. I have a double-barrel shot gun."

Amazed, the lad;s eyes expanded with glee. He practically stumbled over his next words. "Show . . . show it to me!"

"I don't have it with me, tonight, I mean. But I'll show it to you sometime!" He grinned and looked at Lula quickly, and then placed his hand gently on the boy's shoulder. "Would you like that?" With sincerity in his voice that Lula perceived easily, Winfred Jordan laughed along with Oliver. "I thought you'd like that!"

"Lula's got Mose's rifle, don't you, Lula?"

She was surprised. "Well, Yes. Yes, I do, you know that."

Emma appeared in the hallway to announce that supper was ready. This sister was calm despite the heat of the kitchen and her own obsession that each piece of silver was properly in place on the clean white table cloth. With food in place, she stood like a statue with her hands before her apron.

"Mr. Jordan," Lula said softly, "did you meet my sister-in-law?"

"Yes, I did, ma'am. When I got here."

The round table laden with hot food and cups of coffee already poured was a relic. Emma had told everyone in the family that she wanted this beauty if ever her mother wanted to get rid of it. The eight chairs, all matching, made of cedar as was the table, arrived in a freight car, packed and heavy, on one of the first trains out of St. Louis.

Lula noticed, too, the appreciation in the eyes of this guest as he waited politely, with one hand on the back of a chair, the other, whose fingers were tucked into a pocket of his clean trousers. With three lamps all lit and bright, the supper was ready.

Abner first went to his mother who, with hands folded before her, waited until everyone was seated as she had always done for all the time her children were growing. The captain's chair which her husband occupied remained where it had been since his death. Now Abner was allowed to sit in it with her blessing. But the son instead placed his mother in that position, patting her shoulder as he sat to her right. Mr. Jordan sat to her left. Lula moved further away since Oliver insisted on sitting next to this person who had a double barreled shotgun! Strangely silent, Emma remained standing.

The mother of this clan raised her hand. In a soft voice with a reverence that was most exceptional, she uttered her prayer in the only language she knew.

Chapter Fourteen

Spring of nineteen-two arrived but with a threat that the summer would be a hot one. As if a book had closed, the late winter finally bid a farewell but not too quickly. Unusually so, the buds on the trees around the homestead surprised even Ralph Collins. He came sauntering up to the back porch stomping the mud from his boots. His passing through the gate alerted Lula that another noon arrived. The dogs were with him but they were everywhere, all at once, evidently just as hungry as he. Noticing the others working with him, Lula came to the door with a bucket of water and a dipper.

"We got a good head start with the fencing this time," he said as he removed a glove from his dirty hand. "We got some good wheat coming in, some rye, too, maybe a patch of millet here and there." Drinking once, he took a second dipper full.

Lula nodded her agreement. "Wash up quick, dinner is ready." and she returned to her kitchen. Presently they all came in. "Take your boots off, Pete, go on, take them off. They're too muddy." The youth shrugged his shoulders and obeyed. The daily ritual was welcomed and each man took his place at the table. While they ate Lula was attentive to their menu, pouring coffee when they finished and sat quietly to talk. Laredo always wanted an extra half cup to "tide me over" as he put it. One by one, the three men rose to leave, grabbing toothpicks. "I see you got a hole in your right sock, Pete," Lula commented. "you give that to me tonight and I'll darn it."

"I'm having Abner come out tomorrow for dinner so there'll be two more." Lula announced this only to Ralph Collins who waited at the back door as the others walked to the barn. "After that, I've got something I want to tell you, later on, I mean. I'm going to the cemetery in about two or three days to visit Mose's grave. It's been over a year now. For one reason or anther, I just haven't been there."

"You're a good manager, ma'am," Ralph Collins said as he put on his gloves.
"Why did you say that?"

"Oh. Nothing in particular," he answered, holding his hat. "I just see things like that. You do fairly well, this farm, I mean."

This remark was not the first time she noted his concern. While it appeared only infrequently she was still surprised. "Well there's nobody else to do it. I learned a lot from Mose. I mean, other than you and Laredo and Pete, bless his heart. There's nobody else." She was embarrassed so she changed the subject. "How's that stallion doing I got from Mrs. Covey?"

Ralph Collins grinned. "The mare's pregnant again." He moved to the big rock step. "And Pete finished that left wheel on your old buggy. It's strong now. He's a good one for fixing things like that. I got to go."

Lula nodded her thanks as the foreman departed. She stood for a moment on the porch feeling the cool wind hit her face, holding back her hair from falling on her forehead. The girls were in the kitchen but the hungry dogs demanded attention. Their barking was the usual serenade. Lula scraped the food from the dishes, brought it to them in the back yard and she watched each gorge himself.

Her daughters were constantly on her mind with their many questions, with their ample space in which to run and play. Lula developed a ritual of living, of knowing what should be done and when it should be accomplished, of preparing food for the men, of rising early, kneeling at her bedside to offer her prayer as the first gesture of the day which she had done at the last moment of each evening before climbing into her wide comfortable bed. Her time, it seemed to her, was always spent in the kitchen; it always had a fire in the black stove. Ralph Collins loaded it with logs and struck a match a good thirty minutes before Lula shuffled to her breakfast tasks. Once its flames were strong and he heard the kindling taking flame, that he was satisfied Lula would have a good start for the day, he ambled back to the bunk house. Arousing Laredo was easy for he was a light sleeper, but Pete showed signs that he could never resign himself to rising.

Laredo always had a curiosity. "We going to have Texas Fever with our cattle?" He remembered how that disease ravaged cows south of the Red some twenty years earlier in herds as they moved north through the nations.

"What in the world made you think of the Fever?"

"Cliff Covey and I were talking about it last week." His interest always concerned something. "I was just wondering." That fever proved a persistent foe that destroyed herds. It depleted the Perryman fortune until Collins himself was astute enough to understand the situation to alleviate the problem. As a boy, Moses discerned this trait in this Texan. As a young man, he realized that his father's foreman knew how to handle the condition to rid the fever from the cattle. He did not give it much thought, after that.

There came a day, back then, when this foreman had said, "we got no fever and we got no ticks and we got no more dipping vats. We don't need any, now. All that is history now."

Spring was here again as they stood on the South Forty to look at these long horns. Pete would sit down with the wide horizons before them and stare in awe at this heritage. Once again, just as last spring, the blue flowers grew all across the pastures. "How can I learn if I'm not with you?" was Pete's personal logic. That was his reason for being with them.

They were Lula's team. They verified her land, the crevices in the sod, the wide mesa to the south, the areas that extended everywhere on the range, and Coal Creek where they scrubbed themselves with soap to get clean.

"You ever want to go back to Texas?" Laredo asked sitting casually on his pony with his right leg thrown over the saddle horn. He looked at Ralph Collins when he did not get an answer. Pete thought he was talking to him. "No, I'm not, I'm talking to Ralph there."

The soft reply came above the sound of the gentle wind. "Oh, I guess not. I got no family there. I just got you and your pet raccoon, and Pete, and Mrs. Perryman, God bless her heart!" Laredo laughed so loudly that his horse bucked. "We got to make a go of it here, Laredo, you hear me?" He reined his horse to the right and Laredo shifted in his saddle and followed him. Pete tagged along. The birds were above them again swirling and dipping to signal a change in the weather. They meandered northward, aiming their charges to the house which was always on the horizon.

"I saw a deer this morning," Laredo remarked lightly, "down by Coal Creek. I've seen them there before, too, I have!" And with the agreement of Pete and the chirp of a bob-o-link far behind them on the pasture, they reached the little hill just south of the stile block.

From the main road to their right, a black carriage with two brown horses stopped at the closed gate. A man stepped to the ground to open it and then close it after a woman drove past him and waited.

"Pretty buggy," Pete offered. "You know who that is?"

Ralph Collins watched closely. "That's Abner and his woman friend." They drove up the hill. "Mrs. Perryman expects them today. She knows."

"Is that his wife?" Laredo again rested his horse by dismounting to lift the front hooves. A small pebble had lodged in each one.

"Abner's wife died just over a year ago last Christmas, I think it was. Just before little Edith was born. They married young. Come on. Let's go back."

The three men rode past the stile block and waved to Abner who stopped at the south side, dropped to the ground and returned the greeting with a tip of his hat. He came around to her side to help her dismount. A wisp of strong wind caught her large picture hat and she grabbed for it, placing her off balance. Once Abner had tied the horses to the railing, they proceeded down the sidewalk to the house.

"Hi, you young fella," Ralph Collins called brightly "you want me to take 'em to the barn?" A memory surged within him when Abner was just a little boy.

"That's all right, Mr. Collins, we won't be here but just about two hours or so. Thanks anyway." The sun was bright even though the wind did remind them of the winter that just left. The dogs came to greet them, bounding along the sidewalk to bark their usual jovial welcome when they saw who it was.

With the girls, Lula was at the front door. Little Edith was cuddled in her mother's arms, a full year old now. They pushed open the screen door when the couple reached the step.

"You have any trouble fording the river?" Lula asked. "I heard ol' Mr. Tabor died and that the ferry wasn't operating for a day or so. Come on in!"

They entered, greeting the little nieces. The dogs lost interest and disappeared.

"Lula," Abner said immediately while removing his hat and placing it on the halltree, "this is Miss Lucy Stivers. I believe you already know the Stivers, don't you?" He took her coat. "Lucy, I believe you know my sister-in-law."

Dot lifted her arms to her uncle in a desperate wish to be raised and hugged. Cozetta waited her turn.

"What charming children," Lucy replied as she adjusted her hat with her gloved hands. "You have a nice home here, Mrs. Perryman. Such beautiful little girls. This is the first time I've been at the farm. I've heard Mama speak of it, though."

"When we passed through Jenks, I was telling her how Mose built it for you, Lula."

"Mama has a cousin living in Jenks and we stopped to have a bit of tea." They moved into the parlor which prompted many questions. Abner carried Dot in his arms as Cozetta wiggled at his leg to be lifted, too. Lucy stopped at a large portrait on the wall. "Is this your Uncle Josiah, Abe? You were mentioning your uncle Josiah, I do believe." Lula could not discern serious interest in merely a polite remark.

Abner placed Dot on the floor and raised Cozetta who gleefully squeezed his neck. "That's Uncle Legus, Lucy, taken when he was chief." Cozetta pulled at his moustache. "Uncle Josiah is over there on the wall."

Lula pulled Dot aside while Lucy reached to touch the dark oval frame around his picture. She stood admiring it for some time. "This, then, was Josiah, the first postmaster?"

Both Lula and Abner agreed together. When Lucy came to the group picture, she turned to Lula, effusive as usual. "Then this is your family portrait isn't it? This was your husband, isn't that right?" The small picture had Moses Perryman seated with Lula to his left and little Dot standing in the middle and Cozetta to Lula's left. The pose was formal.

Lula studied this picture as she had done so many times. "Taken just three months before he died." Lula cleared her throat as Abner lowered Cozetta to accept Edith.

"You look just like your brother," Lucy replied, taking Abner by his arm.

Abner glanced at Lula quickly before answering. "Yes. Well. When was that taken, Lula?"

While Lucy waited impatiently, Lula removed the photograph from its place on the wall and read the date she had placed on the brown paper backing. "A man was passing through Sapulpa with his camera just taking poses of everyone. I suppose. Anyway. Mose and the girls and I went over and had this taken. I wrote November, nineteen hundred. I don't remember why we took it. Just to take a picture, I guess."

"Pictures are so important, aren't they?" Lucy responded in a bright superfluous manner in which her affected speech belied her comment. Lula remembered that Mrs. Stivers was much like that when Mrs. Clinton announced her daughter's engagement. "I hope I have lots of pictures in my house, someday."

Lula glanced obliquely at Abner but he was concerned with Edith and failed to notice the attitude.

"Well, now, Miss Stivers, I've got a cake in the kitchen," Lula said as she turned in that direction. "The men have all gone back to work and we can have ours at the big table."

"I'm sorry we're late, Mrs. Perryman." Lucy gushed as they entered the dining room. "I just couldn't stop talking with my mother's cousin. She insisted we stay and eat so we did." Lucy noticed the crystal salt and pepper on the table. "Oh, I just love old glass, don't you? And you use it every day!"

"Do you like chocolate? I know Abner does."

"Oh, my, yes, yes I do!" Lucy laughed. "that would be nice because we didn't get any desert in Jenks."

Lula turned to Abner. "Let me have Edith and I'll put her in the front bedroom."

"I'll do it," he answered quickly, and to Dot and Cozetta he motioned grandly. "Come along, girls!"

"Put Edith in the new little bed," Lula called, "that Mr. Collins made for her." Abner did just that, leaving the two ladies to proceed to the kitchen. Lula cut three pieces and poured milk. They could hear him conversing with Cozetta and Dot as he leaned over to spread a red blanket over Edith.

As she lifted the pieces into decorative plates Lula made a silent appraisal of this socialite. She merely deduced that it was human nature to form a first impres-

sion and with this visit, Lula could form her second opinion. On that fateful day
some time ago, when the oil well was announced, Lula had no time really to
become acquainted. It was natural, so she presumed, to draw conclusions based on
how Lucy's mother had presented herself. On a tray, Lucy carried the three plates
while Lula followed her with a white pitcher of morning milk which she took from
the vertical cabinet used as a cooler.

Through the rear window, open now to allow fresh breezes, Lula sighted
Ralph Collins coming this way. "Abner," she called, "Mr. Collins is here. He'll
want to see you, I reckon."

Abner asked the girls to run and play. With a reluctant gesture, they passed
through the front door.

"Will your foreman be joining us?" Lucy asked.

"No, I don't suppose so. He's too busy in the barn."

At Lula's bidding this dainty girl sat, her eyes flittering about the big table,
noting the cloth and the few crumbs that were remnants of the dinner that day.
The two lamps, unlit, on the sideboard drew her attention. "Pretty lamp bases,"
she said lightly, "and the chairs around the table match the design of the wood,
don't they? My goodness!"

Not much for chit-chat, Lula nodded yes.

"Our house on Cheyenne Avenue is going to have electricity. Papa is seeing to
that as soon as the man can install it." She began to remove her gloves. While Lula
poured a glass for Abner, Lucy stood and peered into the kitchen. "Where did he
go, Mrs. Perryman?"

Ralph Collins stopped on the back step when he saw Abner come through the
screen door. The men shook hands happily. "I am glad to see you again, Abner. I
see you brought a friend."

"Want to come in and meet her, Mr. Collins? She's Stiver's daughter. I think
you may know Fred Stivers."

"Can't say that I've met him, no but I've heard of him, I think, once or twice."
When Abner raised his hand in invitation, the foreman objected. "No thank you,
Abner, I just wanted to say hello to you."

"Abner!" The word came from an impatient Lucy.

"I suspect you plan on marrying again, am I right?"

At first, this young Indian hesitated in answering. Over the years it was this
foreman who helped Abner learn to ride, how to milk a cow, and how to tame an
antagonistic mule. This second or two of silence prompted another question. "Is
that why you're here, Ab, to tell Mrs. Perryman?"

Abner slowly made his way from the porch with this man in tow. He had
often thought of this foreman as still belonging to his mother's household, with an
appreciation to listen always to this Texan more so than to any of his siblings.
Ralph Collins, once the loner, now, more matured, appreciated this submission
more as a renewed show of confidence. He was walking beside Abner again. away
from the house, looking sideways into the Indian's face. All those lessons when
Abner was growing up reverberated. A closeness again was apparent that Abner
thought had long ago vanished.

They halted under the trees not far from the rear step. "Nobody likes Lula."
Abner began hesitantly, "I mean, except Mama and little Oliver. Oliver likes every-
body. Down at the store I hear so many stories. I don't know how to take it all."
They heard a noise on the porch. Abner glanced quickly to see Ol' Don lying down

for a nap. The other dogs joined them under the trees. "Mayme, for instance. She's begun to say awful things about Lula. My own sister, mind you!"

Ralph Collins took a deep breath and re-set his hat on his head after he smoothed his hair. "What makes you think that?"

Abner folded his arms. "I think it's really Stewart Shirk who's saying things."

Lucy appeared at the rear door, a bit exasperated. "Abner dear, come on in. Your cake is ready."

"I'll be there in a minute, Lucy." He turned once again to his friend.

"I'm not saying anything, Abner. It's not my place to say yes or no. I've known all you kids since, well, since you were little tykes. Here you are now, a grown man, how old? You're twenty-three, I'd say and been married once. All you Perrymans mean a lot to me. Your father saved my life. I can't forget any of that, no siree!"

"I don't judge any of them ladies, your sisters, Abner. I watch out for Mrs. Perryman, you can bet your last dollar on that." Laredo came through the noisy gate as they continued. "Mrs. Perryman is your age, isn't she? I knew for a fact that she was younger than Mr. Mose. She's kind and good to me and the boys and …well…frankly, I reckon she needs to remarry one of these days." Abner stared at him because he was surprised to hear that this foreman agreed with him. He was curious to think that this foreman might ask for her hand. "Yes I mean that," Ralph Collins concluded.

"How is it you've never married, Mr. Collins?"

By this time Laredo was at their side and heard the question. He slapped Ralph Collins on the back and laughed outrageously.

"Well now, you just shut up, you ol Mexican." It was said in such a jovial mood that Abner laughed too. "You don't need to say a thing, do you hear?"

"I'm going to start a fire in the smoke house, if that's all right with you, Mister Collins!" He gave a gentle nudge this second time, grinned as he looked his friend in the eye and tipped his hat in farewell to Abner.

Lucy was on the porch again. Ol' Don roused and wagged his tail and then relaxed when she ignored him. "Abner, why don't you come in?"

The two men moved from the shade. "I'm right here, Lucy," and then to his confidante, "nice to see you again, sir." And with that, Ralph Collins made his way through the rear gate after nodding to the lady.

Lula covered the cake pan with a cotton cloth as they returned to the kitchen. "Have a nice talk with Mr. Collins? Go in and sit down. We can finish cake now. Your favorite."

Silent but armed with courage that could come only from Ralph Collins, Abner obeyed the ladies and lifted his glass of milk. That conversation , short as it was that he had with this paragon, had generated a strange feeling of weakness.

Seated beside him, closer than before, she cut into her renmant impatiently. "We thought you had got lost," she said, "being out there so long. Eat up, honey. This is an elegant pattern you have, Mrs. Perryman, in the forks. I must remember it. I must remember, too, that Abner likes chocolate!"

Lula sat down opposite the couple and folded her hands in front of her after making certain that Edith was all right, and that Dot and Cozetta were absorbed in playing with dolls under a big tree. Her half-eaten cake was waiting, too, so she finished her piece. "Lucy here tells me you and she are getting married." She looked directly at Abner and waited for a strong, strategic answer.

Lucy decided to speak first which is not what Lula wanted. "As I was saying, Mrs. Perryman, when Abner was out talking to that ...man," and Abner looked at her so sternly that she lost her train of thought. "Well. I mean talking to the foreman or whatever, we really haven't made any decisions yet about when it will be. Daddy wants it real soon because he is planning on some kind of big trip later on in the fall. Mama thinks it is better to have it in the summer just like his brother did last year." Lucy's line of vision went from Lula to Abner, smiling, patting his hand that held the fork.

Abner waited after eating the last bite from his plate. He placed the fork on his right and took another sip of milk. "I reckon we came all the way to tell you that, yes, ma'am."

"And you came all the way to ask if you could have it here like your brother?" Lula chuckled, but there was a taste of regret in her voice. "No, I don't want to go through all that again." She tried to keep a gleeful tone in her statement.

Instantly Lucy had her answer. "Oh, Heavens no, no, Mrs. Perryman." She was all joy again. "Mama and I want it in the church down on Boston Avenue, I think that's the new name of that street. Anyway, it's where that church is. We know the pastor."

"I know him too," Lula said, "especially after last summer."

"It was Uncle Josiah's church," Abner reflected, softly.

"Yes," Lucy smiled, "it was his church and a lot of people go there."

Worship. A lot of people worship there, Abner thought to himself. He sighed deeply and waited before he began to contribute. "Lula." but then he stopped. Lula looked at him just as Lucy started another word. All three halted thoughts.

"Lula!" Abner paused to find his courage again, "There's another reason why I'm here. Why we're here." Lucy relaxed in her chair, wondering what else may occur to surprise her. Abner rose from his chair and walked to the hallway as if he were going to depart. He even touched the halltree where he had placed his hat but he turned to face them just as quickly. "It's about Emma and Mayme." In this silence from the moment that ensued, they could hear the gentle laughter of the girls as they ran around to the south side of the house with the dogs. "My own sisters. My very own family as a matter of fact." He returned to the table and leaned against a wall.

Lula stacked the three plates and gathered the forks with a knowing glance at the startled lady opposite her. "You sure you want to talk about it?" She saw in this Perryman before her the same strong persistence that Moses possessed.

"Well, I don't know what else to do. At first, I didn't even want Lucy here to know what was on my mind."

Lula went to the kitchen and Abner followed, leaving Lucy seated by herself peering perplexedly into space. "Whatever you say won't surprise me," Lula said, placing the dishes on the counter.

"Mayme's having this baby and she gripes about everything. She and Mama have a one-sided conversation because Mama just will not listen and that's kind of funny because Mama can't listen. You know Mama. She's quiet as a mouse all the time, anyway. Mayme acts like she doesn't like you at all."

Lula put the dishes in her wash basin and faced him as she braced herself for whatever was to come.

"I even heard Emma say something about Mose, when he married a white woman." While he spoke, trying to contain a decent measure of objectivity, Lucy sat not too far away hypnotized by this demeanor coming from the man who just days ago agreed that they were to be wedded. For a girl who had been protected from gossip and the "darker side of humanity", as her mother told her recently, Lucy did not know how to interpret what she was hearing nor did she know how to devise her opinions. She thought she had learned all there was to know about this rich family, having been so counseled by her cunning mother and goaded into matrimony by her shrewd father. She was young, attractive, wore pretty dresses, and smiled a great deal. She did not flirt; her mother admonished her for even thinking of that gesture. She was schooled, was intelligent, and she was in love or so she said, to her mother and to her father, and to Abner of course. She was taught the rudiments of excellent deportment in speech and in action. At this moment in time nothing seemed to escape her for a successful future as a Perryman-to-be. The money was there. She did not exactly understand the cattlemen's empire but she was sure the money was there. And so did her father.

"They're out to ruin you, Lula." he said softly, forgetting that he had left his betrothed at the table. Lula did not forget; she hastened to the girl's side. "That's all right Lula, she knows. I've mentioned all of this to Lucy." He came to where she sat. "After we left Jenks on the way up here." It was imperative that he set things straight in his mind, even when he spoke of Lula's desire to sell some of her property. Lucy remembered what her father said. Mrs. Perryman wanted to sell some of her land; and Stivers had an enterprising plan to buy it. This marriage was part of his scheme of things. In an otherwise boring ride from Jenks this confession of Lucy's made Abner's heart pound and his horse quicken that gait.

"Oh, I don't know what in the world you're talking about, Papa," Lucy had remembered saying. "I don't know anything about land or buying anything. I love Abner and I told him so." Over and over, despite what her parents had thrust upon her and the manner in which they had governed her ways, Lucy kept saying to herself that she loved Abner Perryman. Just this once in her life she was going to accomplish a great future for herself without the assistance or connivance of parents. The thought, however, of why her father wanted to obtain Mrs. Perryman's land and of her marriage to this man took on new dimensions which began to haunt her as she sat in her chair at this dining table.

Of course she loved him. Her eyes rested on the empty space before her, on the indentation of the napkin near where her plate had rested, on the few crumbs that remained, scattered on the white table cloth. Then, when she heard the names of the sisters again, her mind returned to listen.

"I really don't know what they had in mind," she heard Abner say, "but I bet you anything it's Shirk that's up to no good. He's talking to Mayme and Mayme is finding fault with everything you do." He sat once again far from Lucy. "I can't think of any reason, Lula, why Mayme should be doing this to you."

Lula folded her arms. Once more she looked at Lucy whose eyes remained lowered. "What is it that Mayme's doing?"

Abner leaned back in his chair. "Lula, she even spoke to me about adopting the girls. Mayme wants the girls. She didn't exactly speak directly to me but I was in the room when she was talking to Emma.

Lula placed a chair at the table, moving it between Abner and Lucy, and she peremptorily sat in it. She began, speaking. "Let me tell you something which you already know. I've known for a long time, before Mose died, that your sisters just do not like me. Oh, maybe Ella does, but not Mayme or Emma. That's not news.

I've known that. I guess that's regular between Indians and whites. Between some of them anyway, at least." She practically ignored Lucy who was still in a trance. "My Papa is a mighty nice and smart man. He said it was all right for me to marry an Indian because I told him that I loved Mose, and I did. I loved Mose because he loved me and he told me so as best as any quiet Indian could say anything of that sort to a lady he wanted to marry. I learned long ago that Indians, the majority of them are silent. They just don't talk much." She paused, thinking she heard a daughter call to her. Then, she rose, listened again, pushed back her chair and stood to finish what was on her mind. "Mose built this house for me. Papa got mad because Mose wouldn't let him help build it! He was good to me, your brother! He was going to build a fireplace in the parlor but he didn't get to do it. He gave me four babies and one of them didn't last, God bless him. His allotment belongs to the girls and I'm along for the ride. We all live here, now, with Mr. Collins and Laredo and Pete and that's the way I want it. This here is our home and land and family and no one is going to take it from us."

Lula stopped and rested. Both Abner and Lucy looked at her, transfixed by such an affirmation, feeling their hearts beat in the stillness of time. All they heard were the girls playing somewhere near the chickens, and their laughter filtered into the kichen.

"Mama!" one of them called. She was all right. It was a joyous sound. Abner made his way to the back door but Lucy remained as if she were cemented in place, her trance broken. Lula walked as far as the cabinet in her kitchen, drying her hands on her apron as if she had washed them clean. In the minute of silence, so profound that she relived all the moments of which she spoke, she first looked to Abner who was answering one of Dot's questions, and then to Lucy, and then to her own thoughts still ticking away inside her. The dogs barked and the girls decided to run to the barn. From afar, practically beyond earshot, Laredo and Pete were arguing about some point of reference that remained obscure. In the parlor, the lovely mantle clock, resting on a table because is still had no fireplace, chimed three o'clock. Lula turned, placed her apron on the kitchen table and braced herself for another verbal onslaught. But none came.

Abner coughed to break the spell. From the door he turned toward the hallway to retrieve his hat.

Lucy stood as he walked by the dining table, "Are we going now?" she asked meekly.

Lula followed Abner and smiled at Lucy. "I guess that was my little welcome into the family to you, my dear. I hope I didn't startle you too much but I guess you might say that a lot of things have been going on."

"Yes, ma'am," Lucy conceded, "I guess so." She gloved her hands and reached for her hat.

Abner eased through the front door onto the porch where he saw Pete at a distance still talking to Laredo.

"Don't worry your head about any of it, Lucy," Lula whispered, "I'm sure not!"

Halfway to the stile block, Abner called, "Pete? Ho Pete."

Both the men stopped and looked. "Yes, hi ya Abner!"

"Go turn the carriage around will you, Pete, please?"

"Sure thing."

Lula and Lucy were at the front door when Abner returned, slipping by them to get one last drink of water from the kitchen. By the time he joined them, they were off the porch.

" Now, don't you worry yourself any by what we've been talking." Lula noticed that Abner was somewhat more concerned by the afternoon than Lucy. "Do you want a drink, too?"

"I don't need a drink," was her reply as she guarded her hat from a sudden gust of wind. Without a further word, she stepped cautiously on the stones of the sidewalk toward the main gate. Pete stood on the driver's side with his hands on the reins that held the horse in place. He politely nodded to her when she stopped to look back at the two.

Abner, purposely remaining where he was, spoke carefully while she was out of earshot. "Don't you even think of selling any property to Stivers or to Shirk, you hear?" Lula was surprised by this. "Stivers is thinking of buying that piece of land you want to sell." He looked at Lucy to see if she had heard his voice.

"My piece of land?" Lula was confused. Again, before he answered, his line of vision fell on Lucy. The girl was waiting beside the carriage, still with one hand on her hat.

"Abner, dear..." she meekly called.

"I'm coming, Lucy." Once off the porch they stopped to verify the weather. Out of the west, dark clouds approached to court rain. Pete, too, looked up at the sky. He removed his hat in a gallant gesture as Lucy paused at the left side. "I am pleased to see you, ma'am," he said. The dogs, too were there to say goodbye. One came too close to Lucy's skirts and frightened her. "He's all right, ma'am, he won't hurt you." Then he moved to her side of the carriage. "Tell you what. You step up on the block and I'll help you. That's what it's for."

"Abner," Lula cautioned, "wait." She was at his side with her hand on his arm, a movement that did not escape Lucy. Lula spoke to him furtively, motivated by his own tone, with an air of complete authority. "Ab, my piece of land that everybody seems to think I want to sell has already been sold."

He blinked his eyes as she nodded affirmation. "When? When did you sell?" He quickly looked at the carriage to see Lucy stepping from the stile block into the passenger seat. Pete was glad to assist. His eyes widened as he cleared his throat. "You didn't already sell it to Lucy's father, did you?"

"No, No, I didn't sell it to Stivers."

"Come along now, Abner," Lucy called again as she adjusted the cushion on the seat.

"But I sold it just last week." Lula spoke up since the wind had risen and birds were flying overhead, chirping and causing alarm. "I went to see Mr. Parker and I had papers to sign so I could sell it. The abstract, I'm talking about. It went to Mr. Atkins. L.E. Atkins. I don't think you know him."

The girls ran around from the rear of the house, calling for their uncle who lifted each one in his farewell. In a joyful embrace he hugged them. 'Wave good-bye to the lady in the carriage." And they did, gladly.

Lucy found her fan on the cushion which she had forgotten. Under the carriage's canopy the breezes became stronger. She managed her response weakly.

Pete's remark made her look directly at him. "You come back and see us again sometime." His sincerity escaped her. A bow with his hat in his hand was cavalier. Subconsciously, Lucy pieced together a puzzle that began to antagonize her. Perhaps it was how candidly her betrothed and this Mrs. Perryman managed to conduct their warm friendship, how their demeanor reflected a compassion that was never evident among Abner's own siblings. She wished she had waited and stood beside him to hold his hand just merely to walk with him instead of being so eager to get to the carriage. She turned her head to Pete's smile for he was still looking at her. "Goodbye," was her answer.

"To Mr. Atkins?" Abner repeated. He was joyful. "Atkins?"

She nodded and smiled as they walked slowly. "I don't think he's part of our relations. I asked Mr. Beaver."

With the wind bringing the threat of rain closer, Abner grabbed Lula suddenly by her shoulders by kissed her gently on her cheek. Then, recovering himself, he retreated backward to a point near the horse whereupon he gave Pete a hardy pat on his back and climbed into the driver's seat. With a cry that startled everyone, he snapped the reins and made a mad dash to the main road. Lula and the girls watched in awe.

Chapter Fifteen

The Shawnee, Missouri, Coal, and Railroad Company was one of the few such businesses that began a concentrated effort to hire the hundreds of cowboys, drovers, even aimless people who congregated among themselves in the territory. For an extended period of time after their competitor finished an impressive station in Sapulpa, one that made James Childers's work easier, lawlessness was rampant in the outlying areas of the Cherokee Nation to the far north of Tulsa and noticeably as far south as Kiefer. Gambling had been popular for as long as anyone can remember. Billy Mack Jones made several appearances at the Sapulpa depot to claim his loot. One time, Arnold Covey stood there while James presented to the man in question the big bundle so well wrapped.

With the advent of the new century, the Marshall's office in Fort Smith dispatched young deputies everywhere into the territory to quell any infraction that resembled crime.

"You can imagine what it's like, Robert," said a judge one day at dinner in the Arkansas border town. "As for a name for yourself, I want everyone from Kansas to Texas to learn of Robert Sizemore and what you do." He raised a glass of tonic water. "You went and married one of the Perryman girls, didn't you? Everyone should respect you since that is the case."

And so Robert Sizemore with his Indian wife moved to Okmulgee, set up housekeeping, and became, overnight the forceful and antagonistic lawman the judge expected him to be. The obvious entrance they made into this small town was systematically endorsed by the Creek Council. And, too, on everyone's lips was the oil speculation that had opened doors of responsible men, all right. Along with the honor of good business came the flood of ruthless artists who cheated and robbed.

"We have crime here in Okmulgee, more crime than ever, simply because the deputy is here." It was the cry of more than one council member. "Before Sizemore arrived we were able to govern ourselves. We were. Yes."

Young James McBirney, the firey Irishman with an Irish temper, had just married Vera Clinton in Vinita. He happily became the forerunner of a bank that was now in Tulsa. Only in the last four years had he maintained a relatively commendable image walking about town with a cane a smile, so often with Mrs. McBirney on his arm. An irate Irishman when it came to assessing robberies, he was quite sure that any gesture committed on his property would first be settled with his own gun and later with the aid of Robert Sizemore. If ever the perpetrators be Indians who would enter his premises to steal money from his tellers, he would certainly be, as he put it, "uncontent to allow the council in Okmulgee to decide the case. Bank robberies in Coffeyville and maybe the unsuccessful one in Catoosa two years ago had certainly better be no precedence for any such action in our fair city." No band of outlaws had need of running down Main Street and shooting the glass out of windows of thriving businesses of all kinds. Hall's Store would never condone such machinations. Robert Sizemore would drink his coffee in Okmulgee and take his time coming north to Tulsa to settle matters.

In a window of James McBirney's bank, on the ground floor next to the wooden sidewalk one of his clerks placed a large poster advertising positions available with the new railroad. In bold letters, it described the hiring of men for the purpose of constructing the tracks from Muskogee to Okmulgee, a mere forty miles. In one corner of the sign prominently displayed for all to see was the stamp that explained the authority from the Creek Nation for this business. On the poster the management of the rail company had penciled in the word Oklahoma because it was becoming fashionable, even for the Creek Nation. The capital for this enterprise came from Missouri, hence the requirement for the name, and for those involved with the monies to pay the laborers.

Mr. McBirney was pleased to offer a portion of his second floor to this new management even though the entrance to the new office, and to the whole floor as well, was an exterior stairway. The steps were new but the degree was steep and a part of these stairs was covered with a wood canopy. To get to these outside steps the men making application had to enter the bank first, pass through the interior lobby and pass through one door. "I wish that I had had more sense to have the architect plan a better stairwell to our upstairs facility," he confessed to the chief teller. "Sure and that's exactly what I intend to do. I'm going to enclose it so we don't have to fret about rain and snow."

The nervous tellers and the disgruntled customers observed these men who had to wait inside the lobby when the line was too long. On this the first day, the crowd was so large that those waiting extended well into this lobby. Excitement about this transportation was generated by word-of-mouth. Construction would, hopefully, begin in April because, by the amount of men present, no problem should arise to deter the success of the new company. The poster in the window was tantamount to a great future for the Indians and for the whites.

Richard Childers heard of this new rail business long before he saw the poster. That was, he said, part of the future for himself and his family which Waller Dunbar found difficult to believe. He, Daisy, and the baby came to Tulsa that morning early in one of Lula's buggies and parked it just one block east of the stylish Stivers residence under a sycamore tree. Many horses were tied all along fourth street and every bit of space was taken along Main and Boston. One of the Perryman cousins was on guard to dissuade anyone from occupying yard area of the House. Leaving a deep bucket of water from Mrs. Perryman's well, along with a basket of oats, was necessary for the long day. "You'll see, Daisy," her husband smiled as he secured the horse, "you'll see. I can work! I'll tell them all about how I was a waterboy on the Frisco on eleven miles from Red Fork to Sapulpa." Luckily, the line of those waiting was oddly short for this time of day. Soon they were inside and climbing the steps.

"There's a bench up here for you to sit, ma'am, if you want to," someone at the head of the line said. Once inside while Daisy waited with the baby on her lap, Richard stood before two men at a wide table who were already tired and irritable even though it was only mid-morning.

One of these clerks studied Richard's paper after he saw that it was placed there neatly. "Laying ties is hard work," he cautioned while looking at the Indian's small physique. He glanced at Daisy. "You think you can help carry track?"

"I know I can. You wait and see. I'll work hard."

Once the two men agreed, they stamped his application. He glanced at Daisy and smiled while he nodded his head. "All right, Indian" and the other coughed another question quickly. "Can you write?"

"Yes, sir, I can," and he gladly accepted the pencil and wrote his name on an indicated line. "That's my wife and kid over there. You want her to sign too?"

"Not unless she is going to haul track too!" and both the men laughed rudely. "Print your name on this line," one continued, "and you can go. That's all. He read "Richard Childers, Creek Indian."

"You know your dad's name?" the clerk handed him the pencil again. "Print it there, if you know it."

Daisy stood, gladdened by the result. The two clerks ogled her, one nudging the other and whispering. Then, to Richard, "Can you read English?" Upon this question, those waiting, especially the white men, chortled.

"Yes, sir, I can."

"You forgot to write your age. Do you know it?"

"Oh, well, I'm sorry. I'm twenty-two, born in 'eighty. My birthday's today."

"Okay. That's all." He handed him a piece of paper. "Here's the place and time to report. You better get you some heavy gloves, the kind that will last a long time. It'll be heavy work." While the one gave Richard these instructions, the other kept his eye on Daisy as she rocked the baby.

"Thank you, sir, thank you!" Richard responded, reversing his steps to the door and grasping this permit as if he were holding a million dollars. They fled down the steps. Much to the dismay of those men who were waiting, one of the clerks loudly announced, "Dinner time! Be back in one hour!"

They pushed back the crowd in the inner lobby as they made their way onto the sidewalk. Richard was indeed ebullient. "I can get Jimmy to get me some good strong gloves. Jimmy can do that. Here. Let me have little Richard, so you can rest." He took the child, held him high, laughing into his little face.

Daisy was thrilled. She thought she had known her husband all these months, all the times when they secretly planned a future or a house somewhere. They were happy even to locate above the blacksmith's shop. This was the first occasion she had seen him so gleeful. He held the baby aloft. "Careful, Dick, with the baby. Let me have him, again."

By late afternoon after fording the Arkansas where Tabor's Ferry no longer operated, they were on the main road passing through the gate to Lula's home-stead. They were earlier than planned. When the buggy passed the stile block the dogs were there to greet them. The sun, just above the barn roof, was bright.

Daisy commented on a new horse. Tied to the railing was a spotted pony unknown to both of them with a shiny new saddle and a tattered blanket wrapped around it.

The dogs always heralded arrivals so Lula came to the door, surprised to see them. Daisy dismounted holding the baby.

"Go on in and I'll be back as soon as I can unharness the horse. Go on in, Daisy, there's your sis!"

Lula waved to Richard. "Hey, I got a good job," he cried as he unleashed the bridle inside the barn. "Mr. Collins, you wouldn't believe it! The job is working on the new railroad out of Muskogee. The company has permission from the council." He unharnessed and led the horse to another stall. "Where is Laredo? I want to tell him too." He grabbed a rag from where it hung on a post and wiped away the mud from the wheels.

"That's mighty nice, Dick," Ralph Collins smiled at him. "I'm happy to hear that." The foreman's surprise came with a realization. Here, he was seeing a change in the boy's countenance, his attitude, the improvement that was apparent in the manner in which he walked and talked. This foreman had not known the young man very long, but in this day and time, getting to know anyone was established on a moment's notice. Richard Childers was talking now more so than Collins had ever heard an Indian of this age speak, with an exuberance that was quite the opposite from when he had first met him.

Actually, if he had had time to think about it, instead of cleaning the milking stalls that afternoon, he would have had to re-think what he heard across the last few months, not of these two Childers boys, for conversation with Mrs. Perryman did not contain such reference but of what the white drovers spoke of Chitto Harjo. On trips to Sapulpa with Pete, he had learned that Crazy Snake was on everyone's mind because at this time that Antagonist caused an uproar in areas of Muskogee and Eufaula. Just very recently, after one such business trip, Collins supposed that Richard had joined forces with this strange Creek Leader. Being the honest and reticent man who he was, Collins did not venture to ask any questions of Mrs. Perryman even though he knew that her sister was troubled, often by this man's absence. Their work finished, Richard still dominated the conversation as they ambled down the path, past the well toward the noisy gate.

"Looks like you got yourself a good life now," Collins managed to say, "so I've got to get to milking, now." He looked to the bunkhouse. "I'm not very good at words, but good luck."

Richard hesitated as he placed a foot on the large step. Before him, standing on the back porch, was a man he did not recognize. The Indian removed his hat and wiped his forehead with his bandana handkerchief. "I guess I don't know you but I bet that's your spotted pony out by the stile."

"That's mine, all right," was the answer, "and I bet you're Daisy's husband." Richard remained where he had stopped, his feet together at the step. "It's nice to meet you, Childers. I'm already acquainted with your wife, sir. I met her about a month ago at Mr. Dunbar's house." He extended his hand. "My name is Winfred Jordan. Pleased to meet you."

Daisy appeared behind them at the screen door. "Come on in, you two."

"You part of the Perrymans?" Richard stomped traces of mud from his left boot. "You don't look Indian." He removed his had and preceded Jordan into the kitchen. Lula, at her cabinet paused to listen as they passed her into the front part of the house.

"No. No, I'm not. I'm just a plain white cowboy, I guess." He looked at Lula. "We're going to the front porch and sit for a spell." He smiled at Daisy as if to confirm this arrangement. She was content to stay and talk to Lula.

Through the kitchen window, the sisters saw the trio of drovers on their horses going to round up the milk cows. They sat at the table with the baby in Edith's old crib.

Lula had been expecting correspondence from her lawyer. She was genuinely surprised to find that Winfred Jordan was the man who brought it to her that day. She reiterated this news with Daisy. In fact, Lula was still pleased by the gesture of concern.

"It was good of you to bring me the papers from Mr. Parker, Mr. Jordan," Lula had said, still staring at the early arrival. The last time, before George's wedding, Daisy slipped at the edge of the sidewalk, causing her to stumble. Now she had been more secure where she stepped with her baby in her arms. The cowboy's reply was still fresh in her mind. "Happy to do it, Mrs. Perryman. I guess I wanted to visit your place ever since I met you. The lawyer gave it to me for you."

"See what I mean, Daisy," Lula continued, "he seems to be a right nice person." Now, later, the ladies could hear these two men talking to each other. Their words were not loud but they were easily heard, the domestic sounds of their voices gently filtering through the hallway for it was a quiet time.

"Lula," Daisy said after a moment's silence, "I guess you might say Dick is content with this new job of his. We talked about it all the way down here. He doesn't drive fast, as a matter of fact." She laughed. "I bout fell out of the buggy when we crossed the river."

Snapping beans in a bowl before her, Lula agreed. "I can see that, all right. You be careful. I know what it is, crossing."

The kitchen had always been the one room in the house in which everyone congregated no matter for what reason, no matter in which season. The habit started with Moses Perryman when he came in from the range, all dirty and tired. His pan and a bucket of water were still on the counter next to the back door. But Moses's drovers, including Mr. Collins, had a special location, far from the back porch, where they washed themselves. In fact, during the hot summers they always said they had two places, on the far west side of the bunkhouse, and the deep hole of cold water in Coal Creek.

"Long about this time I got coffee for the boys including Mr. Collins." Lula offered, "but they've gone for the cows. I guess they plumb forgot it. Call in those two and we can have some. I got plenty."

While Daisy called, Lula arranged some cups on the table. "Well," Lula sighed, sitting again in her place at the small kitchen table, "come in and sit there, Mr. Jordan. It's kind of unusual that I have some time on my hands. But I've finished with the beans and Daisy is pouring the coffee for us."

Winfred Jordan filled the entire door with his height and bulk. "Thank you very much, Mrs. Perryman." With his hands at his side, he did appear tall and when he sat opposite her, he filled the chair.

"We got a ritual we observe at this home, Mr. Jordan. But the men are out gathering in the cows. There'll be milk in another hour or so, then we'll eat some supper. It's a time for us to get acquainted, I suppose." Lula pushed the sugar bowl toward him. "You take sugar and cream, Mr. Jordan?"

"A little of each, I guess." He stirred his coffee with a spoon Daisy placed beside his cup. Then with her mind set on the baby, she rocked the crib. A small pitcher of rich cream was already waiting on the oil cloth.

Richard stood, leaning against the counter with his cup in his hand. "Lula," he began, "with Muskogee and all, I don't have a place yet. I wonder if Daisy and the baby could live here while I set up a place there." He looked straight at Lula and sighed deeply, out of exhaustion more than anxiety. Daisy stopped the cradle, eager to her the response.

Lula's question was immediate. "You go right away, don't you? I mean, from what Daisy told me, you're due now?"

"I plan to go tomorrow if I can get away. Your father said he could lend me a horse. This means I can't help her get to here from Sapulpa. I don't want to take extra time to do that. I just don't."

"Papa's got no place for me and the baby," Daisy offered, "now that he got married again, I mean."

Lula first looked at Mr. Jordan who was silent. Then, she looked at her sister. "Pull up that chair, Dick." He gladly obeyed, placing it between Lula and the cowboy. "Now, let's see," she began, "this means you'll have to get to Papa to get a horse and start off for Muskogee, all, tomorrow. Daisy, you go with him tomorrow, is that it?" She looked at Winfred Jordan and found him looking at her. "Well. I guess Daisy's welcome, sure she's welcome here."

Daisy embraced her sister as Richard grabbed Lula's hands with a big smile.

But Lula was not finished. "I got a better idea." She pushed them away. "You start out from here, Dick. I think we can spare a horse for you. That's going to save you quite a bit of time. That way, you can have a horse there. You might need one in Muskogee. Maybe some of us can come get it later, you never know." Winfred Jordan observed how this woman managed to be so organized in her thinking while he sipped coffee. He stirred more sugar into his cup.

"I can wash your shirt now, Dick, and iron it for tomorrow." Daisy was ecstatic.

Lula stood as she finished her coffee. With one eye on Mr. Jordan, whose eyes caught hers, she started for the hallway. "Mr. Childers," and she sounded so formal, "I think maybe some of Mose's old shirts would be all right. They may be a might big for you but you can wear them and that'll save you a lot of worry. I'll just go get them.

In an area of her house to which she had not gone in over a year a large chest with an oval top waited in a small room. Daisy was beside her as they opened its door off the hallway. "You sure you want to do this?" Daisy asked quietly.

"It's time, Daisy, don't you think?" Lula entered and placed the lamp they had brought with them on a narrow table to their right. "We may not need the lamp, after all." She then went to the one window and removed the blanket that was hanging there, allowing the weak light of the late afternoon to filter through the pane.

The old chest, a relic from Illinois and the Dunbar wagon through Missouri, was to the left of the dusty window. When she raised its lid the top leaned against the wall. Daisy was spellbound by what she beheld. "I've never seen this, have I?" She was awed by what she saw in the portable shelf, articles which Lula ignored as she lifted it to delve into the bottom of this trunk. For a moment, this thin shelf was forgotten. Dresses, a brown robe and a pair of men's overalls demanded their attention. Each was folded neatly as if it was waiting patiently to be worn at some future time.

"Here they are," Lula said softly, brushing them all aside to extract three blue denim shirts, one white dress shirt, and two other work shirts. "Here. Hold them while I put everything back in place."

Daisy's attention now shifted to the shelf, to discover a multitude of photos taken not too long ago. With one arm around the shirts, she tried to identify the prints that were stacked neatly. "Is this you and me?" Daisy was not sure in the poor light. "Yes. I remember when this was taken. We were in Sapulpa about a year ago. One of the Beavers boys was trying out his camera." She looked at another one. "This looks like you and Mose, Lu."

By now Lula had repacked the garments and was waiting for the shelf to be replaced. "I have a few memories there, I suppose," she recalled, "take the one of you and me if you want it. Go ahead. You can have it."

"Oh, good! Oh, and look. Here's one of Richard and me. I do remember when that was taken, Lu, may I have it?"

Lula took it from her carefully and glanced at it, moving nearer the window to do so. "Oh, my! Aren't you the ones? It was your wedding day, I think. Papa took us all down to the photogravure office to have our picture made." She chuckled and pointed. "Look at that hat of yours! Show that to Richard and he'll die laughing!"

"Thanks, Lu. Thanks a million." Daisy slipped them into a pocket of her dress and kissed Lula on the cheek.

Lula patted the garments, shifted the shelf into place, and closed the lid. "It'll probably be another year or so before I get into this room again. Come on. No. Leave the blanket off the window. Actually, I'll get in here tomorrow or the next day and clean this place out. Mose's boots over there, and his big coat. It's a good coat, too. I'll probably give it to Mr. Collins. I just don't know what to do with all this stuff. They're too big for Richard, even for James. It's time for a change, I suppose."

While the happiness persisted, Lula went to the back door. Swinging from a steel frame on a high post was a small household bell which had hung from the same iron catch for over fifteen years at the White House. Oliver always enjoyed ringing it to call workers in from the field for dinner. When Mr. Collins came to Moses Perryman's Homestead to be the foreman, so did the bell. Lula reached for the clangor but changed her mind. Mr. Collins and the other two would be here with the milk so she waited. Very seldom had it been sounded in any such emergency. What she had on her mind was not that important.

Daisy shared her glee and her pictures with Winfred Jordan. "I saw one that must have been right out front of this house! Where is your house, Mr. Jordan? Where do you live?"

Lula was again in her kitchen within earshot making preparations for supper. Richard ventured onto the back porch to watch for the trio after surrendering his son to Daisy.

Winfred Jordan stood with a photo in his hand. "I live in Jenks, actually not too far from this farm. I live with my daddy and a brother. Just us. No one else."

"Daisy," Lula interrupted, "set the table, will you?"

With the baby once again in Edith's cradle, Daisy took the silver and decorated the big table in the dining room. Richard called that the men were coming this way with buckets of warm milk so Lula met them on the porch. "Come in for a spell before supper, I mean, Mr. Collins."

And once inside, Lula continued. "I've got an idea. We can spare that brown mare, can't we?" Ralph Collins stood just inside the screen door with his hat in his hand. "She's old but she's still a good one, isn't she?" Lula could discern a big question in the foreman's eyes so she explained and then finished. "So I figure that the horse ought to be okay for him to take for a while. And, Mr. Collins, please give him that old saddle that is hanging in the tack room. Dust it off, it is still good." And then as an added question, "is the cinch still in good shape?"

"I'll check it out right away, Mrs. Perryman. I'll need a lamp if the youngun can come with me and hold it." He grinned, "Come on, let's go find out."

"Take the lantern from the porch, Mr. Collins, I put some oil in it just this morning." She followed them to the step of the porch, giving Ol' Dan a pat on his head. Then she returned to her duties and addressed the cowboy. "You're welcome to stay for supper, Mr. Jordan, if you've a mind to. We'll be eating in a minute or two. Sorry this kitchen has been so hot but I'm used to it, I guess."

"Anything I can do to help? Bring in some more wood?" He laughed. "Sounded kind of funny, didn't it?"

Lula gave Daisy a bowl of potatoes for the table. "I tell you what you can do, please, sir, if you can." The cowboy leaned against the wall and folded his arms to listen. "I'd like for you to help us by going to Sapulpa sometime soon to get Daisy's things and bring everything here." Lula often maintained a bluntness to her personality but only if she felt that doing so would not offend anyone. In this case somehow, she felt that this directness to aid her sister was well received. She opened the furnace door to her stove into which Mr. Jordan placed three pieces of wood that had been stored since noontime. When she spoke she lit a flame that enveloped the wood. She noticed that this man was watching her action. "I can let you take the hack. That's big enough for what she has over at her place." She stood with hands on hips. "That sound all right?"

He did not answer immediately because Lula turned to get some saucers and plates out of the cabinet. With the silver already in place, she handed the plates to Daisy. "Here. We'll use these tonight. We got company!" Lula's deployment, her manner of working quickly, her very charm were delightful to behold as were most certainly audited by this man. She was younger than he and both realized that, this day. "Can you come back here, day after tomorrow? Early? I mean, early."

"How early?" He hesitated and then smiled. "I guess so. There's nothing much in my immediate future, I can say. No big cattle drive. And I'm not a very good milker. I guess I can become a mover of personal belongings. I can be here at the crack of dawn, if you like."

With all her movement about the kitchen, Lula was charmed by his humor. He appeared healthy and strong yet he possessed a delightful streak not apparent in others with whom she had to handle business. Not even Mr. Parker, being her efficient lawyer, would have the presence of mind to devise an answer of that proportion. With plates, saucers, silver, and two lamps on the table, Daisy admitted that even she was hungry. "Very well, we'll eat as soon as the leftovers are hot enough. If you want to, Mr. Jordan, you can wash up with the others. A pan over there by the bucket, and you know where the well is if you want more water. Here. Take this kettle 'cause I've plenty of hot water in it. Go on. Then you can tell others to hustle up 'cause it's about that time."

The cowboy obeyed as if he had been a part of the whole household for a long time.

"A pan is a pan," Lula commented softly.

Dusk had gathered about the landscape as Pete opened the rear gate south of the barn to allow the cows to pasture again. The summer birds were in the sky early this season in great arcs of flying patterns that delighted Winfred Jordan as he stood by the wash rack. Beyond the barn the sun's rays spread themselves like an Oriental fan. Ol' Don and the dogs played in the mulberry bushes to his right near the path to the bunkhouse.

Lula lit her lamps on the table and an extra one in her kitchen. She noticed that the cowboy had returned but only to the porch where he sat at its edge with his boots resting on the large rock. The last rays of natural light brought on the summer evening slowly. A bit of wind aroused the bell. It began to shift to and fro and once, just lightly, the clangor hit its side as if to serenade the advent of a new season.

For yet the second time, Lula peered at him through the screen door. He thought to himself that the wind against the bell was some type of omen, a good one, of course. He had a wide choice of experience that led to his being here on Mrs. Perryman's back porch on a summer evening. He listened carefully, beyond the wind, beyond the dogs' barking and growling just to be cavorting, as they were, to the domesticity of the women in the house and to the argument and laughter of these men coming from the barn toward him. The dogs were everywhere having long ago discovered a hole in the fence by which they could run to meet them. Then, because they were part of this family, they escorted Ralph Collins through the gate while Pete and Laredo washed quickly. Ol' Don knew how to get into his back yard without the help of the gate. Perhaps it was that he did not enjoy the squeak the old hinges made. The dog came right up to the cowboy and looked with wise eyes directly into the stumbled face which was unusual, for this collie was not so amicable with strangers.

"You staying for supper?" Ralph Collins asked.

"Yep," Jordan answered, rising and stretching his arms. "She is making me stay, all right."

They just laughed. Presently, Pete and Laredo, scrubbed clean with their hair combed, and their hats in the bunkhouse, squeaked through the gate.

Daisy and her husband were caretakers of the children who finished their supper and were allowed to play in the yard. Once their baby boy was asleep in the cradle and with Edith balanced on her aunt's lap, the men wandered in, more slowly this time as was their habit. Lula stood at the head of the oval table, much like the setting at the White House where the other Mrs. Perryman was seated about the same hour.

"Go on, sit down, all of you," Lula said, "I'll stand and say Grace."

An hour later when dishes were in the kitchen and Daisy was sweeping crumbs from the tablecloth, Winfred Jordan stopped Pete before he left. "Will you take some water out to my horse, will you, Pete? and then, "I guess I better be going, Mrs. Perryman."

During the supper they reiterated what was planned. "From what you've told me, Mr. Jordan, " Lula said in response, "you don't have far to ride tonight."

"About two miles north of here closer in to the west side of town. That road curves around." He gathered his hat from the halltree and placed it casually on the back of his head. "I'll be back, coming up the road, day after tomorrow, just like you want." He nodded a farewell to all. "Early. You said early. You better be up, ma'am."

Lula chuckled. "You can count on that. I'll walk you to the stile block." She smoothed back her hair but the wind rearranged it before she could get off the front porch. "It was sure nice for you to do all that work for me, Mr. Jordan, with Mr. Parker, I mean. I'm obliged to you, sir. You delivered to me just what I was expecting." They walked slowly and could see Pete's lantern resting on the ground as he fed water to the spotted pony from an old bucket. "I'll have breakfast for you and Daisy before you take off for Sapulpa. Mr. Collins and the boys will have the hack ready."

At his horse he thanked Pete and tipped his hat again. "I'll be here for sure, ma'am, I will." He mounted and pulled the reins tightly so that they reversed themselves steadily. "It was nice meeting your family." Pete, with empty bucket in hand, grinned broadly. "You got a good foreman, Mrs. Perryman, I feel quite certain about that." Pete laughed as he lifted his lantern.

And off he trotted, into the early evening darkness, making his way down the wide pathway to the main road. As Lula walked with Pete at her side, she heard the movement of the main gate swing open and only seconds later, swing closed again. The latch was heavy but it was located high enough so that a rider would never have to dismount when traveling.

Just for a moment Pete wondered why she had stopped. "Mrs. Perryman, ma'am," he said, "did you know that Tuesday is Mr. Collin's birthday?" He raised his lantern so he could see Lula's face. "Laredo got it out of him when we were milking. I don't know how old he is but Laredo thought you might want to know. He likes chocolate cake."

Lula chuckled again. "I have an idea you like chocolate, too, don't you?" They continued their trek to the house.

"Yes, ma'am, I do. I rightly do."

Cozetta and Dot were on the porch. They were sleepy.

"I thought so, Pete."

Lula, with her girls in tow, knew exactly what she would give Ralph Collins for his birthday.

Chapter Sixteen

"Are you still my cousin?" Oliver Perryman stood at the rear of Hall's Store where he asked the clerk who dipped feed into a wide bucket from a thick gunny sack.

Reubin Partridge stopped, balanced his right arm on his knee and looked at the boy. "What are you doing here out of school? Is it that late?"

"This is the last day and everyone got out for summer vacation early!" Oliver placed his hands on the bucket to help steady it. "Are you my cousin?"

"What are you talking about?" Reubin filled the buckets and secured the top of the sack putting a heavy rock on where he folded it to keep the ants out of it.

"Miss Huntsman at school told me to give you this piece of paper and she asked me if you were my cousin and I said yes. It's a note, I guess."

Reubin accepted the paper. "Well, I'm glad you did." he stood again, took the feed to the front of the store where a customer waited. "Your teacher is my wife's sister. I thought you knew that." He put the bucket at the feet of a stout woman. "I suspect she was making some kind of joke with you!"

Oliver remained at a distance, observing how this woman had grown so big, with ample breasts, while the transaction was completed. He pieced together the puzzle. "Miss Huntsman is Clara's sister? I didn't know that."

While the woman was searching in her purse for coins, Reubin admonished the boy with a laugh. "Oh, Oliver, you know the story. I've told you a million times."

Oliver was all questions all at once. "That makes my teacher then, my cousin! Doesn't it? Wouldn't it?"

"Let me carry this to your wagon, Mrs. Tibbens."

"That's all right, Reubin," she smiled, lifting the heavy bucket easily. "I can manage."

Reubin took her money, smiled, and headed for the imposing cash register. "Thank you, Mrs. Tibbens, and I hope Mr. Tibbens gets better."

The clang of the bell on the large register always interested the boy. "Let me push the key down this time. Let me, Reubin, please." He was already there with his forefinger on the dollar key. "My father and your mother were brother and sister, weren't they?"

Carefully, Reubin moved the poised finger to the twenty cent key. He had explained the family to him many times when he was much younger. Hearing it again was a joy to the boy. Reubin lifted the eager hand clearly away from the register. "Mama was named China..."

"China, like the country..." interrupted Oliver.

"She was China and she died before you were born. Mama was married to Kowicke and she was your father's sister."

Oliver forgot all about pressing keys. "And Kowicke means partridge like the bird." He was excited again about this improvised history lesson. "You are the only cousin I have left, aren't you?" He started to place the finger on the keys.

Reubin pulled him far away from the register keys for fear that he would actually open the cash drawer. "I'm the only one left on my side of the family. I thought I told you all this. Kowicke, my father, died and Mama married again and had some more children." Reubin pointed to the front door. "Here comes Abner. History lesson is over." While Oliver raced forward, Reubin hit the ten-cent key and the drawer slid open.

Abner wore his new black suit but his hat was the same. He was surprised to see the boy. "I hope he hasn't been pestering you, Reubin."

Wiping his hands on his shop apron, their cousin came down the aisle. "Oh, maybe, but that's all right. School was out early today. No more lessons until the fall."

"Come on, let's go home." Abner was anxious. "Where's your school satchel?" But already Oliver was ahead of him picking it up where he had dropped it on the sidewalk. "Say good bye to Reubin."

"Goodbye, Reub!"

They walked south to where Abner had tied his hack. Oliver swung his school kit over his shoulder. "I"m old enough to have my own horse," he remarked casually. "Mose got his horse at fourteen."

"How did you know that? You weren't even born when he was fourteen."

Oliver was two steps ahead of him. "I heard tell."

Abner grinned. "I think Mose was fifteen or sixteen. Can't remember. You have about two more years to go yet."

"Billy is riding and he's my age."

They were careful crossing Second Street when Reubin Partridge suddenly appeared through the front door of the store looking for them amid the turbulent traffic. Spying them as they waited for two wagons to pass, he raced toward them. At this moment, Abner nodded to a passer-by and noticed Reubin's breakneck speed. They stopped.

"I forgot to give you this," he yelled, waving a letter above his head. "It's for Mrs. Lula Perryman," he sighed as he reached their side, extending the important envelope with a canceled two-cent stamp. "It's really addressed to Mrs. Richard Childers in care of Lula." Reubin caught his breath before he continued. "She's Lula's sister, isn't she?"

Abner accepted it as Oliver strained to see for himself over his brother's shoulder. "That's Daisy. She's Lula's sister."

"Let me see, " Oliver pleaded, but Abner slipped it into a pocket. "It's not for you." They were at the hack. "Hop in. Time to go."

Abner turned the horse around pointing them south as Reubin bid farewell. "Thanks, Reub. I can take it to them tomorrow!" And with that, Reubin disappeared in the crowd. Abner climbed aboard and clucked to his horse. "It's not your letter, young man." Abner was laughing. "Who would write a letter to you?" They began their trot to home.

"Can I go with you tomorrow when you take the letter? Tomorrow is Saturday and anyway, school is out, remember?" But he changed the subject prompted by the landscape and the new buildings around them. "We have three hundred and fifty students in our school. Miss Huntsman is a good teacher but I'll have Miss Stringfield next year. Look over there, Abe!" Oliver pointed to the west.

"That's your sweetheart's house isn't it?" and he giggled.

The open field between Main Street and Cheyenne, broken only by a narrow Boulder Avenue, allowed them to view several private homes that were built along this way. The trees were the most predominant feature, having been there on the gently rolling ground since time immemorial. The Council Oak was of course noteworthy since Abner could remember. Standing from time to time with his father and brothers, he had been there for a variety of purposes, discussions, and celebrations.

Oliver was developing into a thinker. Abner noticed this change. "It's about four miles or less to Mama's house along this road." the boy remarked, holding his balance with one hand and pointing south with the other. "Let me drive, Abner, please."

With no traffic to speak of, and plenty of time for possibly another lesson, the older brother pulled reins, stopped, and climbed down on the right side and stepped around as Oliver gleefully slid from the shotgun position.

A man on horseback galloped swiftly, going west. He waved at them as he passed instead of stopping.

Proud and happy, the boy reined well clucking at the horse as if he were teaching it new words. Welcoming the countryside with thousands of sycamores and oak and a pond here and there, they managed a steady pace so that their animal would not be too heated. "You have to be sure of that," commented the driver as if he were answering a test question. "You want me to stop and let him drink from that pond?" Oliver was cognizant of all tactics that were necessary for a good ride.

Dreamily, as if Abner had heard only half of what Oliver had said, he replied. "No, he's all right." And after another minute Abner fanned his face with his hat and unbuttoned his coat. "I'm thinking of marrying again." He watched the hills pass slowly by them. He was more inclined to share such sentiment with this youngest brother than with anyone else. He and his sisters really never did feel any kind of bond among themselves. Moses had been a worthwhile thinker and good cattleman. Many times, unknown to others, these two would exchange several levels of thought, discussing prices, their own futures, the eventual passing of the beauty of Creek culture and how all these transpired at the end of the century, as if that terminus was the provocateur for the eventual dissolution.

A pedestrian passed them and waved. To Abner's astonishment this Indian possessed the very image of their Uncle Josiah. Abner ever turned in his seat to look again to see if, by any chance, such was only his imagination. The man was tall with the same kind of hat, but he used a stout cane, and the postmaster never used any cane. While both Legus and Joseph had been chiefs of the tribe, Thomas and Josiah were the academicians translating English into Creek for hymns at church. Josiah had spoken, not too often, of how his own father himself had carried mail before the big war on a typically pioneer service for white traders and educated Creeks. So it was not unusual in the least for Abner to be carrying this letter a short distance compared to the lonely distances of the 'eighteen-fifties from one end of the Muscogee Nation to the other.

But Josiah, Moses, and Legus were gone now. In such a reverie when Abner had this road to himself either with a buggy or alone on his pony, he often gave some meager thought to that one lady, Gracie O. She had died so suddenly that he and the family hardly had time to grieve. Her three-day funeral seemed so long ago.

But now Lucy Stivers had come into his life and made it a pleasant one. He had been attentive to her amenities when she was graciously establishing her plans for their future. The rain clouds that gathered over them en route reminded him of the bits of opinion that his sisters tossed at him. She was white, too, along with all the Dunbars, and other intruders. But then he, also, became devious to Lucy's methods, even to the sharp glance she had when a questionable motive simmered behind her eyes, when he thought he may have discerned a furtive reason for their new romance. In such a picture she had appeared a duplicate of her mother who effusively manifested to the entire town their sudden wealth. It was to Lucy and to her mother, and perhaps to her father, part of the realm of living at the turn of the century, at the height of social eminence. It was that reference that haunted him, much like the uncles and brother whose ghosts came and went like cool breezes that played against his warm face.

He stopped fanning long enough to remove his coat, placing it and his hat behind the seat, allowing those damp breezes to shift through his long hair and his wet shirt.

"Abner!" Oliver called. "You haven't heard me, have you?"

"What did you say?" Obviously Oliver was in good control or else his reverie would have been interrupted long ago.

"I said is Mama going to give me a horse?" He had removed his own hat and coat.

"I think it's time." That was not much of an answer. "You can drive pretty well, now."

They were at the new road toward the house. "I'm going to show the new road to you now." He turned at the spot where he had frightened Lula. Soon they approached their pond.

"You can take the hack into the barn since you are a good driver." This delighted the boy. Abner gave him a hug. "You are a a a good driver. Do you know how to untie a cinch and take off a saddle? Do you know where the saddle is put?"

Oliver could not believe what he heard. "We got harness, Abe, not a saddle. What are you talking about?"

Abner jumped down when Oliver reined quickly grabbing his hat and coat. "Just wanted to see if you knew what you were doing."

Perplexed as only a boy could be at such a time, Oliver did not know whether to be angry or to laugh with his brother. "I know what I'm doing!"

"Just testing you, my good man!" Abner walked to the porch as Oliver headed for the barn. Another buggy was present. He recognized it as belonging to the Shirks, simply by the manner in which the black reins were looped around a tree limb several times before being tied. It was Stewart Shirk's trademark. Mayme Shirk, obviously very pregnant now and walking unsteadily, met her brother at the door.

"When is it due?" Abner could not believe her condition. She followed him slowly as he placed his hat and coat on the halltree and proceeded to the kitchen where he heard his mother talking quietly to someone in Creek. He questioned his sister as she waddled with him down the hall. "Who's here?"

"Some lady, I don't know, some old woman. I think I've seen her once before, maybe twice. She brings Mama news.

This elderly Muscogee native rose slowly from where she sat when Abner appeared at the door. He greeted his mother and nodded to the guest and went directly to the water bucket for a drink. He looked at his sister again. "You want a boy or girl?" Seeing a bowl of chocolate dough with a large spoon in it, he held the dipper in mid-air. "Are you making a cake?"

Mayme, hot and tired, picked up the spoon. "Just started it." When the old woman returned to her chair, she added, "They've been talking for some time. I used to be able to follow what they were saying, but I guess I lost the knack. Emma is good at it, though." She resumed her mixing.

"Sure is hot in here," Abner said lightly. He went to the rear door just in time to see Oliver and the buggy disappear into the barn. He turned to his mother but waited until the guest finished her comments. An empty red basket rested on the table with a wrinkled napkin in it. "Oliver wants a horse Mama." He waited. He spoke in English for his ability to use the language was quickly disappearing too. He looked at her to see if she understood only to see her quietly continue to prepare her sofkey. Mrs. Rachel did stop long enough to look at her son and smile, with a twinkle in her eyes.

Mayme sighed and checked her recipe. "I hear you and that Stivers girl are giving some thought to ..." but her glance to Abner stopped her in mid-sentence. She changed the spoon and bowl into her opposite hands. "I guess you don't want to talk about marriage, huh?"

His eyes were still on the barn door and he begrudged his answer. "I'm giving thought to it, Mayme." He took the bucket and left the kitchen heading for the well. As he was drawing water he heard Oliver loading the heavy harness and bridle onto its frame. "You okay?" he yelled.

"Finishing up," came the reply.

"Don't forget to wipe him down!"

"I know ." Oliver had learned long ago to keep farm implements and animals in a neat order. His brothers taught him.

A summer storm was brewing. Soft thunder resounded from the distant sky as he pulled the water and splashed it into the bucket. Glancing into the sky to validate the lightning that flashed now and then and once more toward the barn, Abner started for the kitchen. Mrs. Rachel's dogs grouped around him, one, stopping to take a drink from the big dish at the base of a tree. Rain was certain to come that evening.

He thought he heard some slight remark from his sister, much like a groan or a fearful statement of pain.

With the bowl poised over her chest, Mayme's groan became more predominant. Abner came through the back door and placed the full bucket on the table. Mayme dropped her full bowl, the spoon danced across the floor, and the chocolate dough splattered onto the old linoleum near the cabinet.

With no great concern for this overture and with apparent affirmation of what they had been discussing, both the mother and the aged woman came to Mayme's aid. Most assuredly making their way down the hall toward a bedroom, this trio managed every step with precision. Abner merely stood there surprised at how silent they were. His boots were covered with broken crockware and unbaked chocolate. Out of the corner of his eye he saw that Oliver had closed the barn door and was en route to the back porch carrying his school kit.

Giving each other directions, the old woman and the mother placed Mayme on a bed after pulling back the coverlet and a summer blanket. The windows of this small area were already open and the cool wind, drenched with the sprinkles of rain, shook the curtains. Mrs. Rachel slowly removed the calico apron and dress her daughter wore and placed them to one side on a dresser. The place was dark so they decided, quickly, to produce lamps. While the old woman gathered two lanterns from the parlor and lit them, Mrs. Rachel hustled back to the kitchen, poured some water into a black kettle from the bucket that Abner just delivered. With a universal gesture she asked for another bucket full. Faster than he had ever seen his mother operate, she dodged the thick area of chocolate on the floor to account for the two kettles that soon would be hot. Then pushing her son out the door on his errand, she returned to the bedroom for her duty.

Abner ran with his bucket for his second trip and met Oliver at the well where the boy stopped for a drink. "Mayme's having her kid," he grinned proudly. "We need some more water."

Oliver glared at his brother as if he did not believe this.

"Now. Right this instant." Abner lowered the bucket downward. Oliver blinked his eyes in wonderment. "You hold this bucket while I pour." Then, together they fled to the house.

"Don't step on the chocolate!" Abner yelled. "She spilled it. She was making a cake." At a vantage point where the cabinet escaped the splatter, Abner found a pan, poured the water into it, and ran back to the well the third time. "Clean it up," he yelled as he disappeared.

The boy gazed at the dirty floor in disbelief, unable to speak. Edging around the wall, pushing the table so he could move, he reached the archway that led into the dining room. One of the kettles was whistling. He stuck his head into the hall-way in a weak attempt to decipher the subtle sounds emanating from the bedroom to his left. "Mama?" The boy was too frightened to say more.

Mrs. Rachel reappeared, swept past him hurriedly, and from the hall she located a pail. Cautiously she poured hot water from her kettle. When ready she lifted it as she gave advice to Oliver who had followed her every step, not under-standing her at all, but her gesture meant to wash the linoleum. A cry of pain brought her to Mayme's bedside again.

Once more lightning streaked but it was the thunder that shook some sense into the boy. Luckily, the broom was on his side of the kitchen so he began sweep-ing studiously, trying to gather the bigger pieces of the broken bowl into on pile as best he could. He then tiptoed to reach for the spoon that lay against the far wall so he could scoop the mess into the pan that he grabbed from the lower cabinet. Abner returned with more water as the second kettle started whistling. His hair and shirt were wet with rain.

"That's it, keep it up," he laughed, "you'll make a good husband one of these days!" Oliver decided he was teasing again and so he said nothing. He did decide, however, that they would not have chocolate cake for tonight's supper. After numerous scrubbings with three rags, the floor was presentable. The supply of cot-ton remnants from his mother's bottom drawer was exhausted as much as he.

"I could saddle up for a ride for the doctor," came the weak suggestion from the tired lad. He thought it was a grand idea under the circumstances. But Abner, in control now, sat him down in a chair as the table and brushed his hair, from his wet forehead. Relaxed as he himself tried to appear, he explained to his little broth-er that the women of the tribe always knew what to do and how to do it.

"Is that right or are you teasing me again?"

"No. That's right."

The aged woman who came in and sat opposite them affirmed her comings and goings from the kitchen with an eloquence in words which they did not understand at all, but to which they both smiled. This beautiful old woman, in front of them with her basket in her lap, was now resting. The smile that played about her lips foretold of favorable work in the bedroom.

In a tub on the back porch, Oliver drowned the broom and finally cleaned it to perfection. He was forever fearful of the lightning that danced in the dark sky. Time and again he had asked everyone in the family questions concerning thunder, but no one ever seemed to have a minute for an explanation of it. Thunder always followed lightning. That, he knew.

Mrs. Rachel remained with her daughter for a long time. After the birth, which was normal, she sat in a rocker beside the bed, content and generous with washing Mayme's face from time to time. In Creek, she called for the woman. Tired from having played the mid-wife, this ancient lady rose and proceeded to see what she wanted.

At that time, Abner ventured down the hall after making sure that Oliver was to remain where he was for the time being. From the doorway, Abner slowly walked to where his mother sat. She placed one of the lamps nearer the occupants of the bed and by its rays, Abner smiled at his sister. Mrs. Rachel pointed to the baby lying next to her daughter and said in her language, boy. He lay cozy and warm with a soft cotton blanket around him. Then, by the rays Abner saw that his mother smiled. Broadly.

Oliver disobeyed his brother and presented himself at the door, too. With big questioning eyes and a look of wonder on his face, he mumbled, "Am I an uncle again?"

The big brother put his arm around him. "Yes you are! You have a nephew this time."

Even the old woman, who had picked up the apron and dress, paused to admire this picture. Talking to herself she returned to the kitchen with one of the lamps. The silence in this bedroom was deafening and time had passed more quickly than they imagined. The house became darker now with the coming of a damp dusk. One lamp remained in the room and the other lent its rays into the hallway. The tranquil evening, covered by light raindrops was not long. Those crickets that were always present fell silent earlier. Thunder was the only persistent invader, other than the bellowing of cows and the barking of two dogs who thought they saw and heard someone approaching. Abner verified the night sounds through the front door. Even the ducks at the pond were hesitant about conversation.

"Stay with me, Mama," Mayme implored.

Abner confirmed the arrival of strong rain coming in from the west. The strong winds did not move the welcome sign on the porch but Oliver brought it inside the parlor for safekeeping. He felt happy, standing beside his big brother and peering through the rain to study dark clouds forming above the house.

Despite this threat, the old woman, with her empty basket exited the back door and walked around the far west side of the house that had been the old post office. A big shawl was over her head to ward off the wind and rain. Her movement in this startled Abner but she called her farewell in Creek. Soon she was swallowed up by the night.

"Where is Stewart Shirk, do you know?" That was the main question between the brothers. Oliver broke this spell by going to the kitchen. "Can you fix something to eat? I'm hungry."

"Sure I can," Abner conceded "You cleaned up the kitchen. Come on. Mama's got to be hungry. And Mayme, I reckon. Soup is on the stove. You like soup?"

Barking dogs with a tone that heralded the approach of a horse alerted everyone. This brought both of them back to the front porch. Abner opened the screen door. Riding at a slow trot, a man was passing the pond. As he drew nearer he stood vertically in his saddle which alarmed the ducks. The man was Stewart Shirk.

"Go on back to the kitchen, Oliver," Abner whispered. "I'll be there in a minute. Reluctantly but because he was starved, Oliver gladly obeyed him this time.

"You all okay?" Shirk announced as he dismounted and tied his horse with his usual knot next to his buggy. "Howdy, Abe," he called, "How's Mayme?" He flipped rain from his hat before they entered and walked down the hallway. "My horse will be all right. I'll take him to the barn in a minute."

"Mayme's a mother. Stew." Abner replied hurriedly. That stopped the young father in his tracks.

"The baby! It came already? Where? Where is she?"

Mrs. Rachel came to the door and motioned for Stewart who was immediately at her bedside, peering down at his family. He threw his hat aside and pulled the rocker closer, fearful more so now than at any time in his rough life. Emma's babies all died. He had heard of other children succumbing to the recent epidemic. Anxiety was written on his face. Mrs. Rachel was still there.

Mayme was not speaking at all, not even when her mother moved the infant to a cradle which she brought to the room. She left this family to themselves and followed Abner to the hot kitchen. Both were surprised to see that the floor was doubly clean where Oliver polished the boards with scalding water from the kettles. In the rain, now falling in torrents, Oliver raced to the well with another bucket.

The grandmother prepared a delayed supper for her men folk. The stove was still ready. Oliver brought in extra dry logs from the supply on the back porch. A lamp, lit, was on the table. This happy mother beamed at Oliver for helping and he gave her a big hug. He even said thank you in Creek.

Throwing a wrap over his head, Abner went to the well for yet another bucket full. Something startled him in the dark, but it was only a sharp reminder that he had a letter for Lula. In no time, the well bucket brought up more water which he splashed into the waiting bucket. He anchored the rope against the well frame and hurried to the back door. Once he placed it on the cabinet, he raced down the hall to the halltree where his coat and hat were still hanging. He felt pockets in anticipation of confirming the envelope but it was nowhere to be found. He frantically verified his pants pockets but it was not there.

Frozen with a numbness until he could surmise what he must do to think again he methodically began his retreat down the hall to piece together the events of their homecoming. He remained with this mounting fear, dumbfounded. Shirk did move by him to the kitchen where, in broken English and Creek, he argued with Mrs. Rachel over a matter that was not clear. Only noise echoed back to him amid his worry. Oliver exited to retrieve the broom from the back porch.

The front screen rattled with an immediate streak of lightning. Rain was increasing; this spring would be wetter that last year at this time. The thunder also made Abner think.

He raced into the dining room, grabbed a small lamp and paused only to light its wick. Then, with a shocked look on his face, Oliver saw him bounce through the back door and run toward the barn without a wrap this time. Lightning hit the sky to the north and a cold gust of wind blew against him as he unlatched the barn door. It remained open banging against the outside wall.

"What is it?" Oliver yelled as loudly as he could above the wind. The horses neighed at this intrusion and two cats that populated the areas amid the hay bales scampered across the floor to Abner's side. Everything was neatly put away just as Oliver had been taught. Abner quickly looked behind the seat he occupied when Oliver was driving. There, dry and safe, under some hay remnants, lay the envelope where it had fallen. Abner relaxed. By the time he had stuffed it in a pocket, he realized he was breathing again. Always fearful of fire with lamps or lanterns in the barn, he waited, took a moment to pet a cat, and then retreated to the door. He saw that Oliver was still on the back porch, still calling to him. Abner closed the barn door, latched it, and made his way hastily to the house.

With eyes that asked more questions, Oliver followed him to the table where, under the lamp, Abner looked at the letter thoroughly. The postmark was a dim circle with Muskogee, I.T. with a large hand-written name and address to Tulsa, I. T.

Stewart Shirk, in the meantime, tied his horse to the buggy and brought everything around to the barn. He had long ago learned to ignore trees during spring storms and both horses were expensive. He was angry that no one had presence of mind to care for Mayme's buggy and horse in the first place.

He was still mad by the time he got to the kitchen. "Have you got any coffee in this pot?" His hair and clothes were wet so he sat in a chair next to the stove. "Hey, Abe, are you listening?"

Absentmindedly while still gazing at the envelope he held in his hand, Abner lifted the pot and shook it to determine its contents. "I can make some more, I guess."

As yet perplexed, Oliver was again at the table, seated opposite Shirk. The stove was hot enough to boil water. Abner casually laid the envelope between them and he searched for the coffee can.

Oliver slowly reached for it merely to satisfy his curiosity about stamps, but Shirk managed to touch it first with a dirty hand as if it were a prize. He tilted it toward the lamp. The boy thought this brother-in-law was actually going to tear open the envelope and read what was inside.

"Who's this Mrs. Richard Childers, one of Lula's relatives?"

"Put it down, Stew," Abner said softly while he measured the fresh grounds. He was not a good provider when it came to suppers, an opinion he shared with his youngest brother. He did manage a sandwich. Oliver was not too keen for soup this time but kept one eye on Shirk. "While I'm getting this for you, go put a pan outside and catch some rainwater. You'll want to wash up before bedtime."

Shirk dropped the letter onto the tablecloth. "Like I said, who is this Childers? I know some Childers, down around Broken Arrow."

"It's a letter for Lula's sister." Abner checked the sandwich. He preferred a bowl of soup for himself. A dog was barking again but only at Oliver.

"Catch some water for me, youngun," Shirk called through the back door as he rose to shake the kettle. "Enough hot water there for me? Where does she keep soap around here?"

Silently, Abner poured more water to answer the question. He pointed to a bar of soap in a little dish near the door. Shirk returned to his seat to appraise the letter, peering at it as if that alone could answer one or two doubts that had been bothering him lately. He flipped the envelope onto the table again. "How come Lula went and sold that piece of property, huh, you know, Ab? You know why?" He rose again, removed his shirt, and stretched his arms. "I'm just real curious about this. That land was Perryman territory and legally it belongs to the little girls, all three of them. That's Creek law. I don't think Lula owned that to begin with, did she? She sold it outright without letting any of us know. You got some bread around here?"

"Some ham there for you if you want to make a sandwich." Abner poured coffee for both of them. Oliver came through the back door carrying his hat and shirt. His face and hands were clean and his pants were wet where he had washed his torso. He sat down and ate his food, ignoring Shirk as best he could. Between bites he asked Abner, "Can I go with you tomorrow?"

Abner recovered the letter. "Sure." He placed a forefinger against his lips, an action that was not seen by Shirk who was cutting a slice of ham.

Oliver understood. "Can I have some coffee, please?"

Abner hesitated but obeyed. The boy ate and drank in silence because he was tired. The food prepared, and with a cup before him, Shirk sat solidly, resting his stout frame in a chair that was too small for him. "Your mama still in there with Mayme and the kid?"

It was directed to Abner. "She's all right. She'll come in if she's hungry."

With his mouth full, Shirk extended his complaints. "Mayme wanted that land. Why Lula had to go and sell it, Mayme sure would like to know. I'm going to tell her tomorrow when she can hear me." Stewart ate hurriedly, rising once to pour another cup of coffee. He raised the pot toward Abner to see if he wanted one but the answer was no. Shirk leaned against the cabinet. "You interested in that land, by any chance?"

"No. No, I'm not."

Stewart Shirk, always in control, drained his cup and left in on the cabinet behind him. With the kettle in one hand and the soap in the other, he made his way to the porch, prepared his water, and washed. "Go to bed if you want to. I'll turn out the lamps and sleep on the daybed in Mayme's room."

Abner rose and motioned for Oliver to follow him. "Come on, I'll put you to bed. Both of us won't have any problem sleeping tonight." He held the letter this time. Then, to make certain that Mrs. Rachel was all right, he looked into the bedroom where Mayme and the baby were sleeping. He saw that his mother had straightened the comfort over his sister and had, herself, left for her own bed. Soon, only the light from the storm lit the rooms with their streaks and patterns in the wet sky.

"Mama?" Abner called as he knocked on his mother's door. "You all right?" He knocked again and then opened it slowly. She lay peacefully on her wide bed. When she turned her head toward the door she smiled and he said in Creek, good night.

The barn was secured, the front door, shut. The back screen slammed twice as he heard Shirk still roaming around outside. The dogs were under the house at their location where a hole in the foundation was their gate during storms. By now, the rain was gentle but the lightning persisted with the accompaniment of muted thunder. The storm was passing over Tulsa and was destined for the Cherokees. Tomorrow would be cool and he and Oliver would play the important role of postman.

As he lay on his bed, he remembered when he was a small child, how Uncle Josiah explained to him what it was to be the first postmaster here in this very house, to receive and sort the mail for everyone in this entire area.

Abner watched sheet lightning still play about the heavens beyond the trees outside his window. He recalled an incident. One day, when he was ten, he was out there in that old dusty office rummaging through two or three heavy wooden boxes. He was looking for a picture of his uncle and father taken when the post office first opened in 'seventy-nine. Spiders had built webs in the corners of this old room. Abner saw a broken section of the ceiling, holes through which wasps built their mud homes. Even so, layers of dust gathered on Josiah's chair and shelves which he devised as individual mail boxes. But by the time Abner was scrounging around, looking for the print at his mother's request, Josiah had moved the postal operation to downtown at Hall's store. Among his many duties, Reubin Partridge was also a mail clerk.

Mrs. Rachel wanted to keep that picture because Josiah was holding the certification, signed by the President of the United States, neatly framed by the man who stood beside him in this pose. Abner's hands and pants were dirty but he found what he wanted and joyously handed it to his mother. He was so pleased that he forgot to return other discoveries to the box and close its lid.

Shortly thereafter, at Josiah's funeral, when a great deal of mourners celebrated the three-day event, that picture, in its old frame, could not be located. Abner's father was furious and Mrs. Rachel was saddened, indeed.

Just last year, when Abner was at Mayme's house one day, when she opened a box of personal papers, Abner's eyes innocently fell on its contents. Among those knickknacks and papers outside of its original frame and partially covered by a receipt of feed was that picture which he thought was lost. Mayme had it all this time. He did not say a word then to her. And he would say nothing to her now about why Lula sold that acreage. Abner wanted his sister and her husband to presume that he knew why the transaction was made.

Chapter Seventeen

Spring of nineteen-two came at a time when their winter had been excessively harsh. New homes were appearing on the south horizon of Sapulpa along muddy Maple Street and south of Dewey where Waller Dunbar was in the process of building his own big house. His good reputation as a fine carpenter caught the attention of the new lumber company, all by word-of-mouth. Because of this phenomenal growth the people of Red Fork presumed that Sapulpa would expand to the north to overtake their own southern limits, that Red Fork would then lose their own cultures. One politician exclaimed that the seven mile stretch of the Frisco Railroad was built for Sapulpa to grow southward or, possibly, westward. That was a plan.

Mr. J.C. Menifee drove by Mr. Dunbar's house one day to show this carpenter a new buckboard. "It's the latest thing in transportation. I got it in Vinita. Look how sturdy the axles are and the wheels are solid." Then, after circling his new possession in measured steps, he climbed aboard and took the reins. "By the way, if you see young James Childers before I do please tell him that new hunting groups are being planned. He would be welcome to hunt with the other men this fall. Of course, if he wants to join us earlier, please let me know."

"I will, all right," Waller Dunbar agreed. "He's already told me about his interest as a hunter. Jimmy has been busy with his work at the depot. I know that he went to Vinita about a week ago. But I'll tell him if I see him." And then, as a last remark, 'You have a fine wagon there, Menifee. You want me to build you a garage for it?"

The railroad industry became the most productive business to dictate social trends all along the routes in the case of the Frisco, from Vinita, which had become a major transfer point, to Sapulpa, the terminus at this moment in time. The Katy, also, had successfully proved to both the Cherokees and the Creeks that their interests were honorable and that both nations would reap major profits. Exactly what their future plans were regarding expansion and route extension remained a serious secret known only to the respective managers. But James Childers, because of his loyalty at Sapulpa, returned from one such business trip where he met a variety of men up and down the Frisco tracks. He had been told, outright, that the new company operating from Muskogee toward Okmulgee may very easily develop into a growing competitor where the far west was concerned.

The Fort Smith and Western Railroad, yet another company, was not nearly as threatening as was the company out of Muskogee. All these ideas, these suppositions, were pending regarding any such improvement of service. Among many self-declared authorities, this was a universal opinion.

An announcement from the Frisco interrupted a ritual that James wished to sustain, more out of habit of doing so than for any other reason, and that was being able to see his brother more often, especially now that they felt a closeness not heretofore shared. Sporadically, they visited each other in these last few years. That was due to the fact that Richard ventured to points unknown and was not seen for a great number of days. Even when he married Daisy somehow he always eluded his five brothers. But he had hardly known them.

The company advertised that the schedule from St. Louis to Sapulpa would be increased to a twice-weekly service. In fact, this came at a time when James Childers' work was appreciated and when the number of personnel would be expanded. James then would be in one prestigious position to recommend that his brother join him at the station as a new employee in the ticket window. Richard was good at figures. He could easily learn the manipulation of the newest tabulating machine.

Rumor had it that another railroad, and not the Frisco, was applying for a permit from the Creek and Sac and Fox Nations to extend a rail line westward from Sapulpa all the way to Guthrie or perhaps to Oklahoma City, in competition with the Fort Smith and Western. The stockyards for example, which had gained potentiality and prestige in Red Fork, as well as the most repugnant odor that could disturb anyone, might be constructed, then, on the far south edge of Bristow or Stroud.

Spring, this one especially, was a fine season for anyone, James thought. Now would be a good turning point in his brother's restless spirit. But when it came time for all the good fortune to become tangible opportunity, this younger brother and his wife made their decision almost immediately. It came at a time when the company in Muskogee attracted hundreds of men, including Richard Childers. This decision was so rapid that neither of them reported any such intention to James or to say goodbye to him. This was not mysterious to the older brother for life, for anyone, had become too swift with the growth of the Frisco. Not seeing them over seven days' time did not necessarily alter filial admiration and love nor did it raise any doubts as far as James was concerned. But in two weeks' time, with no word whatsoever, with no sudden appearance at the station as Richard was inclined to do, James did take advantage of a nice conversation he had with Mr. Menifee about their mutual interest.

"I appreciate the information you gave me about your plan with those men coming in from the east. Really, you have to think well in advance, don't you?" James had learned good protocol in business relationships.

"Yes, we do, Jimmy," Menifee was pleasant about all this. "I'll let you know more about it later this summer perhaps."

"Oh, Mr. Menifee," James added, not to delay him any further, "if you see my brother, please tell him to come see me or let me know what's going on."

"I will, Jimmy," Menifee smiled. "I certainly will."

"The company is growing and I may have a job for him. But he has to see me, first."

When the formal announcement came from the Frisco office, all of Sapulpa was thrilled. Even the Indian Journal in Eufaula carried a column on their front page of the next issue. The times and schedules, to and from intermediate stations, and most importantly at Vinita and St. Louis where transfers were guaranteed, allowed him to be absent on the weekends. This was only just a portion of the news he wanted to share.

So, reaching a decision, James, with the best of intentions, determined to locate his brother. Hopefully he walked to the blacksmith's shop. Nothing essentially was changed since he sat on the back steps with him. In the light of day, with a small wind blowing, the wide open landscape that surrounded these few buildings looked far more barren than at night. Evidently people did not want to establish their homes in this part of the world. In a sense, it was lonesome. "It's really Claythorn's allotted land," Richard had told him at one time. "Elbert Claythorn owns the land, the building where the shop is and I don't know who lives across the street. That's somebody else's land."

As he came near, a dog met him. He looked apprehensively at the poor structure. It was somebody's home but it had a new swing dangling on a rope from a high tree limb. With the many trees that covered the area, this part was the only liveable section on this side of town. He noticed that the forge was blazing, even in the heat of day, and the blacksmith pounded a horse shoe.

When greeted, the perspiring man looked at him. "They left about two weeks ago, something like that." He paused and rested his hammer on the side of his anvil. "Wait a minute." He wiped his face with a wet towel he extracted from a pail of water. "You his brother, ain't you? I remember seeing you here one night."

Confused by his answer, James persisted. "Two weeks, you say? They've been gone? Gone two weeks?" The heat from the coals made him retreat.

"Well now, let me see. Said something about his birthday, and that they go to Lula somebody, I think it was. And then up to Tulsa. Tulsa, I'm sure about that." He began to pound the shoe again, speaking with the beat of his action. "About two days or so later his wife and a gentleman come back here and picked up their belongings, lock, stock, and barrel." He stopped again to rest. "This here is my place. I'm a renter. But its my place. I ain't no intruder if you're law." He stopped to look at his callus under his right glove. "I 'bout forgot. My wife was upstairs three days ago and found a little book. They must have forgotten it. It's over there if you want it. There's nothing else left upstairs.

James stepped over to a little box lying on the ground at the front of the shop. On it, waiting, was a small book bound with a red edge and a marker extending from its top. It contained poetry, a compilation of several authors on a variety of subjects with three referenced more particularly than the others. Penciled in the margin of one was "this my favorite." The other two poems were dog-eared at the top of their pages, one of Edgar A. Poe and another a translation from the French poet, Beaudelaire. "Thank you, I'll take it." And with that, he tipped his hat and escaped the heat of the shop by moving north on the road again.

He was even more perplexed now than ever.

In another hour James encountered Waller Dunbar who was talking to a trio of businessmen across the street from the hotel. He waited while the men said goodbye. With a hesitancy that bordered on politeness, he approached the carpenter.

"You off work today?" Waller Dunbar announced. "Walk with me to my house. I think maybe we've got some talking to do." As they proceeded down the street, he told James what Menifee had said to him. "So you make up your mind about hunting. I can imagine you're ready any time!"

"Mr. Dunbar," James said softly, "you once said that if ever I needed a horse I could come asking to borrow one from you. I hope that is what you said."

"That's right, Jimmy, I said that. Turn left here. I want to show you how I'm progressing with my new house." They went south for an additional half mile before they stopped at the work site where the foundation and half the walls were waiting for approval. "This summer," Dunbar said while he pointed with a stick, "I ought to be finished and we can move. In the meantime, Malindy and I and the baby will be where we've always been. back over there." He indicated a small house just a half block to the west. "You hungry? How's the business?"

After walking around his new structure and an explanation of what he wanted, Waller was pleased with what he saw. Two men were putting the final wall in place. He commented as he waved to the men. "It's going to be a nice home for us, you wait and see. Lula was here two weeks ago and she liked it."

"I haven't seen by brother and Daisy in a long time. I was just wondering..."

They went through the old gate. Each paused on the porch where Waller adjusted his favorite rocker and sat in it. "Sit over there, Jimmy, in that chair. Let's rest here for a bit." He sensed the boy's concern. "They're all right, Jimmy."

"I was just thinking, maybe, if you don't mind of borrowing a horse and riding over to Mrs. Perryman's house to see what, maybe, she had heard. If it doesn't rain too hard."

"You going to Lula's place, huh? Well. Then you can take a quilt she's been wanting." Waller started rocking. "When do you want to go?"

"First thing tomorrow morning if that's all right. I'm trying to find Richard."

"Well, let me see what we can do about that!"

A short lady appeared at the front door. "Oh, Jimmy," Waller said without rising, "this here is my wife, Malindy. You never did have an occasion to meet her, I reckon."

James rose and shook her hand as she opened the screen. "Pleased to meet you." She was young and obviously pregnant, and she had a pleasant smile when she returned the greeting. Her bright red hair was pulled back in a tight bun.

"Lindy honey," Waller mentioned, "go fetch that quilt Lula and the women finished about two weeks ago. You know the one. I want Jimmy here to take it to Lula tomorrow." With a nod of her head, she disappeared, but a little girl who had been directly behind her waited at the screen door until Waller acknowledged her. "And this is my Ruby, my little girl!"

"Sit back a minute, Jimmy." Waller said as he motioned for Ruby to hop onto his lap. "Daisy sent word to me she and Dick and the baby were on their way to Tulsa to see about a job. In Muskogee the job was. Didn't they tell you?"

Ruby, silent and with large brown eyes, was soon on Waller's ample lap. James sat again slowly with a worried expression. "No. I didn't know about that. It's just that I was hoping." And in that pause Waller cocked his head to hear what he was about to say. "I was hoping that Dick could take a job here in Sapulpa. The railroad is hiring and I was going to..." but his remark trailed off into a heavy sigh. James felt embarrassed.

They heard Malindy in the front of the house as she folded the blanket into a neat package. "Lindy's my second wife, Jim. I don't suppose you ever knew what happened. I had Lula first, then Daisy, then Walter Clyde, and two more with my first wife who died in 'ninety-three." He rose and placed Ruby on the porch. "Better have some coffee with me. Let's go in."

Before Malindy could complete the wrapping, Waller asked her to unfold it. "They worked long and hard on this piece. But it's finished and when Lula was here just a trim was all they lacked."

It was the flower garden pattern made from scraps of calico and cotton cloth from a variety of colors, all in shapes of tiny octagons and all delicately sewn together by patient fingers of several ladies. The art of quilting was pursued in their fair city as long as a large sewing area was available in which to maintain the frame as their work progressed. One recommendation from the second wife was that Waller design a dining room in the new home to be sufficiently large enough to accommodate the frame and about eight chairs around it so the women could work well. As the quilt expanded, the frame was extended and the ladies were to readjust their chairs.

"Easier said than done," was Waller's reply.

Malindy came from her hot kitchen bearing two cups of coffee. "I've got cream and sugar if you want it."

Waller began to drink. "Lula already knows about the quilt of course." He suggested sugar but James declined. Ruby begged to be on her father's lap and he gladly lifted her. "I want you to take it to her tomorrow, please." While he sipped his coffee, he noticed a soft reverie encompassing James. "I always like to have my coffee before supper and you're welcome to stay and eat with us if you want to."

'I just wish Dick had told me what's on his mind."

"Well, you see, Jimmy," and Waller moved Ruby and sat in another chair closer to him. "I had a hard time understanding that situation. I guess you'd call it a problem with the boy." Ruby stood near her father while he combed her hair with his fingers. "He's just that way. As long as Daisy is happy, but she's a strange one, herself. She says she loves him and that's all that matters. Dick just doesn't tell much to anyone."

James secretly concluded that what Waller said was not altogether true but he knew what this good man meant.

A slight rumble of thunder sounded far to the east. James stirred uneasily in his chair. "Rain or no rain, I guess I better go and see what's going on." He waited. "Can I come by early tomorrow to get the horse, Mr. Dunbar?"

"Okay by me. You got a watch?"

"No, I don't, but I'll be here at sunrise, right there on that front porch, if that's all right."

Waller leaned forward to stop rocking his daughter. He put her gently on the rug. "I tell you what, Jimmy. You be here early, all right, and Lindy will have a breakfast for you. By that time, I'll have the mare saddled and ready." He opened the front screen. "Come her, I'll show you."

They walked around the east side of the house to a small barn which was on his neighbor's property. "I built this on condition that he let me keep my horses and buggy in it, too, on this side area here." They stopped when a streak of lightning blasted through the east sky. "Rain or shine, we'll be ready. The mare's not here. There she is, out south of us. Pretty thing I might add. I'll bring her in here if it rains tonight." They meandered back to the porch. Waller waved at two men in their wagons as they passed on the street. "Shouldn't take you more than an hour or two to get to Lula's place by the road that leads off to the east. You know how to get there?"

"I had a horse once when George Beecher got married. I rode it over there for the wedding. Yes, sir, I know how."

This raised the question of borrowing the horse. "Whatever happened to it, Jimmy? Your horse, I mean." It was a gentle reference. Waller Dunbar, with all his dignity and tranquil attitude, would never have implied a wrongful deed.

"Well, sir, I sold him. When I got my job with Frisco and I knew I would be working at the depot, I managed to find my boarding house where I live now. I believe you know it, Mrs. Gray's Boarding House about a mile west. I walk to work. Easy for me. So I sold my horse. I hope you don't mind me taking your mare. I'll take good care of her, I will."

Waller patted the young man on the back. "She's been to Lula's house before. I bet if you lowered the reins, she'd know the way." He extracted his watch from his pants pocket and stepped over to a window where a lamp was shining, where he could read the time. The dial was smudged with lint so he spat on his finger to clean the face and then he pressed it against his shirt. "We'll expect you early, now!"

"Goodnight, then," and with that, James walked away silently, hurriedly, to prepare. Much was on his mind, especially, his brother's new incentive for his own family, and too, his concern for Daisy and the event that she was ready to bear her second child any time. And Mrs. Perryman! She would know what was happening. Mr. Dunbar did say that she was in Sapulpa to talk to him and finish the quilt. He did say that. Lula was there, attending to matters that dealt with Maple Street and her father's new house and property. She sat in a sewing circle fostering her own talent for piecing together those little octagon shapes from her own mother's dresses. Malindy had said that Lula threaded the needle for old Mrs. Stidham who lost an eye in an accident. She joked with them. One of the seamstresses was Mrs. Menifee whose weekly dissertation was a disapproval of what her husband intended to do with his program of hunting expeditions. By now everyone on Dewey Street was aware of his group of ten men who were rambunctious with their sorties for white deer. "I remember you said you had white deer on your property, Mrs. Perryman," Mrs. Menifee said just before she punctured her forefinger with her needle. Immediate attention saved the material from a drop of blood.

So at the time when Richard Childers applied for his job in Muskogee, and after Daisy moved from the two rooms above the blacksmith shop, Lula Dunbar Perryman managed to survey her own expanse of territory. She was organized without being manipulative, disciplined without any trace of commandeering those around her. She rode her own horse over her ranch and attended to matters that Ralph Collins suggested to her as need of repair. She looked pretty, astride her black mare, trotting with her foreman, joking when she could, and noticing from time to time this reticent man was finally able to laugh out loud at some of her antics.

"Pete told me at supper last night that the mare was about to foal."

"Yes, ma'am she is. He may be the one to tell you when. I just didn't rightly know, I guess." Then, on their way back to the barn, he said, "I guess you know Mrs. Covey's son-in-law's horse was the daddy."

"So far as we know, yes. He wants to use him as a business, I suppose." She changed the subject. "Are you planning on slaughtering two or three hogs this fall, Mr. Collins?"

"Two ma'am. Two are really going to be big ones! And we're going to have a fine harvest this fall, too."

"Thank you Mr. Collins," was her reply as she dismounted at the barn and patted her horse. Pete was there, ready to remove her side saddle she admired, mainly because it was birthday gift from Moses two years ago. "Take good care of it will you Pete? I might give that to your wife one day!"

Blushing as he carried it to its frame, and unwilling to comment any further,

Pete nevertheless chuckled, much as she would laugh at some of his own jokes.

Lula did laugh outright as she straightened her jodhpurs. She decided, as they moved toward the house, that the additional comments from her foreman at this time were important to her. She always listened well to him as she did when they stopped at the well to take a drink. "Oh, say, I guess you saw Papa's mare at the stile block. Jimmy Childers rode over this morning and I plumb forgot to tell you. You might want to say hello to him. I'm glad it didn't rain after all." She removed her hat and fanned herself. "I'll have dinner ready in about another hour. Tell the boys."

The dogs walked with her. Once through the noisy gate they went their own ways with the exception of Ol' Don who always walked upon the porch all the way to the screen door. As usual, he curled up there and took his noon nap.

"Well, Daisy," Lula said as she placed her hat on a peg on the kitchen wall, "did you explain all about the new job in that railroad?" Lula verified her wood supply at the stove, "What's that package on the table?"

James stood from where he had been drinking coffee. "It's that quilt your father said was yours. Something about your birthday." He presented it to her.

Lula untied it. "My birthday is two months away yet. But I already knew what was coming because I helped make it." Her eyes roamed over it in silent pleasure. "Mighty pretty it is, too!" Carefully she refolded it and placed it in a chair.

"We've been talking," commented Daisy. "If I was to have a boy, I want to name it James. If I have a girl, she's to be called Virginia."

"Virginia?" Lula asked, as she continued her preparation. Daisy looked at James for help. "Our grandmother was named Virginia." he confessed. "At least, from what I can remember our father talking about her. I don't remember her and I guess Dick doesn't either."

Lula noted often that conversation of any depth, of any significance, were always destined for her kitchen. It was a habit that appeared from nowhere, so long ago, originating by Moses himself who made sure that the big breakfasts would be on time. While Lula cooked his pancakes or sausage he sat at the same table in his strong chair by the window, the same one on which she stowed the new quilt until she could take it to the bedroom. Dot and Cozetta were there, sleepy, until their father would take them on his lap.

Conversations with her foreman were best in this kitchen, whether he was reviewing for her all the requirements pertinent to the ranch or merely laughing at jokes perpetrated against Pete or Laredo. It was in this kitchen that she learned she was pregnant with Edith. The guests on that particular day were the Fred Clintons who were over to prescribe a new medicine for Laredo's bad cold and to have dinner that Sunday.

"Mrs. Perryman, you come to see me at my new location real soon and I'll tell you for sure. But as far as I am concerned you are again with child!" Lula could still hear those words as she patted the baby on her head each time.

And so the habit persisted. The family always gathered in the kitchen to talk. Some vital issue inevitably was the topic. The heat of today's cooking, since the oven was baking a roast, was no detriment to good conversation. The windows were open.

Again the dogs barked their signal that someone was arriving. From their favorite shady spots in the yard, they soon gathered on the south lawn except Ol' Don who was content to remain where he was.

"Jimmy," Lula said, wiping her hands on her apron, "go see who it is, will you? I'll ring the bell for the men." She was able to discern arrivals by the tone of her dogs' welcoming, and for this one, not a warning bark, but a congenial yap. Undoubtedly, they recognized the buggy and its passengers.

After ringing her bell resoundedly and waving to Laredo, she walked to the stile block to see for herself who it was. The sun was bright and hot. She had to peer under her hand at her forehead to shield the glare.

"Who is it?" asked Daisy through the kitchen window.

"Looks like Abner and Oliver. Yes, that's who it is." She joined them.

Pete noticed the arrival too for he was soon at the block. "Howdy, Abner," he laughed as he took the reins. Oliver first jumped down and ran to the house.

"You still not married, yet?" Abner joked, stepping to the ground. The dogs ignored Oliver who had disappeared, and surrounded the buggy. Abner tried to pet them all.

"That's all right. I hear tell you are going to marry again, yourself." Pete moved the buggy to the shade of the nearest tree. "You got a new horse, here?"

"Same ol' horse and buggy Pete," came the answer. By this time Lula was at Abner's side, smiling broadly. It was always a glad moment when they were together. "How are you, Lula?" He saw James on the sidewalk. His greeting was joyous. Dot and Cozetta came running from the porch to their uncle, glad to see him. "I got a message for you, Lu." Abner grinned as he lifted one niece while the other one trailed along. "It's from Winfred Jordan."

"What does that ol' scalawag want now?" she laughed.

"He says he wants to marry you!"

Lula chuckled at this, giving her brother-in-law another hug as they went through the front door. "Oh, he does, does he?" Her glee filled the hallway. "Is it because I am a good cook or because I have a ready-made family?"

They congregated in the kitchen where Daisy was about to set the table. "Hello, Daisy," Abner said, but was inundated with kisses from his nieces. Oliver was at the well bucket for his second drink.

"Comeon, now, girls," Lula herded them away to the table, "finish your dinner so I can fix ours. Looks like my Saturday is going to be busy. Why don't you and James go into the dining room wo wait. This kitchen is so hot and we'll be ready in no time. I already rang the bell for Mr. Collins and the boys."

Oliver replaced the dipper and stared at Daisy's protruding stomach. "You want me to have a boy or a girl?" she asked. To this, with a chivalrous gesture he softly replied, "boy!"

"Oliver," Lula said, "you want to help Daisy with setting the table?"

Abner and James went to the back porch instead. "When is the baby due, Jimmy, do you know?"

James, who was quiet all this time, glanced at Daisy when they left the kitchen. "Oh I imagine, in another monthly, maybe or more. I think she was waiting to get back to Sapulpa. She told me she had no place now except at Mr. Dunbar's house, of course.

"She could have it here. Lula wouldn't mind." Abner then reminded himself "of course, I may be speaking out of turn."

Oliver offered to set the table out of sheer hunger more than being a polite helper. He already looked into two bowls to see what was ready to eat.

"Go wash your hands and face first," Lula recommended and he happily obliged.

James was unusually quiet. He could not dismiss his sadness in not being told by his brother himself. Muskogee was a far distance and on the train by the way of Vinita, transfers were necessary in both directions. The schedule, as he had learned it, dictated an all-day trip and he could never afford the time away from his job. So he sat aloof and still and listened to Abner recount the events at the House. Emma and Ella still objected to the idea that Mayme concocted regarding the upkeep of the farm and the White House. This was strange for in ten years James had erased much of the momentum of living with Mrs. Rachel.

Abner found a moment or two to talk to Lula because she found time to listen. Poised as she was in her preparation of her food, she sat down at her kitchen table by the window and watched how Abner carefully sat opposite her.

"All right, young squirt," she said, wiping the perspiration from her forehead, "you look like the cat that swallowed the canary." She noticed that Oliver returned and had stopped to talk to James on the porch, having completely forgotten to set the table.

"I think I do have something to say, yes, I do." He brought one leg over the other and stared at Lula. I think maybe you should get another husband."

Lula laughed, more strongly than her ususal chuckle. "What have you and that Mr. Jordan been up to?" She saw Daisy walk to the porch and had not heard what Abner had said. "Who is doing the proposing, you or Mr. Jordan?"

Abner, too, laughed at this. "I was just the delivery boy who just might agree with that man. He's a mighty nice man." Lula rose to attend to another chore but Abner reached over the table to stop her. "Lula. Wait a minute. You got a home, now, for yourself. You need a man to look after you. You can't run this farm by yourself." They stood facing each other. "I also know the kids need a father." From a distance they heard the three men talking by the well.

"You've got a lot on your mind, haven't you?" Lula started to remove her apron. "I suppose you want to marry me?"

To this Abner blinked his eyes and grinned. "Well, I hadn't dismissed the thought."

"Oh, hadn't you?" she smiled. "What would Miss Goody-two-shoes say to that, I would wonder! Miss Lucy probably would come out here and scratch my eyes out!" She returned to her stove and began to dish the food. "Let me tell you, Ab, that I guess I am all right as I am. I can't deny I need a man around here and you know what I mean."

"I mean what I said, Lu," Abner replied handing her empty bowls. "I just want you to do some studying about it."

Oliver bounded through the back door. "I forgot," he said, and began his little errand, placing plates and silver. The men were coming through the noisy gate.

Lula stopped her work and pulled Abner aside, out of the line of traffic as everyone passed through the kitchen. "You are just about the best I know, Ab. I always thought so. You got a good idea and I won't dismiss it." By this time her apron was on the back of a chair and she was firm in her gaze.

"You don't even have to wait three years like our women do." That was Abner's last remark. "I mean, you're a white widow."

"I know that Creek law," she said quickly. "Now, let's go eat dinner." She noted, even yet the urgency in Abner's face, "Your little brother is already at the table!"

Lula, with the generous help of Daisy was ready to serve. She grabbed a towel and dried her hands as she moved her men into waiting chairs. Abner removed his coat and placed it on the halltree as James sat to his right. Ralph Collins waited until Pete and Laredo were seated before he was certain that Lula would join them.

"Go ahead and sit, Mr. Collins," Lula offered, "and I'll say Grace. Still standing, she lowered her head. "Bless us, O Lord, this food to our use and us to Thy service, and keep us every mindful of the needs of others."

Oliver was the first to reach for the potatoes. Directly, in the middle of holding the bowl of beans, Abner broke the silence of passing food. "I just forgot! I plumb forgot!" He jumped up, pushed back his chair, and raced for the hallway. Everyone sat mystified and waited for his explanation. "I got a letter for Daisy," he called as he pulled the coat from the hook. "I got it right here!" He returned, excited, to the dining table, waving the envelope.

"What on earth?" was Lula's refection as she sat.

In a sudden coughing fit brought on by too sudden a sip of water, Daisy rose and moved away from the table. The others were surprised by this quick surge of events. James instantly rose and patted Daisy on her back. "You all right? You okay?" He lifted her glass. "Here. Take another drink. Careful now."

Between fits of loud coughing Daisy managed "You open it, Lu...I can't...just now."

Lula stood to obey. She took the envelope, turned it over but saw no return address on the other side. "You want me to wait?" she asked, but saw that her sister was able only to signal that she continue. The others resumed eating.

Lula opened the top with a careful finger while Daisy observed, still coughing and spilling water. Immediately, Lula felt all energy drain from her as if water was escaping from the bucket at her well. A great moan filled the room as Lula fell into her chair. She dropped the envelope but clung to the letter. A sudden silence abounded and even Oliver sat entranced by this strange moment. Others stared.

With her hands at her lips after taking another sip, Daisy glared at her sister. "What is it, Lu?"

At her side, Abner look the letter from Lula's trembling hand and read it quickly but to himself. The letterhead was from the railroad company which hired Richard. It was dated at the bottom some two weeks ago. The writer, who Abner was to determine the manager, was sorry to inform the family of Richard Childers that he was killed in an accident at a construction site west of Muskogee. There was some reference about the body at a local mortuary. Apparently, so the formal letter stated, Mr. Childers had tried to assist a waterboy. In doing so both of them stumbled over pieces of track. They were crushed when a heavy load collapsed on them.

Daisy looked from Abner to Lula, put the glass on the table, and searched Abner's eyes again. "What is it, Mr. Perryman? May I read the letter?"

Chapter Eighteen

The young Indian who carried his Bible in his right hand paused at the corner of Fourth Street and Boston Avenue and verified the time with his new pocket watch. He admired the new wooden frame church as part of the accumulation of homes and businesses. To have a church there, also, was propitious. Like so many men of the past thirty years, he remembered almost daily that this whole area developed more so only in the last decade. On this day the breeze was hot for June was half over and no rain was the everyday expectancy of everyone.

An exterior sign printed in small black letters against a white background announced the worship services. The name of Reverend Hubert Broyles was still there although the congregation knew that he and his wife, a Perryman from Muskogee, had long since moved to Philadelphia. Robert Shaw had an appointment at this church with the present minister. It was obvious that no one had taken time to erase that name and replace it with Dr. Kerr. Below this however printed with authenticity was the date of the church's beginning, October of eighteen-eighty-five. Also on this sign was the word Presbyterian.

Before entering, he was interrupted by another Indian who was passing and who knew him. While stopping to wipe perspiration from his forehead this old man looked twice at Robert and then placed his hat on his head as he greeted him. He asked in Yuchi if he were Robert Shaw, but then he repeated it in English. "You are, aren't you?"

"Yes, I am."

"It's been oh, five or six years, I guess, since we met. I am Wildcat. I live in Sapulpa." They immediately shook hands and entered the lobby to escape the summer heat. Removing his hat, Robert tried to place this elderly gentleman with long braided hair, black boots, and a clean white shirt tied at the neck with no cravat. Then he realized this man knew his parents, for the Shawnees and the Yuchi were close friends and all of them were allowed to live in the Creek Nation. It had been a long time since his parents died.

"I was at your father's funeral. That was long ago. I never did know what happened to you." His beautiful eyes were clouded over with a glassy stare but his smile was ever present. "Your sweet mother was a sister of my wife. I bet you never did know that, did you? That makes you half Yuchi! You look well and happy, Robert. I remember you."

"I don't think I ever knew that, no, I didn't." Robert was captivated by this occurrence. "Mr. Wildcat" he continued. "I've been away at seminary. I don't know many people any more in Tulsa." He paused to think of what to say. "The Creeks were good to us, weren't they, taking us into their care like they did. I feel a little out of place now, born before all that trouble in Okmulgee when all the strife and bloodshed of the Muscogees occurred, and the impeachment of Mr. Legus himself."

Then, Robert realized the man standing before him was living history. His stature and bearing were proof of all that had happened long ago.

With the front door to this church open to allow air to circulate, this old man glanced toward the street and slowly smiled. "Well, it was sure nice to see you again and I ..." and he reverted to Yuchi, continuing with a remark that the Great Spirit may always help you. Mr. Wildcat squeezed Robert's forearms, turned, and left. Robert watched him depart southward along the dirt street.

It had been a long time. Many months. The Wildcat family was not a big one but everyone for one reason or another had heard of them. It was much like the Beaver clan who had stemmed from one of the Perryman sisters. Like his own parents, the Wildcats were received into the Creek Nation right before the Civil War when the entire land was desolate.

Being Shawnee who now spoke three languages, Robert had taken his surname from his bloodline. He was most fortunate and he expressed his gratitude everyday in prayer. Before he entered the sanctuary, while he was still hypnotized by Yuchi words, he heard the reedy sounds of the small organ as played by a lady with her back to the pews. A new treadle type, the instrument had become the center of attraction when first it was installed. Prior to the Broyles' departure for the east coast, Mrs. Ida, as she was known, filled this entire building with her music. With the windows open on a day like today, these sounds penetrated the intersection.

Robert halted midway in the aisle while this organist finished her practice, closed the hymnal, and placed it to one side. She noticed him as she stacked some music.

"Oh, Mr. Shaw," she exclaimed, "I didn't hear you come in. I do think Dr. Kerr is waiting for you. He's in his study." She turned on her bench to face the pulpit. "I'm glad you made a safe trip back to Tulsa."

Reverend Kerr appeared at the far south side of the room. A tall thin man with a clean face, he was the first to admit that everyone in Tulsa should now possess a Presbyterian accent, as he put it. "Except for the Methodists and the Baptists, of course." The organist laughed as she opened another book. "Come in, please. You may continue, Mary, if you wish. We won't disturb your playing. I'll keep my door slightly ajar, if you don't mind."

"When did Reverend Broyles leave? I guess I didn't know."

"Oh, I think possibly in eighty-eight. For a while this church had no minister. Loughridge went to Texas. I've been meaning to change that sign out front but I can't locate any artist, or painter, with a paint brush." He grinned at that.

The study was as simple room with two windows, both open to hickory chairs near the door, the reverend first, then Robert, with his Bible balanced on his lap by his hat. Dr. Kerr removed his glasses as he pinched the bridge of his nose. "In this second summer of this new century," he began, selecting a handkerchief, "we certainly have a lot to be thankful for." He cleaned his lens.

Robert was comfortable in his chair. "I was surprised to see Tulsa growing as it did."

"We've been incorporated since 'ninety-eight, I think it was. But I'm not one to follow progress in that sense." Reverend Kerr crossed his legs and nodded to a picture hanging on the wall to his right. "Being a city now has its problems with a great deal of crime, yet I just preached about a month ago about Reverend William Haworth. That man's strong feelings about lawlessness in this village led to a brief career. One Sunday night he rallied against the sale of illegal drinks. Frankly, I wish I had been there. The following night, as he crossed the street from a store to his house, he was knocked down from behind with a gun butt and left unconscious. That happened, I believe, while you were out of the nation."

Dr. Kerr folded his arms and waited a moment, silently making his appraisal of this young Indian. He opened a drawer in his desk and produced a pad of paper on which he had written a quote. "I'm aware of the Creeks. Even Reverend Loughridge had his problems. He had reported that an old chief said to him, and I don't think this opinion was solicited, 'We want a school but we don't want any preaching; we find that preaching breaks all our customs, our feasts, ball plays, and dances, which is what we want to keep'." He folded the pad and placed it in his drawer. "Well," and he returned to matters at hand. "I am more pleased to hear that you did well at seminary and that you wish to become a minister but I am saddened to know that you had to deliver a funeral the moment you got home."

Robert placed his Bible on a corner of the desk which had nothing on its top except an unlit lamp and two pencils. Another breeze sifted through a window. He balanced his hat. "I'm sure you know the Perrymans, Dr. Kerr."

"The Perrymans." The minister hesitated, for so many references passed rapidly through his thoughts. "Ah, yes. I performed the marriage ceremony a year ago at Mrs...."

"Mrs. Lula Perryman. At her ranch."

"Now I remember, the marriage of young George and a Miss ...oh, dear, I forgot her maiden name. My wife attended too. Only we didn't have an organ there. No music."

"Then I'm sure you already know of Mrs. Rachel, the mother of the groom?" Robert preferred to supply background for the minister. "The funeral was for a young man who, at one time, lived at the Perryman home south of town. He and his brother were orphans there."

"Oh yes, yes! A commendable gesture," Dr. Kerr was pleased to know of whom they were speaking. "A most gracious one indeed. We know of her generosity. So many Perrymans, though."

"I had just arrived back home when I was called to deliver the memorial service. I've known the Perrymans for about fifteen years, and Abner Perryman knew I was home again."

"Then I take it there was no church affiliation?" The good reverend cleared his throat. "I don't think I heard of this funeral, myself. Not at this church, I mean."

Some children ran by the window. Before Robert could answer and while their attention was drawn outside the room by their laughter, the music ceased and they could hear Mary as she secured the organ, pulling down the guard cover over the keys and pushing back her chair. A loud noise ensued.

"Are you all right?" Dr. Kerr rose.

"It's nothing," she answered, "I just dropped some music."

Ever since he was a child, Robert was eager to learn more about religious background of that famous family. He knew Abner had many aunts and uncles who had long ago professed the Christian faith. While at Tullahassee he discovered the hymns translated into Creek. One, maybe two, uncles were destined to become preachers themselves. Reverend Kerr was already aware of Josiah and he knew that Thomas was still in Washington D.C.

While the minister excused himself to see if the organist was all right, Robert recalled what Lula herself said of her church attendance. "I go to Tibbens Church," she said "located just one mile directly south of my land." During the funeral, that was all he could discover at the moment.

Robert Shaw thought, too, of providing a service to the area of the nation in which he matured. Fortunate as he was at Tullahassee under the aegis of his instructors, learning all the lessons they could offer, especially with the quiet and shy Shawnee children, he was grateful for diligent study. His eyes were tired all too often, reading by lamplight far into the nights, and the teachers mad him stop when he did not particularly wish to do so. It was better, they reminded him, that he read by morning light when he would enjoy it.

Throughout his college work and with him at his desk was an artistic pointer given him by Miss Robertson when she had recommended that he continue his education. Only sixteen inches long, it had no tassels but it was niched with an Indian design of red and brown loops that encircled the piece from tip to tip. The mission was certain that with the help of a scholarship Robert would be able to attain his goals. And it was because of the mission that he had introduced himself to Reverend Broyles before he resigned and moved east.

Prominent on his mind was the changing political situation of his adopted nation. A look into the faces of those children still playing outside the church reminded him of several facets of this. He was never quite certain how all the change which he had never foreseen but which he could perceive, affected his total psyche.

Not very many mourners attended Richard's funeral. Abner arranged it as well as he could possibly do so. His sisters and their husbands did not present themselves at the funeral parlor. The Cussetta Cemetery just northeast of Sapulpa, off to the right of the main road to Tulsa, was not large nor was its upkeep super-vised. Weeds and thorn bushes were plentiful and rocks of all sizes were every-where but it was a resting place for many Indians. George junior, with his wife of one year, said he represented the family. Pitifully, the crowd was small.

Driving the large carriage for Lula, Daisy, her baby, and Waller Dunbar was Ralph Collins. On horseback, close behind them, were Pete and Laredo. Daisy was so obviously ready to give birth that Lula thought it best she remain at home, but she insisted on this journey. Dignified, quiet, and beautifully attired in a mourning garb of her tribe, Rachel Perryman elected to travel with her son.

"In God's sight, Richard Childers lived a life that was planned by the Almighty. We do not judge his reason for the accident that separated him from us. With so much change now in this nation, it is difficult to see just how this Indian boy had been able to fit into the realm of mortal things. But God knows Richard by his first name just as He knows all of us, even to the number of hairs on our heads."

Robert spoke of the family that survived Richard, but he did not mention any more reference regarding the change that still was haunting him. He preferred to remain apolitical. He was not all assertive with opinions that dealt with what their chief should do or of what he should ignore. But he did remind the mourners that even Richard at that tender age was yet a waterboy at heart.

All alone now with the bitter realization that he had been acclimated to that condition with a brother he no longer had, James stood at the rear of the cemetery to await the departure of the meager crowd. Reluctantly he saw Daisy leave with Lula, with Mr. Collins and others. He wanted to do so much for this woman he loved. That was most apparent in the eyes of Robert Shaw who stood with him. One by one each gathered dirt in his hand and gently dropped it onto the coffin. Then they dispersed, stepping into a void which, even now with Robert sitting in the pastor's study, could not be remembered.

Dr. Kerr returned and apologized. "She is all right. She just dropped music when the portfolio opened and all those hymnals fell with it." Before he sat again, he poured a drink of water from a pitcher on a table near the door. He extended a glass to Robert but he declined. Before he closed the door he did see that Mary was all right.

"Now," he coughed, as he sat in his chair behind his desk, "please allow me to pass on some opinions I now have to the elders so that we can offer you a stipend for sermons as, say, an interim."

Robert stood, holding his hat. He reached for his Bible from the desk. "Thank you, sir."

"As for your request in your letter which you wrote to me recently," and the reverend clasped his hands before him, "I shall be honored to begin lessons with you on the scriptures. I have even begun to plan this adventure for us. The life of Paul, for example, is a good place to start." Robert smiled. "Do you have your teaching position secured yet?"

"Oh, yes," Robert was thrilled. "Miss Huntsman told me that such a decision was affirmed just yesterday. I am to begin this coming session in September and that the first week is to be started right after the wheat harvest." He hesitated before he disclosed what had been a strong factor in hiring him. "I speak a little Yuchi as well as Shawnee. That helps, according to what Miss Huntsman says." The pastor stood. "I might add the children nowadays all speak English. The majority of them, anyway, I mean."

After an agreement on a time for lessons, Robert left the church, Bible in hand, but with a gnawing pain that somehow he failed to provide the kind of sermon for the funeral that he really had desired. Lula Perryman came to him that afternoon, with the hot wind blowing her gray bonnet and the dust from the dirt that lay beside the grave.

She extended her hand. "Thank you, Mr. Shaw," and she was speaking for her sister as well as for James. Daisy, holding her baby, with tears in her eyes and in agony with her pregnancy, could not utter a word of any kind. "I've known about God a long long time ever since we came from Kansas. I learned a lot from my mama. She died when I was about twelve. The move south into this part of the territory was rough on her, I guess. So my Daddy says. I had never heard that remark about God knowing us all by our first names. I think that is nice! We're all going to the White House to eat. Don't forget. And you're welcome to come to my place, you know. Out in the country!" She gave his hand a squeeze.

"Oh, yes, ma'am, thank you."

"A lot of people came way out here to Cussetta cemetery," Lula continued as she protected her bonnet against the wind. "Not may, but some from where James works." One by one, as James stood transfixed, each shook his hand, gave him a soft pat on his back or a gentle embrace. Mrs. Gray from her boarding house, with her husband, Bert, was there.

Winfred Jordan attended too. At one point when the wind swept over them all, tossing a gentlemen's hat on the ground, Lula glanced at him as he retrieved it and his eyes met her line of vision. He was respectful, nodding his head with a greeting that she felt was directed just for her. Later with his black hat in his hand, with the wind ruffling his curly hair, he managed a handshake with James and offered a quiet word of sorrow. This tall cowboy waited while Lula completed her conversation with Robert. He spoke to Laredo. "I was born in Texas, myself." But both Laredo and Pete were dumb with a grief they had not realized. Standing under one tree, waiting as they were, each was silent and unresponsive.

Winfred Jordan walked to the carriage. 'Excuse me, ma'am, Mrs. Perryman, but I did want to say hello to you." Then, in a soft voice, with hat in hand, to Daisy he waited until she was comfortable in the rear seat. "My condolences, ma'am and I am so sorry for your loss."

That was a side of Winfred Jordan that Lula admired. "That was kind of you, Mr. Jordan," she whispered, adjusting her bonnet after tying the straps under her chin.

"Who is driving you back to Mrs. Rachel's house, ma'am?"

By this time Waller Dunbar had positioned the horses to a point in the road leading from the cemetery. "Our daddy is, Mr. Jordan, but thank you just the same." Lula was correct when she thought that this cowboy wanted to tie his horse to the rear and take the reins himself. "This buggy is daddy's two-seater. It took a big one for all of us." Waller, saying nothing, slid into the driver's seat with Lula to his left. "But I tell you," and she chose her words as if she had suddenly thought of them, "you're welcome to tie your horse on the rear and sit in the back seat with Daisy and the baby, that is, if you like." She glanced quickly at her father who managed a sly grin without turning around.

"Why, thank you, ma'am. I reckon I will." And as he did so Lula smiled back at her father before she supervised this idea. "You can scoot over, Daisy, and make room for Mr. Jordan. When he was settled, she continued. "You're welcome to come eat with us at the White House. Everybody's welcome!"

Soon, the cemetery was empty of mourners save the two Indians who shoveled dirt into the grave and packed it well on top. James rode with Abner in a small hack along with Oliver who had remained politely quiet throughout the day. They were to the rear of George's more comfortable buggy with his mother and Orphia. By this time everyone had gone, the wind subsided, but the heat was thick. It would be a good hour before they were all at Mrs. Rachel's house once again.

Mayme Shirk elected to be at her mother's house for the sole purpose of preparing the dinner. "I don't want to go to that man's funeral," she told everyone. "I'll stay here." With the kitchen door open and the windows raised, the heat from the big stove was unbearable.

Stewart Shirk, still a man of devious thought, made a point to arrange his business so that he would be present in case additional plans may arise that would be concomitant to future sales of Lula's land. He came through the back door bearing three more logs which went directly into the stove.

The Shirks, already frustrated, had arrived that morning early, from their own home, having left their baby boy there with an old Indian woman who professed a gentle hand and loving care for a bite to eat. Mayme never broached her opinion of the two Childers orphans. She never endorsed the compassion of her mother's care for any and all such unfortunate children. Mayme had remained aloof to the needs of others. She and her husband were here solely for the purpose of monitoring Lula, of listening to her, of trying to sift out any possible motive which her brother's widow may possess that could lead to remuneration for only the Shirks and for them, alone. They had no idea where Emma and Ella were that day, for that matter.

"I don't know why in the world Lula has to have all that attention," was Mayme's byline, her trend of thought, and a theme that permeated her life these days. "She's always here at the house whenever she comes to Tulsa. Emma told me that Mama always asks about her, muttering Creek all the time.""Why did we have to come here today, anyway?" Stewart sat at the table after he placed the logs in the stove. "You didn't care for those little kids when they were here, did you?"

Mayme joined him in a chair nearest the window and fanned herself with a tea towel. While she chatted she kept her eyes on the potatoes she was frying in her mother's iron skillet. "They were just two more kids Mama took care of. They didn't mean a thing to me. The one who died married Lula's sister. You know the story." Mayme grew tired of reiterating a tale that she undoubtedly explained to her husband more than once.

"You know what I think?" Stewart picked up a fork and used it as a dirk in his gesture. "You know, I think Lula knows what you did about getting that money from Mr. Simmons." She gave him a stern look as he removed his dirty hat and flung it over a chair. "You know what I mean!"

Mayme turned directly to him, her eyes fixed on his. "I went to Muskogee and talked to old man Simmons. He's my agent and I can talk to him, to give Mama..." and she repeated her phrase more succinctly, "...and got him to give to Mama that money. It was Mama who put her X on the line." She rose, went to the stove and stirred the potatoes.

Her husband waited and then finally chose his words. "You didn't go and buy any tombstone, did you?" She did not look at him. "You told Emma to tell your Mama that you bought his tombstone. For that kid. Didn't you?" He flipped the fork on the table. "I bet a hundred dollars they aint no stone there."

She replaced the large lid to the skillet and folded her arms as she stood above him. "During a three-day funeral, lots of things can happen. That Childers kid was buried in a cemetery so far out in the country that no one goes to anymore, not even Mama. As far as that is concerned, we got our own burying place. It was Mama who wanted him buried at our own place but Emma and Ella and even George said no. Ol' Mr. Simmons won't be around much more, any way. He may be a good agent but he doesn't need to know any more than he does. Now, I am going to set the table 'cause it's late." She gathered plates and stepped into the dining room. "You go and see that the lamps have enough coal oil in them for tonight."

Stewart Shirk reluctantly did what he was told and selected a large lamp with a dirty chimney from a table, raising it to see for himself the amount of liquid in its glass base. He could say no more for he knew that this method to manipulate his mother-in-law's funds was illegal. It was no more of an unlawful system than any of his other adventures.

For the second lamp, for there were always two lamps on the dining room table, he made his way into the front bedroom where his son was born. The whole house was hot so he opened the front door and peered through its screen, past the porch into the yard to the pond where three horses stood, nibbling the grass.

Placing the lamp on the mahogany table in the hallway, he surveyed, for his enjoyment, the interior of the parlor with its tapestry on the wall, the sofa and chairs that old Perryman had shipped from St. Louis. All of this house manifested a modest wealth. To Stewart, the plainest type of comfort in this home was far better than any element he had in his own.

Mrs. Rachel's children had played in these rooms. The orphans too were here, something which Shirk could not appreciate. As he touched the tabletop, the doilies, as he glanced at the pictures in their dark frames, all he could see was the material wealth they represented. Even Stivers managed to possess a better house on Cheyenne Avenue. Mayme always said their allotment of land was too distant from Tulsa. Many more stately homes were growing in the city.

The sun's rays crept through the screen door bringing with them the swift flight of summer birds across Stewart's line of vision. Before he could lift the lamp he saw from the far horizon two buggies making their way from the main road onto the pathway, past the pond, and past the quarrelsome ducks. He recognized the first belonging to Abner but the other one, a newer model with a rear seat, was foreign to him.

He stepped onto the porch holding the screen door open for just a second. "They're here." he called loudly as he retreated with the lamp in hand. By this time the dogs took notice and formed their happy reception.

Mayme lit one lamp and placed it on the dining table. At that point, she stopped to determine how much time she would have before they all sat down to eat. Their horses had to be watered and fed and the ususal delay when they would come to the front porch and wait while additional information would be exchanged and opinions would be reviewed. Her mother would be tired even though no one would realize that. "Go wash," was her quick remark to Stewart.

As he passed her, stuffing his shirttail into his pants, he reminded her again, as if she needed it, of their pact never to mention anything about which they spoke, whether such was innocent remarks or just deft reasoning. Straightening her apron, she went to the front door and tried to smile.

"Supper is going to be on the table so hurry and wash." It was a general statement to everyone. And then she noticed Mrs. Rachel, she called, "Hello, Mama."

Silently Abner and George passed through the house to the back porch. Orphia consoled Daisy in the parlor as James remained in the hallway, immersed for the first time in a long time in memory as one once again in a house wherein he found nothing but love. No one, no one at all, would quite know what all that meant to him. The hallway was still dark; the halltree was tall and still near the front door where he remembered it had always stood. This passageway still went the entire length of the house ending as it did at the kitchen.

Once his brother smashed his right thumb when a door banged shut on his hand. He cried so loud and long that he found consolation only in the soothing and loving care of Mrs. Rachel. "Did I ever show you my two thumbs, Daisy?" Richard had asked her once when they had become acquainted. "See. Look! The right one is smaller than the left. I'll have to tell you about that some day!" Standing in this same hallway, so full of other sounds, James could still hear the great Creek words that calmed the child.

Oliver slipped into the house quietly and went to the kitchen to get a drink of water. He found the bucket empty,

"We needs water, Oliver," Mayme announced. "Go get some."

Lula and her father remained at the side of the carriage for a while as Winfred Jordan waited alone at the porch rail. "Here comes Robert Shaw up the path behind us Papa. Why don't you say something nice to him. That was a fine sermon, I believe it was. That's a pretty mare he has."

"I'll do that, Lu, I'll do that!"

Mrs. Rachel grasped her daughter's hands in hers and looked gratefully into her face. From her eyes passed a smile.

"Oh, Mama," Mayme whispered in soft English, "everything is ready. I'm just glad to help." They made their way to the kitchen. "I'm glad you're home, Mama. It's getting dark."

James, with other sounds still echoing sauntered into the parlor where Daisy found a soft spot on the sofa. At a window, he saw that Lula, her father, and Mr. Jordan had congregated at the Welcome sign. Robert Shaw joined them after he tied his reins near Shirk's horse.

Daisy rose to greet James after she placed her young Richard on one end on the sofa. Because of pain so excruciating she screamed aloud as she collapsed on the rug. James was at her side.

Instantly Lula fled through the front door with attention riveted on the emergency. "You men, here, carry her into the bedroom now." Lula called as if it were a casual greeting at church. "Looks like we're going to have a baby!"

Chapter Nineteen

While Sapulpa was celebrating the Fourth of July with a picnic and horse race, Lula's Homestead was recovering from hot summer heat. Ralph Collins with Pete made a one-day trip to purchase groceries and feed. When they sat down to supper that evening, each had a description of how the town changed. Again, dust was everywhere for hardly any rain fell to alter the temperature. The city's newspaper commented that many of the female population were complaining about how they had to lift skirts when crossing all the streets. Merely managing to pass from one sidewalk to another or from a store to the next one was an involved task. Too many liveries sprouted in each block. Already, other complaints registered the fact that the fair town should have its streets in better condition. The wife of the owner of the newspaper, who was herself widely known in better social circles, longed to return to a civilized city. So the paper was sold. She, with her discontented husband, returned to Kansas City.

"How did you know about the ladies and their skirts?" Lula teased Pete.

With a fork full of green beans poised in mid-air, he was thinking fast. "That's what we heard, didn't we, Mr. Collins?"

"I brought you a copy of the magazine you wanted, the one printed in Muskogee. There was a notice about deer season beginning November first until February first, nineteen-three," said the foreman who explained that deer season was without dogs, this time. "No dogs allowed. Just hunters."

In the few weeks following the funeral, James Childers was quiet for some time. He remained aloof from the Dunbar residence to which Daisy retired with her two children. Her second child was a girl. To respect their original plan she was named Virginia, a pretty baby, darker in complexion than her brother who, by now, was a year old.

The unbearable heat was stifling but the trees bordering the avenue where Waller Dunbar's new house was located provided much needed shade, especially during the small private ceremony when their house was dedicated. Daisy thought James might be attending but he was not there.

Unlike the big city to its northeast this little thriving village entertained citizens with horse racing each Fourth. On this particular one, unlike the previous five, this race was specifically designed for the ladies. Dressed in traditional red, white, and blue, the current riders were more concerned with their appearance in fancy hats and garments than who might win.

James stood on the edge of this crowd wherever his roaming might take him. Every business was closed, even the post office. Luckily, no train was scheduled on that holiday. He stopped his roving to listen to Hall Miller's band play from the stand that Waller Dunbar and two others built especially for this day. For a short while, Mrs. Gray's two children walked with him for they had become great new friends at the boarding house.

"We might as well keep this bandstand," W.P. Root proclaimed, "because it will be good to have for the political rally coming up this fall." Mr. Root was noted for being Sapulpa's optimist on every topic. He could even visualize the banners.

A few Indians spoke to James expressing grief, saying hello, or merely making conversation. From a distance, he noticed that Mrs. Gray and some ladies had prepared a barbecue. "Go get Jimmy, will you," she said to one of her children, "and tell him to come eat something."

"No train today?" was the quick question from jovial old Mrs. Davis who lived down the street from the boarding house.

"No, ma'am, Schedule is tomorrow for arrival and then back north the next day, ma'am." This recognition brought him out of his daze.

"My dear Jimmy," this kind lady remarked sweetly clasping her hands over his. "In time, the healing process will erase all heartache. Trust in the good Lord, my boy, and He will answer all your needs." At this point in time, such was difficult to hear. She smiled, nodded her head, gently touched his cheek with a soft hand, and disappeared in the crowd.

A day or so later James found himself at the blacksmith's shop, walking to the rear beneath the trees that Richard enjoyed. The long flight of steps, the broken board, and the screen door at the top prompted a full measure of memories.

He sat on the bottom step much like his brother did, for all the stairs were in shade at the end of a busy afternoon. He removed his hat and wiped his face again with a red bandana, looking westward, allowing himself to dream. Elbert Claythorn came to mind, the head of a Creek family whose land this was. Mr. Claythorn, tall, regal, with a happy smile was ill. He had lost a lot of weight. His wise eyes were sunken into their sockets. His family was kind to Richard and Daisy. These two rooms upstairs were just enough for them. But now James was sitting there, all alone.

And then he saw the turtle resting among the tall grass to his right as if the round animal had decided to wait, after all, for the return of his master. Spreading the blades with a long stick, James saw it clearly just as the turtle saw him, each respecting this short time element as if it had been a gift, as if even the turtle knew to respect the Great Spirit and to give thanks for the bugs and insects, the grass, the leaves that he would eat this day.

Gently, James reached to place his fingers around the handsome shell, watching its head retreat quickly for protection. The weeds, the shaded wind, the rolling hills to the west together completed the quiet homage that only an Indian and a terrapin would appreciate.

Yes! Ever so carefully, James placed the turtle nearer to him to pet it, as Richard would have done. Laying his hat to the other side, he studied the scene. Presently, the turtle extended his head and legs and attempted to crawl.

James, with ideas racing in his mind, made a sudden decision. Without so much as an additional glance upward he lifted this quiet terrapin and placed it in his right pocket. He pushed his hair back in place and grabbed his hat. He walked fast, declining a ride when a man in his wagon stopped for a short while to talk. He preferred to walk. He held the turtle in front of him as he paused at the steps of the boarding house where the Gray children played. Both of them were elated! "A turtle! Where did you find a turtle?"

"Want to find a place out back where I can keep him? It's a sign of good luck." Whether it was or not, James had no time to prove it. So off they scooted. He

watched them go and then he studied the face of this little creature and noticed
how its eyes blinked. This would be a fine pet, he thought, a nice tribute.

"We got a place," they reported, "let's go!"

When James returned to work, Arnold Covey was present to offer more condolences this time from his mother, his sister, and a cousin whom James met only
once. Arnold was a bright fellow with a large scar on his right hand, the result of
an unfortunate accident at the house. "We were sawing logs, my brother and I," he
explained one day a year ago, "with our big cross-cut saw, he on one side of the
log, I was on the other. We were just about through when he put it on the long
end. My brother, that was Wendell, told me to knock it off with my foot but it
wouldn't budge. so I reached down with my hand and then, that's when the saw
jumped off and cut me pretty bad."

Two days later, James was surprised to find that Pete was standing in the
lobby of the depot asking for him. He had his hat hanging around his neck at his
back. With a big smile he extended a hand for a shake, as congenial as he always
was.

"Hi ya, Jimmy!" and he removed his left glove as well. "I come into town
today to get grub, mostly to deliver this to you." He took from his shirt pocket a
note inside an envelope addressed to Mr. James Childers, Sapulpa. I.T. "This here
is from Mrs. Perryman. She was going to mail it but it would have taken two
weeks to get here. So I bring it." He was all smiles, laughing. "I bet you anything it
has to do with her birthday coming up!"

Putting aside a clipboard, James stepped to the window for better light as he
opened the note. He leaned against a partition that separated one section of his
working place from another. It was indeed from Mrs. Perryman, in her own hand-
writing, inviting him to come to dinner on the twenty-fourth of July, nineteen-
three. He verified the date by looking at the large commercial calendar from Davis
Lumber Company. Its black numbers could be read easily from a distance all the
way across the freight area. Picking a pencil from his desk, he circled this day and
wrote her name above it. Her note did say, also, that she hoped he could attend,
and that he would not have to be working, but if he did, to cancel the train in and
out of Sapulpa. The humor of this letter brought a smile to his face.

"Is that what it say, Jimmy, huh, am I right?"

James took a moment to verify the arrivals and departures because Arnold
Covey had written them on this calendar with a black crayon. No train, Not for
that day. He wondered if Daisy would attend.

"It says that all of you will be at the Beaver place east of Sapulpa. Just tell her
yes I'll be there. I know the house."

The day before the celebration, the men of the Homestead decided to clean the
milk room, rake the floor of the barn, take inventory of the hay bales, and groom
the cows.

Pete was the weatherman. Coal Creek was flooded by a sudden downpour of
heavy rain in the previous day. Even this day threatened rain again. After he gladly went to Sapulpa, he was sent again on another errand, this time to Jenks. He was
to locate Winfred Jordan and give him the same message. "Okay," he told Lula,
"but I know only one guy in Jenks. I imagine I can find him." Lula agreed with
him.

And so he did. Pete's acquaintance was a short, awkard cowboy who maintained a living at a local livery full of horses but noted for having one of three bath-

tubs in town. This basin was popular. Eventually with this happy soul's help, Pete came across Winfred Jordan working atop a second level of a building which faced the town's other two-storied business.

"Here's a letter for you, Mr. Jordan," Pete yelled standing well below the carpenter. "I don't like high places."

With hammer in hand, Winfred stopped and answered. "Wait a minute/ I'll come down." He accepted the note once he was on the ground. "You mean Mrs. Perryman wrote this herself?"

"Yes sir, she did," and again Pete was grinning, "and I took one yesterday to Sapulpa, I did, to Jimmy Childers."

Jordan pushed his hat back on his head, stepped to a shady spot under a tree and read the epistle.

"I know what it says," Pete was still grinning.

"So, the lady has a birthday, does she? It's the twenty-fourth and she wants me out at her place early that morning"

"Yes sir, her day is the twenty-fourth, all right. She told us she will be twenty-four on the twenty-fourth of July! And we're all going to Mr. Beaver's house for a big dinner. Can you make it?"

He scratched his head. "That's real soon, but I can make it all right. Tell her yes. Tell her that my birthday present to her is that I'll be there."

Pete did not understand the remark. "Say that again, Mr. Jordan? You want me to tell her that you will be there too?"

"That's right, Pete. Tell her that I'll be there bright and early and I'll go to the Beaver place with you. Now, I have to get back to work before it clouds over. It's going to pour down, Pete!"

"Okay, Mr. Jordan" Pete said, taking rein. "I'll tell her that, all right, I will. Thanks a lot!" And off he rode.

This carpenter resumed work but his mind was not with the others that afternoon. Once, maybe twice, he misplaced some nails and when he dropped his hammer and had to descend once more to retrieve it, he decided that Mrs. Perryman was indeed on his mind for more than one reason.

He mentioned Mrs. Perryman to his father that evening but that was not the first time they had discussed the young widow. With the elder Mr. Jordan and the brother also all three called upon this charming lady just the previous Sunday afternoon. Winfred Jordan was pleased to find an amicable relationship among the lot. "You go and have a good time, Winfred," his father told him as his brother agreed. "She looks like a right nice lady. You look out, if you don't marry her, I will."

The twenty-fourth was the day when the creek was high. He was there early that morning amid the dark clouds from west to east. He had polished his saddle and cleaned his boots and put on a new shirt that his brother had given him for his own birthday last month. So he rode to the Homestead through the main gate and trotted merrily past the stile block. The dogs escorted him to the barn. Lula was at the long clothes line gathering sheets that had been out over night. She waved to him as she saw him pass her, unable to call out with clothes pins in her mouth.

Pete grinned broadly when Winfred dismounted at the barn door. The drover was grooming a tan filly. "This is the horse I was telling you about, Mr. Jordan. She's my favorite. I'll race her against you any day, rain or shine. You know, they have a race in Sapulpa every Fourth of July but this year it was for females only.

Only females could run. Imagine that!"

"A race, huh?" Winfred answered as he released the cinch. "I heard all about that race. Next year, maybe, Pete!"

"I was meant to ride fast, I do believe that, Mr. Jordan." Pete put the soft brush in its place on a narrow shelf. "I'm thinking about entering her on the Fourth next year, I will. That Fourth should be for men. Here. Let me help you."

"You got that new colt yet?" Winfred folded his blanket.

Laredo noticed his arrival and appeared in the barn. "She is about due, all right," he said, coming into view from the west door. He placed a pitch fork against the wall of one of the stalls. "You just missed a good breakfast. Rain or shine I'm going down to take my bath."

Coal Creek, which approached Lula's property from far to the north entered the border of her land under a bridge that was already too narrow, a wooden flat structure which had always been for six years. the source of accusation concerning a crime. There, the water itself, low but flowing, came from a tributary which no one had ever known. It was, some said, merely southbound heading into that portion of Moses's allotment that Lula had recently sold to Mr. Atkins and which had upset Mayme and her husband.

This bridge had no side rails. The flat boards held together by cheap nails eventually served all travelers as a simple means of crossing this small stream. It had been a scene of a quick murder in the mid-eighteen-nineties when so many such crimes were never solved; far too many of them occurred. The deputy marshalls including Mr. Sizemore, could not depend upon proper procedure to help. The nation was too large.

Arnold Covey often found time to talk to James about his family. One of the stories concerned his oldest brother Bradley Covey who was accused of knocking the construction foreman for this little bridge in the head killing him outright. "He always did have a temper, Jimmy, he always did." The crew attested this to his shocking red hair but Arnold also had red hair and he was just the opposite of his brother in temperament. For a long while, that same crew which went on to finish the bridge, began to call this stream Covey Creek. No one actually ever learned how the name Coal came to be. After it was completed, small as it was, a sign was nailed to a tree at the west end with the newest name printed in awkward letters with the date, eighteen-ninety-five.

This east-west road became the bridge road. The stream widened as it meandered southward arriving just west of Moses's barn. It was bordered by a forest of blackjack trees, some elms and a great many cottonwoods. To the west, on the other side, a host of tree stumps, cut low, was all that remained where Moses and Ralph Collins, with Laredo and a team or ornery mules, had cut down the existing trees and sliced them into sixteen-inch lots for Lula's firewood. Much of this supply still remained just as it was stacked on the far side of the bunkhouse near the wash stands.

It was at this location where the stream was deepest that the men would swim as often as possible, not a long time in it, but enough to keep clean. Lula always knew when they were there. When the breezes were coming from the northwest their laughter would fly over the short distance to the house.

As Laredo and Pete approached their lodging with Winfred Jordan that day, Lula stood on the back porch to provide information concerning the long events ahead of them. "Where is Mr. Collins?" she asked with a ladle in her hand covered with chocolate batter.

It was Jordan who answered as the others continued. "Why, I believe he's still in the barn, ma'am. You want to go swimming with us?" This question came at such a time that Pete, the last in line, gawked at the cowboy and his remark.

Lula chuckled more loudly than usual. "I'm taking my bath up here, thank you very much, after I put my cake in the oven." She posed a question to this cowboy as she opened her screen door. "Can you dance, Mr. Jordan?"

Pete fled, removing his shirt en route.

"Why, yes, I can. I'm a good dancer. Can you dance, Mrs. Perryman?"

"Rain or shine," she laughed, "that's why I'm going. When I learned the Beavers were going to have the dinner there on my birthday, I was tickled pink. That's where we're going, Mr. Jordan! So you better scrub clean." And with that she returned to her cake.

It was a recipe that her mother-in-law gave her four years ago. All that time, she had considered Mrs. Rachel her most trusted friend even though Moses had been on the nearer side of God's Presence, a phrase that Josiah Perryman himself had used. Lula's English was, mysteriously, understood by this quiet matriarch. This Indian managed to do and gesture just what Lula wanted, It was amazing. And it always kept Mayme on the outside of that relationship, peering into it with envy.

"I want our first daughter to be named after my mother," Moses had desired. and so she was. Mrs. Rachel had become a multitude of blessings for all with whom she came into contact. The Book of Genesis in its translation by Thomas Perryman rested on a table in her parlor with Creek artifacts, pictures of her family, and a set of long horns. Emma would read to her at times in the afternoons when the sun was shining its best and a breeze serenaded both of them through an open window.

Lula poured her batter into two round pans, leveled it with a spatula and sighed heavily as she stood to admire it. After she slipped the cake into the oven she sat down at the table with Cozetta. She reached to clear some honey and bread from the child's chin. She attended Edith who was standing in her crib in the dining room. At this early point in time, when it seemingly had stopped, her mind shifted from one side of reality to another side of reverie. She absentmindedly fanned herself with a damp tea towel, with the window open as far as possible next to Cozetta.

She once again was supposing in her mind new tactics she must mobilize just to make certain that life did indeed continue, that she was still young, and very likely that she had grieved too much for too many incidents that she had saddened herself with the recent death.

Richard's passing conjured other such events. Often, when roaming through her house late at night after the girls were asleep, she could hear a rain owl call, or she could imagine that Moses, himself, was about to come through the back door after milking or after sitting and joking as he did with the men in the bunkhouse. She had heard the rain owl call as before, or at least she presumed that she did.

While her cake was baking, while the men were bathing at their favorite place the dogs barking brought her out of the reverie once more. Lula was here in her hot kitchen with her children, with yet another day ahead of her, with some food to take and with a new friend down there getting clean.

She was fortunate. She forced herself to accept this statement. Mrs. Covey had

come for a short visit with her daughters just last week in the heat of a busy afternoon. This strong woman had borne seven children in eleven years, the oldest of
whom was Bradley who disappeared and was never seen again. To the embarrass-
ment of her girls, she reflected, "It's a cross I have to bear." Perhaps that amount of
sadness was responsible for this lady's aged countenance, as if she were twice her
chronological age. Lula was nine years her junior but the rigor and toil of housekeeping made her sixty. Wisps of grey hair about her face confirmed this. Her
daughters reflected hardship. There was no Indian culture in that family. The
Coveys were intruders. Many full bloods came to that decision.

It would not be that way for Lula. Part of her stamina was her unyielding
strong determination. She spoke to every flower along her east fence and to every
seed she put in her garden. She doubled her fists at first sight of adversity. She
made herself stand tall, even now, when she rose from the table, smoothed back
her hair, removed her apron and tossed it aside as she lifted Cozetta high in the air,
prompting a delightful squeal!

"Where is sister?" Lula laughed as she carried little Cozy to the door. "Let's go
find Dot so we can get ready to go!"

This was a refreshing gesture as if Lula had no care in the world, as if she had
all the time in the world which she did indeed have! On the back porch she pieced
together more plans for them. Once she had placed Cozetta on the ground to run
and play with her sister, she walked to the gate, turned around where she could
see the entire house from a rear view with the dogs who were so mystified by this
stance that they stopped their playing. With a cloudy sky becoming darker she
breathed silent prayers with words that explained her happiness. She was the mistress of this Homestead now. This was a home, now again. The dogs, sensing that
all was well with her found a reason to scatter again; off they went to the barn.
Only Ol' Don stayed to receive his usual pat on the head.

She passed through the gate and walked to the well with a bucket she carried
for her bath water. That well made her aware of who had planned it, that Moses
was once again walking down the path from the barn, that Corzetta and Dot were
there pleading to depart for the Beavers now, begging for a drink when they saw
that their mother poured from the well bucket fresh cold water. "Come, daughters,
let's go get ready!"

The men splashed and played as if they had all day. Pete and Laredo were
naked, waist deep, passing the soap from one to another. Their guest ducked himself to take away the soap from his face as the bell sounded. Then, their bath was
finished and they grabbed their clothes. The shade from a large tree was cool for
the most part but as they hurried toward the house, heeding Lula's call, Laredo
broke away from them to report to the foreman.

"The new carriage is big enough for all of us. I checked on that already. Mrs.
Perryman told me yesterday she wanted to take it today." The bell sounded again.
They knew it was time to go.

While Lula fed the dogs and cats, Pete slopped the hogs. "You look real clean,
Pete," she called, "you stay that way."

"Yes ma'am, I intend to. I don't have time for another bath."

Winfred Jordan went back to the barn to roll the carriage out to the stile block.
Laredo hitched two horses. "Mr. Jordan," he began casually, "you ever want to go
back to Texas?"

"I thought maybe at one time I would, really, but not any more. I was too young when daddy and the family left. Texas doesn't really mean that much to me anymore." They worked the harness. In no time, the girls in pretty calico dresses and matching bonnets, with Lula sporting a big umbrella, hastily marched down the sidewalk.

"Mrs. Perryman, ma'am," interrupted Ralph Collins, "if you don't mind, the carriage holds six. I will ride along side. It will be more comfortable for all of us. Laredo can drive for you, ma'am, unless you prefer Mr. Jordan to take the reins."

Lula was too busy with Edith and the girls to explore the reluctance she sensed in her foreman's voice. "Very well, Mr. Collins," she said as she settled the girls in the rear seat.

In the current year, different roads began to take shape throughout the nation. The wagon trails became one-lane highways, the cow paths grew to be thorough-fares such as the one down which they moved southward. The main road just east of Lula's house extended all the way to a wide place in the area that the Indians called Kiefer, only one-half mile south of Lula's property line. There, another east-west roadway started merely as wide ruts but proceeded over one hill after anoth-er until it reached Sapulpa, a distance of some ten miles. With the day cloudy and dark the journey was pleasant. Within two miles from where they turned westerly, and before the road encountered steep hills which bordered on the east side of the blacksmith's shop, Samuel Checote Beaver maintained his allotment of land in the Creek Nation.

From what Lula learned by listening to Moses, his father's sister, Lydia, mar-ried a Beaver. Together they raised only four children and Samuel was their first. If other children were born but died in infancy, no one ever knew. Presently, only twenty-nine years old, he married a lady known as Aunt Ollie. Their modest home stood on the south side of this road but it was commodious enough to entertain a host of Indians who came that day from as far as Broken Arrow. None knew that this day was also Lula's birthday. It just happened that way.

After Samuel, two other boys followed, Amos and David, and the last was Alice Mary. They were all there attending their father's celebration.

Alice Mary had married a man name of Robert Atkins and, together, they were proud of Charles who pushed up five fingers when anyone asked how old he was, and Helen, now three. It was Alice Mary, sitting in a rocker on the front porch, who first saw the two horses and recognized Lula's carriage. Laredo was driving and slowed as he prepared to turn into the wide space between tall trees. While Alice Mary knew of Lula as the widow of her late cousin, she did not ever have an occasion of becoming fully acquainted with her. She, herself, had become Mrs. Robert Atkins and had raised her own sons and daughter so independently from much of Indian culture. As she stood to welcome the new arrival, her brother, Amos, came to stand with her.

Laredo halted the carriage as he saw Amos raise his hand. To their left under the trees were five smaller buggies that brought others to this event. "I'll just park over there, Mrs. Perryman and rest the horses. Let me help you out, ma'am."

One by one they dismounted and a conversation ensued among them all, with Pete and Winfred Jordan remaining aloof until they were introduced. Amos admired the girls. Lula walked to the house with Alice Mary where she was able to say hello to Ollie, a mere twenty-two and obviously pregnant. "Well now," Alice Mary smiled, "let's sit here. I'll get more chairs from the kitchen while the men get acquainted."

"I bet you didn't know you'd be seeing so many people, Lu," Ollie said softly as she cuddled a baby in her arms. "Oh, and this here is my Alice Evangeline, Lu, just less than a year, now. I got my three-year-old running around here some-place!"

She patted her pregnancy. "I hope it's a boy this time." Dot, Cozetta, and Edith gazed in wonder at this stranger.

"Ollie, honey," Mary Alice interrupted, "today is Lula's birthday. I don't think I knew that, Lula. Lot of people are here today so we'll help you celebrate it." She was sincere in everything she did and said which was the trait Lula remembered of this cousin. On that cold day when Mary Alice represented the Beavers at Moses's funeral, she was most gracious and honestly reverent when even family members were inclined to be less so. "Oh, before I forget it, a Mister James Childers arrived not more than half an hour ago and is here, someplace, I'm sure."

The three ladies sat in their chairs and fanned themselves as they surveyed the crowd. The sun disappeared behind heavy clouds that crept in from the west. "Run and play, you two," Lula spoke softly to her daughters, "be careful. And don't get dirty." She lifted Edith onto her lap who whispered that she was sleepy. A refreshing wind passed over the house and barn and in a matter of minutes it threatened a positive rain.

"Well, I guess it's finally going to rain after all." It was Ollie's comment that brought affirmative replies.

Winfred Jordan milled through some men whom he recognized from Kiefer and Broken Arrow, Indians all with a quiet manner and easy gait. From this con-vergence he found his way toward the porch railing and tipped his hat to the trio.

Lula was first to speak, "This is Mr. Jordan. He's my guest you might say. The more the merrier." Alice Mary smiled and Ollie nodded her head. "Now if you'll excuse me," Lula continued, "I'm going to try and find Jimmy Childers. Come on, Mr. Jordan. No use talking to those two." Alice Mary laughed more loudly than did Lula.

Despite the stronger threat of rain, other ladies had two tables set under the trees on which the food was placed. Several full bloods, in white shirts and tall black hats, were silent as they monitored every movement these efficient women made. Samuel Beaver, with an eye to supervise this preparation, paused in his rounds to speak Creek with these men, Lula waved to him as they sauntered past.

Laredo and Pete made sure the horses were watered while Ralph Collins leaned against the carriage. Lula gave Edith to his care so he placed her on a blan-ket on the ground. "Guess you can have my umbrella too, Mr. Collins. It's going to rain."

They walked further. "Mrs. Perryman, ma'am," Winfred Jordan cleared his throat as he spoke, "I thought this was just going to be a little party for your birth-day." He gestured lightly to everyone. "I bet we see close to thirty people."

"I thought you'd be noticing that, Mr. Jordan," Lula grinned "I don't know where or how it all started. Moses once told me that visitors can come and stay two or three days. There's a stomp dance in Tulsa near the Council Oak but we aren't to have one here. A fiddle and banjo, maybe, I hope. You did say you like to dance, Mr. Jordan?"

"Oh, yes, ma'am, I do. Yes, I did say that, ma'am."

"Well, hang around, Mr. Jordan. The majority of these Indians here, like our music, I guess. Fiddlin' is so contrary to a stomp dance. Those full bloods over there, for instance, like to watch." Thunder sounded far to the west and again the crowd looked to the sky. "We might not have a fiddle at that."

A few of the men tipped their hats to Lula and offered a greeting and a smile.

"Howdy, Mrs. Perryman," said a tall Indian with his large black hat in hand. "I'm Homer. I was at Moses's funeral. I'm Legus's grandson. Nice to see you, ma'am."

"Mrs. Perryman, ma'am," another young Indian spoke up with a shy maiden standing quietly beside him, "glad you could be here. I'm glad the rain didn't drive you away."

That threat became more apparent. When the breezes turned cool, Lula let her bonnet fall to her back so the wind could dance in her hair. More clouds crowded others from the west.

Edith began to whimper softly and Lula saw that Mr. Collins gathered her from her blanket to soothe her. "I'll go see what it is," Winfred said, and left Lula beside the food tables.

"Oh, Mrs. Perryman." It was James Childers appearing from out of nowhere. Hat in hand, his smile was practically nonexistent. "Looks like we're going to get rained out. Oh, and Happy Birthday, ma'am. that from your Papa and from me, too."

Lula noticed his neat hair and clean hands. He was quiet. She expected that, seeing him for the first time since Richard's passing. "I hope you find people here you know." She made a point to look into his eyes. "I think I saw some of my daddy's carpenter friends. He was teaching one of Wildcat's nephews to wield a hammer! That's him over there if you want to say hello." More thunder sounded. "It rained on my birthday three years ago if I remember. I guess it can rain again." Her eyes shifted to the carriage, to the two men who juggled Edith. She had stopped crying and both the men were pleased. "There's not much we can do about rain though. Never turn it down, I always say."

One by one as if it were an overture to the storm brewing, big raindrops lightly fell across the whole side yard underscored by the neighing of the horses. Ollie and Alice Mary stood on the porch and beckoned children to come inside the house.

"We should have known a storm was coming," one of the women grumbled "now what on earth are we going to do?"

"To the front porch!" With this command they recruited the men to lift the tables. A few full bloods hesitated. "If you don't help, you don't eat!"

"I'll go check my horse, Mrs. Perryman," James said quickly. "It might rain a long while. I'll tie her to your carriage."

At first the rain was not as severe as it seemed. The drops were steady and cool, just enough to keep everyone dispersed under the trees or on the porch.

James untied the mare and walked her toward the carriage. He was about to select a spot when he came face to face with Abner Perryman. He was so startled that he could not speak. They were under stout branches of a tree that protected the carriage and its contents. Pete had covered the cake with an oil cloth he found in the hamper.

"I saw you with Lula and Win Jordan. I am glad you came." Abner was dressed in a new suit, sprinkled as it was with a profusion of raindrops, holding his hat in his left hand and with his right, holding the arm of the girl he was escorting. "James," he began, "this is Miss Lucy Stivers." He was under the umbrella she held to shield them from the rain. "Lucy, I want you to meet Jimmy Childers who lived with us ten or so years ago. I guess it was, I can't remember."

Over the noise of the crowd James noted a bit of laughter that was crude and forced. "How do you do?" she giggled, "I'm mighty glad to meet one of Abe's friends of yesteryear." The threat of dampness came so intermittently that no one was at all concerned. Both Ralph Collins and Winfred Jordan removed hats and smiled. Pete climbed into the rear seat.

Lucy Stivers was never one to be a wallflower, not at any occasion. Instantly, as if to dominate conversation, she put her hand through Winfred Jordan's arm and proceeded to ask a variety of questions, keeping one hand on her new hat. Abner pulled Lula to a corner of the table where the food was covered with a table cloth from the house.

"I just bet," Lula spoke first, "that you are going to ask Lucy to marry you." She gathered her umbrella en route. "Here. Get under this, or we can step over under a tree there."

Abner hesitated but finally found words almost too soft to be heard over the palaver of those who began to form a line. At first, he thought the remark was a test of some sort. His first wife had died so suddenly. At the moment, he was not so certain he could remember the depth and beauty of that marriage. Frustrated, he gave her an answer. "Yes, I guess so."

She did manage to pull him away from the crowd. "You guess so? What's going on here?"

Abner pulled her farther from the others. "She asked me! And I asked permission from her father." The remark was so abrupt that Lula placed the umbrella handle in his hands and folded her arms. He detected a look of annoyance. "He's weird, Lu, a strange one."

She gave him a stern glance. "Do you know very much about that Stivers family?" Lula was not cruel. She was never that when she offered a negative implication to any situation but Moses had taught her to be careful in social intercourse and never naive when it came to business transactions.

Abner took a deep breath. He did not know what he detected in her voice. Then, after someone greeted them and vanished, he added, "I thought you'd be the first to wish me joy, Lu." He glanced quickly to see that Lucy was still talking to Win Jordan. "Come on Lu. Be on my side. Gracie has been dead now these two years." Then, he added as if Lula had not already known, "Creek Indians are supposed to wait three years or is it four? I don't remember. I don't care!"

They stood there both very quiet, peering into each other's eyes, pleading for some kind of suitable answer. It was not a drastic situation but it did require some answer.

Lula blinked her eyes and with a gentle grasp of his arm, she apologized. "Well, it works that way with squaws so I suppose it works with Indian men who lose their wives." Thunder again blared at them from the west where a thicker layer of clouds loomed. "Of course," was all she could say. "Of course I do wish you happiness. Of course I do." Abner smiled again and embraced her dearly. They returned to the others and she interrupted his fiance. "Lucy Stivers, Abner here just told me of your decision to marry." This remark surprised them all including Winfred Jordan. "I do wish you good fortune, indeed I do!" Lula realized that this may have sounded too forward, especially when she also realized that Winfred Jordan looked directly at her. "The world is full of surprises, isn't it,

Mr. Jordan?" She reached for her bonnet and placed it on her wet hair.

"Yes, ma'am," he replied softly, "it sure is!"

Those in line balanced their plates and sat in different locations, under the trees, on the porch if there was room, and anywhere they could be comfortable. But the crowd dispersed because already the first wave of heavier raindrops peppered the dust of the fields. The low areas around the house gathered water.

Lula, her girls, her drovers, and her guest ate at their carriage where Pete had hung a cotton blanket on the side to keep out as much rain as possible. The leather roof protected them from the increasing downpour. Edith was still with them but Dot and Cozetta were inside the house. "Don't forget the cake," was Pete's glad remark.

"So much for the dance I guess," Lula shrugged her shoulders. "We won't have a fiddle now, I suppose."

From that moment, Abner was judicious as he introduced Lucy to only those whom he knew in the family than others. Some of this gathering were important to him. The Beavers were just as dear to him as other closer cousins. Lula sensed this. But Lucy was gushing with flamboyant remarks of kindness, while Abner, his hat squarely on his head looked embarrassingly to the wet ground at his feet. It was too apparent that many Indians ascertained how shallow this young social upstart was. And because they were Indians they said nothing. Presently, Abner and Lucy said their goodbyes to everybody, despite the downpour, and quietly departed.

"Abe," Lucy said trying to dodge the water splashing from the wheels, after they were out of earshot, "Abner, dear we forgot to tell them the date. Or did you?" She struggled to remain comfortable in the speed he drove the buggy.

"I'll do it." His eyes and mind were on the road, already muddy, and the rain was pouring. "I'm going to the ranch myself and talk to Lula. I'll do it soon. Hold tight, Lucy!"

She obeyed gladly. "Now you be sure and tell everyone the end of August. I'm going to the church on Tuesday and talk to that Mr. Kerr about it." She grabbed his left arm to steady herself. She saw his concentration and a firm jawline. "Abe, honey, you're happy, aren't you?" that was more a statement than a question.

The rain drifted in from the west but the wind blew it around from the south so Pete designed another panel with the other oil cloth that Lula thought to bring, tucking the edge between the frame and the roof. The rain was warm and did not deter any spirit. "Everybody sit down under here," Pete took charge with his invitation. They were glad they did for soon the light downpour became more of a summer storm. By now the tables, with the help of the full bloods, were moved from the wet porch to the front parlor. And, too, many who attended began to leave.

"Happy Birthday, Mrs. Perryman," James laughed as he held Edith while Lula cut the cake. She thought it is so good to see him laughing again.

"I tell you what," Lula said as she lifted a piece onto a small plate, "Jimmy, you may call me Lula. Everyone included."

Lula finished serving, saving a piece for herself. From her front seat vantage point she was able to see Cozetta and Dot waving to them from the comfort of a parlor window. "Oh, I don't know what to do! I was all set for the fiddle to be here with the banjo so we could dance." Once more, she untied her bonnet and let it fall to the seat.

"I tell you what we can do," suggested Winfred Jordan. From the rear seat he jumped down and pulled Lula to the ground, in the rain, before she knew what had happened. Pete, remaining in back with his piece of cake resting on his knee, was dumbfounded again by such antics. Laredo, in front, gnawed on a chicken leg. The perpetrator pulled off his hat and threw it to Ralph Collins. Then he placed his hands squarely on Lula's shoulders, looked directly at her again and after selecting his words carefully, he took a deep breath.

"Mrs. Perryman," he began, "with these crazy yahoos as my witnesses. I'm asking you to marry me. Will you do me the honor to become my wife?" He quickly glanced at Laredo. "How's that Laredo, did I do that right?" Then again, he spoke to Lula. "I've already spoke to your Pappy."

"You done that right, Mr. Jordan," Laredo shouted above the sound of the rain. "You sure done that correct!"

"I imagine you know by now I love you, Mrs. Perryman," he said as he blocked her attempt to climb into the carriage. "I don't have very much, I guess, but I do have my love for you rightly, that, I do!"

"Well now, Mr. Jordan," Lula paused, pushing her wet hair from her forehead, "I must tell you I've been thinking about this situation myself." She turned to her foreman in the back who grinned broadly. "Now, Mr. Collins, you listen to this." Stunned as he was, the foreman listened. "I'm going to say yes Mr. Jordan, yes, I will marry you. I just realized today that I do love you, you ol' cowboy! I'll say yes mainly because I'm getting wet out here in the rain!"

Chapter Twenty

In the heyday of the cattle business, when the Creek Nation reconstructed its council house with exterior rocks and thick interior walls, George Beecher Perryman selected a plot of ground less than one-half mile south of the Frisco tracks. This was at a time when his first son asked for the hand in Christian marriage of Louise Amelia Dunbar. This gesture gave permission to his siblings to follow suit. All of them did.

The elder Perryman, in his declining years, as was that century, with the permission of his wife, built a large two-storied structure for their home "in town" as their children identified this location. Its turret over the main entrance protruded well above the second floor, commanding the tallest vantage point of any building at that time in young Tulsa.

Facing east this magnificent house included a fenced front yard. At its rear, on the southwest portion of his land, Mrs. Rachel wanted a well so one was engineered and dug. It soon became a focal point of the village, the landmark that everyone appreciated. "Thirty-five feet deep," someone contended, but even others doubted that depth.

The House was well known for it was the only private home in that immediate area that became such a grand showplace. It was completed only four years before the century ended. Even so, the husband was not able to enjoy its outstanding beauty with its sumptuous interiors and its reputation for big dinners. He expired at the century's end, not in this House, but in the White House. This showplace became a large and empty shell for the widow and Oliver.

Mayme Shirk tired of her small cottage on her own allotted land with her baby and a disagreeable husband. She began to take matters into her own hand almost from the moment of her father's funeral. Later, the autumn of nineteen-two brought with it a refreshing sort of impetus. She outlined her plans to everyone who would listen. She would make certain that the noteworthy abode would no longer remain unoccupied. Her mother and little brother both returned to the White House for that is exactly what both of them wanted. Mrs. Shirk did not even think to consult with her two sisters nor did she care to mention anything to George junior or to anyone else, for that matter.

So, at a time when she managed to meet with her two older brothers at the House she felt compelled to voice her ingenious ideas. To comply, they agreed to rendezvous. George junior suspected some scheme but he was not certain. He did however ignore his wife's desire to build a home for only them. Armed with a possible idea, himself, he joined this sister to hear what she had to announce.

So Mayme Perryman Shirk, attired in the latest fashion of the season, parked her own buggy on Main Street, removed her white glove as she opened the tiny gate because it was dirty and proceeded into the house as if she owned it.

Abner Perryman, whose marriage was forthcoming soon at the church, as planned by the fastidious Lucy Stivers, was late in arriving that afternoon. He was to meet her at the church at five o'clock, escort her the short distance to the House and then, according to her calendar, go to dinner with the Reeds.

While Mayme waited for these brothers to appear, she sauntered through the entire lower floor, into the kitchen where her mother easily prepared abundant meals for anyone who was hungry, into the long parlor that always attracted the Important and Wealthy, as well as the poor and less notable. She ambled through the wide dining room making mental note of a portrait of Legus Perryman hanging properly over the elegant sideboard. Upstairs, she verified the bedrooms, the dressers, the beds, the carpets that her father brought from St. Louis. The original plan, somewhat forgotten now, was to move everything from the White House into this newer home. Tulsa was on the verge of growing into a bigger town. Everyone who drank from the well out back agreed to that.

Even though Mayme was able to dress well in the last year she still felt ill at ease in her own modest house. Something must be done. Before she could engender more ferment she noticed Abner on the sidewalk from her mother's bedroom window. She walked quickly to the landing where she called to him as he was about to disappear under the porch roof. "Go on in. I'll be right down!"

As Abner sat in one of the big chairs near the fireplace, Mayme lost no time hovering above him there like a domineering schoolmarm. "What are we going to do with this white elephant Abe? Mama's not here anymore. Only seven years old and it's like a tomb."

Abner was not so concerned. Mayme did not wait for an answer of any depth. She walked to one of the front windows that overlooked the dirt street from whence he had come. "You left the gate open, Abe." Her mind was, unusually, on Moses and what he would have said to her had he lived. Instead, what did echo in her brain was what he told Lula in the first year of their marriage. Shirk was never able to prove such devotion to her as what she had been able to perceive in Moses's plan with Lula.

Mayme allowed Moses's own comments to penetrate her mind more than once as they did now with her standing in the parlor. When her oldest brother had escorted his young bride into his own house that he had built for her, they had stood on the far west side of his allotment and looked to the horizon full of trees, the stream, and to the great barn.

"My land is as far as you can see," Moses told Lula, and then to the south, he acknowledged, "and just to the ridge of hills out there. I will need help with our foreman. I'll bring some Indians and white men to work our farm, and Mr. Collins already has Laredo with him. This belongs to us, Lula." That is what haunted Mayme. Her thoughts became audible. "I just wish Moses had never done what he did with that woman."

"What did you say?" Abner turned his head toward her.

"Nothing." Mayme dismissed her thoughts because she could see George racing down Main Street amid traffic. He managed to close the gate. As he hit the porch he stomped the dusk from his shoes. He saw his sister staring at him through the parlor window. She could see him mouth a question but she decided to wait until he was inside.

George bristled into the hallway and closed the door. "What is it this time, Mayme?" Then he saw Abner sitting, relaxed in a chair. "Have you called the whole family on some secret mission?" He stopped at the fireplace. "Where's

Mama?"

"I don't think she likes it here any more." That was Abner's quick response.

George took a deep breath and leaned against the hearth. "Sure she does." He was ready to ask questions. "Papa always made it more comfortable for her. Out there, that old place is so run down." He moved to the large sofa with its new anti-macassar doilies on its back. "I wish Emma was here." He looked at Mayme. "Have you asked Emma and Ella to show up?"

Mayme ignored them both. "I'm going to the well to get some water for us. It's stuffy in here." She left them and passed through the kitchen and to the rear path where a bucket and dipper were still waiting at the rope.

George sat on a quilted cushion and leaned back, putting his hands under his head. "I remember when Mama told us about seeing a bear." With a sly grin on his face he looked at his brother. "You remember that story? Mama went to the well one night and saw a bear!"

Abner rose and walked into the hall to look at the stairwell he always admired. Its bannister was intricately carved with a newel that was designed expressly for it. Hardly more than a week had passed after this home was officially opened that he and their father stood on the first steps to have a picture snapped by a roving photographer. "Where's the picture now?" He thought aloud and did not realize it.

"What did you say?" George asked, still seated.

Again, Abner ignored him. He placed himself on that step.

George laughed at his own memory. "A bear! Right here in town. Now, I've heard of deer roaming around, but a bear?" He was giggling all through his words. "If Mama had seen it at the other place, that would be more logical, wouldn't it? But this was downtown!" He looked toward the hallway but Abner had softly crept upstairs. The back door slammed and Mayme's footsteps echoed down the empty hall.

"I got a bucket of water and put it on the kitchen counter if you want any. I found some of her good glasses. They're still in the cupboard." then she yelled as she sat opposite George. "Abe, get down here, we want to talk." They heard his footsteps just overhead and, dimly, that he opened and closed several drawers in a dresser. "I want us to sell this place. It's a big house in a small town. Sapulpa is growing faster than this town. It's worth a lot of money. Mama is content to live out her days at the old place with her dogs and horses, her crickets and her ducks. She can have her memories."

"Orphia is pregnant." George announced this so casually that one could assume he was reflecting on how tired he was. The sudden statement did not inter-rupt his sister's trend of thought. She merely rose, stepped to the long mirror on the wall and removed her flowered hat. From her bag she selected her comb and began a ritual of rearranging the tresses that had fallen due to the wind.

When George repeated his words, she snapped. "I heard you. It just so hap-pens I'm going to have a baby too. Another one. And poor Emma. I just hope ours lives." She stood back to admire what she had done to her hair. "Emma told me last week she was pregnant again. Courageous soul she is!"

They heard Abner's slow descent, waiting on each step as he monitored the change in his view. When he came through the archway from the foyer, Mayme turned, placing her hat on her head. "When are you and that snip of a girl going to marry? I want to know soon."

"I'm meeting her here," and he looked at his pocket watch "in about thirty minutes." He was not thinking of Lucy but of Emma and her melancholy pregnancies. Apparently the sister was never destined to have children. Roaming around upstairs he tried to study objectively his family, all of whom at one time or another observed the construction of this House. With a multitude of people who admired the architecture as it was growing, from its foundation to the top of the highest roof, the siblings stood with their father and mother in critical appraisal. It was such a huge edifice, a monumental undertaking that received the respect of everyone.

"That house belongs to the Perrymans," people would say as they walked down Main Street. "Even the tiny wire gate to the sidewalk was imported."

Abner should not have been so exhausted, not at twenty-four. While the sister, vociferous as she was infrequently, prattled, Abner was actually thinking again of Moses who was the magnate of them all, the cornerstone, the paragon. Many times when they were on the range the older brother ventured to speak of their brothers and sisters but only to Abner. The cattle and land were fortunes to them all. They must remain wide in dealing with every transaction that came their way. "I don't know that I like Mayme," Moses had said.

They were all such young people. The reputation of this family was such that eager businessmen compared them to the new century. Since eighteen-seventy, the foundation for good business tactics was well established in the wide, sumptuous pastures all the way south to Eufaula and east to Broken Arrow."I wonder what is going to happen to that house," people would ask as they wandered by it. "Too bad about old George dying like that. and Moses himself going so strangely. In an accident, wasn't it, up in St. Louis?"

Abner covered his eyes as he resigned himself to listen to Mayme's pronouncements. She seemed too vague. Her words were overpowered by the vision Abner imagined once again of Moses standing there in the hallway, hat in hand, when this House was completed and resplendent with all the loving care that their father had brought to it.

Mayme broke his reverie with her caustic remark. "Well, I don't want to be here when Lucy comes. You'll have to attend to her, yourself, Abe. You and George both know I don't like that family. Stewart socialized with Mr. Stivers but her mother and I just don't see eye to eye." She manipulated her one earring and tightened it. "Abner, now listen! I want you and George and anyone else to know that this house is a burden to all of us. When Papa was alive it had some value. I'm going to ask Emma to talk to Mama about this."

George stood from where he lolled about on his chair, hardly ready to comment. "I'm meeting Orphia after a while. I'll mention this to her."

At the archway Mayme stopped. "You'll do no such thing. I want Emma to translate to Mama what we just said, first, before you go sharing it with anyone, especially Orphia. She's not very intelligent, I have to tell you."

George frowned. "What do you mean by that?"

"She's a dumb Indian, George. I thought you knew." She opened the door just as Lucy opened the gate. Squaring her hat, she quipped, "Here's your betrothed, Abner," and Mayme sped by her, only nodding her head in passing.

"Good afternoon, Mrs. Shirk," Lucy called brightly but it was too late. Mayme untied her horse and was gone. Abner was quickly at her side. "Hello my dear," she said sweetly. "What a beautiful entranceway." He closed the door as she nodded to George. "I have always enjoyed coming into this pretty house so often. My daddy can see it all the way from our front step over on Cheyenne Avenue. Did you notice the new street signs put up in the last month? This intersection, for instance, is Fifth and Main. My Goodness! The tallest house in town."

"Please excuse me, Miss Stivers," George said as he grabbed his hat from the mantle over the fireplace, "but I've got things to do. Goodbye, ma'am." He was gone as swiftly as his sister.

"Well!" Lucy removed her hat and placed it carefully on the table that rested below the front windows. She focused her attention on the man before her. "Dr. Kerr says that our plan is all right with him. We have reserved the Saturday we wanted before Thanksgiving. Nineteen-two has been a good year for us, don't you think? Let us be happy, Abner." She sat on the sofa, rearranged her skirt, and placed her gloved hand on the cushion beside her. "Come, sit down."

Abner did so, quietly, with no words.

"Now, may I say that I am very happy, very happy, indeed. Thanksgiving is not so far away at that. Mama is just as happy as I. Oh, I wish your Mama could speak English so they can talk. Together, I mean. Your Mama probably doesn't understand a word, does she? Mama wants to know," and she paused in her statement, "she wants to know, and so do I of course, why your Mama returned to that country house out there. It's..." and here again she paused, "it is so old, I guess, isn't it? When was it built?" She did not wait for an answer. She selected her words carefully. "My dear, if this house remains empty, why can't we live in it? It's here. It's downtown. The church is right over there." She started to say something else but Abner lifted himself with a breath of careful assurance that what he was about to say would not be too much of a surprise. He made his way slowly to the front windows peering into the mirror where, just moments before, Mayme brushed her hair. "I thought of that some time ago," he spoke softly, "and I'll pass this idea along to my brothers." then, in an effort to complete his thoughts, he returned to the fireplace. "I was thinking of maybe moving to Eufaula. Uncle Legus gave me some property. I have some property in Red Fork, too."

This startled the girl so abruptly that she rose and walked to him. He could see a glint of panic in her eyes. "Oh, Abe, now, really! Eufaula? That is so far away. Why not here? This is a perfect house for us and I know that your Mama doesn't want it anymore. I mean, your future is here, in Tulsa. The stores, the cattle out there." She returned to the table and reached for her hat and pulled him into the hall. "But let's go tell Mama and Daddy our good news. They're home, or should be. We can leave your buggy where it's tied and walk over." He could see she was eager to leave. "Come on, dear, let's go tell them what we've planned."

As they walked the three blocks, Abner was not listening to Lucy's gossip. His mind had shifted south of the city where Lula lived. It was there.

In the autumn of the second year of the century, Lula went about her business on her Homestead, with her acreage, with the barn, with the men who were loyal to her. More than once she thought about the foundation that Moses provided for her. She stood at her kitchen door and looked to the north, past the noisy gate, to her garden, past the bunkhouse, above the tree line. Her grief would reappear like tiny bits of bittersweet candy. But always the laughter of Pete, with his genuine smile, and the barking of the dogs, even the crickets at night would sing her to a sound sleep.

Last week she made one more trip to the little room that contained the clothes that Moses once wore. She particularly noted the boots, still on the floor where she left them when she and Daisy were there. With no more thought, she reached down and lifted them, one in each hand, and placed them outside in the hall. Then she closed the door. It was as if she could call upon memories at any time if she elected to do so. That room reflected all those who had come and gone, the mother she definitely remembered, pictures of Richard and Daisy for Daisy did not take them all, the gladness that was hers as she placed the coat on the dining room table in front of a surprised foreman. That evening, again, to an equally surprised fore-man, those boots became his possession.

"This is another birthday present for you, Mr. Collins about five months late. Go on. Take them. You can wear them."

And the century was already drastically changing as well. While she did see Moses in Abner's eyes, the way both of the men carried themselves, the way they both lifted bales of hay or brought in a bucket of well water or stood erect and respectful at a pow wow, proud to share Creek blood, her own father always told her to look beyond her immediate troubles.

This tall good-natured cowboy called Jordan came into her life. He was her future now. He was here, the breath of winter that manifested itself, sweeping into her life as a cold nip of a sudden surprise that made her stop and think again. It was a time to take down the portrait from the parlor wall of Moses and his family. It was a time to go to dances in Jenks and Sapulpa. It was a time to cook for a new man. Mrs. Rachel would understand.

The winds of autumn now spilled over her land. She no longer gave much thought to any of the people who had so recently populated her world, with the gentle exception of Abner and his mother. Somehow just those two managed to escape the obtuse relevancy of the clan. She was not a reader but she did come to a conclusion that with the coming of winter she felt she was passing from one chap-ter of her life into another as if she had just finished a small book of recent history. With a final turn of many pages she closed the book. That chapter resounded as an echo that died away.

But she would retain Abner and Mrs. Rachel, of course, as bookmarks for the next years ahead of her.

Lula even began to talk to herself, reaching the decision that, after all, such a habit was most propitious. She and Mrs. Covey discussed this once. Her father's new wife agreed, vocalizing one's thoughts, of mental prayers from day to day was not uncommon among many young mothers. Moses had not altogether disap-peared from her mentality. He was known to pronounce great and significant statements. If Lula should stop her daily toil and listen, she would hear echoed across the network of her psyche a dogma that Change is the only permanent pos-session one has. Moses told her that and he learned it from his Uncle Thomas. "Then I'm changing," Lula surmised.

Abner Perryman was going to marry the second time. The announcement appeared in the local paper from Vinita to where he and Lucy had gone to obtain a marriage license, at a time when he could conduct cattle business. Lula was not to think too stringently about the union. A second marriage for many people, Indians as well as white, was not uncommon. Mr. Winfred Jordan of course entered her mind. As part of the unconcerned attitude about people she did not enjoy, Lula hardly spoke of the Stivers girl anyway, except to learn as the days passed that this young lady, much her same age, was traipsing about Tulsa with loud rhetoric that she was marrying into the Family.

Lucy wanted the whole Muscogee Nation to know about it. She was disappointed by the four-line reference in the newspaper. One Sunday, Abner and she came to dinner shortly thereafter. "Dear," Lucy said when Lula served her famous chocolate cake, "why can't we have a much larger notice in the Chieftain?" And Lula did not say one word to Abner before they drove away in a new buggy. She vocalized, among other things, to keep her mouth shut. Dot and Cozetta stood there watching as the Buggy disappeared. "What did you say, Mama?" Dot asked.

And then one day when rain was drenching the entire land surrounding the house and barn, when Laredo and Pete were out rounding up the milk cows, Ralph Collins came onto the back porch, drenched. He scraped his boots and removed his old red slicker and slapped his hat against the porch pillar.

"I've made you some coffee, Mr. Collins, at least, some of what was left over from dinner today. Still good." Lula had a cup before her where she sat at the table. "Not much you can do on a day like this. Pete and Laredo okay?"

"We'll be all right," the cold foreman remarked, heaving a deep sigh as he pulled up a chair. When you going to marry that ugly galoot, Mrs. Perryman?"

Lula shoved the sugar bowl to him and chuckled, "You'll be the first to know 'cause I want you to be giving me away."

This brought a hearty laugh from the wrinkled face. "Giving you away?" he asked. "Why can't your daddy give you away?" He put two teaspoons of sugar into his cup.

"He's too busy having daughters!" She laughed out loud. "Fall is a good time for building houses and winter is coming on. Besides," she joked, "you got no family except us so I chose you this time." She monitored the change of expression that altered his eyes. He held his cup not by the handle but by the mug so that the heat would envelope his hands.

He sipped again before he spoke. "What do I have to do? I don't think I'm good at any of that stuff."

She relaxed when she heard that. "Just wait till we make up our minds, then take a bath, comb your hair, and I'll have a clean shirt for you." Their laughter was contagious. Cozetta strolled in from the other room to see what happened. After glancing at Ralph Collins with a grin on her face, she made her way to mother's lap. "We'll let you know so don't you fret yourself. Pete and Laredo will be there to hold your hat while you walk me down the aisle. I want all three of you at the church." She giggled once more. "We got to get Abner married off first."

"Well, I guess I can do that, all right." And so he did.

Waller Cornelius Dunbar with his wife and little daughter visited the Homestead earlier that week. They came calling, merely to sit in the parlor and learn all about the current agenda of the Creek Nation. He combed his large walrus moustache and placed himself in his favorite captain's chair next to the stove, drinking coffee as part of the ritual to keep warm. While Malindy crocheted, he and his oldest daughter exchanged stories.

Very recently, on a sunny day, Waller Dunbar drove James Childers to the Cussetta Burial Ground to make certain that the grass around Richard's grave was neat and trimmed. It was at a time when Daisy felt she should go, too. James smoothed the ground and moved some large rocks before he finally decided that they had done their best to improve the new grave. "Look here Jimmy," Daisy commented, "here's an old grave. The date on it is eighteen-seventy-nine!"

Daisy stood silently then, alone with her two babies as she watched him work. "That looks nice, Jimmy. That's pretty the way you rearranged the rocks to the edge like that." She did not wish to visit her sister on this trip this time. She felt, as did her father and others, that all time, efforts, and endeavors of any kind were at a hiatus.

This is what Lula explained to her foreman on that rainy day over coffee. She was astute enough to realize that he had more persistent questions on his mind. "My Papa is a good man and a good carpenter." She drained her cup. "Who knows when we will need him to building something for us!"

"When did you learn to milk, Mrs. Perryman?"

Surprised by the question but not by his curiosity, Lula rose to pour more coffee. "Just a little girl I think in Kansas before we moved south. Papa said we were on our way to Texas. We brought our own cows, two of them. We were intruders. Moses often used that word. 'Course Mayme didn't like it at all." She settled again in her chair by the window. "You know, I'm glad we came to I.T. I've heard Papa say time and again that if we'd stayed up there we might have been caught up in a terrible disaster. Up there in Kansas corn was sold as low as ten cents a bushel." She leaned back and laughed and with her right forefinger she signaled, "I can out-milk you anytime, Mr. Collins!"

Again he grinned and Lula was pleased to see this, "If you want some more cows like you say, you may have to join us! It is slaughter time anyway and you may just have to milk while we finish with the two hogs. One of the Covey cousins is to come over to help us. Fresh meat, coming up!"

Ralph Collins learned long ago he could joke with this lady. She was always pleasant when riding with him as she had done on many occasions when he rode with him and the others over the fields, investigating accidents that had left some of her long horns with scars. They recalled when a cow grazed too closely to an arroyo and lost her balance, fell, and broke her rear legs. It was an odd accident. Laredo mentioned that the land south of the house had far too many arroyos on it.

"Yes," agreed Lula, "I remember he told us that. Good man, Laredo. Maybe he can teach me some Spanish I hear from him." She tried to look southward but the rain was too heavy. "Here they come, Pete and Laredo now with the cows."

Ralph Collins rose and took his hat from the counter. "Can you make some more coffee for supper, please, ma'am. Laredo likes coffee at supper time, you know."

"Yes, I know. I reckon I can." Lula nodded as she gathered the cups. "You take care, now, and stay dry. Is that slicker warm enough for you?"

He nodded and smiled and left the kitchen. She could hear him pass through the gate on his way to the barn. The winds became angry and brushed against the bell. Its clanging made the foreman turn to look at the house. Lula came out to wave him onward as she halted the movement. She stood there for a moment, feeling the rain against her face, gazing through the raindrops to see the last of the cows as they waited outside in the weather. Cozetta wanted a drink and Lula obeyed.

With Cozy and Dot seated at the table there, Lula found Edith in the hallway. Despite the rain which had not slackened, she took her littlest in her arms, opened the front door and gazed out to the south pasture well past the stile block. The child extended her small hand as if she could touch the water as it dripped from the eaves. Lula kissed it gently and waved a hello to birds as they sped away

dodging the rain as best they could. It was a cold rain. In another month, very likely, the rain could turn to snow and January would be another anniversary. Edith
would be two.

"That is such a beautiful tree there, Edie," Lula said as she pointed south to
the tall oak in the yard. "I bet sooner or later you will be climbing in that tree with
Oliver. Your cousin is always up there in that tree whenever he comes to see us."

Thanksgiving was a week away and surely the family would be expected
here, the Dunbars, especially. Lula lifted Edith high in her arms as the girl called
out in her tiny voice to the rain. In a moment which Lula often felt was too expensive to enjoy, she sang to her daughter one little song which her own mother had
taught her when she was that age. Lula uttered a prayer to God to Whom she
spoke when she was experiencing a milestone in her life. Lately, Lula had her
share of them.

Dot and Cozetta walked into the parlor where three dolls and a toy awaited
them. Lula felt Edith's arm around her neck and she saw, through the downpour,
two cows as they finally reached the muddy corral. Laredo was there scolding
them for being late.

Lula made up her mind to accept the edict about Change, that she would
appreciate what she experienced and to appreciate anything that arrived mysteriously into her pattern of living. She smelled the fall weather seeping into the fabric
of her life, filling the land with an invitation to expect it and its autumn brilliance.
The leaves of that tall oak tree were already turning and falling. She spoke to God
just as she would speak to Ralph Collins or to Winfred Jordan, or to her own father
for that matter. She spoke to God in the same way her mother-in-law would talk to
Him. But soon Mrs. Rachel would no longer be her mother-in-law.

Three black crows flew in and landed in that tall oak tree. She and Edith heard
them call to each other. Lula closed the door and released Edith so the child could
join her sisters just as the rain owl swooped over the house.

Chapter Twenty-One

Of the crowds of Indians and white people who attended the wedding of Lucy Stivers and her groom, only Emma Perryman Drew gave thought to the differences between the girl whom her brother married first and this socialite. Emma was never conducive to comprehending the motivations of the young lady. This had to do, to a great extent, with the fact that her Indian blood alienated her from what many full bloods accepted as the change that occurred when the century changed. She was not adept at discussing such matters, anyway, not even in a language she spoke but not wrote. Her brother had married a full blood for his first wife. Her death had been so sudden. Other siblings once voiced the opinion that she was too fragile and ill. The epidemic that took Emma's babies also took the first wife.

Emma then came to another decision and it did not set well with her nor with her two sisters and not with George. Oliver was too young to grasp the characters of the two wives. Miss Lucy Stivers was a white woman.

Emma could not surmise that because Moses had married a white woman that the Old Regime would now be tainted with a mixture of another foreign element. Mixed bloods had invaded Indian Territory. This sister, and so many others, apparently preferred to ignore the fact that her tribe had intermarried long before Moses met Lula.

Emma was not a sociable woman nor was she inclined to profound perception. Her ample knowledge of the language of her mother alienated her to an extent from her brothers and sisters who did not ever profess such a linguistic interest. But her one strong trait grew when she least expected it. She was herself almost too melancholy when she lost her children. It was when she perceived the faces of the old men strolling up and down Boulder Avenue next to the railroad tracks that reflected an enigma that no one was able to solve. And another trait, as is seemed to be, was that she was able to condone this situation. The church to which she went for the wedding represented a religion that, at a time, was anathema to Creeks, but now it was acceptable if that was a word she could use.

Sixty years ago this very church was subject to dismissal where the nation was concerned. The full bloods did not wish for the services. Missionaries met with a negative approach. How, then was this one church existing on what was territorial soil? Emma sat in a pew that afternoon and did not think any more about it. She was tired. She did not know if she were happy for Abner or simply if she had arrived at a station in her life where she did not care for anything anymore. She did know one thing. Her husband was not there beside her.

Ella Perryman Horner was late because her husband had no interest in anything either. She came through the front door adjusting her windblown hat and proceeded to sit with Emma.

George and Orphia acted as official host and hostess while Mrs. Rachel remained seated at a decorated table to one side. Oliver, now fourteen, sat next to his mother, completely enthralled by the sounds and inflections of the Creek language as she conversed with the full bloods. Every time the front door opened as more guests arrived, he glanced at his friend Billy who was outside in the crisp, cool weather.

Mayme Shirk, in a new dress, hat, and gloves sat by herself. She explained to Abner, days before the event, that she would be attending alone. She preferred it that way.

Emma was unable to contain her curiosity. She rose and excused herself from Ella's whisperings and slipped to the rear of the sanctuary where, luckily, she encountered Abner. She placidly counseled him. "Come over here and sit down, back here where no one is. I'm afraid you're not going to have very many people here anyway. The organ hasn't started yet. We've got some time before you stand down there."

Abner did not respond well nor did he say one word to her. His eyes were focused on the door to Dr. Kerr's office. This wedding was not designed to be a big affair much to the disappointment of the bride. Her parents were not feeling at all well. Emma touched her brother's arm. "What do you want?" was all he could ask.

"I guess we've never been much like a brother and sister ought to be. I'm not important to you, I suppose, as Mayme or George but I am your sister, too."

This was not a time for such philosophizing. With all the confusing thoughts penetrating his mind, Abner frowned at her. "What are you talking about?"

"You do what you want with that House, Abe. Mama doesn't ever want to live in it. Anybody can see that. It served its purpose. That Childers boy stayed with Mama in it after the other one ran off."

Abner interrupted her. "Emma, I don't have time..."

"I talked to Mama the other day about the House."

Her words frightened him. Quickly, the groom wanted to conclude this dialog. "I guess Mayme is after you to sell it too, is that it? Emma, I got to go down by the alter now."

Emma adjusted her hat as she continued almost in a whisper. "I talked because I was the only one to talk. I talked to her mainly because she wants to live in the White House now and I don't blame her. That Townhouse is going to seed if we don't use it one way or another."

Abner was noted for a quiet thinker but the organist came from the anteroom with some music in her hand. "Why are you telling me this now, Emma? I got a wedding." He started to rise but her hand, gently on his arm, forced him to remain.

"Because I don't see you often enough, that's why. Everyone in this family just ignores poor Emma, that's why. I have a husband that don't care whether the sun rises or sets. Let me tell you something before I return to my seat." She looked directly at him, ignoring the crowd that took their seats near them, her hand still holding his forearm. "Mama is going to sell that property. That is what she wants to do. And sometime, I bet real soon, you are going to have to explain to that white bride of yours, that schemer, that you and she are just not going to be living in that mansion on Main Street. Not any length of time." She stared at him.

Abner took one deep breath and tried to relax as his own eyes darted from his meddlesome sister to the office door. He tried to remain the disciplined thinker even under the trying circumstances, even for questions raised that were not to his liking.

The organist was at her instrument and sat waiting for a signal from the door. George slipped into the alcove. As Best Man he motioned for them to go immediately to the altar. When everyone settled and was quiet, Winfred Jordan and Lula managed to enter and sit in the back of an alcove. Emma gave Abner one final squeeze. "I'll talk to you next week." Dr. Kerr joined the wedding party. Lucy, dressed in an expensive gown with two maids of honor appeared from the outside and walked down her aisle.

And in such a short time the ceremony was completed. The pastor began the line of greeting while the organist played. Only a few spectators remained to shake hands with the groom and his bride while others loitered to watch a host of women prepare the cakes they had brought.

Mrs. Louise Clinton and Vera McBirney prepared the tablecloth. "A perfect event for my little daughter," Mrs. Stivers beamed as she poured punch. But at one time she left the bowl in Mrs. McBirney's care to accost her own husband for bringing a flask of whiskey into the church. In one ugly moment, she escorted him out the back door as witnessed by Mrs. Clinton. "Now don't you dare let me see you do that again do you hear?" In a violent gesture she struck the bottle out of his hand. "What an awful thing to do on your daughter's wedding."

Mrs. Kerr found Lula Perryman midway from the alter to the rear doors and graciously extended her hand. "Dr. Kerr and I haven't had an opportunity to tell you that it was a genuine pleasure being at your country house. It was well over a year ago, wasn't it? At a wedding of another brother, I believe. A Mr. George Perryman, I believe it was!"

Lula instantly noticed the beauty radiating from this woman's kindness. Mrs. Kerr's line of vision was anchored with Lula's brown eyes. For just a second she included the attention of Mr. Jordan. "That's right, ma'am," Lula smiled, "it was George junior and Orphia." She pointed. "There's Mrs. Orphia, right over there. This year, it's Abner and Lucy, and next year..." and Lula paused and looked at Winfred Jordan who stood drinking punch, "It looks like another wedding."

That remark was not loud, but Mayme, standing outside the perimeter of this group, heard it and stopped her own conversation with Mrs. Stonecipher. "I want you to meet Mr. Jordan," Lula continued. "Mr. Jordan lives in Jenks and I guess you can say I live in Jenks too. My homestead is now part of that township according to the latest explanation I got."

"Well, I'm pleased to make your acquaintance, sir," Mrs. Kerr said, again extending her hand, "and I'm sure my husband will be wanting to meet you too. I'll try and bring him over to you." Several children ran past them down the aisle with cake and cups of punch. "Don't spill your drinks in church," Mrs. Kerr gaily called. She watched as they fled through the front door. Then she turned to the couple. "I hope you can attend church with us here, Mr. Jordan."

Lula was pleased by his answer after he cleared his throat. "I've settled in Jenks now, ma'am. It's a far piece from there to here and we got churches." He placed his empty cup on the table behind him. "I'm going to be married after the first of the year, Naught Three." He did not look at Lula but wiped a drop of punch from his chin.

With sudden comprehension, the pastor's wife laughed. Her reply was delightful! "Oh, my, I take it, yours is the wedding, then." She nodded her head to them both, pushing a strand of greying hair in place under her big hat. "Well, my dear Mrs. Perryman, oh, my goodness! We'll have to have your wedding right here at the church, that is, if you wish. Oh!" With a gentle pat on their hands, Mrs. Kerr cheerfully dismissed herself in search of her husband. The music ceased at her signal and the organist packed her portfolio with added care.

Winfred and Lula moved toward the table where Mrs. Rachel waited with Oliver but the boy had grown restless and disappeared. Emma departed after saying goodbye to her mother but not to the betrothed. The guests vacated the premises with the exception of Robert Shaw. He managed to wind his way easily through the pews, talking to Yuchie and to Creeks for it was to Mrs. Rachel that he was going. He was soon at her side offering to translate for her.

It was time to leave for the Townhouse.

"I'm so glad we have to go only two blocks," sighed Mrs. Clinton. "I gave the rest of the cakes to some poor folks who needed the food more than we. I'm sure that was all right."

A few Indians walked with Abner while their women escorted Lucy. Mrs. Stivers was still irate with her husband but she never allowed her anger to manifest itself again.

Ralph Collins was at Lula's side almost immediately while en route the short distance. "Ma'am," he said, as he pulled his horse behind him, "if you'll excuse us, Mrs. Perryman, Laredo, and Pete and I will trot back home now and get to milking. We can make it in time. We give our best wishes to Abner and the missus a while ago." He put on his hat.

"Where are your horses, Laredo?" Lula asked.

Pete answered quickly for them. "Over there behind the big House, ma'am. We'll be going now if you don't mind. Sure was a pretty sight." He scampered ahead of them. "Save some cake ma'am, if you will please."

"Food is waiting at the big House," Lula shouted but that did not stop them. Ralph Collins called. "We'll be all right ma'am," and he mounted. "Goodbye, ma'am. Goodbye, Win!"

"Wait here, ma'am, while I check our buggy," and Winfred paused beside the brown hack that they rode this day. He inspected the harness and from the bed he picked up a bucket for water. The fall weather had made the air comfortable and the shade of the cottonwoods and oaks kept the leather cool. With buckets in hand he was soon at Mrs. Rachel's well.

"You hungry, Mr. Jordan?" Lula's question was less important than the manipulation of her hat. "I should have left it in the buggy," she said as she untied it, "I don't need all this fashion!" She combed her hair with her hands. She walked with him to return to the horse.

"I guess I'm always hungry ma'am," he answered. The horse drank quickly from the bucket under its nose.

Lula succeeded in hiding her large chapeau beneath an old blanket that she had permanently kept in the buggy. "Let's go check on the girls and eat a bite. What do you say?"

"I agree to that, ma'am, I agree to that, all right!"

The reputation for Mrs. Rachel's food was the magnate for bringing many wedding guests into the House. Such knowledge was well in progress since the eighteen-nineties. Dinner was popular at the White House but the habit was extended to the House downtown for as long as her husband was alive.

The remark, from Ella, that their father's sudden demise at the end of the century was such a disappointment, in that he did not occupy this home very long, was shared by all with the exception of Mayme and her husband. But the House became a home and from it Oliver was the only Perryman who began to appreciate it from his very early years.

Mrs. Rachel, though pleased by its location and its comfort, often felt compelled to venture back to the White House. Her children, with various attitudes about all of this, were occupied with their own families and careers. Having the stamina that amazed many people including the recalcitrant Shirks, Mrs. Rachel was often seen at her well watching the newly installed windmill pump water, or walking down the street with a grocery basket and assuredly the most surprising, that she was driving her own buggy south to her other home.

Her remark to Emma was translated often. She goes to that other house because it had memories that she wished to keep.

But this House with its tender reputation also possessed a beauty that made all of Tulsa agree that this edifice was an outstanding example of modern architecture. By the autumn of nineteen-two, a variety of buildings was appearing on the city's horizon with young businesses sprouting along Boulder and Main near the railroad tracks with its depot and a host of private homes and four churches. "Real Estate is a force, an economical force which is big business now," said a vice-president of Mr. McBirney's bank. And, of course many people agreed.

Mrs. Stivers discussed this very topic with two other women as they made their way down Fourth street toward Main. "That is such a magnificent house," she gushed at the matrons, "and from this angle it is so impressive, with nothing around it except the trees to block this view. Lucy is very lucky, very lucky, indeed, to be a part of the Perrymans."

While at play Oliver watched for the trek to start toward the House and he joined his mother. Robert Shaw helped her along, dodging the dust of those who drove their buggies those two blocks. The boy got a drink from the well before he went in through the back door. Soon, the lower floor was crowded.

Tired as she was, Mrs. Rachel wanted to escape. While gleeful noise invaded her parlor and spilled into the dining room, this matriarch made her way gently and slowly past the crowd and up the stairs, one step at a time, to her second floor and toward the bedroom with her big oak bed. There the sounds of hilarity were less definitive. Amid this crowd, no one saw her. She paused and turned to the left listening for the sound of her old friend who had come, once again, delivering eggs, and who was upstairs minding the grandchildren. When Mrs. Rachel looked through the door, Dot and Cozetta ran to her with an embrace.

Having determined that all was well, she thanked the nanny, hugged the girls, and walked down the hall to her bedroom. Removing the shawl, she folded it neatly and placed it at the foot of her bed. From a narrow drawer in a tall wardrobe she extracted a small bound set of papers, tied with a lace from a brown shoe, that was part of personal manuscripts written in English. They were all in a clearly inked script and dated October, eighteen-ninety-eight.

Through her open door her attention shifted to the stairwell where she heard footsteps slowly ascending. She turned, and with parcel in hand, she stepped into the hallway to see Robert Shaw, paused at the landing to catch his breath.

Quietly and with a slight smile enveloping her face, she explained why she wanted him to meet her upstairs. Away from the reception she began her story. Robert felt himself growing more fascinated by all the intricate background. He told her he was honored to help translate just for her.

The noisy group downstairs grew in volume. Since no one to her knowledge knew that she was upstairs, they were expected to be alone. She told her old friend to keep the girls occupied.

With the assistance of Thomas and Legus, her beloved husband wrote these papers in English. Only recently a year ago she discovered the packet while moving some clothing. Across the years, not knowing English, she never asked about business nor had she ever intended to learn. Her husband was the head of her family. She always respected that, whether it was an Indian tradition, which it was, or an extension of a Christian attitude. In either case, she accepted this promise.

So now as they sat together on a comfortable settee, Robert saw in her eyes a curiosity that demanded answers. With her wrinkled hands resting in her lap, she watched as Robert untied the folder. Emma could have translated but Mrs. Rachel did not care to impose any such information on her daughter. Only this mother needed to know what these papers contained. This was to be between this Creek lady and this Shawnee man.

She remained quiet but alert while he perused the material before he began to explain. They heard no sound other than a happy playful room just down the hall. One window was slightly open to keep their area fresh with the fall air.

This was a type of diary with annotations from six months prior to that October. The pages were unsoiled and the words were still very clear where George had scribed his opinions. One smudge on a margin of a page preserved a fingerprint. He studied it diligently, eager to help, but was burdened often by lack of vocabulary. Even so, he was able to make sense of each paragraph according to what Mr. Perryman intended to imply. As Robert softly gave her words from this diary, she nodded, periodically vocalizing her agreement, pleased that she heard again what was strong on her husband's mind. Being a disciplined thinker, Robert reiterated.

Its first references were written at a time when the Muscogee Nation was in doubt about its future, before Josiah's demise in 'eighty-nine, as if so many points of interest had to be solved before the new century was to begin. It contained vital sections that related to specific details, much of what was on the minds of the chiefs and of the council. Personal in context, it could very easily stand as a manuscript capturing a bygone era.

George Beecher Perryman was not ever the academician like his brothers. But they remained close a strong family in the last twenty years. This cattleman was concerned more with his pastures and rail shipments. His talents lay in numbers on a ledger. He drew attention in this diary to a concern that the Creeks must modify their concept of land tenure. Among many men of authority, and not just merely the Creeks, land was held in common and not subject to individual purchase. That is why so many of Perryman's friends opposed allotment since eighteen-ninety-one. All the tribes opposed the termination of their local government as well.

It was an historical document. Robert stopped to look at his hostess. He interjected the word "brilliant." He wanted to make sure what he translated was a piece of history that she was able to comprehend. She returned his gaze with eyes that confirmed this. So many incidents from across the years fell into place. She then nodded her agreement but he took it to mean that he should continue and he was pleased to do so. What he encountered had actually been a portion of this man's personal approach and study of a nation that begged for survival.

Well before Legus Perryman became their chief, a growing dissatisfaction was most apparent, at the encroachment of the whites upon the Indians' domain. Too, a desire by some of the Creeks to return to the early cultures they enjoyed prior to their removal from the Southern locations. When young boys, this is what George and his brothers heard from elders. Ironic for Mrs. Rachel to hear this while she was encompassed in this modern mansion.

Again, Robert paused to monitor this woman's reception of all that this parcel inferred. He had been as complete as he possibly could be for the English words had been so beautifully selected. He was not quite satisfied with a translation here and there but the total implications were placed in the mind of this lady. She settled back in the comfort of her sofa with a stronger realization that her husband had been indeed a man of success and wealth, and not only in cattle.

This young Shawnee closed the packet and breathed deeply with a prayerful hope that he had spoken well.

Mrs. Rachel took the parcel and held it in her lap to look at it again for a while. Then, with a genuine gratitude only her eyes thanked him. He was happy to be at her side and to learn more of the majesty of the man who had been kind to so many people. Robert could not help but assume that this paragon learned graciousness from the lady who sat next to him.

So he rose to bid his goodbye but his statement was interrupted with the clamor of Oliver running up the stairs. Mrs. Rachel stood, holding the packet. As the boy reached the top both could see tears welling in his little eyes. He embraced his mother, embarrassed that a fourteen-year-old Indian boy was weeping.

Mrs. Rachel cupped the boy's face in one hand and escorted him gently into the bedroom, placing him on a chair, while she returned the document to the dresser drawer. Robert's work was not finished for he had to translate why Oliver was crying.

The sobbing ceased when he explained that he was told he was adopted and, for a while Robert could not discern who it was who had informed him of that statement. Between the tears Oliver would gasp a word or two and wait for Robert to translate. This provoked discomfort among the three of them. Robert then pulled the boy onto the settee where they sat. Mrs. Rachel hovered near them.

Robert grabbed they boy's shoulders and wiped tears from his cheeks. "Now, listen to me, Oliver," he stated bluntly, "are you listening?" He gestured to Mrs. Rachel. "This is your mother standing there. She's always been your mother from the moment you can remember." Mrs. Rachel muttered a question in Creek. "She wants to know where you heard this."

Oliver heaved a big sigh. "Billy. Billy told me. Just now out in the front yard. He said...he said she's not my real mother. That I'm one of the orphans that she took care of for a long time." Oliver, quite perturbed, glanced at Mrs. Rachel and back to Robert. "Mama, you're my mama, aren't you?"

The agonized look in the child's face needed no translation. The lady answered in Creek and with a definite yes in English! Then, she looked to Robert for additional help. The boy relaxed but still whimpered and moved to the edge of the sofa. He looked at Robert's stern face and then back to Mrs. Rachel's. "I'm an Indian. I know I 'm an Indian." A bright smile passed over his tears.

After Robert looked once more for any more questions, he pulled the boy to him and said softly but definitely, "You're a Creek Indian and you're the youngest Perryman of the lot!" Then he added, "Whether you like it or not!"

Alerted by the noise, the nanny appeared at the door but was quickly dismissed by Mrs. Rachel. For this moment, Oliver had time to calm himself. He slowly rose with Robert and lowered his head and took Mrs. Rachel's hand in his, turned and with the other hand he grasped Robert's arm. Together, with Mrs. Rachel carrying her shawl, they descended the flight of stairs as if each step was beckoning each one into an exciting future. Once at the foyer they were able to view the remaining guest who had just completed a sumptuous feast. And Billy and his mother had gone.

Robert signaled to Abner who was talking to one of the Covey girls. His whisper into Abner's ear brought the groom instantly to Oliver's side. "Well," Abner called to the boy, "I didn't mean to ignore my little brother." Oliver looked directly into Abner's eyes as he continued his banter. "Have you had some cake and cherry pie? Which do you want, I'll get it for you!" As he guided Oliver to the table still laden with desert, over his shoulder the older brother nodded to Robert and his mother. "Let's see what we got here."

Before doing anything else, Oliver halted a foot from the food. "Are you really my brother? Along with George?" This apparently was a test question. The boy surveyed the remnant of a chocolate cake that Mrs. Rachel had made earlier at the White House.

Abner claimed a plate. "You forgot Mose. He was our oldest brother, yours and mine." He chose one slice with a spatula. "George junior is older, than I and I come next. And then you. That's the way it's always been. You came alone in eighteen-eighty-eight. I was about ten when you were born." He placed the cake on a plate.

Accepting all this, including the chocolate, as his eyes went from the cake up to Abner, Oliver asked, "what about Emma and Ella and Mayme? They are our sisters, aren't they?"

Abner shoved the plate toward the boy and laughed. "Oh, sure! Sisters, all." Again quickly, Abner glanced to his mother who was smiling. "And you want me to tell you one more thing? He handed him a fork.

Oliver said nothing but nodded in agreement.

"You want to know where Lucy and I are going?"

"You mean now?"

"Yes now."

"On your honeymoon?" came Oliver's final query.

"I'll tell you if you don't tell anyone else. Even your mother. Even our mother! Okay?" Abner waited for some kind of signal from him. It came with another nod of the head because his mouth was full of cake. With a voice that was quieter Abner pulled Oliver to the corner of the dining table. "We're going to Vinita and stay on Shanahans' Ranch for a while. I told you about the ranch. You've heard me speak of James Patrick Shanahan and his eighteen children? Well. That's where we're going. We'll be back in a week or so and we'll live in this house for a while." Throughout this conversation with his brother, the same kind he had maintained over many of his younger years, Oliver listened well. Abner had never sounded patronizing in any way. With a matter-of-fact tone in everything he had said Abner always was able to reach Oliver's intelligence in every case that required tack and honesty.

"Are you going to have a slice? It's your favorite." Oliver pointed with his fork to two remaining pieces. And then, wishing to prolong the moment, Oliver asked "Mama likes our house in the country, doesn't she?"

"Mama likes that house, yes," was Abner's reply, glancing to see if he could spy where Lucy had gone. "Yes, she does. Now that you're a big boy," and his voice was genuine, "you can ride your horse to school." Oliver could not believe it! "Yes, I already checked on that. Mama says you can, now."

This delighted him, to hear again what he had been doing since the first of the school year. "I'm a good rider."

Mrs. Lucy Perryman appeared suddenly from a conversation with three ladies in the kitchen. "There you are," she said, "and you, Oliver, my new little brother-in-law. How's the cake?"

"It was good." He did not know how to relate to her.

"I'm about ready to go, Abe," she continued, putting on a traveling hat. "I noticed you brought the bags down. Is George still going to take us to the train?

Abner gave Oliver a manly embrace and they meandered into the hallway where a few people still tarried. "I'll take them out front, now," Abner consented, "we've got plenty of time."

Observing this entourage from the parlor was Mrs. Louise Clinton who, with her daughter, was careful to say the right word at the right time. "Vera, my dear, will you go get that Mr. Shaw so we can talk to Mrs., Rachel? Those two full bloods already left or I'd ask them to help us."

Soon, after so many of the guests departed, the interior of the House appeared vacant. The dining table was littered with cups and saucers and plates but two kitchen helpers had remained to clean. A third lady retired to the pantry to repair the damage of the table when someone spilled the remaining punch by leaning against the bowl.

Winfred Jordan stood by the front windows to view the few guests who were saying their farewells to the happy couple. Mrs. Rachel found a place to sit in a chair directly behind this tall cowboy.

Abner and Lucy rushed in. "Goodbye, Mama," he said, and she smiled. Then they fled down the sidewalk to the carriage with George at the driver's seat. Just as quickly they were gone and out of sight. Vera's husband stood by the gate.

Upstairs Lula made certain the girls were awake from their naps. "We going home now, Mama?" Dot asked. Cozetta slipped into her dress. As Lula descended she met Mrs. Clinton.

"Why don't we retire to the parlor, Mrs. Lula," Mrs. Clinton said as Vera came into view. "I see Mrs. Rachel is there and I have been trying to find time to talk to her and of course I need someone to talk to me. Do you know Creek? My, what a long day! Weddings made the day extra long."

Lula was more or less in the background. When she managed to say goodbye to Abner, Lucy was not in sight. It was just as well. With the noise subsiding, with the table cleared, Mrs. Rachel remained in her chair. A peaceful dignity pervaded the lower floor.

"All I would like to do, Mrs. Lula," Mrs. Clinton professed, "is say goodbye to this lady properly. I think she is such a dear." And then she saw her daughter with Mr. McBirney and Robert Shaw who had entered the foyer. "Oh, my dear," she was so relieved, "please, Mr. Shaw, if you will kindly translate for me." She pulled the Shawnee more closely to herself and to Mrs. Rachel. "I want to offer my best wishes to this wonderful..." and she hesitated so she might select the most appropriate word, and in her sincerity she could not, "to this wonderful Indian lady."

And then as an afterthought, she said, "I don't know what happened to the Stiverses but we're here, now. Mr. Shaw...if you will, please."

Mrs. Rachel watched this lady move and speak so much the social etiquette that any such gestures no longer astonished her. She listened to the translation, smiled and nodded her approval. In English she said, "thank you."

The Shawnee edited these remarks but he added some explanations. This lady was the mother of Doctor Fred Clinton who lived in a new abode just three blocks east of her. This interested the matriarch who had no doubt passed their cottage when en route to her errands in the city. Several businessmen had already noted the independence of this woman as she made her way along the streets. Mrs. Gray in her Sapulpa home learned long ago of the fearless woman that Mrs. Rachel was.

"Oh," continued Mrs. Clinton "and please tell her my other son, Lee, has a new daughter and they've given her the name of Celia." She caught the smile on Vera's lips and the joy in Mr. McBirney's own countenance.

Robert did. He also mentioned that the daughter, Vera, who proceeded to shake his hand, was the wife of the banker and that his office was approximately three blocks from her door. That man over there, Mrs. Rachel. He is Mr. Hugh McBirney. Yes ma'am, the banker.

When the party retreated finding their way out the front door, Mrs. Rachel commanded the attention of the young Shawnee once more. Rising from her chair she asked him to detain the tall Irish gentleman for a while, if he could stop him. The House was quiet now except for a gleeful commotion upstairs. The girls' laughter was more definitive once she walked into the hallway. Robert hurried through the front door.

"Mr. McBirney," he called loudly to get his attention. "Mr. McBirney, sir, if you will please." His call stopped the trio at the gate and the expression on Mrs. Clinton's face was one of dread. "No alarm, ma'am," Robert continued, "but, sir, if you will kindly return? I believe Mrs. Rachel wants to talk to you!"

"Me?" This man, with hat in hand, obligingly turned to him to follow instructions. To Vera he said, "Wait a moment, my dear." But his wife and her mother decided they would go on to the house. "Very well, I'll see you shortly, then."

Mrs. Rachel returned to her chair. With Robert translating she wanted to know some answers about money. "This may take a while, Mr. McBirney," the Shawnee said quietly. "She wants to come see you at your office soon. I'd have to be present, you understand, because she doesn't want her daughter to speak for her." He looked at the lady and then again at the banker. "So when would be a good time, sir?"

The banker thought a moment. With his Irish brogue his answered in a strong voice so well known in the business world. He looked directly at this lady. "Tell her, Mr. Shaw, that I can see her almost any time she wishes. I can easily make an appointment," and he extracted a leather notebook from his pocket, "...an appointment, say, for next Tuesday exactly at two post meridian." With a bejeweled pencil he noted the time, writing it as he spoke. "Tell her that, please, to see if it is suitable."

The Shawnee did so and agreed. And with this, Mr. McBirney smiled an Irish smile. "Then bid her goodbye for me, if you will, sir, please." He tipped his bowler and opened the door and was soon through her gate.

From her front door Mrs. Rachel watched as he turned to his left and disappeared among the traffic on Main street. With a happy glint in her eyes, she thanked Robert who departed almost as quickly. Then, pleased with herself, she turned in time to see Lula descending the staircase. She carried Edith. The tall cowboy, who interested this Indian lady greatly, was carrying Cozetta with Dot trailing behind them.

Mrs. Rachel gave each of her granddaughters one big embrace before she sent them all on their way.

PART THREE
1903

Chapter Twenty-Two

Two weeks before Christmas, snow started falling slowly just as the men finished milking. Such precipitation lingered for seven or eight days much to the surprise of everyone at the Homestead. Laredo had seen snow before this holiday time in North Texas as well as in Indian Territory.

"This will be a great Christmas for us," Pete offered his opinion from a cold milk stool one evening. "This cold hurts my hands." After milking, he was glad that the cows remained in the corral where they huddled together on the south side.

But winter was harsh. By the end of January, Nought Three, the Creek Nation suffered, reminding so many families of the loss of many infants to epidemic. The week between the Yuletide and the New Year contained another bitter session that made travel impossible. Lula and Winfred did not get to any authority for a marriage license so they waited.

"Knowing full well what this crazy weather can bring," Lula told Winfred, "let's plan this wedding of ours real soon."

And so they did. With no mild fanfare, such as was the Perryman-Stivers nuptials last November, Louise Amelia Dunbar and Winfred Morris Jordan became man and wife in the subdued parlor of the House on Main Street.

Two days before the ceremony, with thick snow thawing on the fields, Robert Shaw came all the way on horseback to consult with Lula. Not much activity was noticeable outside the few chores that were still required regardless. Bundled in a heavy mackinaw against the cold, his strong figure astride a black horse was handsome silhouette against the pure white blanket that hung across the landscape. Pete trudged to the stile block to meet him. Shaw thanked him and made his way to the porch as Pete took his horse to the barn.

"I am happy to say that I think of you, Mrs. Perryman, as a woman who knows her mind and how to apply common sense. The most noticeable trait you women have is a perseverance which I must say that I admire. Grit, I believe the word is. Despite hardship, despite chaos." He looked solemnly at her as she poured hot chocolate from a pitcher. "When you do become Mrs. Jordan, I am sure that the stream of consciousness will continue and bring you and Mr. Jordan good fortune. Might I say that that is my prediction. That is, if I were to be one who predicts!" He smiled at this.

Without saying so, Lula thought he had a good command of English. For a very long time from the moment her own family arrived from Kansas, she realized that a bilingual person was utilized in almost every phase of endeavor. That was evident moreso when she was surrounded by Moses's uncles and others of the Tribe. With Edith perched on her lap, and Dot and Cozetta standing there, hypnotized by the Shawnee's handsome features, Lula chose her words. "I asked you to conduct our wedding and I'm glad I did. Oh, and thanks for coming all this distance on a day when the sun is trying to shine!" She put Edith on the floor, rose from where she sat, and went to the black stove to add two more logs to the fire. "Winter seems to keep me tired all the time, I guess. Being couped up like my chickens, I suppose. I've got to tell you I do thank you for your sermon when Dick died. At such a time, grief can surmount just plain courtesy. Oh, that was a terrible time for my poor sister." She settled again in her chair.

"I understand," was his tactful reply.

"I feel like I've aged ten whole years instead of just one since that poor boy died." Her remark registered a sadness on her visitor's brow. "I once met a woman who was far more religious than I, I reckon, and she experienced four deaths of her own children with only two surviving. It's hard for me to weather the storm of losing loved ones. When Moses passed, did you know that wasn't my first big grief?" She allowed the girls to run into the kitchen when they became restless. "I guess you never did know. Mose and I lost a little boy. Born after Dot. He didn't last but about two months. But after losing four!" She paused to take a sip of chocolate. "Another lady I know asked me one day just how I fare now that I live alone, so to speak. I guess I just about laughed. I've been too busy right here. I told her I just have the farm and Mr. Collins and the boys to help me. Come to think of it, I don't think she knows I'm going to be married in two days more, come rain or shine!" She looked into the pitcher. "You want some more drink, Mr. Shaw?"

"You have a comfortable place here. No, thank you."

Her demeanor changed a bit as she looked steadily into his face, noting how he sat and listened with his eyes. "Now you asked me how I love Mr. Jordan. And you should, I guess, being the good pastor you are. Mose and I just got married without such service from anybody, let alone a preacher! That's the right of a minister, I guess, isn't it?" He agreed that it was. "Well. In this day and time, Mr. Shaw, despite my being less than thirty years old, I've learned a lot of things in my life time, you can bet your boots on that, yes sir."

A sound of some kind from the outside made her rise and go to a window. Pete and Laredo were just passing the house and their laughter was contagious. "If you had been married once," she chuckled, "you could understand." She turned once more to his attention. "I grieved once, maybe twice, and certainly when Daisy's husband was killed, but I suppose that's all over now. I'm ready to move on. You've got to do that nowadays."

She placed her empty cup on the table as her eyes fell on the portion of the wall where a picture of her and Moses had hung. "I feel so sorry for poor Daisy, left with two little ones, like that."

This remark, coming from this stalwart person, mystified this pastor. Their conversation had been good. The pioneer spirit remained a favorite subject of this Indian.

She joined him again at the stove. "Oh, I know what you're going to say. But with Daisy, it's different. But. We've got to go on don't we?" She adjusted her chair and sat, looking at him until he felt self-conscious. "Our Papa taught us good religion, Mr. Shaw. I may look like a little silly girl riding my pony around this ranch of mine, but I got more sense than most. When my Mama died, I guess that was when I first realized what God means. I didn't grow up doubting anything. I grew up believing in God and all that stuff. I still do." Lula began to feel more comfortable. "I do love that man, Mr. Shaw. I do. Winfred and I had a long talk the other day, one day, it was, after Christmas when we took down the stale popcorn streamers. We talked it out. We talked about every conceivable aspect of living. It's going to be right here, yes siree, in this very house, 'cause it's all we've got. About a house, I mean, this property, this building you're sitting in now. It's ours. This home is a good house and it's going to stay that way. Mose built it but I live in it now."

The dogs began to bark in the back yard and the noisy gate opened and banged shut as if more than one person had passed through it. Lula rose quickly, smiled as she did so and offered an apology. "Come in the kitchen with me. That should be the men coming in before milk time." She gathered the pitcher and the cups. "Talk to me while I get supper on. It's already dark outside. Glad you're staying for eats, Mr. Shaw. No I'm not his wife yet, not until you marry us day after tomorrow, but it's a wife's duty to have food on the table when her husband comes in from the fields, summer or winter. You can help me set the table."

And then, two days later, with the help of four elderly Indian ladies with whom Mrs. Rachel chatted in Creek like several happy and contented magpies, Lula became Mrs. Winfred Jordan in the House on Main Street. Not very many people attended. From a discrete distance in an aura of silence, Abner caught Lula's eyes from time to time. Lucy, however, insisted they leave early. George and Orphia escorted Rachel and Oliver. Obviously missing were the three sisters and their husbands who had not sent even a greeting of any kind.

Before he did go, Abner pulled Mrs. Jordan aside to mention that his mother was about to complete a transaction and that possibly Lula would care to see her in a week or so. "Lula," he continued, "listen to me quick! I think Lucy is anxious to go so I'll make this short. George doesn't know, yet, what I just told you about Mama and her big business deal. Not even Emma. I think I can say..." but his conversation was halted by Lucy, putting on her new winter coat.

"Come along, dear," she said, "I'm ready now." Her smile to the bride was forced. "My best regards, Mrs. Jordan." And off they went.

The few others who congratulated them erased Abner's reference from her mind but not for long. The receiving line dwindled and soon the pastor himself was at her side. Then he waited until the last person departed.

"Mrs. Perry..." and he corrected himself, "I mean, Mrs. Jordan. Before I, too, leave you, I want to add one more bit of information I failed to disclose when we met at the ranch two days ago." The groom presented himself at their side with a cup of coffee. "Mrs. Rachel is selling this property. She and I met already with Mr. Hugh McBirney at his office, and he would like you as a witness next week or so along with myself to talk to Mr. Parker. He is Mrs. Rachel's lawyer."

"Well, yes," Lula answered, "he's our lawyer too."

"Shall we say then, in mid-February. I can easily talk to Mrs. Rachel within a day or two. Can you make it the second week?"

Lula would always regard this lady as a dear and trusted friend. But she did not quite know what to ask about Emma's position as family translator. The Perrymans were no longer her major concern. She looked at her new husband and repeated, "the second week of February coming up! We'll just have to remember to expect some kind of notice from Mr. Parker."

Robert Shaw sensed a delay. "Thank you, Mrs. Jordan. And thank you for the remuneration and the food, too. It's an easy walk to the church and I have plenty to do. Goodbye."

Winfred Jordan learned a good lesson from an old Indian at his wedding that day, a week ago. It was about weather. Here in Indian Territory, weather was strangely so varied even between Cherokee and Creek Nations. The winds and clouds seemed to venture in from the northwest. One day, possible two, the threat of rain could easily discourage the best of farms while the very next day the sun would promote the warmest of afternoons and perplex even the best of predictions. Jordan was now a country farmer and he had to adjust to working in all kinds of weather even in late January. Together with the others he traversed the land and counted his blessings.

"This wind is awful, Mr. Jordan," Pete groaned as he carried his two pails of milk to the house. "But, I reckon tomorrow we'll see the sun again, if I remember my times growing up." While Winfred went on ahead of him, Pete walked silently with his foreman. With an ingenious manner about him to solve any major problem that arose at the farm, the young drover never was able to solve the question of cold hands. At one time he begged Lula for a pair of old cotton gloves. He cut open the fingertips and managed to reap an extra bucket, so he said.

"You want me to believe that?" Lula laughed, "then where's that extra bucketful?"

They placed their brimming pails in the usual place in the milk room for Lula to tend. Jordan sat down at his place near the window and drank his coffee. Laredo brought his regular bucket but left immediately to wash for supper.

Pete stood grinning at the whole lot. "You want a cup of coffee now before supper?" Lula asked. "Warm you up!"

Pete started to answer but Ralph Collins nudged him. "We can wait, ma'am."

Lula noted the disappointment. "Supper be ready in no time so tell Laredo." She checked the contents of her kettle. "Oh say, before I forget it," and the men were practically out of the warm kitchen, "I'll have to go into Sapulpa tomorrow if the sun is out. Pete can go with me, please, sir. We'll take the wagon for supplies and we can stop by and visit with my daddy. That is, if you don't mind, Mr. Collins."

Pete grinned. "Yes, ma'am that'll be right nice. Tomorrow you say?" Then he raised his eyebrows to Mr. Collins. "Please?"

"I reckon." The foreman agreed nonchalantly.

"I plan to leave right about mid-day, Mr. Collins," Lula said, "we can go and get back before too late."

"I just bet the sun will be shining all right." Pete was ecstatic. "Maybe I'll get to see somebody I know." He left with a happy smile as pleased as a little child.

"You don't mind staying here with the girls, do you, Mr. Jordan?" Lula went to her stove to load more wood. He did not answer her immediately so she looked at him. "Do you?"

"No, I guess not." He finished his coffee and shifted his chair so that he sat sideways. He brought his right leg over his left knee, a habit that Lula noticed for quite some time. He raised his coffee cup and wiggled it in mid-air.

"Well, we're married Mr. Jordan." As she poured more coffee for him she sensed a soft silence about him. "What's the matter, you having second thoughts?"

"No, oh no, nothing like that." He mused aloud. "I just am glad I won't be alone now, ma'am."

Lula talked to him over her shoulder as she continued her preparation. "Is that why you married me?"

"I asked you to marry me because I love you. I was just thinking. My daddy is alone much of the time since my Ma died about three years ago. She worked herself to death, I suspect. My brother..." and he stopped to sip his coffee, "my brother is a good person but he's hardly around, out scrounging for work in the territory where he can find it. He's so sunbaked from the neck up that he could pass for a Creek Indian!" He laughed at his own comment. "I wouldn't be a bit surprised if he's down at Muskogee working for the railroad."

Lula paused as she lifted plates from the cupboard. A quick pain raced through her memory, of Richard and Daisy, and of James at his freight window at the depot.

"You know, Lu, I guess I was just meant to stay in Jenks. I worked once or twice with your daddy, did you know that?" She agreed and listened, "I don't have much to offer you ma'am. I'm not wealthy." He stopped. "As some people I know. Maybe I should have been in the cattle business. I could have done what Ralph Collins did, bringing them cattle from Texas like that. Laredo and I have been trading stories."

Lula paused en route to the dining room with her plates. "Well, Mr. Jordan," she said flatly, "wealth doesn't have to be only in money. Besides now, you are in the cattle business." She put the plates down, took his cup from him but spilled a drop or two in his saucer. "Set the plates, please sir. And drink up, Mr. Jordan. My granddaddy from Illinois drunk from a saucer. He died in Kansas before we came on south to here. Did I ever tell you we were headed for Texas?"

He tried lifting his saucer to his lips and spilled some on the table, laughing as he attempted the feat again. "Did I ever tell you I was born in Texas? Maybe we were destined to meet in Texas somewhere around San Antone. But in fact, I started to stay in Missouri when I was a kid so I could have met you up there! I guess it was just Fate brought us together ma'am. There's not such a thing as a coincidence. You told me that yourself."

"Yes, I guess I did once upon a time." She handed him five knives, forks and spoons. "We're eating on the big table tonight." She joked as she preceded him. "Meet too many robbers and thieves in Missouri or were you one of them? A lot of them, from what I understand." She chuckled and together they returned to the kitchen. "You are a sight, you are!" She straightened his denim collar. "Your neck is as dirty as your brother's! I'll finish setting the table. Go on and wash. Oh you can bring in some more wood, too, please." Her eyes were happy; he could see that. He gave her a quick squeeze before he verified the wood supply. Outside the house the cold wind was quiet but bitter.

After supper, after the men returned to the bunkhouse, Lula was weary, judging what had to be done to close her kitchen for the night. The bucket was full of well water and the pot for morning coffee was already waiting to be placed directly on the fire. "Did you say you want to talk to Mr. Collins?"

"Go on to bed if you want. I'll be along after awhile. I'll stoke the fire for you on my way to bed."

Lula nodded, removed her apron, and placed it over the back of her chair for it to be ready.

Dot appeared in the doorway dressed in her heavy flannel nightgown without shoes. "Well now what in the world child? What are you doing out of bed? Come here!" Lula gathered her into welcoming arms and rubbed her feet. "Say goodnight to your daddy!"

Sleepily little Dot cuddled against her mother's shoulder. She opened her mouth and repeated the word but no sound came.

He watched them disappear down the hall with Lula holding a lamp with her other hand. From the parlor, resting on the table nearest the archway, Lula's fancy black clock chimed ten. He verified his own pocket watch. He slipped on a coat that was hanging on a peg on the back porch and noticed that a light was still shining in the bunkhouse. The men were not a bed yet for he saw shadows pass across the small window. He turned up the collar, passed quietly through the gate with a look to the dark heavens and decided to talk first before he collected the logs. He knocked on the door and Pete opened it.

"Oh, hello, Mr. Jordan."

"Mr. Jordan," Ralph Collins called. He was dressed only in his long underwear and jeans and stocking feet. "Please, sir, come in." Winfred did not hesitate en route to the stove, well lit, with its inviting warmth. "Sit down on that stool yonder. Laredo, bring it nearer for him." Then, Laredo and Pete both sat on their cots. The smaller of the two rooms was cozy and neat with the other room shut off during the winter.

"I saw your light so I thought I'd mosey in." At first he was more hesitant as he sat. The one lamp provided light and shadow for them to see each other fairly well.

"Something on your mind, Mr. Jordan? Ralph Collins exchanged quick glance with Laredo as Pete moved to the other side of the stove for a better view. "Take your coat off."

He did so. "I don't think anything special. I think my wife was...uh....is lucky to have such fine drovers here." Pete was more embarrassed than the other two. But when Winfred smiled at this good man, the drover relaxed and pulled a chair to the stove. "She told me how you came to be foreman here. That was a good story. Got our name in the paper."

"Oh, that was a long time ago, it sure was." Ralph Collins did not exactly know what to expect. This visitor hardly ever presumed to step inside the bunkhouse and never would the occasion be so late as it was.

The next question was another surprise. "How old are you, Ralph?" It was odd and direct.

"'Bout fifty or so, I reckon." The foreman blinked his eyes and tried to smile. "You're still a yearling." He reached to place the lamp on the table so that its light would shine on their faces. For Ralph Collins, it revealed more of his wrinkles in his features than those of the young cowboys. "I mean that as a compliment, Mr. Jordan." Pete laughed. Laredo was silent. He rose and opened the door quickly to place his pet raccoon outside. Collins continued, "How old are you?"

"I was born in February of 'seventy-eight. That makes me twenty-five come next week." Winfred put his big coat across his lap. "Sometimes I feel older maybe. That makes me twice as old as you, Ralph!" Their laughter was so bright that even Laredo forgot to shut the door.

"Close the door, crazy!" Ralph Collins shouted.

Winfred continued. "I'm pretty good at figures. Mathematics. I wanted to get married on my birthday but she didn't want to wait that long."

"I'm glad for you, Win." Ralph Collins, though older, had begun to call him by his first name since the wedding. This sincere remark settled well for this new husband. "Mrs. Jordan told us she wanted to have a talk with us after a while, and I guess you'll be in on that talk, too." Ralph Collins raised the lamp slightly to see the quanity of coal oil remaining in its glass base. Pete and Laredo were so silent that this short moment became tedious. The foreman was expecting almost any decision to be forthcoming by the mistress and her husband. He rubbed his hair. Pete and Laredo sat very still. "I can say Win, if I may, that we sure would like to stay on with you and Mrs. Jordan and your family, sir, here on the place." A second of time passed that seemed like an hour. "Well. You know what I mean."

Winfred's eyes fell upon the shotgun resting in notches, hanging on the wall directly above Ralph's cot. "Is that your gun? I mean, is that the one that killed Mr. Childers?"

Without turning to look Ralph nodded. "Yes. I keep it oiled but I hardly ever use it anymore. It's an old piece, now, and probably not worth too much in case I'd ever want to sell it." His eyes were still on Winfred's shadowy face. "I'm not interested in going hunting as some men are," and he nodded toward Laredo. "I don't know whether I like to hunt, even. On the plains we needed to have meat and rabbits to eat. I guess I'm getting old." Again, he grinned. "Maybe I am, at that. I seen a lot of violence in my lifetime. I think I let Laredo use it about a month ago when deer season opened. We got them around here, you know." He waited a moment. "I don't like to see no deer killed, mind you." The oiled springs in Laredo's cot squeaked as he began to remove his boots. "Mrs. Per—, I mean, Mrs. Jordan, I don't think, now, she doesn't want me to kill any of the wild deer around here, so I don't. No sir I won't." Laredo said nothing to that. Pete was engrossed in what he had heard.

Winfred Jordan came to a conclusion. "I came out here tonight, I guess, to offer you an idea, I guess you'd call it. I got a plan and I want to know what you think of it."

Ralph Collins became more curious than fearful of his future. "You're master of that house now I guess you can offer your plan, but I might not be able to help. But I'll help if I'm able to."

"We don't particularly want to leave, Mr. Jordan." Pete was more than frightened.

"Be quiet, Pete," put in the foreman quickly, "let the man speak."

"It's nothing personal, mind you, or anything like that." Winfred cupped his hands over his coat. "I got this aunt. My daddy's sister. At least, that's all I ever knew about her."

They were relieved. Ralph Collins heaved such a sigh that he secretly hoped the new family member could not suspect he was worried as much as Pete. He was too old to try to locate Mr. Daugherty again.

Winfred Jordan did not suspect. He continued. "She is my Aunt Sally. I guess she was from Texas like the rest of us. You remember when my daddy and brother was here at Christmas last? When they was here, they told Lula about how Aunt Sally was to come visit us, visit daddy, I mean. Well. Sure enough, she shows up out of nowhere all right. I guess she had no place else to go. I was thinking maybe she could come out here and live and work in the kitchen for Lu. That's what I want to know from you."

"Here?" interjected Pete, all shocked. "You mean bunkhouse?"

"Course not, silly," Ralph Collins said, "sit down!" That this man had asked him for his opinion was such a startling surprise. All questions, even from Pete or from Laredo, disappeared. "Almost like it was planned," concluded the foreman as he held his hands over the stove." She a nice woman, Win?"

"You ask me if my aunt is a nice woman!" He was at a loss for words. He needed the best answer to this man's question. But he had to stifle the laughter bubbling up inside him. "I will have to ask you one, myself "You've known a lot of nice women, have you, Ralph?"

Pete, trying to keep up the conversation, was prepared.

"Well. She's your aunt, you should know!" Laredo, having managed one boot, sat intrigued.

"She can cuss like a cowboy!" Winfred's laughter was so contagious that Ralph Collins joined in.

"You're a cowboy yourself, Mr. Jordan!" Pete tried to interrupt. "What did she say, huh, what?"

Ignoring him, Winfred giggled. "Well, yes, she uses quite a vocabulary. She's quite a gal she is. I can't imagine what Lu would say and think if ol' Aunt Sally lets go with a word or two from her list." In his glee, Laredo pulled off his other boot. Winfred rose and put on his coat. "I can't imagine where Sally's been but daddy has his own story."

"Well, I tell you what," Ralph Collins had not laughed so much in months, "Bring her out to the ranch and just see what happens. If she's a good cook, we'll overlook the words."

"Sure, Okay." their visitor was at the door ready to leave. "That's what I'll do, all right."

"Goodnight to you, Win." Ralph Collins remained where he was, by the stove, but Pete insisted on walking to the gate.

"Is Mrs. Jordan still wanting to go to Sapulpa tomorrow?" He ignored the cold. "It won't snow. The sun will be out and real pretty. I bet we won't have no trouble at all, not a bit."

"Tomorrow, Pete. That's for sure. Tomorrow is Saturday and I bet you can find your friends up and down Dewey. Goodnight to you, Pete." Winfred Jordan passed through the gate without arousing even the dogs.

That is exactly what they did. The day was bright. By nine in the morning Pete swept out the wagon and stowed two extra blankets directly behind the driver's seat just in case they needed them. He harnassed the mare and drove the wagon to the stile block. The sun made his appearance through the jungle of trees from across the main road and their day had begun.

"We're stopping at the Beaver place for dinner before we go on into town." Bundled against the cold with Pete driving, they moved out, waving goodbye to the men as they made their way south.

"When we get back tonight. I'll think about making you a chocolate cake, Pete. You'd like that, wouldn't you!"

"Oh, yes ma'am, I would. I dearly would." Pete watched for the narrow road on his right that led to the Beaver house.

"But in the meantime," Lula continued, pulling her scarf tighter under her coat. "We want to get groceries. I hope I got a big enough box for our supply. Remind me to get boxes. We got to do this before we spend time with Papa and Malindy and the neighbors." She looked directly at the youngster. "You are a good driver, Pete. You get along mighty nice with horses. Yes, you do! I've noticed that."

"I want to race one I got, Mrs. Jordan. I already talked about wanting to race in the Fourth of July come summer. It's a good fast pacer, Mrs. Jordan. I'll win."

Later that afternoon, once again on Maple street Lula realized how that little town had grown with additional houses, a great deal of businesses, and a new hotel bearing its name on a huge wooded sign over the door painted with large green letters. Lula had heard that its proprietor was proud of his name, Ripley, and that he must be another Irishman with that bravado. Someone parked a long buckboard with siding near the south wall of the train station. Pete reined in to wait for a carriage to cross in front of him. Another wagon casually interrupted their journey to the Dunbar home, but this second delay did not rile Pete at all. "Lots of people, Mrs. Jordan. Town sure is growing."

While they waited for this traffic to clear, Pete pushed his hat to the back of his head so he could feel the winter sun against his face. He confided in Lula. "Mr. Jordan tells us we may get someone to help you in the house."

After waving a greeting to a lady, Lula confirmed this. "He's got an aunt who is in need of a home, I gather. I told him to bring her on out. I guess I could always use new help washing dishes," and she grinned at him, "unless you want to come in sometimes and wash while I dry."

To this he grinned, himself, and called to the horse.

"In a minute," she continued, "you can turn left at the next corner. There's Mrs. Gray's boarding house where Jimmy lives. Okay. My Papa's new house is up along the street. I'll show you where. We won't be long because I want to get back home."

The street was narrow and flat. In another five minutes, they approached the block. Through the naked tree limbs they say the fence and front yard. This portion of the street was a steep hill that terminated just the end of Dunbar property. Her father told her he preferred that his new home sit on an incline thereby making it easier to excavate an ample cellar for Malindy's canned fruits and vegetables and any other food for cold storage. In this weather, she did not have any problems about that. Waller Dunbar built plenty of shelves. The home was so new that it lacked paint on the eaves and porch line.

A delapidated buggy was waiting in front next to the gate with a horse pawing the hard ground and snorting in the cold breeze. In the seat on the left waited a large woman bundled well with a dark bonnet and fur mittens.

"Pull up over there, Pete," called Lula as she pointed to her right. "Looks like you got plenty of room." After they stopped. Pete hopped down to check the reins and harness, bit, and nose piece. Lula looked at the woman sitting by herself. "Hello, ma'am," she called politely, "are you waiting to see Mr. Dunbar?"

"You're Mrs. Perryman, aint you?" this woman answered.

As Pete tied the horse, Lula climbed down and went to her side. "Well, I was. But I married Mr. Jordan a while back. I am Mr. Dunbar's daughter. Get down and come inside with us."

"I'm Mrs. Gray. I own the boarding house." She peered down at Lula with a sad and wrinkled face. She waited a moment and gestured weakly toward the house. "My husband is inside talking to your daddy." And then, "No thank you. I'll wait here."

Lula wheeled around when she heard the front door open and close quietly. Instantly, and in a surprised moment, Waller Dunbar stood on his front step, coatless. He saw Pete approaching. "What are you doing here, Lu? How did you know?"

Lula did not hear what he said because of a passing buggy and wild driver. Pete tipped his hat to Mrs. Gray. Again the front door opened and out came Daisy, wearing a heavy shawl over her shoulders. In this late afternoon light Lula noticed her sister's dark eyes and sustained tears. She only stared.

Waller was insistent. "Come in, Lu, come in, all of you. I wish you'd come in, Mrs. Gray." He spoke softly and carefully. With his hat in his hand, Pete followed them. With some trepidation, Lula halted just inside the warm, neat room because she did not recognize the two men standing there like sticks with a solemn look about them. Pete remained directly behind her and closed the door.

Lula looked at her father for some kind of greeting. Then her eyes roamed about the room toward Malindy who was lighting an additional lamp on the table that occupied the center of the large dining room which satisfied her quilting stipulation.

"Lula," Waller began in an unusual monotone, "I don't think you know Bert Gray." Here was a man who wore a thick mackinaw and carried his black hat in his nervous hands. To this man, Waller said, "Bert, this is my daughter, Mrs. Jordan, and that young man over there is Pete, her drover from her farm."

"Howdy, ma'am," Gray mumbled. Lula could sense something was totally out of focus when Gray only nodded to Pete.

Daisy found her way to her sister but merely to give her one more sad look. Then, pulling the shawl closer about her, she disappeared into the bedroom. Lula removed her bonnet.

Waller ignored the second man. "Lula," he whispered, "Bert here is a part of the group, Mr. Menifee's group, that goes out hunting, you know, on hunting parties." He hesitated when the bedroom door opened and Daisy reappeared. They heard the baby daughter crying in the back room.

"Well, Lu," her father tried to continue, but Daisy interrupted, grasping his arm defiantly.

"It's about James, Lu," she spoke unhesitatingly, "Jimmy was killed about noon." More tears stopped her completely.

She wept so that Bert Gray intervened and spoke for them. He attempted a vaild explanation but his emotions destroyed his poise. "I'm sorry, ma'am. Jimmy there was trying to get through a fence. We was out west of town, west of the blacksmith's place. He was just a step or two ahead of me, he was, and we was joking and carrying on. He put his new shotgun against the barded wire, I guess, and I just looked away at a bird, I guess it was, and he crawled through and that's when it went off. He was killed outright."

Lula's bonnet and scarf fell from her hand onto the carpet. She collasped onto the sofa.

"I am so sorry, ma'am," Bert Gray mumbled as he fingered the brim of his dirty hat. He looked at Daisy and then again at Waller Dunbar. "I better go now, Mr. Dunbar." At the door he turned. "We taken his body to the undertaker if you want to know about that." Then quietly he left, closed the door, and joined his wife in the buggy. He wept silently as he took the reins.

Chapter Twenty-Three

The final days of February came and went with a gradual thawing of cold sleet into heavy rain. The entire nation was affected with added drudgery at Eufaula due to an accidental fire that destroyed a house and barn. It was all so unfortunate. In Tulsa the streets became quagmires. On a single one-day trip, Mrs. Covey's wagon was bogged down a block from Mr. Jedediah Parker's office and twelve men helped free it while her two horses pulled.

Mr. Parker, with his new found cat, discovered accommodations for himself at a newly established rooming house with the address of Two-O-Six South Boulder. Along with his cat, which he always took with him to his office each working day, this house entertained a menagerie of four other felines all noted for keeping the two storied structure free of mice.

Mrs. Foster, his landlady, upon hearing of the conflagration at Eufaula, proclaimed as loudly as she could her set of rules for those who used tobacco products. Under no circumstances did she intend to lose her commodious building that had only been completed just two months ago. This rotund lady with a loud bark that was heard a block away was not satisfied, after all with the performance of her cats. She wrapped herself with her old coat and marched down to Mr. Hall's store with a determination that conquered all problems. People who knew her moved out of her way.

"I want some poison, Mr. Partridge," she exclaimed that day, "no, not for my cats, no siree, how dare you think that, but for the mice that keep pestering the kitchen and basement."

"I knew you liked your cats, ma'am," Reubin tried to be pleasant, "do you still want what you say?"

"I certainly do. My cats are lazy." When she returned home she had a difficult time opening the container. "Mr. Parker," she called to him as he was about to leave, "before you go to your office this day, please help me with this lid."

"Of course, Mrs. Foster."

"You have to be real careful with poison, you know," she smiled at him. "Thank you. You're very helpful, sir."

Jedediah Parker had become not only helpful, he had become successful. Among his clientele were the Stivers family, the Stewart Shirks, and Mrs. Rachel Perryman, now that Mr. McBirney requested that Mr. Parker represent this dear lady who could not sign her name, even in Creek.

That cold day, after the session of opening the container, Mr. Parker met with a man by the name of J.D. Hayward in anticipation of the more important rendezvous the next day. With the advent of traffic increasing along this famous Main thoroughfare with its muddy and sloppy ruts, pedestrians had to become more careful not to slip and fall. Only one minute after saying goodbye to his landlady, Mr. Parker's boots would be layered with mud. That is why he carried his cat in a bag slung over is shoulder. Once at his office door he changed into house slippers which he placed just for that purpose. On this cold morning, he instantly prepared a small fire in his pot bellied stove since his client was expected that morning. With each piece of wood, garnered from a young chap who sold such wares, the decree about fire from his landlady haunted him. The businesses that surrounded his own humble place were close together, made of wood, and subject to their own holocaust if anyone should be so careless.

By the time that Mr. Hayward arrived, his new fire warmed his small area. The man had no trouble locating this office. He had an inbred sense of direction and always knew where he was going according to where north lay. He came from a family of seven, including his virile parents, who was most conscious of finding a means of making a living in Kentucky with brain and brawn. Two of his brothers were lost in a boat accident on the Ohio River just north of Owensboro. When Mr. Hayward sat in Owen's Cafe that morning, he overheard a conversation about that river and the name Hoskins was spoken. He remembered he had a close friend by that name when he was in his early twenties. Kentucky seemed so distant. As he sipped his coffee on this cold morning he was glad he dedicated his endeavors to money instead of agriculture. He was comfortable, even here, in this Creek Nation. It was the first time he was outside the United States.

Mr. Hayward was elegantly dressed in a black suit that proclaimed wealth. With his hand on his diamond tie pin to insure that is was not loose, he crossed the street on boards that were placed there only minutes earlier so several women holding their skirts high would not soil their hightop shoes. With all of today's traffic soon the boards would be submerged in thick mud.

Mr. Parker saw him step gingerly and when he reached the sidewalk safely the lawyer bid him welcome. "I trust all goes well," he called, "since we last saw each other?" He took Mr. Hayward's coat and hat and hung them on the new halltree just to the right of the door. "I have no secretary, Mr. Hayward," he obliged, "just myself in this modest office on Main."

"I mean to ask you, Mr. Parker," Haywood said as he adjusted his vest, 'I have heard about Judge Isaac Parker. Are you related, sir?"

"You ask about a time that was notorious twenty years ago. No, I am not related. This whole section of the territory was a hideout for criminals from every part of this country, of the States, I mean. That Parker lived and died in Fort Smith and under his jurisdiction the only law in the Indian nation was a handful of scattered deputy marshalls working with him. That judge died recently, I believe in 'ninety-seven I think it was." Then, picking up his cat, he added, "This is Tabby. He goes where I go." He offered a chair nearest the stove to his client and he brought his own from behind his desk.

"I've already met some Perrymans, Mr. Parker, but I don't think I've had the pleasure of meeting this woman you say who lives south of town. I've been to the town of Red Fork but no where else. Are they full bloods, as you say?"

"I would venture to say that they are all full bloods, sir," Parker announced, "but this lady whom you will meet tomorrow is the nicest of them all." The cat cuddled in his lap. "When I first met you shortly after your arrival, I took you walking by the house, the one on Fifth and Main, just up there. Everyone in town knows that house, Mr. Hayward. Real Estate is a big business now in Tulsa. I specialize in consultation regarding real estate and you have sought the right lawyer. As for crime, I leave that to the deputies who are undoubtedly still influenced by the Hanging Judge."

Mr. Hayward shivered as he placed his hands near the stove. "I asked you to find out for me what this woman thinks of my offer." He rubbed his hands together. "Were you successful in obtaining information for me?"

He crossed his legs and stroked his cat. "Since you are from Kentucky," he ventured an answer, "you may not be aware of the honesty and inherent beauty of these Creek people. I'm to understand that this lady, Mrs. Rachel Perryman, now fifty-three years of age, or thereabouts..."

"Fifty-three years old!" interrupted the client, "goodness gracious, I would not ever think that woman that age when you pointed her out, just by her merely walking along the street with her basket on her arm."

Mr. Parker smiled in agreement. "..that this lady has been planning to sell the ground on which her house is located. I reckon." The cat purred noticeably. "Mr. McBirney informed me what she wanted. I believe I'm correct when I say that I was able to locate you and your own commitment around early January, last, right after Christmas. You agreed, I believe, to wait a month."

"Well, it's two months now, sir." Hayward said softly.

"Yes. Well. I was unable to locate the other bidders for her land."

"What about her other house? Does she want to get rid of that land?"

"No, no," came the quick reply, "just the block of which we speak. Being a relative of a chief of the Creeks, she consulted with Mr. Porter..."

"Who?"

"Mr. Pleasant Porter. He is the chief of the tribe. Mrs. Rachel wanted his opinion on several matters. She speaks only her Creek language, although rumor has it she may understand some English. No one knows for sure."

"How on earth does she communicate?"

Mr. Parker relaxed and leaned back in his chair. This very question had become a delicate problem recently when Robert Shaw confided with the lawyer that only a few people were aware what was on this lady's mind about such a transaction. Jedediah Parker took a moment to explain this to his guest. Her three daughters maintained such an antagonistic attitude with their own mother that it was again difficult to explain this predicament to a stranger from the east. The Shawnee Indian, himself a character from yet another portion of history, reflected a lesson which this lawyer had no time to mention. For this moment, he kept to immediate detail. "You will meet Mr. Shaw, the Indian who speaks for her tomorrow. He is a local minister, I believe, of the Presbyterian Faith."

"And that's another thing," interrupted the Kentuckian, "I can't get over how civilized they all seem to be. I guess I mean Christianized."

The lawyer frowned a bit. He had no time to elaborate on the government of the Muscogees. But he did feel compelled to mention quickly some conditions wherein the man's statements were not altogether valid. "Not all of the cases, Mr. Hayward, but with Mrs. Rachel, we will have no problems arising. Evil does abound in Indian Territory, but not in her realm."

"Have you mentioned my price for the land? It's the land I want, remember, and not the house. That building will have to be removed," and he cleared his throat, "based on my plans and my clients bid for the block. I represent more than just myself on this business deal."

Mr. Parker rose, placed his cat on the floor, and went to his desk. He opened a neat parcel. "I have here in your brief the asking price of fifty-five thousand dollars. I must tell you that I am often amazed at the amount of monies that pass through the hands of barters who visualize the growth of our fair city. This town has lost its moniker of being a "town." They heard the logs crumbling in the stove as they turned to ashes. "We even have an Opera House here. I believe that your figure that you have proposed for transaction still exists?"

Mr. Hayward uncrossed his legs and stood on the opposite side of the wide desk. "It does."

"May I ask, sir," Parker closed the folder and he continued in a business like tone, "do you have the funds here in Tulsa with you?"

"I do." A loud scream from the cat broke the formal atmosphere and Hayward jumped. "Oh, I didn't know the cat was under my feet."

'"No harm done, sir," the lawyer conceded, "people step on him all the time. He's a very loving cat, all right."

Mr. Hayward spied the animal at the far end of the room by the rear door hiding behind the waste basket. But it's tail was still undulating. "Do we meet here tomorrow and at what time, Mr. Parker?"

"Let's see," he thought, "that's another thing. Tomorrow. Mrs. Rachel wants to meet with Mr. McBirney, and with us, at the House in question, to be there," and he stopped to point over his shoulder southward, "at eleven, if that's all right with you." By that time, the lawyer had come from behind his desk to locate the cat. He then gestured toward the halltree.

Mr. Hayward accepted his coat. "I suppose. Eleven, it is. Tomorrow. I'm going to the bank now to pay my respects again to Mr..." He had a problem with the right sleeve.

"McBirney. Mr. James Hugh McBirney."

"Yes. All right," he said, looking at the cat as he took his scarf from a pocket. "You have muddy streets here in Tulsa, sir."

Mr. Parker smiled. "And in the summer time we usually have cows or maybe a pig or two stepping along the avenue, right out there." He handed him his hat. "Our town is becoming a city. With your help, it will be more so, I'm sure. Goodbye, Mr. Hayward. Until tomorrow, then, sir."

The foreigner nodded agreement, laughed at the thoughts that his shoes would soon be dirty, but did not close the door as he stepped into the cold morning.

Jedediah shivered from the blast of cold air that managed to find its way into this office and closed the door rapidly. He picked up his cat en route to his desk. His mood changed considerably. While he never did know the full extent of the complications of which he was only the attorney, he frowned again as he studied the papers in front of him. He sat in his chair and the noise outside his perimeter of thought soothed his mind. The cat jumped from his lap.

The Perrymans had become a fascinating subject in the last three years. In the eleven years that he had been in the Muscogee Nation, he lived first in a cold tent, hearing stories, meeting cousins, all while establishing himself and his reputation. Several times he had to negate cases that dealt with criminal matter.

While stoking the fire again, his mind recalled his family. His mother was Irish so he was more inclined to speak well of the few families that reflected that ancestry. He kept a picture of his parents, brother, and sister hanging on a wall in his bedroom. Everytime rain fell here and he watched the Arkansas rise, he could not dismiss the flood in Jamestown that took his father's life.

But he was a successful lawyer. He told himself that from time to time. Mr. McBirney's own father was a pastor with a strong accent that complimented gentle conversations across these many months. With both, Jedediah sat and argued, even contemplated an aspect or two or social and economic differences of the potato famine and the wheat fields of Kansas. "I am glad my father came to Kansas when I was a wee boy," This thought was confessed by McBirney many times with the lawyer.

It was the Perrymans who intrigued Parker since eighteen-ninety-five when he first glimpsed the foundations. The house was to be large. What fascinated this lawyer who remained on the outskirts of this whole clan, was the amazing ability of the mother to care not only for her own children, who had become so enigmatic in his own mind, but those of other people who either discarded them for inexplicable reasons, or who had died, leaving many orphans by this woman's Welcome sign.

Mrs. Lula Perryman Jordan had been the person to introduce him to this family. It was not just a simple indoctrination, such a large extent of the siblings, Mr. Parker, as others, was bound to note a variety of temperaments. It was as if at the turn of the century a great many new facets of this clan were emerging. Spread out over the Creek Nation was this clan with its many limbs sprouting from the central tree. Protected as it was by treaties that had come and gone, with those that had been observed and discarded, their nation had been ignored, finally, by a government that was setting precedences for them from afar.

Being the lawyer who he was with so much to consider the surging of activity around him, he was consistently amazed at what he beheld just on his street alone. The two-storied hotel bordering on the railroad tracks put on a fresh coat of paint and its sign was broadened so the public could read it from two blocks distant. A man by the name of Byram, whom he had just met, bought the rights of the store across the avenue from where he moved his expanded office business. And one day about a week ago, Parker was able to tip his hat to Mrs. Mayme Shirk, certainly one the principals of this drama, who was walking with her sister. Neither lady returned his polite gesture.

With the help of Robert Shaw, he set about industriously to put into motion the location of businesses that particularly vied for valuable land from Fourth to Sixth, and from Main to Cheyenne. Somehow, no one was too concerned with the popular well which quenched thirst for many pedestrians even in winter.

His work continued by taking Mrs. Lula Jordan to lunch at Owens Cafe at a time when the Dunbar family had survived the recent sadness. Mr. Parker had not become acquainted with the Childers boys nor with their legend. From Lula he learned the intricate network of the many stories and faces that had become the fabric of the Perryman empire. Hopefully, with the coming of spring, the pain of James's passing would fade with the grey pall that fell about the Homestead.

"Please extend to your sister and your father my deepest condolences." They walked across the street toward the cafe. "I believe it was Mr. Shaw who delivered the funeral sermon."

Lula added, as they waited for traffic to clear, "That poor man had done nothing but preach funerals. One of Mrs. Covey's grandchildren died just last week."

The ground was frozen. Lula was careful where she stepped. "You may not remember an accident that happened. It was right over there." She pointed to an open lot. "Archer's store stood there." They paused at an intersection where she finished her story. "One of the first stores in town. Mose had a cousin, just a year younger, and they grew up together, name of Andrew. So Andrew came riding on his horse and went in to joke and carry on with Mr. Archer." By now, she pointed to the dimensions of where the foundation of the store rested which was now a knoll with some trash lying at different spots. "James Childer's death reminded me of what happened right here, Mr. Parker. Andrew was a good Indian, Mose told me, but that day he was full of spice and ginger and I reckon whiskey, too. Inside the store, surrounded by kegs of gunpowder, he fired his pistol into a barrel of it." Jedediah Parker was astounded. "That explosion killed both of them, right then and there, it was. Andrew left a widow and a one-year-old name of Homer. I saw Homer recently at the Beaver house. He's about thirteen, now, I guess. Same age as Oliver."

"You sure Mr. Jordan won't join us, ma'am?" He held the door open for her.

"Oh, this is fine, warm in here. No. Mr. Jordan is tending to some business today in Broken Arrow. So I drove the hack up here by myself this morning."

The cafe was still the same small room with large tables each with four chairs. They sat near the door to the kitchen to feel the heat from the stove. A young cowboy reminded Lula of James Childers, the manner in which he entered, shy, composed. When the lad sat alone, he removed his hat to run his fingers through his red hair. He was not Indian but a unique appearance suddenly brought Jimmy to mind again. "I guess by now I've learned what makes the world go 'round. I don't forget Mose. I guess I won't ever forget him. But Mr. Jordan is in my life now and I'm pleased to admit that."

A tall waiter with a dirty apron took their order. He was new and was not too alert at what the menu offered. After he left, the lawyer smiled. "You know, when I first met you, my dear Mrs. Jordan, I took you to be a rather quiet type of woman. I see a great deal of passers-by. Sometimes when I have time, I try to conceive of why they are in town or what they are thinking. And I believe I learned a great deal from you." Lula giggled and removed her gloves. "No. I really mean this. Ladies out here in the territory are a breed apart from any who remain where I came from. I don't ever intend to see Connecticut or Pennsylvania again." Then he changed his mind. "I guess I may like to visit again sometime one of these days."

After their coffee was brought to them, he broached the subject of the financial agreement. Lula was helpful. "Mrs. Rachel doesn't care for that monstrosity. Oh, at one time, I think she did, as long as her George built it for her and was alive. It was a beautiful house with the kids growing up, especially Oliver. It still is. I didn't mean to say that it's not." She spilled some sugar into her mug.

"I understand," was his reply, but he did not intend for it to sound patronizing. The city was a small one from a business standpoint. Such interests became acquainted with others. Along with those communications developed the reputations of this lawyer, the banker, and the client.

Therefore, when the first of March arrived with a suddenly bright, new sun. Lula and Winfred rose early, he, for a return trip to Broken Arrow to attend a sales of horses, she to leave the girls with Mr. Collins and to drive to Tulsa again to attend to her matters at the big House.

Specifically absent that day at the request of Mrs. Rachel were her three daughters and their husbands, the two sons and their wives, and of course Oliver who was at school.

By some stroke of luck, or an arrangement desired by Mrs. Stivers, she and

Lucy departed for Vinita when the second Mrs. Shanahan gave birth to another daughter. The Stivers ladies wanted to pay their respects to this large family who owned a valuable tract of farmland southwest of this important rail center. Mrs. Lucy Perryman was invited back for the first time since her honeymoon. And Mrs. Stivers was pleased about that.

Standing on the front porch of the House enjoying the new day was Mr. McBirney, smoking a fat cigar, as he watched the Jordan buggy find a place to park. Mr. McBirney went to meet Lula. "Mr. Shaw, Mr. Hayward, and Mr. Parker are already in the parlor," he said casually. They shook hands as they turned through the gate. "You're right on time, Mrs. Jordan."

Lula removed her hat and gloves in the foyer and she said hello to Mrs. Rachel in Creek.

Mr. Hayward remained at the side of the fireplace and directed a question to the Indian. "Am I to understand that you explained that I want to buy the land and not this house?"

"Yes, sir," Shaw agreed. He looked at the quiet lady who sat on her sofa, waiting. "She knows this." He spoke to her. By this time, Lula found a chair and sat. Her hair was mused but she was prepared to listen. Within the context of business, she noticed that this stranger was thorough, alert and polite. His grooming and apparel were immaculate. She even noticed a small diamond on his right ringfinger which she had not seen when she met him four days ago.

"Then," Mr. Hayward continued, "I suppose I can repeat my offer in front of Mrs. Jordan, the witness, and the banker?" Lula nodded in return. Mr. McBirney, who had left his cigar on the porch railing, coughed and cleared his throat.

Mrs. Rachel Perryman," Hayward began as Robert translated, "I am authorized and willing to pay you fifty-five thousand dollars United States currency for the terra firma on which this house rests, this day, the first of March, nineteen-o-three, eleven thirty ante meridian."

Jedediah Parker, standing next to the windows, was amused by the formality. He had hardly said a word since he had arrived thirty minutes earlier. He wondered just how this Indian would be able to be as succinct as the man from Kentucky.

But he did repeat it. The purchaser, the banker, and the lawyer waited for her answer which did not come immediately. The wall clock that hung near the stairwell sounded half the hour. Its chimes echoed throughout the entire lower floor.

Mrs. Rachel waited also, thinking, as she smoothed her long wool skirt. Lula turned to look at her. The noise of traffic along Main was extra loud, noticed, because the front door had not been completely closed. Mr. Parker closed it and returned to the windows. Mr. Hayward straightened his stance beside the fireplace and cupped his hands behind him. "Did she comprehend you, Mr. Shaw?"

The Shawnee looked up from his notepad on which he wrote him communiques. "Oh, yes, that, I know!" He then smiled at this lady. When she spoke in return it was a soft murmur. He bent low over her to verify her remark. Then, he stood erect and replied to all. "She talked to Chief Porter. She asks for sixty thousand dollars United States currency."

George arrived outside the front gate and distracted every one. Mr. Parker was first to notice him as he tied his horse. "Mr. Perryman is here," the lawyer announced. But Mr. Hayward concentrated on his transaction. "What did she say?"

George came through the front door, leaving it open as he surmised the crowd. "What's going on?" Then he stepped back to shut the door. He looked at Hayward with a frown.

"Her figure is sixty thousand dollars, Mr. Hayward." The repeat of the statement left everyone silent.

Lula rose quickly and escorted George from the foyer into the far corner of the dining room. "Your Mama is selling the land, George, this block where the House is."

"What do you mean block? You mean the House?" He tried to look into the parlor but she detained him.

"No, She means, the land."

George was so perplexed he tried to move the second time. "Mama?" he questioned, "I don't understand. How can anyone sell this...land if you can't sell the...what's going on? Who is that man in there?" He stopped and looked again. "Why does Mama want to do something like that?" Again, he looked past Lula into the parlor where he saw his mother. "Mama....Mama?"

Lula was at his side. "George," she tried to present him, "George, this is Mr. J.D. Hayward. He's here to..."

Jedediah Parker intervened to help. "George, this man here is intending to buy the property on which this House sits."

The son sat beside his mother. "To buy? Why?" His eyes told her what was in his heart. He looked at Mr. Hayward. "I didn't know this House was for sale!"

"Not this house, young man." Hayward corrected, "the land."

George jumped up and confronted him. "Well the land then, whatever!"

"Mr. Parker," Hayward called, looking past the figure in front of him, "am I to assume that this woman's family...?"

"Mr. Hayward, sir," Parker answered quite suddenly, "your transaction in which we are currently involved concerns this lady and the business at hand, namely you and your constituents and does not include any other family members." To this, George reeled and was totally silent, frowning at the lawyer and then down at his mother. "And now, Mr. Shaw, if we may continue. This lady is requesting a sum greater than what you offered."

"Well, she certainly has, Mr. Parker." The gentleman from Kentucky was flustered. "I am obliged to remind you, and her, that I just may not be able to agree to that increase."

George was stunned. He returned to the sofa but did not sit by his mother. Robert Shaw tried his best to keep up with the conversation.

"Ask her again," demanded the purchaser. But that was not necessary since Mrs. Rachel translated the expression on his face. From a wide pocket in her skirt she extracted a paper on which was written in cardinal numbers the figure of sixty thousand dollars. The signature of the chief was the seal.

George sank onto the sofa beside her. "Oh, Mama!"

Mr. Hayward, at a loss for words, heaved a sigh. "Oh. Are you sure?" Shaw politely took the paper and showed it to Hayward. "Then please ask her to sign this paper and date it today." He offered his pen to her by first removing its cap.

"She will make her X and I will witness it, or Mrs. Jordan can witness it."

"Oh, very well." This was his conclusion. "I'll go to the bank with you, Mr. McBirney and draw up a check for her."

Mrs. Rachel, following closely, uttered one word after she made her X and returned the pen to its owner.

"What was that? What did she say now?" The perspiring gentleman extracted a handkerchief from the breast pocket of his suit coat and wiped his face.

Again Robert Shaw verified the word with her and she nodded in agreement. "Not a check, Mr. Hayward. She wants cash."

That word penetrated the silent room. "Cash!" Hayward was confounded! "Why cash, my stars! Why not a check? A check is good legal tender even in a foreign country. Just ask anyone, ask a banker, there!"

The translator remained polite. "She wants cash, Mr. Hayward." George was so upset that he stumbled into the foyer.

This request astounded even Mr. McBirney who, exasperated, offered his own pen to Lula to sign on the witness line. He caught the eye of Mr. Hayward in a plea for help. "Attending to this matter may take me more than the rest of this day to determine if we can oblige this lady." All eyes were on the banker. He continued. "Today is Friday. The bank is closed at three p.m. and will not open until Monday morning at ten. I will see what I can do." He retrieved his pen. Shaw translated. "But it can be done!"

"Good grief!" was all the purchaser could say. "Well. All right. I'll have to agree with this figure." Resignedly, he handed the paper to the lawyer. "Take care of this, sir, if you will, please." He extended his right hand to Mrs. Rachel which she took with one simple grasp. He then spoke to George with an effort to calm himself. "Sir, I take it you are this fortunate lady's son. My name is J. D. Hayward from Owensboro, Kentucky, sir, and may I say you have a fascinating mother." He smiled when he signaled Mr. McBirney to leave with him. To Shaw he remarked, "Please tell this lady that we will contact her when the money...when the cash arrives. Mr. Parker, don't lose that piece of paper. I trust you will conclude the transaction at your office?" He reached for his hat.

"I will, sir."

He replaced his handkerchief, nodded politely to all, and preceded the banker. Lula walked to the window and watched them walk down the sidewalk and turn north toward the bank.

Mrs. Rachel remained still, very still, on a sofa that reflected hardly any wear, with its high curved back and round arms. Her son collapsed next to her, placing his head in his hands, only to stand immediately, to glance perplexedly about the parlor as if he were searching for the most correct word to say to anyone. He was much older now and the onus of bearing his father's name was more obvious than ever.

This century did not begin well for this young man. With Abner and with his other siblings, of course, he bore the loss of a great and honorable spirit. Also with Moses gone, George looked to Abner for help in managing their cattle. The herds were even yet predominant but they were also depleted.

As his mother rose and went to her kitchen, George slumped on this sofa deep in thought. Lula said goodbye to Mr. Parker who departed for his office.

To the siblings, the beginning of the century meant more consternation than merely the loss of their father. The winter, when nineteen hundred arrived, was one of the coldest as was the previous one. Perryman cattle died by the hundreds at Legus's farm in Eufaula clear north to Moses's Homestead. 'The weather, while certainly bitter, was wet. Ralph Collins voiced deep concern.

Wrapped in his current thoughts, this contemporary George Perryman groaned with worry. Even Robert Shaw noticed how silent he was after the principals of this drama departed. The Shawnee was near the pantry, with Lula ready to leave.

"Is he all right," this translator asked.

"I guess he is," Lula replied quietly while putting on her coat. "But I've got to go. Goodbye, Mr. Shaw. Good luck." She discovered Mrs. Rachel returning from the well with a bucket of fresh water. She called to her, "Goodbye, Mama," and left.

Again George sat on the sofa. Absentmindedly he found the stubs of two railroad tickets, remnants of the recent trip, in a pocket of his vest. Having just returned from Kansas City, he and Orphia had not unpacked yet. The trip and its reasons were still strong on his mind. In order to manage the cattle as well as Abner would expect, this brother carried on the business largely by borrowing capital. This negotiation was imperative. The numbers of remaining long horns, steers, even milk cows, including Angus, dwindled pitifully by the fall of nineteen hundred. Even so, they were herded by the few loyal wranglers who persisted to remain under Perryman aegis. "We will be here, for you, Mr. Perryman," was their cry.

Mrs. Rachel appeared in the archway with a glass of water.

"Oh, Mama! You didn't have to sell. I borrow money! It's natural. The Livestock Commission gave me plenty of money to see us through this winter. Oh Mama!" He realized she did not understand him even when she saw the tears in his eyes. There was no way to talk to her. "It's commission money, Mama. Mose taught me this."

She offered the glass; he took it and drank.

It was easy to arrange for monies in Kansas City at the office where everyone was well acquainted with this family. "We have a good reputation," the father proudly stated, long ago. But his son's agonized thinking brought everything up to date. Abner mentioned a thirty percent loss a year ago with possibly more during this past winter. The two brothers were faced with the sudden reality that their intended profit and their borrowed capital were now lying on frozen ground over hundreds of acres.

And the kind face of his mother was always there, waiting. George returned the empty glass to her. He had always been organized and disciplined, much like the other brothers. He desperately wished Abner were here. He was like a rudderless ship on a sea of dismay. It was he who inherited the cattle empire, what there was left of it. Moses, by now, had become a figment of an era that began disintegrating when he died. Everywhere that George went, he saw this change, this immense and overpowering annihilation of traditions that he learned as a small child, strolling hand in hand with his uncles and teased by them, loved by them all.

"Oh, Mama, I wish you could talk to me. We always had people to talk for us, Emma, when she was there, the old men who came to the White House when we were growing up. Uncle Thomas was good at that, he, with his hymns. Uncle Josiah, I remember him, too. That's all gone. No one to speak Creek anymore. Oliver doesn't know hardly a word of it."

Mrs. Rachel was ready to leave. She pulled down the shades in her parlor, opened the front door and gestured to her son to leave, also. So George rose and followed her to her buggy. He tied his own horse at the tailgate, helped his mother get on board, looking back at the House as if it were one final effort to erase the day's milestone. "I'm taking you home."

Across the street, hidden by noon traffic, coming a block away from the south and dressed in her finest garment with a new hat was Mayme Shirk, driving her own new carriage. She had stopped when she recognized Lula Jordan. With reins yet in her hands, she watched her leave in her own buggy. Mayme sat for a while, protected by partial shade from the closest elm. Then, just as she was about to proceed, Robert Shaw walked through the gate and continued to the church. She reined in again the second time. She deliberately dismounted and hid herself behind a tree that was one of many on the east side of Main. Those leaving had not seen her.

She wished Emma were with her, going to the luncheon, so she could stop and talk because she was certain of what she beheld, a brother to whom she had not spoken in two weeks and her mother whom she had not visited in a long time. All, after that Mrs. Jordan left. George and Orphia must have come back, not that it mattered to her.

Mayme did not enjoy the idea of Lula being a part of her family now that she no longer bore the Perryman name. Adjusting her hat when a low tree limb struck it, she frowned at the exodus. Lula should not even be living on Perryman land. That was Perryman allotted land. That woman was impertinent!

From somewhere in the back of her mind Mayme recalled the lessons that an old Indian man disclosed to the children. The old Creek was ancient but the Perrymans and everyone learned respect and honor and history. To them this man spoke through Uncle Thomas. Outside, under the trees, at Wealaka Mission, Mayme, more than others, learned Creek tradition. She had even learned to dance with turtle shells tied to her legs. But she grew up. She married Stewart Shirk and she became, if anything, the woman who hid behind elms. She had not danced in years.

What was Lula Jordan doing here? She had no right here. She was not to own land nor raise cattle, nor own her house. She could be ejected at any time. She had no business here.

With his mother to his left, George turned on Fifth Street, absorbed by the frightening episode, the menacing crowds.

Chapter Twenty-Four

Rachel Perryman welcomed the return to her domicile south of the burgeoning city and away from the deep-rutted streets, the din of traffic, the congestion that changed her own placid scheme of things. She returned to her daily sewing in the afternoons when the late winter sun spread its rays through her west windows and covered the quilt she was making. It was a time when the layer of cloth, thick and new, was off the rack and balanced on a nearby chair as she sewed on its borders. In her tranquil manner she worked diligently until her eyes grew tired before her hands did. Then she stopped. In another chair which she moved to a position to gather the most warmth, she napped.

And Oliver Perryman had reached that pleasant time when he and his horse galloped over the south side and near the pond on school days when he talked to the ducks and they answered him. They knew him, so tame were they that they waddled over to him, begging for food. If he had crumbs, remnant of his sandwich in his lunch pail, he let them spill on the ground. One duck was a favorite. But they were all favorites. He was riding his horse everywhere with the blessing of his mother. It was an arrangement both had made since she allowed Abner and his bride to live in the House, for the present, that is. In another month more or less they would have to vacate, plans for which were not devised yet.

But for the moment, Mrs. Rachel was pleased. When George brought her home that Friday, he filled her bucket with well water, carried logs of firewood into her kitchen and peered into every room, upstairs and down, to see that she would be comfortable. For whatever her purpose, for whatever her gain, he was happy if she were happy. When she started to prepare her bowl of sofka, he knew she was all right.

Before he left, George stood for a while at the front door to look to the pond, the trees south of it, to the cattle that roamed about the plain, to the low pastureland that reflected the myriad of thoughts that roamed through his own head. Finding grass for herds to eat was difficult, moreso, than it was previously. Leaning against the pillar of the porch where his mother always had her Welcome sign, he heard her at her usual pace, unhurried, quiet, systematic, contributing. With so many sudden reveries his mind centered on his baby he and Orphia lost. He knew now the anguish Emma felt. This past winter was harsh, cruel and so very cold that pneumonia claimed tots who had not reached their first birthday.

With the sun on his face the wind was not cool. In a narrow wicker chair that had been resting on the porch for ten years, George sat down and crossed his legs, folding his hands over his vest as if he had no care in the world. This was his home. He was born in this house and he learned to milk cows here. The amount of cattle on the plains was four times what he saw then, that afternoon. More than once his eyes fell on the pond where he used to run and play. Oliver inherited that joy.

He remembered the story how Mr. Collins saved his father's life right out there not more than thirty feet from where he sat in the chair. He felt the wicker arms, the broken pieces that mirrored the wear across the years. Wind fell across his face. This was home, not the City of Tulsa, not Owen's Cafe, nor Hall's Store, nor Parker Attorney at Law.

To his right, coming on the path from town was Oliver on his pony from school. When the boy saw his brother standing to greet him, he spurred his horse to a trot and then reined just a few feet from the steps. After a gentle wave, Oliver dismounted, placed his satchel by the door, and sat on the porch. He was very much the young boy of fourteen now, with his shirttail out of his waist and his cap on the back of a head full of long black hair. His horse ambled to the buggy, its reins trailing on the ground.

"I want you to take good care of Mama, will you?" was the brother's remark, more a statement than a question.

That sounded odd. "What do you mean?"

George rose and tended to the buggy, untied his own horse from the rear and checked the left hame. "Mama sold the land downtown to a buyer from the States." This did not register with Oliver at first. "She sold it," George continued, "without saying a word to any of us."

"I never did like that House much anyway," Oliver confessed. "She didn't sell this house, did she?"

George felt the cinch and tightened it. "I hope not. No, I guess not. No. She didn't. It's still ours." As he mounted he added, "Park the buggy in the barn for me will you? I don't have time to do it myself. Make sure that one gets feed and rub him down good, will you?"

"Sure." Oliver walked over to George. "Is Mama all right?"

"Yes, she's just fine. She's inside the house. Look after her." George's remark was casual yet it sounded odd to him. Oliver always considered that a joy and not a chore. "You're growing up, now, little boy! I can see that. How's school?" This question made Oliver retreat, shrugging his shoulders. "Goodbye, then," George said, and turned his horse toward the pathway now worn away into a narrow roadbed. By the time the boy took the two horses and the buggy to the barn, George was out of sight hidden by trees that had grown so tall they became land-marks long ago. The sun was practically on the same horizon.

Almost forgotten from time to time, Emma was the translator only in the past three years, yet she had been obviously missing from the day's dialog. This too was on George's mind as he turned north. She learned Creek by rote from the uncles, her father, and from the many elderly tribesmen who refused to learn English. Every early lesson was disciplined and orderly. At such a young age she even wondered why her brothers and sisters had not wanted to pursue such an interest. "English is very much the language of the Council, now," Josiah had once told her before he became ill. "Mr. Porter wants it from now on. Mr. Berryhill and Mr. Grayson have already agreed and it was such an agreement long before Porter became chief. But still she persevered, for it was a culture that was quickly fading from the landscape.

"I don't know why you don't learn it, either," Emma argued with Ella when they were little girls. "I know Mayme doesn't ever want to learn it so I don't even bother with her." Growing up, Emma was always ready to help people in some way for any purpose. The uncles infused the spirit of Indian lore in the brothers;

Emma never did understand why they ignored the females. She was just as proud to be a Perryman as the rest of her family.

This pride was not an easy project to maintain. Clifton Drew, who was elusive and eccentric, voiced no objection to what his mother-in-law succeeded in accomplishing with the House on Main. He was too absorbed with his own Reason, as he called it. On his horse at different locales, Eufala, Okmulgee, Muskogee, he attended to business that concerned the memories of only the full bloods. For the rest of his life, he was destined to remain on the perimeter of reality as far as his mind could fathom. He traveled to and fro forever enveloped in the sadness that his babies were buried in Perryman Cementery but with the inevitable hope that others might survive. Clifton Drew always partook of the tribe's traditions which were most appreciated when he caroused with the best of Indians, drank prohibited whiskey from a mysterious source in Sapulpa, or when he was most respectful while learning of the Great Spirit. In either case, he was always just beyond the realm of comprehension. Being Emma's husband was to conjure the most significant mystery of them al. That, then was the way it was to be.

Mayme Shirk, tallest of the Perryman women, had attained her height from her father and his father. Both were tall and the grandfather was slim, but not George senior. Her uncles were practically all six feet and her Uncle Thomas, being the thinnest, was one inch higher than any of them. Mrs. Rachel was noticeably short. Everyone who knew her remembered that.

Mayme's strength was not in height, alone, but in her own inner self, setting her apart from the others. The time had come, now that the word got back to her about the House and the land, when Mayme was more concerned with her own worth as a blood member of this family. She asked Emma outright just why their own mother refused to discuss the sale before she committed herself to this Mr. Hayward. Emma was too fretful to venture a guess. Poor Ella remained aloof. Mayme mused about her own house, often going out to the rear to watch the river on its lonely trek to the east. Her house was small, too cold in the winters, too far from the White House and, like the Arkansas, too lonely. To make matters worse, in her eyes her house was not an important home as was the one that her dead brother built for Lula in eighteen-ninety-five.

Mrs. Lula Jordan was the reference for conjecture. At opportunitites which Mayme devised, she would make her sisters talk about this woman. Mayme would no longer visit her mother unless Emma was present. She wanted to be certain Mrs. Rachel was listening to words which Mayme contrived.

Mayme even presented her opinions on the situation of the House with hardly anyone except Mrs. Stivers. Lucy's mother was acquainted with the three sisters but not too well. She was a prudish matron who was more concerned with her daughter's new social status than with any other phase of endeavor. Lucy and her mother returned from Vinita and learned of the recent exploit. At her breakfast table that morning, Mrs. Stivers dropped her coffee cup. The hot liquid shattered her nerves and stained the new table cloth as well.

Mayme felt obliged to discuss the matter with someone, so she and Mrs. Stivers met in the house on Cheyenne Avenue. "I can't figure it out," Mayme complained. "I will say this." Together they left this residence and were able to view the House as they walked toward it through the many elm trees along Sixth street. "Your Lucy and Abner are going to have to move. I guess you know that. I suspect that the House is coming down. Abner told me they have mice, anyway."

"What do you mean, 'coming down'?" Such a threat was inconceivable to Mrs. Stivers whose presence in social circles around the city was never in doubt. This matron made sure that her Lucy's name was dropped everywhere as Mrs. Perryman, Mrs. Abner Q. Perryman. Frustated as she already was, she felt an enigmatic committment to solve this dilemma. It was a bright and beautiful day. They walked past the House and to Owen's Cafe where they had lunch.

Mrs. Lucy Stivers Perryman was furious and she had been so since returning from the Shanahan Ranch in Cherokee Territory. Her amazement to learn about the births of so many children threatened her very soul. The latest baby was the eighteenth, a daughter, and the threat was that she, herself, could easily become a mother of eighteen. When Abner told her recently that his own father was one of eighteen, she could not accept it.

"I'm just telling you what Mama has already done, Lucy," Abner tried to explain. "I don't know what else to tell you." The threat of eighteen children disappeared like a flash of lightning the moment Abner exposed the situation.

"To give up this house, Abe," was her retort. "Why, I just can't quite grasp what she means. This is our home, Abe. To surrender this House . . . Oh, Abner!"

The next day, George came to consult with his brother. And Lucy, still so fragmented, fled the House and raced up the street to the comfort of her mother where both women emphatically agreed that they were required to solve this predicament.

Reubin Partridge was never one to adhere to reports of any descrepancies, rumors, or gossip. He went about his work at Hall's Store gladly, even effortlessly, watching the spring come on with gladness and gratefulness, always grateful for every good and precious gift from God, as he put it. Reubin was a good man and a solid rock, as strong as Gilbraltar about which he read this past week in a book he found in the trash behind the store. He became an avid reader who pestered his wife with wild stories about going to Africa or sailing the Seven Seas. But he did remain home after all. At this moment the wild stories were not on his calendar. He returned to the store after delivering a large order of seed to Lloyd Cooper where the river bends westward. He positioned the empty buckboard at his usual spot on First Street and unharnassed his mule.

"Through for the day? asked a lady as she waited before crossing Main. "What time is is, Reubin, do you know?" He extracted his pocket watch, squinted his eyes to the sun, and uncovered the dial. He smiled, "Five to four."

"How's your wife?" She decided to chat.

"She had her baby all right. We got a boy, our second one."

"That's nice, Reubin, you've got the start of a good family." She waved goodbye. "There's one of my youngon's. Gotta go."

The railroad tracks were just to the north of Hall's Store where everyone within earchot could always hear the train as it approached. Often times the soot from the smokestack lingered in the air, depending on March winds. This caused the town to cough and wheeze if any traffic lined the streets at the time the engine slowed and stopped at the station. By now the town had grown so much that hardly anyone accounted for the twice-weekly schedules. Other than the mischevous children who put pennies on the tracks so the cars' wheels could flatten them, few people elected to stand and watch arrivals. Mr. Hall and the city council petitioned Frisco to place the engine two blocks farther west so that those on Main Street would not have to suffer the noise and confusion. That way, the passenger car would stop directly at the Main Street intersection, convenient for everyone.

Lucy Perryman, with her right arm poised, ready to accept Abner's escort, spoke about this subject of the railroad with the populace. She stood on the front porch ready to walk with her husband to the store. She decided to walk rather than go in her new buggy and a new horse, and to allow Reubin to deliver her order later. Her ire subsided for a time and she agreed that the bright afternoon sun helped to alter animosity of any kind. "If we go now," she suggested as she opened her parasol, "we'll miss the arrival of that dirty train."

Abner walked swiftly. When Lucy complained, he slowed a bit but not for long. Their conversation was not original nor did it spark any significant conclusions about important events. Mr. Shanahan had had two wives, not one; the first one died. Both were Cherokee. Vinita was larger in population than Tulsa. The Fort Smith and Western Railway operated as far west as Weeltka, possibly farther. Too, their words were sprinkled with simple phrases about the ordinary minutes of their life together and their lifes apart from each other. Just before they sighted the store, three large wagons with ornery horses hurried by them. One of the drivers called out to Abner. Lucy bounced backward to miss the mud that splattered on the dusty walkway.

"If it isn't one thing, it's another," she commented when she looked at the hem of her dress. "Abe, the drivers offered no apology whatsoever. Do you know them?"

He did not answer. Eventually they reached the store front where they encountered Reubin, sweaty and tired, from his trip west of town. Abner stopped to talk to his cousin while Lucy folded her parasol and entered by herself.

Abner motioned for them to stand to one side out of sight from those inside with the customers. "Looks like Mama sold the land, Reubin. I suppose you heard about that." He removed his gloves.

"Already did, Abe," he answered. "I knew for a fact George and you were having trouble with your cattle. Sales, I mean."

"A slump in prices, Reubin. But it's not the end, by any means. We still got our heads above water." Abner nodded to a passer-by. "George took it pretty bad, though."

His cousin listened and then, with his wide hand, gave Abner a strong pat on the back. "Come on in. I bet Lucy probably has a list a mile long. She walks alot, now, doesn't she?"

"She goes to see her mother every day, I guess."

Reubin's smile did not help, for he noticed Abner remained preoccupied. "What's wrong? Is it the House business?"

"Oh, I don't quite know it all. I'm worried about Lucy, I guess." Abner glanced through the front entrance to make sure she did not hear them talking. With her list in her hand, she was busy talking to another lady. " I do want to talk to Hall, though. Is he upstairs or in the back?"

"He's upstairs, I suppose. I just got back from the Cooper place. You go on up. I'll see what Lucy needs."

Abner moved through the aisles with a hesitancy that was foreign to Reubin. but the clerk was soon at Lucy's side, as the other lady left with her bag of groceries. "Well, now, Mrs. Lucy," he smiled graciously, "let's see what you have there, written down."

Lucy was kindest at its best, turning to Reubin with her gloved hand extended, with her greeting and a curtsey, so unlike what Reubin heard from other sources in town but which he had learned long ago to ignore. "Did my husband leave you, Mr. Partridge? Where did he go?"

Reubin's eyes left the paper he held. "I believe he is upstairs yonder, ma'am, talking to Mr. Hall. That's what he said to me just now. My, that's a pretty hat you're wearing."

"I got this in my favorite store in Vinita, when Mama and I went to say hello to the Shanahans. They're a big family now, and Mr. Shanahan has the thickest Irish accent I've ever heard, thicker than Mr. McBirney, I reckon."

"Excuse me, ma'am, and I'll see to gathering these things and I'll just place them on the counter over there for you."

Lucy sauntered among the rows of wares, food, tools, and farm merchandise that Mr. Hall stocked every month. She noticed the warning signs regarding gunpowder and one big one advertising that dynamite may be ordered, with a deposit and purchased later. She stopped at a display of goods where her eyes fell on a shelf two feet from the floor, not very wide, but stocked with multiple boxes painted red with large white letters. She reached for one and read its small print. It was chemically manufactured expressly for destoying ants, mice, cockroaches, and spiders. Holding the tiny box carefully in her hands, blowing away the thin layer of dust that had collected on its top, she walked slowly to where Reubin placed her items on the counter. She included this box with others. She waited patiently.

Abner finished his conversation with Mr. Hall. "I really don't know what's going to happen with Mama selling that property. I can't begin to think what we'll do to save the House." He rose from the chair by the south windows. "I can see it, coming down, tearing it all out, just for the sake of the sale. You've got a pretty nice view of it from up here. We've had a lot of bad luck in our family lately. You heard about Emma losing her babies. And of our cousin Nora, married Andy Scott and already they lost a little girl, too. We've had some bad winters." He started for the door that led to the stairs.

"Wait a minute," Hall interrupted, "I'm through here. I'll go down with you."

Reubin obtained a strong packing crate from storage and put it on the counter. "I'll deliver these tomorrow as you say, Mrs. Lucy."

Her casual reply was noticeably different from the other times when she bought her groceries. "Except that I'll take a few, if you don't mind. I can manage them. I'll have Abner tote them for me." As she spoke, she set aside three small selections from the larger order. I'll just take these with me now."

Preparing for paper work with a new pencil and separating them, Reubin accounted for each, first, absently noting every one with a soft movement of his right hand since he was left handed. He started his list as he saw Mr. Hall and Abner entering from the rear. "Cocoa, toothpicks, and poison," placing them in a neat brown bag. "Very well." While he continued his tabulation on the credit slip, Lucy folded the top of the bag and handed it to Abner.

"I'm making a chocolate cake tonight for Abe! His favorite, so I've learned. I've everything else I need."

"I bet you're a real good cook, Mrs. Lucy." Reubin laughed as he leaned against the counter.

Lucy adjusted her gloves. "Come, Abe, may we go now?"

On the walkway still caked with mud from the recent rain, Lucy opened her parasol. "Why look, Abe," she nudged him, "I believe that's Mr. Shirk across the street. It sure looks like Mayme's husband." Two men were talking to each other.

This stopped Abner. Through the heavy traffic he tried to signal both men. "Lucy," he muttered, " you go on home 'cause I want to say hello to those men over there. Please."

"That other man looks like Papa but it isn't." She shrugged her shoulders. "All right. Don't be long. Mama and Papa are coming over to eat with us, you know." She stopped him suddenly. "Abe, dear, give me that bag. I'll take it with me."

"Stew," Abner called loudly. It did not carry so he yelled again. "Hey, Stew, wait a minute." He made his way carefuly across the street and shook hands with the two men. Stewart Shirk's hair was longer under his tall, dirty hat. He was too casual in his return greeting. The other man quietly dismissed himself and was lost in the crowd. Shirk never maintained any formal postition with his wife's brothers and sisters. He never wanted in any way to express any reference to his business nor what he wanted his business to become. His black suit was never pressed, he wore no tie at any time, and his dark Indian skin seemed caked with grime. He waved goodbye to the man who was taking to him and then he turned to Abner. "What is it you want to see me about, Abe?"

"I'm going to Vinita either tomorrow or the next day and I thought you might want to go with me. I've got to see some stock and pay a bill."

"I don't think so, Abe, thanks anyway. You got cows to sell?"

"Mama is selling the land on Main . . ." and Abner paused to see how this information may affect Stewart's composure. He merely waited for Abner to complete his statement. "I guess you know that . . ."

This brother-in-law was one Indian who searched for news that would enlarge his money schemes, even his pocket change. There was a time when he proposed eloquent plans to his wife and she was asked not to broadcast them. While some succeeded mysteriously to bring them wealth, especially where real estate was concerned, the other so-called opportunities backfired and made him callous and cruel. That was just his manner. As the months passed, Abner and George eventually became aware of this man's tactics. In time, they had to accept the brother-in-law for who he was, his personality, his grooming, his image. "I know that.." He spit tobacco in the street. "And Mayme is downright mad at everything, including your ma, that's happened. That land is worth more than sixty thousand dollars. Anybody would know that. You people . . . you should have talked to somebody before going off the handle . ." Shirk was so angry at just the mention of the transaction that he could not complete his statement. Obviously, neither he nor Mayme knew that Mrs. Rachel had discussed this at length in Creek with Chief Porter. "Now, then, just when is this finally going to take place?"

Abner waited until an ancient wagon full of noisy children rattled by them. "The ninth," he said, somewhat reluctantly," that's next Tuesday. No, Wednesday. In the lawyer Parker's office." He pointed. "That one, right over there."

Still wearing his poker face, Shirk commented, "That's still a lot of money." He casually waved to an acquaintance. "Mayme ought to be there. I'll tell her."

Abner dared to ask a question. "Wasn't that Atkins who was talking to you?"

"Yes it was." That is all that Stewart Shirk volunteered. That name, Atkins, was prominant in the Creek Nation. It was an Atkins to whom Lula sold that section of her land at the intersection of those two country roads, one leading west to t he bridge over Coal Creek, the other southward to the Homestead. That Atkins had plans for a one-room schoolhouse to be built soon on the corner. One of the

Perryman cousins married an Atkins and already had two little babies, but the man who walked away was not a relation to any of them. Shirk listened as if he had never heard Abner's subject. He seemed much too disinterested by Mayme's brother. At a lull in conversation, Shirk dismissed himself with a curt "goodbye', losing himself in a surge of pedestrians.

Lula's children sat at the kitchen table a day later eating oatmeal and drinking milk that Laredo brought to them. Dot, now eight, was in charge of washing dishes while Cozetta, six, had the everyday duty of setting the table for dinner before the men, including Mr. Jordan, came in from the fields. Edith would stand and watch.

Their mother realized the order of the day, of the week, of the year, better than anyone. In the heavy week that followed James Childers' funeral, to which the children did not go, snow fell for three days. That seemed, to Lula, to be a good time for her to set the daughters on the sofa near the stove in the parlor to explain, first-ly, that they would never see Jimmy again. With assistance of Robert Shaw who found eleoquent words regarding Heaven and Little Girls, he managed to surprise them with news that Mr. Atkins was building a school at the crossroads to which they will go instead of having to consider the arduous task of education in Sapulpa. It was an answer to a prayer.

Secondly, and much easier for all concerned, was the explanation of adoption, in that Mr. Jordan was to become their new father. At one time or another, Lula tried her best to explain what happened to Moses. Edith had never known her father. Dot and Cozetta had their own remembrances, a fleeting moment or two somewhere in the back of a child's mind when the father's care of his daughters was recalled in embraces that was disappearing, now, but reflected in a picture or two that originally hung in the parlor. Dot looked at the wall but her mother had removed those pictures. They were not on that wall anymore. When she nudged her sister, Cozetta said they were in a box in that room off the hall. So the little girls sat obediently with their hands in their laps, with their little feet in black boots, like those in the pictures that were no longer there, hardly touching the throw rug in front of the stove. The three of them were warm and attentive. They listened. And they promised to be good little girls.

Such was a difficult time. They were never to see Jimmy again, but they were to see spring again and spring did come, and they began to run and play around the house, outside in the fresh clean air, to tease the dogs, to joke and laugh with Pete who carried them around in the red wheelbarrow and told them wild stories about Texas and where it was located, aided of course by Laredo's unquestioning authority.

So one morning early they had their baths, they dressed quickly, and had a good breakfast as promised by Pete for he was the interim cook until Aunt Sally arrived. Then, with hair combed, with pretty ribbons, and long dresses, they rode all the way to Tulsa to visit Mr. Parker.

"Will we still be part Indian?" Dot asked softly.

"Will we still be part Perryman?" echoed Cozetta.

Such questions haunted the girls especially after a nice long talk with their Uncle Abner. "Papa is dead," Dot mused. "I remember."

"Yes, but Mr. Jordan will be your new papa now, Dot, " replied an eager Lula most assuredly. "He's going to live with us in the big house on the hill . . ."

"Where I was born. . ?" Dot was full of questions as they prepared to go.

"Yes, " she continued, " and he is going to be the head of the family now."

"And will Pete and Laredo still be here? And Mr. Collins?"

"Yes, they'll be right here." To this answer, Laredo felt tears well up in his eyes for the first time, at least, for the first time he could remember. He brought the two-seated carriage to the stile block and waited by the horse with his hand on the bit, looking to the north to see how the weather was changing for the better in these last two days. He placed a blanket in the rear seat for the girls to use in case they got cold. Wearing her new bonnet, Edith was to sit between Lula and Winfred.

Pete walked to the carriage with them. "Now, ma'am, don't you worry," he confirmed, "everything here will be just fine. I'm washing the dishes right after you leave."

The three men waved at them as they moved away from the farm. They rode through Jenks, nodding to several people who knew them and arrived well ahead of their time at the ferry, but they did not find Mr. Tabor. The old gentleman had always been the master to take the fares across the Arkansas.

Slowing his steed, Winfred Jordan reined in and dismounted to lead the horse onto the flat boat. He spoke to the new man. "You Tabor's boy?"

"Yes, sir," the youth answered with a big smile. "Name is Donald Ray Tabor, sir. My daddy died, Mr. Jordan. He died about a month ago. Howdy, Mrs. Jordan. You folks coming back this way tonight?"

"I reckon we are," Winfred said, "Tonight, early, I guess." The wind increased and waves slapped against the boat. "We're supposed to get a new bridge across here, aren't we?"

"I hear tell," Donald answered as he manipulated the ropes. "May be some time, though, yet."

As they crossed with the water gently lapping against the sides, Dot and Cozetta giggled when the carriage dipped with the waves. It was a simple crossing. Once on the east bank, Winfred led the horse up the incline to level land.

By the road northward which became more accessible in the last few years, as they passed dwellings, they did not stop to say hello to the Shirk home. No one was on the porch and no one apparently was there. Several of Mayme's chickens roamed about the yard and two dogs ventured to bark as they passed. Neither did they stop at the White House, being, as it was, out of the way.

The fourteen miles from the Homestead to Tulsa was a long journey. By the time they encountered traffic, the horse was not tired but the passengers were.

"Two buggies out in front of the House," noted Lula, "did you see that, Mr. Jordan?"

Mr. Jedediah Parker was sweeping the wide sidewalk in front of his office with a new broom. Luckily, Winfred found ample space to park. While he tied the reins, Lula stepped down, helping Dot and Cozetta to the ground. Then she claimed Edith who lost her bonnet in the seat.

"You folks are right on time," Mr. Parker called, leaning the broom against the outside wall. "Noontime and I just got back from eating beef at Owen's Cafe. I kept my eye out for you." He opened his door. "Come on in."

"We brought a picnic lunch with us, this time," answered Lula as she shook his hand. "We'll eat when this is over."

Trailing the family after he secured the horse, Winfred closed the door. He removed his hat and gloves.

"Make yourselves at home, all of you. I got three new chairs from Hall's Store. I ordered them some time ago and they came in last week on the freight. Passenger train it still is."

Lula found the new chair comfortable and put Edith on her lap. The other girls remained standing near her. Mr. Jordan sat to her left as Mr. Parker took his seat behind the desk. The business at hand was orderly and neat, as disciplined as was the reputation of this attorney. Adoption papers, to be witnessed by Reubin Partridge, who was the new notary public, were resting on Mr. Parker's desk ready for signatures. They were completed in a matter of minutes. Lula took pen in hand and signed just as Mr. Jordan was to do afterwards.

Reubin burst in upon them in time to observe. "I saw your carriage there, Mrs. Per . . excuse me, Mrs. Jordan, so I hustled right over." With his stamp, he pressed his authority at the proper location on the pages, nodding to everyone and then he smiled at Cozetta en route to the door. Dot fingered the paperweight that showered its scene with snow. When requested to return for payment, Reubin halted halfway to the store. "No. No money. Not fom kin. I guess you're still kin."

"You might want to stay around this afternoon, ma'am," the lawyer commented, "this is the day when Mrs. Rachel gets her money. In cash. Right here in my office in case you want to know." He folded the papers and placed them in a drawer. "Mr. McBirney has two armed men stationed across the street, just in case. But I don't think anything is going to happen."

Winfred Jordan lifted Edith high in the air and gave her a big kiss on the cheek. "I'm your daddy now," he laughed," to all three of you!" By this time he was on the sidewalk with Dot and Cozetta trailing along after them.

"Thank you, Mr. Parker," Lula concluded while reaching in her purse. "This is a big day for us, but I guess you can appreciate that, rightly."

"I'd stay clear of the part of town just three blocks west of here. The stockyards haven't been moved yet. Sometimes the smell is just really too strong for all, here on Main Street. Especially at the cafe. A lot of people have complained but it doesn't do any good." He walked with them to the carriage. "Go past the church over there and stop just over the little hill on Seventh Street where there's nothing except trees." He assisted Lula as she climbed into her seat. " That's a good place. Did you notice the new street signs?"

"Thank you, Mr. Parker," Lula said.

The lawyer's day had just begun. In another hour a messenger from the bank arrived, an efficient young man in a fresh shirt and arm garters but no vest nor hat. This clerk, merely twenty or so, was aghast at what was to occur. He remained at the door for he was due to return immediately. "Sixty thousand dollars," he gasped after verifying that the lawyer was waiting, " I seen sixty thousand dolloars!"

"You want to be a banker, don't you?" Mr. Parker asked him.

"Why, yes sir, I do, I do that!" was his reply before he trotted the short distance to the bank.

When the Jordan carriage disappeared over the hill to the picnic, Lula removed her right glove, reached over Edith and clasped her hand in Winfred's busy reins, and smiled at her husband. It was a tacit confirmation of a moment that became a new existence for them all. They did not notice the people around them.

Riding north in a buggy with Oliver proudly seated as the driver, Mrs. Rachel held only a satchel in her lap. Erect and pleased, the boy held his position well with strong hands at his reins. They passed many who knew them. With his mother's permission, he was out of school for this occasion.

Mr. J.D. Hayward thought, right from the start, that producing cash was so out of order, that the bank here in this new town was fully capable of completing a transaction with a simple piece of paper. That morning he sat opposite Mr. McBirney over coffee when the banker outlined for the Kentuckian the whims and eccentricities of Creek Indians about whom the Irishman learned by being in the nation a short time. His wife and mother-in-law brought all types of variances of the culture to his attention including the busk games, the Green Corn Dance during mid-summers, the Oak Tree on Council Hill, and the turtle shells which the female dancers wore around their ankles.

"I'm sorry you won't be here for the stomp dances, Mr. Hayward," James McBirney casually mentioned as they rose to meet their obligation. "The Property is yours of course and I imagine you have some valuable plans for it." He buttoned his coat and took his hat. "Sure, and when I walk about this town my own imagination works overtime, I suppose, and I begin to dream a bit, of businesses here and there, constructed with brick and mortar, among the trees, naturally I like nature's trees, don't you?" After Mr. McBirney personally garnered the money from the wide-eyed clerk, the two men began their quick walk. The banker signaled his two guards to step into place. "I do believe she has arrived," he said," that buggy belongs to the Perrymans, I am sure."

"I've never felt so conspicuous," Hayward remarked as he professed nervousness with so many bills. "I wonder what in the world she is going to DO with the money?"

"Probable turn right around and take it back to the bank, I would think." McBirney was more relaxed.

Reubin Partridge came from the store with his stamp tucked in a bag, this time, to verify his aunt's 'X'.

Once inside Mr. Parker's office, McBirney hoisted the canvas container, as big as a carpet bagger's valise, onto the desktop. "Mrs. Rachel will make her mark on the proper line. That's all I require. Parker and I will witness." He turned to the door to welcome Mayme Shirk and her sister, Emma, who were late. By the time the ensemble was in the room, hardly a space was available for business. After Mrs. Rachel sat in one of the big chairs near the desk, in the awkward minutes that followed, Emma translated. Mayme remained quiet. Oliver stood near the door.

"It seems to me," Emma said to everyone, "that bag Mama's carrying is too small for all that money." She spoke again to her mother.

"Mrs. Drew," the banker replied politely, " and if it is, she may take my canvas bag after we count it in her presence. I of course don't know what whe wants to do .. with it . . ." This satisfied both Emma and Mayme whose only response was a simple nod of the head.

The larger bag was opened and Mr. Hayward began to count the bills all packaged in one hundred and five hundred allotments. Before he could complete the first stack, Mrs. Rachel gently lifted her hand and stopped his work. She looked into his startled face. Patting his hand softly, she smiled at Mr. McBirney. Then, in her quiet manner, she whispered to Emma that she was ready to leave.

Saying nothing, Mayme opened the door and waited outside.

"I have the abstract and the title, Mr. Hayward," Parker reported. To Emma, he said, " and Mrs. Drew, if you will ask your mother, please, to make her mark on," and he pointed "on this line, here."

"I don't quite understand all this," Hayward confesses, "but I suppose as long as I get a receipt."

"You will, sir," Parker answered quickly, " I have it here."

Mrs. Rachel made her 'X' and returned the pen to Mr. McBirney. She rose and lifted the heavy satchel herself as if it were a bag of groceries she purchased from Hall's Store. Noticing her effort, Oliver carried it for her. She smiled at Mr. Hayward and took the arm of the banker whom she followed. Both McBirney and Mr. Parker spied the guards, alerted now, at the street locations.

"Take her to your bank, Mr. McBirney," Emma translated.

Shaking his head in disbelief, J.D. Hayward was transfixed while staring at the receipt. The moment was incredible. The others remained in line with Oliver instantly at his mother's side. A few pedestrians gawked at this parade, surprised more in viewing a Indian lady escorted by a sophisticated gentleman than by the innocent appearance that belied the contents of an unusual carrying case.

To Emma, who walked with Mayme at the rear, her assistance was no longer needed. Their mother was a determined soul and both had learned that trait from her since they were little girls. This lady, so appreciated by everyone, walked steadfastly to her destiny. Emma had so hoped for a life as good as her mother's. She wanted that almost at every moment that she was in her presence.

Emma recalled a story told her by her father, an incident that occured during the 'eighties. With all the traffic noise surrounding their trek to the bank, this one tale echoed resoundedly in her mind as if it were yesterday. After delivering a large herd to Kansas City with Ralph Collins and Laredo, the father met with some highwaymen. It was a valid moment in a time full of fearfull excitement , especially when they were confronted by six masked horsemen. When these outlaws recognized who it was on their way southward from selling cattle, they allowed Perryman and his drovers to return to Tulsa. The whole affair was without further incident.

"Why did they let you go, Papa? the children asked.

George senior settled back in his chair and with Emma on his lap, he explained. "Because just two months earlier when the U.S. Marshalls were roaming this part of my land, seeking these outlaws, I put them in my barn. That barn right out there. No one knew they were there. Not even Judge Parker."

No one, for that matter, knew Mrs. Rachel had sixty thousand dollars in that bag when she casually walked with Oliver to her left and Mr. McBirney to her right. Across the street and through the bank door she made an astonishing impression on the tellers behind their cages. She was majestic. She was quiet in her own way.

Her husband always dealt with cash. Somehow, his spirit had walked with her that day. It could have been that the Great Spirit made the sun shine brightly that afternoon. She looked at Oliver and smiled as the young teller began counting.

Chapter Twenty-Five

During the following summer, after the wheat was bundled and the corn was
cut, Oliver Perryman rode frequently to Lula's house in the country. He was doing
well at his studies. Gladly, also, he was in charge of chores at the White House
whose blessings he took for granted just three years earlier. Once, last fall, when
Abner talked to him, when the Shawnee confirmed his blood line of his family, he
began to realize that he was alone, now with his mother on this land with the wide
pastures and long horns that he could see for miles all the way to the south horizon. No one had really pointed out the values of this land to him but he perceived
them, nevertheless, of these pastures, the cattle, and even the milk cows in his
mother's barn. But he still enjoyed his trips to visit the Homestead.

Had the Dalton Gang really hid in the hayloft? Or was it some other notorious
outlaws that his father protected? Despite these questions, his own life continued.
Work was necessary. The new calluses on his palms and the dirt under his finger-
nails meant a status important to him. He would stare at them for minutes as if
they would help him attain manhood. His brothers had these when they were
working and growing up. So he was glad that rough hands were an integral part of
the Indian's Way of Life.

And he began to think. Was it the Dalton Gang, really?

Moses had lifted Oliver high in the air and placed him in a saddle when he
was a child; he remembered this quite suddenly one hot Sunday when he crossed
the Arkansas alone with no help, not even Tabor's Ferry.

"Did you know?" Lula told him, "I used to cross all alone when I'd take my
trips to Tulsa. My horse was Ol' Bill and he was a good one. He knew more about
crossing the river than I did, so when we got to the shore I'd just let him find a low
spot and he'd take us across just like he owned the river!"

All the bloodline came surging back to him, the Sunday afternoons with Uncle
Thomas delivering a prayer before dinner, with Uncle Josiah taking his little hand
and walking down to the pond to converse with the ducks where they had been
long before Oliver was born. And those inevitable trees, and the crows flying
around him as he passed through Lula's gate and up the hill to the stile block. In a
matter of ten miles, he had been immersed in memories but now he was here.
Once more he was at Lula's house.

It was another Sunday, a hot Sunday, with the cicadas singing their usual
anthems, with the Bob-O-Links whistling from afar, with the deer that he saw
waiting to greet him, near a hill he always thought was his. Lula probably baked a
chocolate cake which she usually did for Sunday dinner. That was not why he
chose to ride to see her and his nieces that day, but it was part of it.

Dismounting, Oliver waved at them. They were on the porch playing a game.
He called, but they already came running to greet him, with Edith plodding along
as best as she could, deliriously happy because they had an uncle who had come to
run and play with them.

They did not enter through the front door. Together they moved slowly around the west side of the house so Dot could show how Laredo built a nice swing from a limb of a big tree.

These two years were a drastic change for Oliver. When he joked with Pete and Laredo he was embarrassed by their chiding. If he were big enough to ride all the way from the south side of Tulsa by himself, he was old enough to flirt with the girls. His long hair was straight and ebony as much as that of the crows that met him at the main gate and presently sat on the crest of the roof line.

"Come on in," Lula called from her kitchen door when she saw everyone together. "Girls, get ready to eat. Dinner will be ready in a little bit. Go wash up, Pete, and tell the others." She embraces the boy. "You're growing up, Oliver. You okay?"

The dinner, like all dinners at Lula's Homestead, was magnificent. But by now, rituals of this sort were commonplace, with many blessings taken for granted that the men, the boy, and the family fell into a day-to-day method of living that ignored such benefits. Even so, a visit to Lula was always in Oliver's plans.

The folk around them, those of Kiefer, of Jenks, of the Indian populace, began to recognize this Homestead on the hill. "Who lives up there in that big house, Papa?" a child would ask. Every passer-by driving his buggy with his family would always point and explain to their young that this was a Perryman House and this was Perryman land but the lady had married a cowboy from Jenks so now it was the Jordan Homestead.

So on this Sunday when Oliver visited again, Lula did not go to church on Tibbons Hill. In a sense she was glad she did not attend. If her buggy were not in its place when the boy put his horse in the barn, he would be disappointed, she was certain of that. Lula was Mrs. Jordan now. As the days passed into weeks, slowly, she began to lose communication with the Perryman clan. Only three memories, those being Abner, Mrs. Rachel, and of course, Oliver. She thought of this as she called to him again.

In his own shy manner, Oliver did mention to her that his times spent here had become a close affinity that had become a part of his bearing. Young, shy Indian boys would never make that thought a vocal analysis, but Lula knew. Ol' Don wandered to him, looked into his eyes as he sat on the south porch and longed to be petted. More than two buckets of well water were needed; he would fetch them. Even on Sundays, the chickens begged to be fed and their eggs were ready. Since he usually had his mother's permission to stay the night, he was ready to milk when Ralph Collins said so. On summers' nights the sun set at this time and Laredo drew their attention to the wonder of it all.

Winfred Jordan came in from the fields and while he was washing his face and hands, Lula delivered a remark to him, more so for Oliver's benefit. "No work on Sunday, Mr. Jordan."

"The corn needed to be plowed, regardless of which day it was," was his return. "Better the day, better the deed!"

Oliver sat at his usual place at the oval table, always the same, when he visited, his face and hands scrubbed clean, his hair combed neatly. Pete was glad. After supper by lamp light, he showed Oliver how he and Laredo learned to read and write English. In the bunkhouse, their ledger contained many an exercise involving cursive letters both upper and lower cases.

Time, as the boy knew it, would stand still when he was at the Homestead. Perhaps it was because he was there that he felt more like talking, being more alert to conversations. He had a word to say about his mother, how she was sewing in the afternoons with the sun just right coming through the window and how she would never turn away an orphan or hungry child.

"That's part of her charm," echoed Lula.

"That's like Mama, all right. And did you know George and Orphia are going to have a kid? I think. And Abner and Lucy are just fine, I guess, living in the House until it is to be moved. How can they move a house, Lula? How can a big house like that be moved? I heard Mama and Emma talking the other day and I asked Emma to tell me what it was. George bought a lot on the street called Elwood down by the river just south of what they call Eleventh Street."

When Oliver saddled his pony and left the next day, the whole house was strangely empty. The girls quickly found joy in their playthings but they enquired when Oliver would come back to see them.

Pete and Laredo were concerned also. They asked him about each word, about phrases that seemed awkward to them. Pete's bookmark on this occasion was Oliver's name printed in bold letters with its cursive counterpart under it. Ralph Collins stood by acting as if he were not at all interested but that indeed, he was. When the lessons were completed and the ledger set aside, when Pete and Laredo went about their chores, he opened the pages and mumbled to himself all the key elements of new words, of new attitudes, as he called them.

Such thoughts came to Ralph Collins at a time when astride his own horse, inspecting the barbed wire fence that stretched along the west border, he could ponder his own fate, as he once told Moses quite some time ago. Laredo, with Pete, was more in control of the major chores than he. This allowed him to monitor the range down by Coal Creek to watch the rabbits scamper ahead of him, to feel the breezes against his sweaty face. There, on that spot, is where Moses Perryman led us in branding some mavericks. And there, over there, in the bend of the creek, was Pete's favorite swimming hole complete with the slippery mud steps that he carved from the niche made by the roots of the biggest tree that bordered the stream.

A gust of wind, one of many, brought back the spirits of all those men and boys who died on the route from Texas. How strange it was that this breeze, these gusts, would command such a vivid memory! He did not dismount at another location that attracted him, but merely stopped, allowing his horse to nibble at the Johnson grass. The great fertile fields of cotton and wheat surrounded the farm. Moses made a wise choice when he agreed with the commission for **this** portion of land.

Returning to the barn slowly and with a gratefulness he had not heretofore experienced, Ralph Collins remembered the creaking leather of yesterday, the roll and slicker behind his saddle, the sunshine and rain of Texas, the dust, the hail, the muddy water of the Pecos and the Guadalupe, the inevitable streams they had to cross, the cinches, the sting of rawhide with stirrups turned time and again to resist the cruel wear of boot heels.

The laughter and glee of the girls welcomed him home. This matured drover, older now, was home again.

"It's nice to have memories, Mr. Collins. Little Oliver and I were talking about that the last time he rode in." Lula was busy but compatible in her kitchen when he came to inquire about the arrival of Mr. Jordan's aunt. "Why, he went to Jenks to fetch her. They ought to be coming in any time now."

Finally, when the men sent the dogs ahead of them to round up the milk cows, when the sun was just beyond the roof line of the barn, the old buggy with Winfed Jordan and his aunt slowed for the turn, rattled up the hill and stopped west of the stile block. At this time, just before the red summer sun settled over the pastures, he dismounted so his aunt was able to see the house. She was old but alert, older than he imagined but certainly more alert than he expected. "This is it," the nephew announced. "We're home, Aunt Sally."

"My goodness, what a nice big home you got, Winfred!", Aunt Sally said as she stretched her limbs before she climbed to the ground. "I get my satchel, youngin', before you hit the barn." She managed to pull her bag and let it fall beside her.

"I got to go help milk so you open the gate there. Around to the west, you'll see a swing for the kids and then you'll see the back porch. Lula is expecting us. I imagine she knows already we're here with all the dogs barking."

Aunt Sally, short and nervous, frail with years of toil obviously embedded in her face, did just as he said, following the sidewalk to the subdued front porch, then making her way carrying her belongings through a welcoming committee of inquisitive dogs. Ol' Don merely observed from a distance. "Now you and I are going to get acquainted soon enough, " she answered them, "just you let me be."

Opening the screen door, Lula heard this weary relation drop her bag. Sally, exhausted but smiling, looked at Lula. "Well, I'm Lula. This is our place so welcome to it." The girls, curious , stood silently beside their mother's skirts and peered directly at this creature. Sally removed her bonnet, disclosing tresses of uncombed hair and a withered face that exploded in a wide grin and hearty laugh. "Say now, I'm your father's aunt, too. How be ye, Miss Lula? I'm glad to be here." She waited and caught her breath. "I didn't have any place to live and you and Winfred are most kind to me, I'll have you know." She curtsied and extended her right hand. "My Winfred told me all about you, ma'am. He sure loves you, ma'am, you and the youngin's. I just got one bag, right there, that's all the material possessions I got. I'll have you know, my soul is the Good Lord's and that's all that matters. At least, that's what I think." She stopped talking to return the girls' stare at her. "They sure do look Indian, all right. I don't have candy for you, kids, I'm sorry, but I make good sugar cookies. I sure do!"

In the kitchen, Aunt Sally sat in the chair next to the window. When she sipped coffee put before her, her eyes fell on Dot who came and sat in her lap. Cozetta waited her turn. Edith was still undecided and remained three feet away from this newcomer.

Of all the characters that Lula ever encountered from the host of Indians that the Beaver House entertained, to one or two drovers that her foreman knew, Aunt Sally quickly became more notable and exceptional. She took command of the kitchen as chief cook and bottle washer, as she called it. She commandeered the meals from sunup to way past sundown. She invaded the bunkhouse making sure it was clean and neat. But most assuredly, with her unlimited conversation, she proved to the men she was a new friend. Pete fell in love with her. Laredo especially liked her apple pies. Ralph Collins learned how to tease her and get away with it. And she was always one step ahead of everyone else.

Those were this woman's traits which Lula found difficult to understand. The fact that she was here, and now, mystified Lula. If she had been one of the many homeless wanderers who came and went throughout the nation, Lula would be satisfied. But Aunt Sally came into their home, a strong paragon herself, full of willful energy but flavored with a vibrant nature. It was planned. And, more so, by merely Mr. Jordan getting into the old buggy and bringing her here. Lula was astounded. This relation was guilty of painting a pure picture of goodness yet her innate philosophical demeanor was flavored with a crude sense of vulgarity. And she cursed like a sailor.

"Where were you born?" Pete asked her.

"Winfred's daddy and I were borned in Texas, along with a couple of others that we lost. I don't rightly remember when. I look old and I am old. I got wrinkles everywhere. I can cook pretty good. God knows me by my first name and I'm glad for that, I am. If you ask me about church, well, then, I don't know much. I like Indians and I just hope they like me. Living in the territory has been a treat. I got no place else to live out my days. Now, Pete, if you want some supper after milking, you get out of the kitchen."

Later in the bunkhouse, Pete rejoined, "Boy, she can talk a leg off you. As long as she makes pies, though."

The question of eternity, always present in Aunt Sally's vocal exercises when cooking, entered Lula's curious mind often. While it was there, flittering about her brain like a hummingbird, the question remained a question, especially when Lula stopped to watch the cumulus clouds while holding Edith in her arms. The majestic mystery of it all was everywhere, in the wheat, the family, the food, the memories. While Lula often tried diligently to grasp for answers, they never appeared. At best, she found a thick layer of security in the words of the Shawnee preacher. His visits underscored what he previously told Lula just before she became Mrs. Jordan. Lula had all the time in the world, now. She was a fortunate woman. With Edith in her lap, with the house in order, with Winfred Jordan, with Dot and Cozetta, and with a propitious future, Lula sat in her chair to listen to the pastor. And with her, during his latest trip to the Homestead, listening also with sharp ears, was Aunt Sally.

Shortly after that last visit, in the heat of August with no rain in sight, the milk cows and long horns were thirsty. Lula prayed for more than a mere drop when she heard a rain owl sounding his mournful call to another one. At night, almost every night, when they were forced to take their bedding outside to sleep on the south porch, she thought she spotted this old owl high in the trees, a great white bird that sat looking straight down on them all. It was there not too high but on a limb that spread over the east part of the yard. It would rest in each tree for a while to determine whether or not any one limb would be more to its liking than any other branch. When it swooped down, Lula nudged Winfred. "See," she said softly, "it's the rain owl. I know it is. I can feel it in my bones. We'll get rain for sure. I can see that old owl every night."

They rested on thick pallets spread over an old mattress that Lula forgot she had. "You happy, Lu?" came a question.

"'Course I'm happy, Mr. Jordan. Whatever makes you think I'm not?"

From his standpoint, he was a good cowboy, an earnest and loving person who entered Lula's life at the precise moment when she needed for him to do so, as if that, too, had been planned like some road indicator, the likes of which were being installed all along the main thoroughfares of the nation. Lying on this bed with his wife beside him, looking into the heavens of this summer's night, Winfred Jordan was never the one to doubt the reason for his being there. "I don't reckon I have any doubts at all about how happy you are. I reckon I love you for sure, Mrs.

Jordan."

Gently she took his hand and turned her head to view his profile. "I'm pregnant again if that's what you want to know."

Smiling, he raised himself on his left arm and looked at her closely. The rain clouds came just as the owl predicted. "When? How did you know?"

She took his hand again. "I went to Tulsa to see Dr. Clinton the day or two before you went to get Aunt Sally. Remember? His office is in his new house, just one block from the Perryman House where Abner lives. Anyway, he said I'm with child. That's the way doctors talk, you know. I'm ready. I'll have another one."

"Well!" he laughed and lay back on his pillow. "I'm sure glad Aunt Sally's here, finally."

"I was just thinking, I'm talking as much as Aunt Sally!"

Winfred laughed again. "I don't reckon Mr. Collins has ever delivered a baby. Other than a calf or two."

Lula squeezed his hand. "I'm glad Aunt Sally is here, too. Good night, Mr. Jordan."

A pervading thought passed through her sleepy mind. She thought about Abner for she had not seen nor heard about him in well over a week. It was a random reference which passed from her consciousness into the sky above them. On the previous Sunday, Oliver did not visit but he was not altogether as frequent a guest as that. Oliver kept them informed.

But on his last trip Oliver said he encountered three men who raced ponies. One of them asked him to learn to ride fast so that he could make some money quickly. He shared this invitation with Pete who was equally impressed with the joy of racing. this new sport became a sudden preoccupation and Oliver, so he was told, had the stature and weight for being a good jockey. Racing ponies was not unique but it was new to the city. Maybe, just maybe, that was why the boy was not at the Homestead last Sunday.

Oliver Perryman, protector of his mother, of the land around the White House, the pond, the pastures, the remaining cattle, and even the ducks, stood on the front porch of that country home and watched as two men galloped over the horizon, coming swiftly down the road, past his pond, under the trees. They stopped directly in front of him, not more than ten feet away. Their dust loomed everywhere. At first, he decided they were part of a plan to build a racing stable on a section of allotted land east of Tulsa. As they drew nearer, Oliver detected feathers in their black hats. They were not those who had talked to him. One of the riders had paint on his face. He dismounted immediately. Fear surged through the boy's body that they had come to do harm, at least, they had the appearance of that type. When this Indian came closer, his hand still holding reins, he spoke in the Creek tongue. The other, still astride his tan horse, said that the boy did not understand at all what the first was saying.

The front screen opened and shut. As the dust cleared, Mrs. Rachel appeared with one of her dogs beside her. She answered softly but well. This was Perryman land. This was her house and the two men, though presumptuous, were not to be rude or caustic.

The painted one reversed his horse slightly and looked to the other rider for assistance. His own horse was nervous as it pawed the ground and snorted. The mounted one, with difficulty at controlling his steed, became antagonistic. They only wanted information.They were remnants of Chitto Harjo.

Mrs. Rachel was aware of this crazy snake and his men. They wanted to make sure that this brave woman and this frightened boy were still Indian enough to respect what Crazy Snake was still trying to accomplish.

Their two horses became more nervous. Mrs. Rachel said nothing to this. She motioned for Oliver to stand closer to her and to hold the dog in place.

It was not unusual for this faction to exist in Tulsa. The majority of full bloods were still traditionalists. They intended to establish their brave tribal government and to retain some semblance of tribal order.

Because he did not understand any of this talk Oliver entered the house, hesitant at first to leave his mother. In the kitchen, out of breath from moving quickly down the hall, he saw Emma.

"I know!" she cried, grabbing a towel and drying her hands, "you don't have to tell me. I heard them talk."

"They're full bloods, I think, Emma," was Oliver's reply. "Come on, come back with me." He did not wait for her but Emma was at his heels.

Pausing at the front door to monitor the situation, Emma then stepped to the edge of the steps. Her feet hid the Welcome sign. She confronted these two in Creek.

She thought primarily that they were totally out of place to be disciples of Chitto Harjo. This leader they purported to follow was a thing of the past. The immediate past. Yes, Emma knew of their exploits more than any other family member other than her mother who remained gallantly beside her with an arm around Oliver. The boy had a stern look about him. Her uncles knew of the problems Crazy Snake wanted to solve. But this renegade declared himself a martyr for a Cause that had grown weaker as the months passed.

The two messengers had an answer for it all. The treaties that the white man's government made with the Creeks were not valid. Why did the men from Washington come with laws when those laws ignored what the treaties gave to us?

Yes, my mother and I are aware of that, too.

It's not a losing fight Harjo is waging.

All that happened over a year ago. Why did you paint your face? Why do you persist in causing so much trouble?

We tried to play their game but the white man changed all the rules.

Get off our land. Go back where you came from. My mother doesn't want to have anything to do with you. You and your kind are defying the laws.

Out leader warned his people that allotment of land would be the final step in the white man's dominance over us.

"What's he saying, Emma?" Oliver questioned, pulling at her apron. Mrs. Rachel gently tugged at his shoulder. "Be quiet."

Before Emma could answer, the other Indian dismounted but remained beside his pony. He interrupted.

"We know who you are, Mother Perryman. We know your clan. You are good people. But Chitto Harjo tells us he denounces his people for straying from the ways of his forefathers. He is a good man. He tells us to warn you that the destruction of the Muscogee Nation is soon". Less antagonistic than the painted one, he repeated the word in English.

"All of you were arrested in Muskogee two years ago. Why do you persist in going around like this?"

The painted one uttered a cry but the second one stopped him. "We admit we're not like you. Many of us are poor but we'd rather remain poor than mix blood like so many of you have. We can't live on the land the Great White Father in Washington promised us. We want to be left alone. Chitto Harjo has enough courage to defy everyone. Our bodies were in jail, but our spirit remained free."

"What do you mean by that? What do you want to do that you haven't done already? You were in jail because of defiance, anyway!"

That threat of looting was always on the horizon prefaced by many of the young full bloods who were inspired but only by Harjo himself, but by his adherents, the older generation who convinced everyone of his group to balk and remonstrate.

"We heard what your men did west of Sapulpa, how you went into the land, taking the law into your own hands, tearing up things, burning houses. You won't burn this house! It's a Perryman house. Allotment is legal. You ought to know that by now."

Emma was losing patience with these two who persisted in looking at her mother and brother with a threatening stare. Oliver was just as perplexed, listening to a conversation he could not enter nor understand. But he did hear one quick remark coming from his sister who, in a fit of pique, uttered in English, "they're not going to burn **this** house." The boy's ire welled up inside of him, a furious anger that moved him bodily toward the painted face. But Emma stopped him, grabbing him outright, holding him against his will. Their attention was riveted instantly to the road opposite the pond.

Rapidly galloping toward them with clouds of dust behind him was a third snake, standing in his stirrups, calling wildly in a prolonged yell. The frightened ducks fluttered their wings and scattered as best they could as this rider rushed by them. To the two who by now mounted and turned to him, he called for them to retreat, to leave the grounds, that they had better feats to accomplish. So off they rode together not saying goodbye, even in their language, to the trio standing as their dust filtered through the porch.

Immobile with relief, Emma watched them disappear. Her remark to her mother resembled a strange assortment of ghosts from the recent past, of stories about the leader, this Chitto Harjo, this malcontent who did not accept anything that anyone had tried to achieve in all of Indian Territory. Trembling yet with fear, she escorted her mother into the hall and to their kitchen where she lifted the lid off a pot of beans.

This concern was still on her mind. Those Creeks had molested a little community. They had even roamed about the land whipping those who accepted their allotments from the Dawes group. If there had been four or five with painted faces instead of merely those two arrogant riders, her mother and she would have been hurt. Her brother would have been flogged.

Oliver was not with them. Emma dropped the stirring spoon and ran to the porch. The boy was still there. Their Welcome sign lay face down on the porch where her foot had hit it.

"Set it right, Oliver, and come on in." she remained at the screen door. "They're gone now." While Oliver sulked, she returned to her cooking.

Over the months Emma heard this. And obviously her mother did, too. Mayme and Stewart Shirk talked about it when they wanted a topic of interest to which they could relate. In the cafe, different diners exchanged gossip about the fierce man. On the streets, the accounts of his threats were widespread, not only

among the vociferous white community but the quiet Indians. It was learned that
these quiet Indians were not so quiet, after all.

Oliver came to the kitchen and sat in a chair. When Emma used the word
warpath to him, he began to wonder just how it was that so much violence should,
at this point in time, enter his civilized life. In the back of his mind, through a lesson or two, he sat fascinated when Miss Huntsman told his class of Custer and
Wounded Knee.

Noting that the boy waited for some kind of explanation, Emma confessed she
had no time to qualify the events as they happened. The sister was still shaking
with an intense fear.

The one frightened aspect of all that occurred was that these men, so indoctri-
nated by the philosophy of Chitto Harjo, repeated a reference that she, and possibly her mother, had heard somewhere along the line of turmoil. The white man
was going to destroy us. They were there to commit themselves to counteract such
a future. Oliver had another lesson in history right on his mother's front porch.

Pregnant with another child, Emma replaced the lid and sat on a chair in the
parlor to get away from the heat. She asked Oliver to bring her a glass of water.
She had to think. All she was able to do was to sit, fan herself with her apron, and
stare at a picture of her father still framed, hanging on the wall. Silently, and with
drops of sweat matting her hair, she wished he could have been on the porch with
them or at least George or Abner. It was as if the ghosts of some weird chapter in
their lives reappeared but with a threat instead of a blessing.

"I'm going to milk," Oliver called as he regained his sense of direction. "The
cows came in and are standing at the gate. I got to go. You going to be all right?"

"I don't know," Emma responded. "I'm still thinking." She rose and went to the
kitchen again.

For these snakes to deliver their sermon to this house was not unusual. Their
leader, purporting such an edict from his capitol, had been on the minds of everyone. Even after their own arrest, such a continuance of this depth became a matter
of dire circumstances. Two years ago five thousand such full bloods, a great number indeed, began a rampage to no avail. Just as they quickly appeared in anger, so
did they elect to become suddenly covert for a time. The Council House in
Okmulgee demanded all kinds of adherence of laws from them. At his site near
Henryetta, Chitto Harjo proclaimed himself a new chief. On his orders a new government was to evolve from the old one which had become decadent and mean-
ingless, or so they said. Harjo's threat was still abounding. The white man was
destroying the Indian.

It was just as well that Emma was in the house. She told her mother that she
was leaving to find Abner and inform him what happened.

I'll ask Abner to speak to George and I'll have Mayme and Ella come stay with
you because we don't know what to expect. It's apparent. We don't know those
men at all. They're from Henryetta or Eufaula, but they're not from Okmulgee.

Don't fret so, Emma.

Well, I'm going anyway. I'm going to Abner. He'll know about what to do.

The late afternoon sun beamed on the front porch to where she went for yet a
second time. With her hands over her eyes shielding them from the bright summer
rays, she looked across the wide pastures but no riders were there. She was too
fearful to eat; food was least on her mind. From the back porch she was able to see
the cows and to hear Oliver. He was all right. For some reason, the birds circled

over the house and she detected a slight breeze that prefaced a possible rain.

For the first time in a long time, Emma was genuinely afraid. She stood before dirty dishes which she had overlooked. The beans were ready but she lacked interest. She moved to a corner of the table and finally sat, motioning for her mother to join her. She folded her wet hands before her and her nervousness began to show.

Are you all right, Mama? We don't have to worry, really, do we? Really? Why did they come and pester us like that? Wasn't this whole business of Crazy Snake finished? I thought so.

Mama, I've lost babies and I don't know why all that had to happed to me! I've got another one, now, Mama. My husband goes away and I don't see him for a long time.

She rose and went to the dishwater again.

Now, you just sit there and relax, Mama.

Emma dropped a glass and it splintered all over the floor. Desperately, she sat again, tied, worried, and began to cry. Mrs. Rachel with broom in hand swept up the pieces carefully and then came over to her daughter, lifting her tearful face in her hands.

Dry your tears, Emma, before Oliver brings in the milk. We want to be ready for him, then you can go for Abner. I will see to supper if you want to leave. When I feel low, I always talk to the Great Spirit as soon as I am free to think. I always tried to obey what Thomas or Josiah and my husband said about talking to the Good Lord. Sometimes, I put down my sewing when my eyes are tired and I walk to the pond with dogs, and I speak just as if I am talking to Oliver's ducks. I wear my bonnet because it's hot, and I talk to the trees. We did not ever have to rip out one tree to build anything. Not even this house. My husband knew just where to put it here on the crest of a tiny hill. You were born in that room upstairs.

A lull in their conversation augmented the silence of the house. This was a good time as any to do chores. They heard the cows as Oliver pushed each one from her stall, returning them to pasture. The clock chimed the quarter hour. Mrs. Rachel sat at her table, her hands in her lap.

Mrs. Rachel sat quietly but her mind was active.

Mose wasn't born upstairs because this house wasn't built then. He was born at that little house we had. Then my John. We lost John so early. Then you were next. I can't remember but then they built this house. And then Abner, and Ella and Mayme and then my last was George.

Emma managed to put the broken pieces in a bag. She paused almost as abruptly as did her mother when both realized what the mother had said. The barn door slammed shut as Oliver, now finished with milking, managed two buckets Mrs. Rachel rose to look through the kitchen window at his activity. She turned to meet Emma's surprised stare. The dogs were barking and Oliver trekked toward the back porch.

Oliver!

He's not yours, Mama?

The lady shook her head slowly and painfully, aware that the subject of their furtive discussion was close.

He was never to know that he was adopted almost from the very first month of his existence. You remember the Haikey boy, Edward Haikey? He was our ward. But Oliver was adopted. I know where he came from, but my husband wanted to think other thoughts. He was a full blood.

wanted to think other thoughts. He was a full blood.

The dogs told them Oliver was on the porch.

Oh, Mama, you kept him! Without his ever knowing!

He became my last child and he grew up with us in the family. He was ours. Much like Mr. Shaw did. Shaw's parents were Shawnee but he was adopted! From a lost and forgotten Creek family. So many families, lost and forgotten.

Her mother's stare at this daughter was a fervent plea, a look in this Indian's eyes that Emma had never seen there at all, ever!

I'll take care of the dishes, Emma. You're welcome to stay if you want but I know you want to go see Abner. Ask the boy to bring me some more firewood, please.

With one bucket full of foamy milk, Oliver opened the back screen to put it on the counter. Before he went to claim the other bucket, he caught his breath. "Tell Mama, Emma," he said, "that I think Bossy is going to have her calf." He stopped, heaved another sigh, waiting for a response. Neither sister nor mother looked at him. A part of his duty, he selected two clean jars from the pantry and poured from his first bucket.

"Mama wants some more firewood, please."

After attending to his second bucket he obeyed and placed the logs in their box by the hot stove. Emma removed her apron and hung it on its peg. Gently, she touched his arm and pulled him to a chair at the table. "I have to go see Abner, now. I'm going to have a talk with him." she peered into his eyes for a long time.

"We'll be all right, " he answered softly as he wiped his perspiration from his forehead. Continued silence from this sister worried him. " I know where father's old rifle is. I'll use it if they come back tonight."

His remark sobered her. "Now you be careful, Oliver, with that old gun. You be a good boy." She pushed him to the front of the house. "Walk me to the door, will you?" With one baleful look at her mother she passed him without waiting for an answer, selecting her gray bonnet from the halltree.

Still worried, Oliver trailed along after her. "You want me to go with you? It'll be dark in another hour."

Emma untied the reins to her horse that had been waiting the hour since she arrived. "No, I don't. You wait here and eat your supper. I'm not saying those men won't be back, but they could." she climbed aboard. "You stay here with Mama!" She clucked at the horse as she made a sharp left then. "You are the man of the house, now!"

With no other word, Oliver saw her depart. She disappeared in a burst of dust with a concentration he had never noticed in her. Emma had always been there, standing at the edge of the line of family, waiting for a picture to be taken. Emma was always the tranquil lady in the kitchen, wearing her calico aprons, working diligently, making noodles, separating cream from milk, seasoning beans, alone while others talked among themselves. She hardly ever said anything because she was the chief cook during the big family dinners. She was always the supervisor of the table setting, the one to speak to full bloods when they came to the White House. Emma had clean dresses and a determined look about her with latent creative energies deep inside her, baking in a hot kitchen, allowing her pies to sit on a shelf to cool, never complaining aloud if indeed she had anything about which to voice an objection. And her Christianity was more than just an ounce or two during a Sunday morning service. When she married Clifton Drew, she insisted on a

Creek ceremony but with one in the church, also. Emma was that way.

By now, with the road traversed so many times in the last ten years, the journey to the House was easy. She sped along as the accomplished driver she was, the reins held securely in her gloved hands, her bonnet tied deeply under here chin, the wind blowing against her and her constant awareness that the horse needed water.

She had no time to poll the number of new houses that had sprouted up on this road to town. If her husband were driving she would nod to the people who waved at them. She may even have a greeting. Several neighbors passed her going south. One man, whom she thought she recognized, fled by her so fast on his steed that she hardly had time to speak.

Emma was tired. Her day was at an end. The sun to her left was sinking behind the tall cottonwoods that lined this avenue with rays that peeked at her as she moved swiftly. At one place, at an intersection with a tiny sign indicating twenty-first street, a herd of lazy cows caused her to halt. Three young boys with them gave her sorrowful glances to apologize for her delay.

Onward she went. Once past Oak Lawn Cemetery up an incline and around a corner, she saw the imposing House penetrating the dark sky with its tall steeple-like gables easily recognized from all directions. As she drew near she noticed buggies and horses along Main Street with several men and women grouped around them.

She reined in, waiting in her seat to determine the reason for this crowd. One buggy approached. She twisted the reins around the headboard. "What's the matter here?" but she got no reply as they sped by her. She climbed to the ground and passed through the people. Solemnly the men removed hats and women lowered their heads. The gate was already open. She saw two men on the front porch whom she knew. Dr. clinton, bareheaded, was one. He walked to meet her and extended his hand.

"Mrs. Drew," he greeted softly, "my dear, please come inside. Who told you?"

Through the entrance and into the foyer she followed, never taking her eyes from his face. "Who told me <u>what?</u>

Closing the door to the curious, the doctor remained in the hallway. "Mrs. Drew," he began, "oh, my dear, please go into the parlor and sit down." At first she hesitated, her face full of questions. She even objected, but he escorted her to the sofa but she remained standing. " I have the sad duty to inform you and the family . . ."

An interruption came from Lucy who stopped on the stairs, a few steps from the bottom. "Oh, Emma!" she gasped, bracing herself against the railing. Mrs. Stivers descended directly behind her.

The doctor continued ". . .to inform you and the family that Abner is dead."

Lucy hurried to the fireplace, trembling. "Emma! Oh, please, Emma, Abner's dead, he's dead!" Mrs. Stivers strode quickly to console her daughter. "They think I did it. I didn't kill him, Emma." She was sobbing, even yet. "I didn't!"

"SShh, Lucy my child, of course you didn't!"

Dr. Clinton gently sat on the sofa with Emma at his side. He said, simply, "Your brother died because of poison. I saw that immediately upon viewing him. I'm calling in Dr. Shepard and he's due any minute." Emma untied her bonnet and started to object. "Just a minute, my dear, let me explain further."

Lucy and her mother were petrified.

"It's going to take time to determine the cause. I sent a messenger for your brother George and for Mrs. Shirk, too. A man on a fast horse has gone to your mother's place." He took her hands in his. "I'm so sorry, Mrs. Drew."

"Poisoned?"

With more questions surging through her mind, and with a look to Lucy who sat next to her, shaking, Emma remembered a man who fled past her riding southward.

Rising slowly, the doctor placed his ear-piece in his bag and snapped it shut. "Please accept my condolences. I did all I could but I arrived too late. He was lying on his back, on the dining room floor." He took Emma by her arm, her bonnet fell to the floor, and they walked into the foyer where they could view the food still on his plate. " A very distinct odor on the plate, Mrs. Drew, I would suggest you not smell it. Sometimes it's necessary for me to play the role of lawman." He turned her away from the scene. "Evidence is for doctors to test, Mrs. Drew. I'm sure you understand."

Emma refused for a time to look at Lucy. Her eyes stayed with the doctor. "Where . . .? she attempted her question, " is Abner?"

Dr. Clinton remained calm. "His body is lying there in the pantry. I've summoned the marshall who I believe is Mr. Sizemore. Someone told me he's in town. and I want to hear what Dr. Shepard will say."

"I want to see him myself," and Emma slowly made her way around the table, still laden with food and glasses of water at both places.

"Please wait, Mrs. Drew."

There, on three chairs that had been placed side by side with a tablecloth spread over it lay her brother's body. An Indian stood at one end who disallowed her attempt to raise the cloth from his face. In Creek, he negated the gesture.

"Please come back to the parlor, Mrs. Drew," said the doctor softly, "Dr. Shepard has just arrived and I want to talk to him, now, please."

Stunned, Emma tried to obey. She turned and found her way to the hallway where she met the other doctor coming through the door. A clamor outside the House forced her to wait in the archway. Through the gate, Reubin Partridge plowed his way past the crowd and into the foyer, stopping only to get his bearing. He sighted Emma and to her he came in tears.

Both doctors went to the pantry to consult.

Emma embraced her cousin. "Oh, Reubin, don't cry, please."

Ignoring Lucy and Mrs. Stivers, they broke away from the front area to secret themselves deep in the hallway. One of the church matrons burst into the parlor, noticed Lucy, and went to console her.

In a matter of seconds a revelation raced through Reubin's brain. He pulled Emma out of earshot of the others, off into the hot kitchen. Already an army of men was assembled to follow the directions from the doctors.

Reubin sobbed. "I heard it was poison. I was out in front of the store and old Issac Stidham and I were talking and we saw someone who came to get Mr. Renfro. He's the new undertaker and when he saw me he stopped before he knocked on Mr. Renfro's door. He told me Abner was poisoned, just like that. I had a hard time trying to understand that man."

Emma was trembling now. She forced herself to listen to what he was whispering, so low sometimes that she had to ask him to repeat a few words.

Reubin was frantic. "Some men came running past us and one of them yelled that Abner was dead and for me to come to the House right now. That's what he said. By the time I could reach Mr. Hall to tell him, I couldn't get the rest of it."

Emma heard other conversations, of the two doctors, of Lucy weeping in the parlor, of the men who were to assist.

Reubin continued through his tears. "Emma, listen, please listen! I don't know what to think. You've always been the stable one of the family. If it was poison, then, oh my good Lord, help me, please help me!"

"What is it, Reubin? Tell me!" Emma implored. With this question she saw another person entirely, different from the Reubin she thought she knew.

"I sold some poison to Lucy!" Nervous, he paused to look toward the parlor where Mrs. Stivers was embracing her terrified Lucy. "I did, Emma. If it was poison, then . . . and Lucy bought poison from me." He wept uncontrollably, burying his face against the wall as Emma fell into the nearest chair.

George arrived and dismounted and ran into the hallway to stare at his sister and cousin. "Oh, George!" and with tears streaming down his face, poor Reubin embraced him.

Mayme's buggy halted in billowing dust that seeped into the curious crowd. Both she and Stewart Shirk plowed through the people and made their way into the House.

Emma rose and walked past them. Standing by the chair that Abner occupied, she commanded a vantage point where we was able to spy on Lucy. And, then the widow looked beyond her mother's care and realized she was staring back at her sister-in-law.

The din of frustration was loud. Emma could not erase the thought that exasperated her soul. The white man had killed the Indian.

—— PART FOUR ——
1911

Chapter Twenty-Six

The passing of the seasons weighed heavily on the mind of Oliver Perryman. In the autumn of nineteen-ten, he began to realize this simple fact. He had completed his twenty-second year in the spring and also he was able to relate to a wide range of people who came to Tulsa. A German settlement made its home far to the northeast of town in what was the Cherokee Nation. The railroad increased its operation to the east with three trains a week from the new station that was built north of First street. The Creeks and Cherokees, along with the other tribes, were swallowed up by the hordes of every other race. The Glenn Pool, with electrifying swiftness, located just eight miles south of the Jordan Homestead, brought oil to the new state and made all of that possible.

Oliver's habits changed with these times. Hall's Store remained noteworthy, especially with a new streetcar track in the middle of Main Street where the river bends westward. From this important thoroughfare, he walked to Owen's Cafe, past the barber shop and the new drug store, only two months old. Then, he came to Boston Avenue. After tipping his hat to two ladies who had known him all his life, he continued south to the old livery stable, still in business to talk to Tom Bolton. Tom was two years younger and undoubtedly his only longstanding friend with whom Oliver pondered when he felt despondent or sad, or, in other cases, happy.

Oliver took this route south in order to escape the view that was so odd, that of the vacant lot where once stood the handsome tall dwelling that had become, in its day, a landmark for Tulsa, that of the Perryman House. It was gone now, all of it, removed practically piece by piece by a pack of professional house movers who was hired from St. Louis. Four years ago — or was it five? — he stood not too far on the south side of Sixth street near Boulder, to watch their beloved structure as it was dissected. He marveled how these men manipulated the entire House, cutting it into gargantuan pieces so to transport it on thick slabs of timber, away from that block, down narrow streets to Elwood. He remembered standing on that same spot of ground a long time ago when only seven years old with his little hand in his father's big one to see that same House grow.

After the building was dismantled and gone, the well remained. The prodigious Mr. Hayward could not determine what to do about the famous watering place, whether to tear it all out or to place an impressive sign on it for the while until he was able to resell the land, as most assuredly he had in mind, to the highest bidder to construct a tall building for Tulsa. Mr. Hayward, with all his well-meaning attitudes, returned to Kentucky but his agent in Tulsa did, in time, provide him with an answer. With statehood came the propensity of the Court House whose skeleton framework of steel filled the northeast corner of that intersection. With reluctance it also erased all reference to the well that had, for so many years, been the oasis for thirsty Indians and white men alike.

Oliver gave no thought to that new building. He decided to ignore that block each time he walked in the vicinity. A few houses blocked his view anyway, if he did glance westward. A lawyer, not Mr. Parker, bought a plot of ground and built his dreamhouse on one corner. Dr. Clinton's home, with a fence, still occupied the other corner. It was to this house that a maid ran with a command to attend to Abner who had collapsed. Along with other parts of the city, this house reminded Oliver of all sorts of memories that persisted. And the trees were still plentiful, the spruce, the cottonwoods, the elms, and a sycamore or two along Boston.

Oliver remained at that corner while he thought of Reubin. With a present for his cousin, the young Mr. Perryman had just come from saying goodbye. Reubin was changing jobs now that their third child was born. And it was in Hall's Store that Oliver tipped his hat to Miss Huntsman, once his teacher.

Her words were still with him. "My, what a nice young man you are, Mr. Perryman! With all the changes, I'm glad to know you are the proprietor of the Perryman store. I understand you are going to marry Addie Mae soon. My very best wishes to you, sir."

Walking, he did not look at the church as he passed it for it reminded him of Abner. When he was at the old house, Abner always waited for him to come in after milking. He was that brother who cared most for him, to give him Moses' horse after Lula said yes. Six years ago, in the House that was no more, Abner ate supper and Lucy poisoned him. That was Emma's contention. That was what the court proceedings intimated. That was what Emma was never able to prove so she added that loss to the list of her many others. With a persistent effort to console Emma, Lula was the only one who tried to locate her. With a broken heart, Mrs. Clifton Drew disappeared.

Tom Bolton saw Oliver walking toward his stable from his hay bales there and covered them with a canvas tarpaulin when it rained. He put down his pitchfork, wiped his sweaty face with a blue bandana, and retreated to his front office.

"How do you like my new sign, Bolton's Livery? Brand new. Kind of pretty, don't you think?" Tom offered his one chair. "Your mare is ready. I gave her a good wash for you."

"Thank you, my friend."

Tom wiped his face the second time. "You heading home?"

Oliver did not answer, for at that moment, a fire alarm's shrill horn sounded from the north side of town. He glanced backward, over his shoulder, curious along with the crowd at the street down which he had just ambled. Faint as it was but definitely a scream that everyone comprehended, the penetrating siren sound-ed as far south as the livery.

Tom joined Oliver in the dirt street to search for a better view northward. "It's a fire, all right." Tom said, it's farther north of the train station this time. Looks like it's up on North Cincinnati." This was too far north for them to become spectators even though several men ran by them.

His friend, prompted by the cone of smoke that billowed above Archer street, was first to comment. "Third fire Tulsa had this year. Well, come on in, it's cool in the back. I got some ice from Herschel's Ice House. Plenty of water for you."

Oliver found a comfortable bale not too far from the back doorway. He saw his mare in a stall waiting for him. Just as his memories flooded him when he walked into Hall's Store, so did them come rushing back in the tranquility of this livery with only the neighing of his horse when she saw him. At the bucket for drinking water, Tom reached for his tin cup and a clean glass for his guest and poured fresh drinks. Then, in answer to a customer, he went forward to his office.

Oliver recounted in his mind what happened that spring. It was Lula, once his very own sister-in-law. It was she who kept coming and going in his mind, in his reveries, his whole way of thinking. It was Lula who made him pancakes every morning when he spent the night at the Homestead. It was Lula who gave him a male collie from a new litter. And it was Lula who with her husband stood at the stile block to behold the turmoil that occurred just one week ago.

The house which Moses built for his bride was no more. That beautiful home burned to the ground one night in a matter of three hours. Oliver was aghast, numbed by a recurring fear of an episode, long ago, at the White House when poor Emma suspected arson from the Harjo revolutionaries. But that was so long ago. Still, the idea persisted.

But he learned a different tale. Aunt Sally, exhausted after spending the day canning green beans, was the first to smell the smoke coming strongly from the kitchen. At her alcove where she slept on her cot she raised herself, disoriented from deep sleep, in time to see sparks flying all around her. By the time she rose and was near the back door, too many flames prohibited her to control the wild fire. She screamed and screamed again, running past the flames, out the back door to the bunkhouse, even rattling the noisy gate.

This brought Pete and Laredo first from their cots, with Ralph Collins hobbling along, trying to slip into his pants and run at the same time. Pete was first to account for it. Barefoot, he fled to the west side of the house, shouting as he went. When he reached the main bedroom, again he shouted names, banging on the window frames and outside walls.

Laredo circled to enter through the front porch to reach the girls, arousing them, grabbing blankets. Carrying Edith, he pushed the others frantically out of their sleep.

Knowing where Winfred Jordan kept his ledgers, Ralph Collins followed Laredo, grabbing what he could locate. In short time, the entire area of the house was engulfed with sparks and flames blown by the night winds that were too hot to extinguish.

So Lula and Winfred Jordan, the girls, a frightened Aunt Sally and the men retreated to the stile block hopelessly to witness what they could not accept. Beside them, hovering in fear, the dogs were silent. And they stood there for such a such time with Lula desperate to soothe the weeping children, grasping Winfred's arm for some meager amount of reassurance while she saw utter anguish reflected in his blue eyes. "Our beautiful house, our beautiful, beautiful house!"

"Hey, Oliver." It was Tom Bolton, shaking him out of his reverie. "Mr. Stidham says hello to you. He just came for his horses. I told him you were back here but he couldn't stay." He got some more water. "You all right?"

Oliver rose and stretched his arms. "Sure. I'm okay."

Having known him for all of his own years, Tom took that answer as gospel. He took the glass and poured water for his friend. "Sure is hot!"

"I got to get home, Tommy. I promised Mama to get some of the chores done before sundown. Tomorrow we're going to ride over to Lula's place, I mean, what's left of it." He slipped the bridle on her head as they walked forward. "You get that right hoof shod okay?"

Tom was always a positive thinker in many ways especially in business. "She needed one, all right. Her other shoes are just fine." He removed Oliver's saddle from its stand after he put the blanket in place. "I was down on Elwood yesterday and I noticed the House. Looks like it was built right there on that lot. Instead of moving it to it, I mean. You want to ride over there and see it yourself? I remember when it was moved. All that machinery and those men sawing it into those sections." He put the saddle in position, adjusted the cinch and looked at Oliver who had become noticeably quiet. Waiting a moment in silence, Tom then began to wrap the reins around the saddle horn. 'I'll get your bedroll. It's over there."

"I never did go over there to see the House, Tom."

"Well, I can understand, all right." The mare was ready. They went to the front with her. "I never did know what happened, no I didn't. Wasn't my business, anyway. My daddy said so. For a long time everybody talked about that court action. Nothing seemed to be resolved." Oliver placed his hat on the saddle. "I don't mean to pry, Oliver, really I don't."

For that matter, Moses' death was never resolved, so the family understood. Lula accepted it. He died in St. Louis and that was all there was to it. He died. Anyway, Oliver was too young to understand all the whispers that transpired between Ella and her husband, all the unanswered questions about it, months later, between Ella and Mrs. Rachel. Such did not make much difference now, a whole decade later.

But in the case of Abner's demise, the reason behind his passing was far more poignant. All that occurred reoccurred in that exact moment when Oliver stood there staring at Tom. It was still fresh in his mind. Much of the talk and speculation as to the precise cause of death endorsed three theories and each was so extreme in nature that Oliver was unable to accept any of them. Not many believed in suicide. Abner was far too competent a business man. Poison self-administered without suicidal intent or administered by other hands with murderous motive added to the profound quandary. Emma held to the latter. And she took the matter to court.

"My sister, Emma," Oliver replied quietly at first hesitating before he mounted. "I tried to follow it, Tom. It was the paper and Emma that prosecuted Lucy." He paused as his mare became eager to leave as most certainly he was as well. There being no provision in the territory's judicial system for the investigation for poison, Doctors Clinton and Shepard made a personal commitment. After a quick autopsy, they discovered a large quantity of laudanum. These bits and pieces of facts which had lain dormant in the back of Oliver's psyche were there in the front of his consciousness ready to be answers for Tom. "But Emma lost. That's about all I remember." He squared his hat. By his tone, so sad and lonely, he ventured no further explanation.

Tom extended his hand upward to his friend. "I'm sorry, Oliver. I guess I just never did really know about it." They shook hands.

His mare wanted to move but Oliver held her back. "I don't know what to think, anymore. Tommy. There's not much left of my family. You're lucky. You still got the clan. The Boltons are strong. But with me, well, I don't have much 'cept Addie Mae. George wants to move to Kansas City. He thinks he has good opportunities there, what, exactly, I don't know. Orphia doesn't want to go. That would mean selling their house. And Ella. Nobody sees Ella and her husband. He's her second husband. I don't know what happened to her first one, the one I remember. You remember my sister, Mayme? After her first son she had two more. And one of them I think is...well, I won't say. I never see them, though. She never talks to Mama anymore, well, hardly ever, I mean. Mama is Mama and always will be." He clucked at the horse and she bolted into the street. "Mama is okay." he said as he pointed the mare south and patted her nose. "I watch over her just like Abner told me to. And Lula." His eyes sparkled in the late afternoon sunshine. "Tom!" he called brightly, "you remember Mrs. Jordan, don't you? Think back. She used to be Mose's widow."

Tom Bolton waited a moment, his thoughts racing through his past, and then he laughed. "Oh, I reckon I do at that! I remember, sure! She laughed a lot, had a nice chuckle. It was Mr. Jordan himself who came through here and left his team by my first stall while he went to do some business. He had some kind of presents for his children, he said. "I recollect that."

Oliver calmed his horse. "Lula had another daughter. She must be four, maybe four and a half by now. Her fourth girl. Lula said it was all right for me to call her my niece, too. They're grown up, they sure have!"

Oliver's attention was drawn to yet another siren calling from that fire to the north. The mare balked but he soothed her. "I guess you never did know about the fire, burning that big house Mose built for Lula when they married." He looked westward as if he could visualize the block on which the new court house was being constructed. "Two houses, both of them gone." Then when another thought passed his mind, he laughed and extended his hand again. "Thanks for fixing the shoe, Tom. Don't go buy a new coat with all the money I gave you. It'll be milk time by the time I get home. I'll be back. So long."

The next morning, at the beginning of a new week and with instructions to a young Yuchi boy who helped with the chores, Oliver and his mother climbed into their old carriage, turned the horse south, and rode past the pond. On shore, a new generation of ducks jumped out of the way as they sped by them. The old road had become a numbered avenue now, forty-first, with several houses located on the portion which George sold to a real estate firm. The trees and landscapes were plentiful but a commitment that the section of the city, far south, would remain vast and wide was soon losing its promises. The acreage between this street and the Perryman Cemetery was to remain open to pasture but with less cattle. Mrs. Rachel had been courted to sell but George refused to negotiate.

"I want this land," he told his mother with Oliver present, "for my children." This delighted the mother.

The old road south to Jenks took them past Mayme's original property with a house that lost its adequacy. It was yet nestled among taller trees, more now, than when it was built so long ago. The carriage did not stop. The sharp curve further south had a name now, so designated as Cline's Corner.

They came to the new bridge across the Arkansas. In town, they did not stop when several pedestrians waved. Two children, resting on a pipe fence shouted a greeting. They continued turning south again with the road bending around a steep hillside. Westward again, on a narrow road that took them to Pogue's Corner where a one-room school house was entertaining adults and students with a picnic. Atkin's Store was on the opposite corner.

Then, to their right, as they went south again, the view to the hill that had invited families to slow their horses' gait in order to remark at the majestic sight was frightful. The house of the Homestead was no more.

Mrs. Rachel, who had remained silent the entire trip, exhaled with a slight whimper and uttered a few words. Oliver understood the agony; across his line of vision he beheld the groan from her lips and the pitiful tears that she could not halt. The sounds that came from her soul made him move his head toward her. He visited the ruins once already but this was his mother's first moment to see the remains. Once they entered the main gate and proceeded to the top of the road, they could see that the stile block was not scorched as were the trees that surrounded the empty space. Before they dismounted, for Oliver did not quite know where to park, they sat very still, hypnotized, visually taking in all the charred areas that were still untended.

From where they remained for an additional moment, annoyed by pesky flies, down the sidewalk which was not blackened or molested, they saw the stubble of the foundation that survived the destruction. That sidewalk was still secure. And in those few days since Oliver himself gazed in awe, the rubble was cleared with only a scant amount of evidence that a devastating fire actually occurred. What the two beheld now was a remarkable yardstick for reconstruction.

The first of the family to see the carriage's arrival was Dot, a young lady now and proud of her fifteen years. Coming around the two tables under the south trees placed there for today's dinner, she signaled to Cozetta. Together they greeted their grandmother and a happy Oliver.

Edith ran to join them. Oliver hopped down and helped his mother to the sidewalk. He folded the cotton blanket she had over her lap en route while she smiled at the girls.

The bunkhouse was spared for it was too far from the heat to ignite. The gate was still upright. The two large boulders that formed the rear steps to the back porch were all right but now, they led to nowhere. The barn, that great majestic edifice built one year before the house, loomed to the west, with its east door open. The nine milk cows roamed about the corral. Ralph Collins with Pete and Laredo had the long horns under control. With only the foundation visible, the overall scene was strange and sad.

Edith wept as she explained to Oliver again of the ordeal with her hand in her grandmother's elbow and Cozetta walking with them on the other side. They started for the others.

With Winfred speaking to three other men, Lula left a trio of women and met Mrs. Rachel. She carried her latest daughter but placed her on the ground as she embraced the old woman. "Oh, Mama," she intoned, "I sure wish you could know what I'm saying to you today." Lula looked into her eyes for they had her answers. She looked at Oliver. "I'm glad you are here, I am! I just wish I could talk to this dear woman!"

Mrs. Rachel lowered her head to smile at the youngest. She bent down to lift the little girl. Oliver spoke for them all. "I missed seeing you, Alice," he said softly, "when I was here last week. You sure are growing!" He took the child, himself as the others sauntered along the yard with Mrs. Rachel. He could see that the crowd was busy.

Lula again squeezed the young man's arm. "Oh, Oliver," she sighed as they strolled arm in arm toward the tables, "I am mighty glad you brought Mama today. It means a lot to Cozetta and to Dot and Edith, too. Just look at them, now, they found one of the full bloods so she could talk. I don't know who he is, he's one of the carpenters my daddy rounded up."

Waller Cornelius Dunbar, with a sweaty face and hands that carried gloves, met them immediately. "Howdy, Mr. Oliver Perryman, sir, glad to see you." They shook hands. "Course, you know, we can get all this cleaned up in no time, yessiree!" He gestured to the north, encompassing the entire foundation from west to east. "Lots happened since you were here last."

"Yes, sir," Oliver smiled, "I can see that, already." He put Alice to the ground. "Run and play, now, hon!"

"We've got help already," Lula cried, "with the women there to bring food to us almost every day. I don't know what we'd do without church women."

"That's what I came over for, Lu," Waller interrupted, "I guess you're ready to eat now that Mrs. Rachel and Oliver are here." To this, Lula nodded yes. "I'll get Win and the boys."

"Come over here with me," Lula announced, "I want to show you something." They walked as far as the sidewalk went to a piece of the porch that had not burned. "See that new stack of lumber over there? It was brought in just day before yesterday all the way from Coffeyville."

Winfred Jordan joined them. "I sure am glad to see you, Oliver. This is a good day for all of us." He glanced at the black hole surrounded by the stone foundation. "It looks bad now, I guess, but we got plans." He remained at their side as others prepared to eat.

Lula spoke proudly. "They're anxious to get working on the new house. You can see how much they got done already cleaning up, getting ready. Let me show you."

Together they stepped off the sidewalk. "The new house will actually face east and we want a porch all the way around it from the east end, there, to the south and on around to the west, a wrap-around porch, so to speak." Lula placed her arm in Winfred's clasping them together with her hands. "Three rooms at the east side, stairs going up from the center one to the second floor. And then, the dining room about there," she said, pointing, walking to their left, "extending toward the west and the kitchen there with that big stove Mrs. Covey and her son-in-law gave us until Mr. Jordan and I can get the one we want. There's the stove, right over there. Mr. Jordan put a tarpaulin over it so the rain won't get it."

Oliver saw the joy radiating from her hazel eyes. Without a bonnet on her head, Lula felt the warm breeze against her happy face and a new excitement as if she encountered a new toy for Alice. Once again, her newest daughter ran to her.

"She has pretty eyes," Oliver remarked. The child reached her little arms to him and he lifted her high in the air. "I am your Uncle Oliver come to see you again, Alice."

The noontime was perfect. The breezes escorted the beauty of autumn across the pastures that formed the original ranch when Moses first set his boots on the land. As Lula and Winfred returned to the tables, arm in arm, Oliver felt suddenly alone. His mother was talking to an old gentleman whom he had met at the White House last year. The girls were already at the tables waiting. Standing slightly away from the crowd, Oliver sensed Moses' voice coming from the stile block.

With his father beside him and with his allotment plans ready to be submitted, Moses nudged the patriarch and said, "Papa, this is where I want to build a home for me and Lula. This is where I want my family to grow. We are really lucky, aren't we, Papa? Uncle Josiah says we got a lot to be thankful for 'cause we're not gathered here alone. Uncle Josiah believes that. I want my ranch house right there and I want my stile block right here so the women can mount their horses. And my sidewalk will go all the way from here to the porch. I can get a team of mules to haul the rocks from Kiefer. Stidham said he had a team he'd let me use. And over there, see, away from the house, west, I want my barn. And my long horns can graze all they want. And I want my well dug back there so Lula won't have far to go to get water. You'll like Lula." His words echoed across time. Oliver heard them.

Mrs. Rachel parted from the full blood and stepped slowly over to where her son stood alone. She took his hand and in another moment she brought him back to the Indians with whom she was speaking. "You are a nice man," one said, surprising him with a strong voice in English. "Your mother speaks highly of you. You are Creek. I can see that." Oliver shook hands with three men who wore black hats and long hair. While they continued in their own tongue, he wondered if Lula had heard Moses's words, too.

"It's time to eat, Mama," he said and the full blood said it for him.

The men had stopped work for dinner. With Aunt Sally ready to guide everyone down a line by the tables, the women were on the opposite side with church fans guarding the food from flies. Mrs. Covey was there with two daughters. Mrs. Gray from Sapulpa came with her husband that day. He knew how to hold lumber just right. Winfred's father was first in line.

Laredo interrupted Lula. "Mr. Collins is coming from the barn," he told her, "he told me to tell you to go ahead and eat if he's late."

To verify this Lula glanced in that direction and saw the old man with shovel in hand trudging as well as he could. He waved. "Come along, Mr. Collins," she called when he passed the well, "Hompuksce!" And to that Creek remark, Mrs. Rachel smiled broadly.

Some of the trees were singed but nature has a way of taking care of that problem. That is what Mrs. Rachel said to her friend who removed his hat when they noticed that Lula placed herself at the end of the table, with Mr. Collins to her left and Mr. Jordan to her right. As if by magic a gentle hush fell over this encampment of workers. The other men, on cue from the old Indian carpenter, took off their hats, too. The children, the women, the drovers who came to help, bowed their heads. Pete began to weep.

"Our Dear Heavenly Father," Lula intoned reverently, "it looks like this day's going to be a good one and Your blessings are going to be quite a lot all right. We're just humble people, Lord and we do give You the thanks for the food we're about to receive, and for all these people who came to help me and Mr. Jordan and the girls to get started again. Thanks to You and everyone who brought these victuals for us, especially the chocolate cake. And we give You all the glory and we pray earnestly in Jesus's name. Amen."

And sitting on a limb, high above them, in a tree not too far above the bunk house, peering down with sharp eyes was a white owl.